"So that was a good-bye kiss?"

"If you want to call it that," Reece responded. "Personally, I'd call it 'See you later.'"

"You really are a cocky bastard," Jess said.

He laughed out loud, liking that someone finally had the nerve to tell him what they thought of him, especially here in the building he owned. "Yes, I am a cocky bastard. Admit it, though. You like that about me."

"Keep telling yourself that."

"All joking aside, Jessica, whatever happened Friday night, whatever mistakes I've made since the day I first saw you..." He leaned close enough to brush his cheek against her hair, inhaling to capture the tropical scent. "You want me just as much as I want you."

I'LL BE WATCHING YOU

ALSO BY LESLIE A. KELLY

Nowhere to Hide

I'LL BE WATCHING YOU

LESLIE A. KELLY

FOREVER

New York   Boston

Forever
Hachette Book Group
1290 Avenue of the Americas, New York, NY 10104
read-forever.com
twitter.com/readforeverpub

Originally published as *Watching You* in ebook and print on demand by Grand Central Publishing in March 2018
First mass market edition: March 2020

Forever is an imprint of Grand Central Publishing. The Forever name and logo are trademarks of Hachette Book Group, Inc.

The publisher is not responsible for websites (or their content) that are not owned by the publisher.

The Hachette Speakers Bureau provides a wide range of authors for speaking events. To find out more, go to www.hachettespeakersbureau.com or call (866) 376-6591.

ISBN: 978-1-5387-3514-5 (mass market)

Printed in the United States of America

OPM

10 9 8 7 6 5 4 3 2 1

Young Starlet Falls to Death

Hollywood Tattletale Reporter J. Federer

December 12, 2000 | Reporting from Atlanta

Hollywood "it girl" Rachel Winchester was found dead early this morning outside an Atlanta hotel. The teenage actress's body was discovered in an employee parking lot below the balcony of her twenty-eighth-story suite. Police have not yet determined the cause of the fall, but sources say the troubled star has been secretly struggling with drug addiction.

The late sixteen-year-old gained fame playing a high school detective in the popular television series *Breaking Rules*, and was in Atlanta working on her first feature film. Recently receiving a Kids' Choice Award for her work, she was also known for her romantic relationships, which were often portrayed in the media as a wholesome example for teens.

The oldest of four children, Miss Winchester paved the way for her younger brothers to enter the industry. Rising star Reece has already surpassed his sister's fame, appearing in several films before the age of twelve. Lesser-known Rowan and baby Raine appear poised to do the same. How the tragedy will affect the new Hollywood dynasty is unclear.

CHAPTER 1

As a film director, Reece Winchester was used to watching life through a camera lens, picturing angles, depth, color, and texture. He lived as a voyeur, removed from the action he oversaw, the unseen god of the worlds he created for moviegoers everywhere. Some people might see him as being aloof or uncaring. Hell, maybe he was. But he'd learned hard lessons throughout his life about trust, about grief, about tragedy and loss. Better to put a layer between yourself and the outside world, as far as he was concerned.

Maybe that's why he was able to remain calm during this latest catastrophe. He only sighed as he stared at the charred remnants of his house, eying the wisps of smoke still rising from the ruin in the early morning light.

"Damn, Reece, I'm so sorry," said his brother Rowan, who'd been the one to call him at two a.m. to tell him about the fire. He'd repeated the phrase about a dozen times.

Reece had been shooting in the New Mexico desert, so his Beverly Hills home had been empty when it went up in flames last night. He'd spent most of the flight back being thankful he'd left his dog with his brother and had given the couple who looked after the place two weeks off. During other trips, he'd left Cecil B., his golden retriever, at home with the Scotts. He didn't even want to think about what could have happened if they'd been there.

Shit could be replaced. Lives could not. The loss of a couple of statues of a guy named Oscar was nothing compared to the singeing of one hair on the heads of his employees or his dog.

"Any idea yet what started it?" he bit out.

"I talked to the fire investigator. He already found accelerant."

Accelerant. Arson? Jesus.

"Somebody hates me enough to burn down my house?" Reece murmured, a little more stunned by that fact than by the fire itself.

"It could have been a frustrated stalker who expected to find you at home."

"And when I wasn't, they decided to make sure I didn't have a home to come back to?"

"You know it's possible."

Yes, it probably was. He'd had overzealous fans before, mostly during his acting days. They occasionally slipped from pushy into obsessive. He'd been dealing with a particularly bad one lately, who'd found out where he lived and had been leaving notes stuffed into the security gate. Perhaps that was who had gotten past the fence last night and decided to send his home up in a giant ball of flame that had, reportedly, been seen by people miles away.

"Do you ever wonder if we're damned?" he asked.

He'd had this thought many times over the years but had never shared it with his twin.

"Don't say that."

He didn't push, knowing Rowan had done a better job moving beyond all the dark episodes of the past. Reece, though, had found letting that go extremely difficult to do.

"You know you can stay with me for a while. At least until you find another place," Rowan offered.

Reece nodded. "Dad has a spare room, too."

Reece, his twin Rowan, and their baby brother, Raine, had bought their hardworking father, who'd supported them all his life, a big place on the beach a few months ago. His dad would hate to hear about the fire but would probably love some company.

Reece watched silently as firefighters walked the site. They carefully looked for any sputtering embers trying to reignite. With the drought, they also had to be sure no sparks landed on a nearby roof, spreading the conflagration to the entire neighborhood.

"Why don't we get outta here?" Rowan asked. "You've given your statement. You don't have to stay. Want some breakfast? We can pick up Cecil B. and take him out for pancakes."

Seeing his dog sounded like a great idea to Reece. "Sure." He was hungry, as, he suspected, were the sweaty, exhausted firefighters. He'd already put in an order for cold drinks and food for the guys who'd tried so hard to rescue his six-thousand-square-foot house. *Just a house. Just a building.*

Right. Frankly, the worst part wasn't the fire, but the

realization that someone had set it. He was in somebody's crosshairs. The knowledge unsettled him.

"Surfing after?"

They hadn't surfed together in months, both of
them having busy schedules, and Reece being too easily
recognized to hit any of the local beaches. One of the
many pleasures his fame had cost him. Rowan was
lucky they were fraternal twins, and that he no longer
lived in the spotlight. "Maybe later. I think I'll stop by
and see how Aunt Sharon's doing at the gallery."

"Okay. Pancakes, followed by weird art."

Their aunt did have eclectic taste. She also had a good
eye, which was why Reece had been glad to finance the
gallery in Venice Beach. Considering she had helped
raise them after their own mother had been committed,
there wasn't much he wouldn't do for her.

Which was why, three hours later, he stood with her
in the office of Venice on the Beach Fine Arts, actually
smiling. The gallery was filled with pieces that only
the pretentious, rich Southern California type could
afford. To him, many paintings looking like plates full
of spaghetti smeared around by preschoolers. Sharon,
however, loved all types of art, and was thrilled with the
gallery, which pleased him.

"You're sure you have everything you need?" he said.
"You know you only have to ask."

She ruffled his hair like he was still a thirteen-year-old
kid...not that he'd felt like a kid at thirteen. "You've
done enough! Now stop thinking about me and start
focusing on yourself. I still can't believe you came here,
today of all days."

"I'll be fine." He'd already asked an agent to look for a house he could rent—one with great security—while he started rebuilding.

Sharon kept talking, but he didn't hear her. Because something bright and colorful on the security monitor in the office suddenly caught his attention.

Red hair. Shiny, glorious red hair, with gold highlights.

Captivated, Reece turned to fully face the image. He immediately went into director mode, glad the state-of-the-art security system displayed everything in full color.

The woman had come into the public part of the gallery downstairs, jogging in off the beach. She was young, midtwenties at most, with that long mane swept up into a bouncy ponytail. She did things for spandex that would make cotton lie down and weep with jealousy. Yet it was her face he kept staring at. Her body might be perfect, but her face wasn't, at least not classically so. But it was interesting...arresting. Strong—so determined, it told tales of struggle and adversity not often seen in faces so young. Most of all, she was *different*.

The nose was a little crooked, a little pronounced. Most self-respecting Southern California women would have had that straightened and daintily tipped before entering high school. The eyes—he couldn't determine the color—were a bit too far apart, but big and heavily lashed with highly arched brows above. The mouth was wide, the lips full. Kissable. She had a cleft in her chin that he wanted to taste, as he wanted to taste the slick sheen of sweat riding across her chest, gliding down into the hint of cleavage shown by the scoop-necked jogging top.

It had been a dark and difficult morning. But the sun had come out and it was wearing running shoes. "Who is *she*?" he murmured, not taking his eyes off the screen.

Sharon bent to peer over his shoulder. "I have no idea."

"Not one of your artists?"

"Does she look like an artist?"

"Not exactly."

"But not a typical beach bimbo, either."

"Definitely not."

She appeared to be the type who would be much more at home in a place like this than on a boardwalk. He pictured her in a gown and jewels, hair up, one long curl hitting her shoulder. Or screw it, no dress and the hair down and loose, draping over her bare breasts.

He watched her through the camera, saying nothing, envisioning how she would catch the light, where she would be best framed, how she'd move, how she would take direction. It was how he always reacted to initial encounters with strangers, picturing a series of shots and takes, cuts and stills.

A woman he had briefly dated had once accused him of being calculating, always the director, no longer an actor, on film or on the world stage. His brothers, though, and closest friends, saw the real Reece. He was a man of long vision, not the quick, immediate scene. He saw the key moments, the turning points, the journey, the climax, the resolution, and how to get there.

He wondered how to *get* there with the redhead and was determined to find out.

"What the hell?" he whispered, wondering where his sanity had gotten to.

Because this was crazy. He'd never had such an immediate reaction to a woman he hadn't even met in person. Something about this one made him revert to a hormonal teenager. The sight of her had hit him like a punch in the gut, leaving him anxious and a little dizzy. He had never gotten involved with a woman based on looks; it was always about shared interests, intelligence, and, of course, attraction. For all he knew, the redhead downstairs might have the personality of a bag of rocks. But even reminding himself of that didn't slow his pounding heart.

This was physical. It was fascination.

It was completely new.

Reece swallowed, took a deep breath, and regained his control as he continued to watch what was happening one floor down, waiting to see something—anything—that would break this spell he was under.

A minute later, after showing the floor manager, Sid, some invisible-from-here photos on her cell phone, the woman frowned—Christ, even the frown lines were sexy—nodded, and departed.

"Can you find out what she wanted?" he asked Sharon.

"I was just waiting for you to ask," his aunt said, tapping a text on her phone. Sid looked down at his own, receiving Sharon's message. He jabbed at the screen, typing something back.

"Her name's Jessica. She has a sister who's in the arts."

Doesn't everyone in LA?

"She sent Sid a link to a photo gallery of the sister's work." Sharon was silent for a moment, and then she whistled, swiping her finger across the screen, her eyes growing round.

Reece watched her react to whatever she was seeing. He could have feigned disinterest, but Aunt Sharon knew him well enough that she'd have seen right through it. "What is it?"

Her brows were up, her expression a bit stunned. "The artist hasn't had any professional showings, and the sister is trying to help her set something up," Sharon explained, handing him the phone. "And she's good. Damn good."

Reece took the phone, glancing at the screen, far more interested in the woman than in the artwork. At least, until he took a closer look. "Holy shit."

"Tell me about it."

The sculpture displayed on the phone was of a life-size naked woman. But it wasn't a classical, museum-type study of the female form. No. This one was sexy and erotic, displaying a woman in the full throes of pleasure, with her hand between her legs and her head thrown back. Something about the model looked familiar.

"The throat," he whispered. "The shoulders, the hips, the legs." He recognized them. He'd been staring at them through the security monitor for the past several minutes.

"Interesting, no?" Aunt Sharon asked.

"Interesting, *yes*." He swiped the screen, seeing

another piece, and then another. All were stunning nudes, though most were not as sensual as the first. Only that initial one had a recognizable—to him—model. The artist had talent and reason to be proud. So did her sister.

"You've been looking for new and newsworthy pieces," he said, handing back the phone.

The older woman nodded. "This would certainly get attention."

Yes, it would. All kinds of attention: press, buyers. Having a display of nude art wasn't unusual, but the raw talent of the artist made her work stand out. It could help Sharon make a go of this place. Reece didn't really give a damn if the gallery made him his money back, but he knew his aunt was too proud to remain indebted to him.

She definitely shouldn't feel indebted. She'd stepped in as a mother figure after his own had become unable to. He would have given her the money for the gallery, no questions asked. He'd become a silent partner because she'd insisted it was the only way she would accept his cash.

"You want me to have the artist come in for a discussion?"

"Yes."

Aunt Sharon smirked. "I suppose you want me to ask her to bring her sister?"

He didn't reply. He didn't need to. His smile was probably answer enough.

Thinking about how his day had started—with a phone call saying his house had burned down—he couldn't help but be surprised by his own good mood. All because of the beautiful stranger he'd spied through a camera. One he would never have seen if not for the fire, pre-dawn flight, and his presence here in the gallery this morning, at the perfect moment.

He couldn't have planned the scene better if he'd tried. It was as if it were meant to be.

CHAPTER 2

By the time Jessica Jensen arrived at the Venice Beach gallery for Liza's showing, there was a line out the door, winding to the end of the block. Trendy hipsters jostled against grungy millionaires and diamond-decked socialite types, the crowd as mixed up and melted together as only a Southern California social event could be. Apparently, word had spread about her BFF/adopted sister's rave review on the *LAArtscene* blog, which called Liza's work "wildly innovative and breathtaking, both exquisite and shocking!" The masses had come here to see and be seen, to shock and be shocked.

The open bar probably didn't hurt either, at least for the trendy hipsters, whose high-end taste didn't always reflect the size of their low-end bank accounts.

The turnout was thrilling, and her heart pounded in her chest as Jess realized the person she cared for most in this world was really on the verge of the success she so richly deserved. A long line wasn't the endgame, though. The true test would come in the morning when Liza found out from the owner just how many of these desperate-to-be-cool types had actually shelled out money to buy any of the pieces, the cheapest of which was priced at around five grand.

All of Jessica's crossable digits were metaphorically crossed, and not just because she wanted Liza to be successful. There would be a more immediate benefit. One sculpture sold meant their rent wouldn't be late next month. Two might mean they could actually drop the air-conditioning thermostat from ninth circle of hell to eighth. *Dreamy.*

"Miss Jensen, did you find it?" the bouncer asked as she skirted around, cutting in line.

She lifted her hand, in which she held the silver charm bracelet she'd raced home to get when Liza had realized she'd forgotten it. "Crisis contained."

He grinned, having watched her tear out of the gallery an hour ago, right before the show opened. "Her good luck charm, huh?"

"Yeah, literally." She flicked the four-leaf clover. It had been the first charm on the bracelet. "Our mom gave it to her for her sixteenth birthday."

"You're *sisters*?"

He sounded shocked. That made sense. Jess was tall, Liza petite. Liza was a brown-haired bundle of creativeness, Jess a red-haired bundle of attitude.

Oh. Plus Liza was black, and Jess was white. *Details.*

"Yep," she said, not feeling the need to reveal anything more to a stranger. Especially not about the adopted family she'd been blessed to land in.

Liza had been fortunate enough to have her mom, Beth, all her life. Jess had only been lucky enough to get her at age eleven. Her own mom had died when Jess was nine, after which she got to play here-we-go-round-the-foster-care-system for two years. Beth was the prize she'd won at the end of the game. The adoption had saved her life, and not just figuratively, considering Jess's final foster mother had had the maternal instincts of a snake.

Wait. She probably wasn't being fair…to snakes. They vibrated their bodies to warm their eggs. Her last foster mother wouldn't have warmed Jess with a cup of her own spit, and her creepy husband would have just spit on her for his own amusement.

She shoved the memories away. They were phantoms from a past she barely recalled.

"The bracelet must be pretty special. I hope it works for her," the bouncer said.

"You and me both," she murmured, picturing Beth and how proud she would be tonight.

Thinking of Beth still made Jess cry, eighteen months after her death. Liza had to be feeling the loss even more drastically, knowing that but for a few cancerous cells, her mom would be right here with them. The cruel twists of fate had been especially cruel to Jess and Liza when it came to mothers and fathers. They were both orphans now—Liza officially, since her dad had died in an accident before her birth, and Jess technically, since hers had skipped out when she was two. Neither one of them was whining about it, though. They were both gonna be okay.

The bouncer opened the door for her. "Tell her if she doesn't get a taker on the *Touch Me* statue, I'll give her part of my salary for the next twenty years to pay for it."

As he wagged his brows, she forced a tight smile and

hurried in, fearing he'd ask if she'd ever modeled for her sister. She'd been asked that too many times, by too many people.

The short answer: No.

The long answer: Sort of, but only from the neck down. Well, maybe the jaw down.

The longest answer: Yes, and oh, God, wasn't it freaky-weird to lie there naked while her best friend/sister drew tons of sketches of her?

Jess was the woman alone in bed, gaining pleasure in the only way she could.

Art imitates life.

The number of people who would ever know that: two. Jess and Liza.

Inside, she took a second to gawk at the crowd. When she'd left, the building had been practically empty—only Liza on the floor with the management and the staff. On her way out, she'd sent up a good luck prayer, noting how the tastefully arranged gallery had been thick with possibility, waiting for something to start.

Now, sixty minutes later? Well, hot damn, it had started. Her BFF was taking the art world by storm. The place was jam-packed, a strange cross between an art exhibit and a rave. Potential buyers sipped fruity vodka and gushed over the classical-yet-sensual pieces of art surrounding them. A deep thrum of evocative music pulsed; the very air throbbed with it. She felt it reverberating through her body, each thud of the bass timed to the beat of her heart. God, anybody who didn't get a rush from this display was obviously half-comatose. Because the music, the food, the ambient lighting, the thrill of expectation and excitement all added to the atmosphere of sensuality inspired by the nude forms filling the room.

Some artists were inspired by beauty in nature, in architecture, in landscapes. Liza was inspired by naked bodies. If she photographed them, she might be called a pornographer. Instead, she sculpted them, and was a hot artist on the rise. *Gotta love SoCal.*

"There you are!" Liza squealed, grabbing and tugging her into an alcove near the exit. "God, that dress. It's like Cinder-freaking-ella's godmother was Christian Dior."

"Thanks," she said, amused Liza was sticking to her goal to stop swearing. "Did you think I'd show up here in my hideous prom dress, the only long one I own?"

Correction: the only one she *had* owned. Now she had this pale blue designer gown. She'd bought it from a consignment store in Laguna Beach, for probably one-twentieth its original price. That had still been just about enough to break her clothes budget for the year, but she wouldn't have come to Liza's opening in a ratty outfit for anything.

"Nope. We're both the belles of the ball." Liza extended an arm and Jess hooked the bracelet on without interrupting her sister's babbling excitement. "Can you believe this?"

"Of course I can. I knew you could do it," she said, loyalty winning the race over honesty out of her mouth. Because, the truth was, she'd been scared to death that Liza's dreams would be shattered, the whole thing would be a bust, and they'd end the night doing tequila shots in the roach-infested dive downstairs from their not-infested-but-still-sometimes-roachy apartment.

Liza deserved success. But, in Jess's experience, things like this—acclaim, wealth—didn't happen to chicks like them. Ever since they were teenagers growing up in a tiny Illinois town, Liza becoming a famous artist was her fantasy, a daydream, like Jess's was to see her name on an Academy Award statue for Best Original Screenplay. She had never *really* thought they would come true.

Now, though? Surrounded by rich people oohing and aahing, whispering about the beauty of Liza's creations, and pretending they weren't turned on by the naked or nearly naked bodies? Well, Jess wasn't exactly rehearsing her acceptance speech, but perhaps after tonight she'd be willing to admit such things were at least possible. And thinking about what she'd say when seated next to Benedict Cumberbatch on Oscar night.

Whoops. Inner Sherlock *fangirl moment. Down, Cumberbitch.*

"Well, it's all thanks to you."

"Oh, sure, I'm the one who spent sixty hours a week for the past couple of years in a sweltering storage unit making amazing art out of clay."

"No, that was me," Liza said, her smile impish, which went well with her sweet, heart-shaped face, deep brown eyes, and mass of curly brown hair. "But you are the one who got Sid to give me an appointment with Sharon, which resulted in me getting this opportunity."

Jess frowned, not comfortable going down the *I'm so grateful* road. Not with Liza, the person she loved most in the world. What wouldn't she have done to help Liza get her start? She couldn't think of a single goddamn thing.

"That wasn't me, it was my cleavage," she replied with a shrug. "Sid didn't look above my collarbone the first time I came in to talk about your awesome art."

"Well, thank heaven Sid's a creeper."

"Pervert is more like it." But perviness had worked to Liza's advantage. So Jessica hadn't spit in the jerk's face or punched him when he'd made a really gross suggestion after looking at the cell phone full of pictures of nude statuary.

Liza glanced down, addressing Jess's chest. "Thank you, ladies. I've been jealous of you half my life, but you really came through for me."

Jess laughed, knowing what Liza meant. She'd been out for a run, all sweaty and slick, when she'd seen the sign for the new gallery. She was not the type to use T&A to get what she wanted, which was why her usual nonworking uniform was jeans and a geeky fandom T-shirt. On that occasion, though, the she-bits had come in handy. Sid Loman was obviously into college-aged young women wearing tight workout clothes.

She wasn't really college-aged, though she *was* still in college. At twenty-five, she should've graduated three years ago. But when one started late, and then had to work forty hours a week and go to school part-time, it took a lot longer. After this summer session, she'd be within six credits and one internship of that elusive diploma.

"For all your hard work, you deserve some big, strong, man hands," Liza added.

Jess purposely misunderstood, lifting her own. "I'm happy with these."

"I wasn't talking about *you*." Liza nodded toward her chest. "I meant *them*."

She cleared her throat. "Yeah, that's not happening."

She hadn't had anybody else's hands on her body for quite some time, which frankly was fine with Jess. Man hands were attached to men. And men could be...well, she'd leave it at *difficult*, and ignore the other words sprouting in her mind: *bastards, jerks, stalking pricks.*

"Come on, not all guys are..." *Bastards, jerks, stalking pricks.* "Bad." Seeing Jess's reaction, Liza backed off. "Sorry. I forgot I'm talking to Sister Jessica, patron saint of celibacy."

"I'd be happy to end my sainthood if I could meet someone worth sinning for."

"I could name a hundred guys who would line up to help you sin."

"You don't know a hundred guys."

"Fifty then. Fifty guys."

"You don't know fifty guys either, unless you're referring to the jerks we went to high school with." And if she hadn't slept with any of them then, she sure was not going to now. Even her prom date hadn't succeeded in getting her ugly dress off her, though he'd tried groping her through it. Which was why she'd ditched him and walked out of the stupid high school dance.

"You're such a pessimist."

"I don't need fifty guys. One would be fine...as long as he's the right one."

"There are nice men around. They're not all like *that*

bastard," Liza said with a shudder. She knew how bad things had been when Jess ended her last relationship, about a year ago.

Her sister had been her rock, moving without complaint—twice—so Jess could remain away from her ex, Johnny, who she'd dated for eighteen months. They'd both changed their numbers because he'd kept calling, first begging Jess to come back to him, and then growing threatening. He'd also harassed Liza, blaming her for breaking them up.

They both knew the guy was unhinged. It had been a nightmare scenario, for sure.

Fortunately, he had finally backed off...or so she hoped. A tiny hint of worry had been tickling the back of her mind for the past few days, though. One of her neighbors told her a man had been hanging around the building and had asked about her. *Private delivery man.* That had to be it. She didn't know if she could handle it if Johnny reappeared on the scene, wearing his crazy like a crown.

It's been complete radio silence for two months. He's gone, it's over. So maybe she would consider reentering the dating world, if only she met someone who (a) interested her and (b) wasn't a psycho jerk who would stalk her if she ended things.

As usual, Liza read her mind. "You'll find someone. Someone wonderful. You have to let yourself be open to it and not worry every guy is going to go Michael Myers stalker on you."

Johnny had never gone serial killer crazy, but he had once threatened to kill her. That threat had been the final straw. She'd told him she never wanted to see him again, moved, and changed her number. Only he didn't get the hint... or the blunt statement.

Not wanting to continue the dark conversation on this oh-so-bright evening, she said, "Emily doesn't get off work until nine, but she promised she'd be over afterward."

Their new roommate had been with them for only a month. It hadn't been easy bringing a stranger into their tight little family, but they needed a third to make their rent. So far things were working out. Emily was a lot of fun—she worked with Jess at the restaurant—but was also respectful of the longtime bond her two roommates shared. She didn't take offense when Jess and Liza wanted some sister time.

"Great, but you're not getting away with the subject change. It's high time you put yourself back into the dating game. Or at least the sex one."

Sharon, the owner of the gallery, came gliding over, looking ecstatic. "Liza, darling, you must come with me! We've sold *Making Love*. The buyer wants to meet you."

Not only was Jess thrilled the priciest piece in the collection had sold, but she realized she'd been saved by the bell by Sharon's announcement. Her sex life was not something she ever wanted to discuss, especially not when in public. And sober.

"Seriously? *Making Love*'s the first one to sell?" Liza asked.

"Did you think it would be a subtle, small-penised, classical nude?" Jess replied with a snort, not surprised a supersexy sculpture had found a buyer right away. Everyone in SoCal wanted to be considered cutting edge and daring. "Of *course* some studio hotshot wants sex-in-stone. It'll be the centerpiece of the marble-tiled foyer of his Malibu mansion."

Liza merely sighed. *Making Love* was the biggest piece in the collection, depicting two nude forms, not one. It perfectly captured the beauty of human sexuality between two people who loved each other. But it was also full-on statue sex, and there were a bunch of discreet, classical pieces Liza liked more.

"It's not the first to sell, it's the second." Before Liza could ask for details, Sharon went on. "And the buyer *is* a rich studio hotshot who might buy more, so let's go."

Sharon grabbed Liza's arm and tugged her away. Jess smiled as the women disappeared into the crowd, then decided to walk through the exhibit. She'd watched these items develop from sketch to completion, but she had never looked at them on proper display.

First, though, she needed fortification after her race home and back. Skating around the chatty gawkers, she headed for the bar and smiled at the good-looking bartender.

"Tonight's special is a Flaming Orgasm," he said with a confident smile.

"Interesting."

"Can I give you one?" His words were low, suggestive.

"How about you just *make* me one," she replied with a chuckle.

"I'll make sure it's strong and powerful...something you won't forget."

The guy was obviously angling for good tips, offering hot orgasms to every person who came up to the bar, male or female, so Jess don't take the flirtation seriously. But when his fingers lingered against hers as he slid the glass across the bar, she took notice. His smile was intimate, his eyes warm. So maybe the invitation wasn't as generic as she'd imagined.

"Whenever you're ready for more, you let me know."

"I think this'll be enough for tonight." Because real flaming orgasms were nice, but they so often came with strings attached. Or men. Same difference.

Sipping her strong, fruity drink, she moved through the gallery. Clumps of people whispered around some of the most beautiful pieces. The biggest crowd was gathered around *Looking in the Mirror*, a stunning piece showing a woman weeping as she undressed. The woman's eyes and posture conveyed such sadness— a statement on society's pressure on women to look perfect—that the heart ached to behold her. She affected everyone...well, everyone except Sid the Perv, who looked so pleased you'd think he was the artist, not the salesperson.

Suddenly, something changed.

A frisson of tension slid through her, and a tiny quiver shook her body. The fine hairs on her arms stood up. Her breath shortened, and she began to hear the pounding of her own heart as her pulse surged.

She was being watched.

Jess took a calming breath, knowing her panicked reaction was excessive. Because, well, of course she was being watched. Everyone in the place was watching everyone else, looking for reactions to the art, or for a subject of future gossip. Jess suspected this art show would inspire more one-night stands than Marvin Gaye night at a singles club. Everyone was watchful, wanting to know who wasn't going home alone and all that critically important stuff people in this zip code loved to whisper about.

That didn't calm her. Jess's skin actually began to prickle in goose bumps, and a tiny throb in her lower back made her almost want to arch it. It was odd, but the small of her back, with its delicate vertebrae at the base of her spine, was one of her most erogenous zones. A lover intuitive or patient enough to discover the vulnerable spot on her back could turn her into a puddle of need with the faintest brush of his fingertips. Not surprisingly, Johnny never had.

That was how this felt...like a delicate touch. This stare, this attention—it was intimate. The hint of panic receded, utter awareness taking its place.

With her history, thinking someone was watching her every move should make her nervous or afraid. But she wasn't. Just because she was being stared at didn't mean any ugly remnants of her past were lurking in the shadows of the gallery. Her instincts whispered this was something different, something new.

She lifted her hand and swiped her hair back over her shoulder. Trying to be unobtrusive, she looked around, hoping to discover the person eyeing her. Her stare slid over the crowd. She didn't see anybody focusing on her enough to make her react so viscerally, though she did catch the gaze of more than one guy who offered a smile. She ignored them, even while the heat of someone's avid attention bored through her skin.

And then she saw him.

He stood in the back corner of the gallery, half-hidden in shadow. He appeared to be the only person in the place not pressed in the middle of a group. Something about his posture—ostensibly relaxed, but with an almost tangible element of tension—warned anyone not to get too close.

The lights from two nearby alcoves cast enough illumination to show he was tall and wearing a dark suit. His brown hair was shot with gold, but Jess couldn't make out any of his features. Still, she knew he was the watcher. His eyes reflected a gleam of light, and those eyes were staring at only one thing. Her.

Jess looked away, swallowing nervously. She resisted the urge to lift her hair off the back of her neck again, not because she needed a distraction, but because she was suddenly hot. A thin sheen of perspiration had emerged on her skin, to go along with her thudding heart and choppy breaths. The spot on the base of her spine still tingled. She knew it was bizarre to be reacting like this to the watchfulness of a stranger, but thought wasn't part of the equation. Her senses and instincts were in charge. She felt as confusingly aroused as a virgin on prom night.

Unable to resist, she glanced at him again. He hadn't moved, still standing silently in the corner, alone, unapproachable. But when he saw her looking, he leaned forward to meet her gaze, so the light shone on his entire face. Jess sucked in a gasp, pure feminine appreciation flooding through her, and she literally wobbled in her spiky heels. She hadn't had so much as an ankle tremor when darting between cars on Venice Boulevard, but she was ready to fall over because a stranger's face shifted the world on its axis.

Calling him handsome would be like calling Mount Everest a hill. He was utterly magnificent, from the top of his tousled hair to his strong forehead, slashing brows, high cheekbones, hollowed cheeks, square jaw, and luscious mouth, so serious and unsmiling. The shadows of the room emphasized the stark, sculpted lines of his face, and as he shifted, the light caught those strange, arresting eyes again. She couldn't determine the color but realized they were practically glowing, the effect nearly animalistic.

Her fanciful writer's imagination went to dark places and scary stories of vampires and werewolves. Sexy ones. Damn, she really need to reglom *True Blood*.

Yes, she had a TV obsession. A movie obsession. A Hollywood obsession.

Which made it even crazier that she hadn't *immediately* recognized who was staring at her the second she laid eyes on him. But when she heard a whisper nearby—*Is it really him? Is that Winchester?*—her mind finally kicked back into gear and she realized who, exactly, he was.

Reece Winchester.

The six-year-old girl within her who'd liked him in a Nickelodeon movie smiled. The thirteen-year-old girl who'd crushed on the rebellious, smart-mouthed gang member trying to break out of his deadly world sighed.

The fourteen-year-old girl who'd been devastated by the fate of the golden-haired lieutenant who'd stormed the beaches of Normandy wept. The fifteen-year-old girl who'd gone wild over the dreamy nineteenth-century writer with the tragic life and death quivered. And the seventeen-year-old girl who'd fallen wildly in lust with the hot intergalactic playboy/fighter pilot who saved the universe got a little damp in the panties. Every movie in between had only deepened her crush.

Reece Winchester: inspiration for dreams and fantasies. Childhood star turned adult box-office golden boy. Actor. Director. Screenwriter. Moviemaker. Oscar winner. Millionaire. Recluse. Mystery man. *And he's looking right at me.*

"Oh, my God," she mumbled when it all sank in. Her jaw unhinged, but she quickly snapped it shut, wincing as her teeth scraped her tongue. She was supposed to be a professional; she wanted to be part of the movie world, and soon. Getting all tongue-tied and fangirlish over a sex god who was miles out of her league was not the way to get ahead in this town. At least not the way she wanted to get ahead.

Besides, she must have been mistaken. He hadn't been staring at her. No way. Reece Winchester dated heiresses, models, and actresses. Glamorous sexpots. Not twenty-five-year-old waitresses/college students. Nor could he be as handsome close-up as he'd always looked on the screen...though he looked pretty darn good from thirty feet away, too.

Forcing away the crazy idea somebody like him would give somebody like her a second glance, she deliberately shoved her shoulders back and her chin up, and stepped close to the nearest piece of art, studying it like she intended to do a dissertation on the thing.

Mistake. The piece was a male nude, and she was about eye level with a thickly muscled thigh and a coyly draped crotch.

She fanned her face, remembering the nude scenes from the last movie in which Winchester had appeared. *Twisted*, an erotic thriller released five years ago, had been scorching. The film had earned its R rating by the skin of its teeth, and it was Winchester's most popular of his acting career, even if it hadn't been the one to earn him the Best Actor nomination. After its release, and despite its popularity, he'd stopped acting to focus on scriptwriting and directing. Since he'd been only twenty-five at the time, and was the hottest young star in Hollywood, the moviegoing world had been shocked, twenty-year-old Jess included. But the career-change didn't appear to have hurt him any.

Jess was so lost in thought about Reece the Superstar she forgot the man was in the room, and that she'd imagined he was staring at her. Which was perhaps why she nearly dropped her glass when she felt a tall, solid form move behind her and heard a man say, "Interesting."

Smooth voice. Deep, silky. A voice she recognized. She'd heard it on the big screen and the small one, since she had copies of every movie he'd starred in—seven from his childhood years, eight from his adult ones. Was he *really* talking to her?

"Yes, it is," she murmured, all calm and collected, like she was not shaking in her consignment store shoes.

"Possibly one of the artist's earlier efforts."

Hmm. How had he known? "Yes," Miss Conversational Genius repeated.

"I'm not interrupting, am I?"

The hint of confidence in the tone told her he knew the answer. Had any woman ever told him to go away because he was bothering her? Huh. Doubtful. "Not at all."

"Good. What is it called?"

"What we're doing? I think it's a conversation." Jess didn't know where the snarky response came from, or where she'd gotten the nerve to be all quippy with the guy, but there you go. That was her, always a mouth-off away from catastrophe.

"I meant the sculpture," he said. No laugh. No humor. *Crap.*

Realizing they *were* actually going to have a conversation, and knowing it might require face-to-face interaction, she wondered if she was ready for it. Hesitating, she licked her lips and replied, "It's called *Naked Man.*"

"Subtle."

Knowing it was rude not to face him, she took a deep breath and glanced over her shoulder. *Lord have mercy.*

Deep breaths might be calming in normal situations—like when one was confronted by a repo man repossessing a car. *Been there, done that.* But they didn't work at all when looking into the clear amber eyes of a man every woman on the planet fantasized about. His looks made you silently gawk while you tried to figure out why the arrangement of cheek and jaw, mouth and eyes, was so arresting and unforgettable. She interacted with scruffy, shaggy-haired surf-bum types in the bar where she worked, so she'd almost forgotten how appealing a conservative haircut and a smoothly shaven face could be. Not to mention the sexiness of a perfectly tailored power suit, the charcoal color interrupted only by a splash of red in the necktie.

She finally cleared her throat and pushed a few words out. "It *is* from very early in the artist's career. How did you know?"

"She draped the sex organs, as if she wasn't quite ready to go there."

Jess nodded, wondering if she was truly talking about men's packages with the sexiest freaking man alive. Was this really happening, or was she hallucinating? Had that stupid bartender slipped GHB in her drink? Damn, if she woke up tomorrow with no memory of what happened, and then found videos of herself on YouTube, she would rip him a new one.

"Even for an early work, though, it's very good," he added.

In case this was real, she decided to go with the conversation. "Yes, I'm happy to have seen it coming together."

"You watched the work in progress?"

"Yes. The model's a neighbor."

He was also an actor. Jess had heard he was talented, but she had no firsthand knowledge. His movies were the kind shown in shady theaters on Santa Monica Boulevard, where the guys in the audience wore trench coats and the only women were looking for customers. But he was a hell of a nice guy, as well as being hilarious at parties.

"And the artist?"

"She's my sister."

"You have different last names."

Shocked, she spun all the way around and gaped at him. "How do you know?"

"I asked about you, Jessica." He didn't seem at all embarrassed or coy about it; his bluntness was unnerving.

"Asked whom, *Reece*?"

A faint twinkle in the eyes. "Sharon."

"You know her?" She was starting to feel like a parrot. "I mean, why would she tell you?"

Why would you ask?

"She's my partner."

Confusion dug at her. "Partner..." Then it sank in. "Wait, do you co-own this gallery?"

"I do."

Wow. She'd had no idea, and she would bet Liza hadn't either.

Before she could question him again, he elaborated. "Sharon's also my aunt. She has a good eye, and she likes art. So I supply the money and she does the rest."

A silent partner. It made sense. A guy like him couldn't simply open a business. He was too busy running his movie empire, writing and directing hit film after hit film, achieving the kind of superstardom his fans from his childhood-star years could never have envisioned. He might have had only one Oscar nomination for acting; so far, however, for writing and/or directing, he'd added another three nods and two wins. In under six years. Amazing.

"I stay out of it, for the most part." His voice dropped, and a hint of intensity was audible in his tone. "I just show up when there's something *interesting* to see."

He wasn't staring at the statue now; he was studying her. Those fascinating brown-gold eyes—a lion's eyes—swept over her as he assessed her hair, her face, her throat, her lips. Jess's breath didn't quite reach her lungs. She got the feeling he was trying to tell her something, as if he'd come here to see *her*, not Liza's work, which was crazy since he couldn't have known she existed until a few minutes ago.

"And you knew there would be something interesting to see tonight?" she prodded, feeling light-headed. His stare was so captivating, the appreciation in his gaze overwhelming. She was probably fumbling, but she had to know if she'd totally misread him.

"I knew."

He continued to stare, but didn't smile, nor did he go on. He was cryptic, his speech clipped and deliberate, his mood mysterious. He had sought her out, come over to talk to her, but he wasn't flirting, and he didn't appear to be trying to pick her up. *As if.* Still, his attention was searing, every bit of his focus directed at her. It felt as if they were the only two people here.

Being the object of Reece Winchester's unfiltered interest was a feeling unlike any she'd experienced before. It had nothing to do with him being a movie star, or even that he was a drop-dead gorgeous, rich, successful one. There was something magnetic about the man himself. A sort of powerful energy throbbed when he was near, and she found herself completely unable to resist the pull of it.

He turned on his heel to look at the sculpture again, the abrupt change of mood startling. "I prefer your sister's female nudes."

"You and every other straight dude here."

He didn't laugh, or even acknowledge the comment. "In fact, I've already bought one."

"Let me guess—you're the studio hotshot who snapped up *Making Love*?"

A slow shake of his head. Right. Left. Center.

The man was so serious, so darned intense. And she was so far out of her depth, she had no idea how she was still even a part of this conversation.

"I had my new purchase removed to a private suite upstairs before the opening, and will have it shipped out to my place tomorrow. I didn't want anyone else seeing it. I wanted it reserved strictly for my own viewing pleasure."

Huh. She hadn't even noticed one missing, and Jess was familiar with all of Liza's work. Then again, there were sixteen pieces on display, and every display alcove was packed.

She was curious, though. "Which one was it?"

"Come. I'll show you."

So much for his own viewing pleasure. She had no idea why he was inviting her, nor did he wait for her to agree to come with him. He simply tried to steer her away by placing his hand on the small of her back to edge her through the crowd.

A tiny moan escaped her lips. She quivered and almost stumbled.

Her dress was extremely low cut, front and back. A silky scoop descended to just above her rear. She'd never worn anything like it, mainly because she had never wanted to inflict dreadful boob tape on herself, and there was no way this dress could be worn with a bra. But now she knew the dress was worth the tape, even if she ripped away skin trying to pry it off later. She'd been so worried about the front, and containing her *assets*, she hadn't even considered how exposed her lower back would be in the dress. It had never occurred to her to wonder what might happen to her if that oh-so-sensitive spot was on display and practically invited touching.

Now she knew. Fire happened. Lava and wonder and desire and need happened.

As his fingertips brushed against her bare spine, his middle finger dipping low, a hot wave of pulsing desire radiated throughout her body, making her shudder involuntarily. There was the faintest contact, the tiniest stroke of skin on skin, but she felt utterly electrified as sparks of heated sensation spiked through her.

He leaned close to murmur, "Are you all right?"

She swallowed hard, trying to find her vocal cords. "It's warm and overcrowded."

Understatement. The tiny touch had aroused her to a point of near insanity. She didn't imagine that was his intention, but he'd succeeded nonetheless.

"It will be more comfortable upstairs."

"Maybe. Or maybe it'll be a big mistake."

He dropped his hand, not urging her, nor trying to lead the way. It was as if he knew Jess was fighting an inner battle between want and wisdom. He even stepped back an inch, touching her only with his magnetic aura, the decision entirely in her hands.

"It's your choice. Do you want to come with me, Jessica?"

Damn. She was not the type who wanted a man to call the shots, but it sure would be easier to justify anything that happened by saying he'd swept her off her feet. But he wasn't going to let her off so easily. It would have to be her choice.

Then she reminded herself: *nothing's gonna happen*. He was an unusual man, here alone, probably looking to escape the sycophants by engaging someone as equally alone in conversation. That was it. There was nothing personal, nothing sexual, about the invitation, despite the ambiance.

But his eyes—oh, those eyes—they glowed with something that looked like promise. And, at last, that mouth quirked up the tiniest bit, the sparkle in his eyes accompanying what might, for him, be the beginning of a genuine smile. It was as if he were daring her to give in, to at least go along and see where he might want to take her.

A wise woman would know her limitations and stick to her own side of the playground. This guy played in a whole different league.

The hint of a smile tempted her, though.

She knew Reece wasn't any of the characters he'd played on the screen; he was a unique person who was good at disappearing into other people's skin. But she had beheld his gorgeous smile in films, seen the way laugh lines fanned at the corners of his eyes when he was happy. What she was seeing now didn't come close. She wanted to witness the real thing. Full-throttle warmth and broadly smiling charm from the man himself, not a character he was playing.

She wanted a real smile directed only at her.

So while she knew the wise choice would be to say no—two little letters, one small syllable—she found another word coming into her mouth.

Before she could say it, however, his jaw clenched the tiniest bit. "You decide," he said, glancing over the crowd toward the front door. "I don't want to pressure you."

Little did he know his hint of a smile had already done the trick.

Jess had never pictured herself as the Cinderella type. Well, she'd understood the sitting-in-the-ashes, worked-to-death part. Her days in foster care had given her a graphic lesson in playing that role. She'd just never imagined there could be fairy godmothers, gorgeous gowns, and Prince Charmings whisking girls into their happily ever afters. Or at least their happily-upstairs-in-a-private-suite-with-a-movie-stars.

Hmm. Beth certainly had been her fairy godmother. She *was* wearing a killer dress. And a Hollywood prince was trying to whisk her away from a big party.

Shit. Maybe she *was* freaking Cinderella, with Christian Dior as her fairy godmother.

"So I'll tell you what. I'll wait for you by the elevator in the back hallway in ten minutes. If you're there, I'll take you up and show you everything you want to see."

Oh. He was giving her time to change her mind. In ten minutes, she would certainly come up with a thousand reasons not to go with him. Crap.

You're going. It's a once-in-a-lifetime chance, and you're not going to blow it.

Right. She was so gonna be there. Almost certainly. Definitely probably.

But something impertinent and unpredictable made her ask, "And if I'm not?"

He looked down at her. Hesitated. And then said, "If you're not, I think I'll regret it for the rest of my life."

CHAPTER 3

One minute Reece had been with the most stunning woman here, touching the soft, creamy skin at her back, entranced by her husky voice and the sparkle in her brown eyes, more fascinated with her by the second. The next, he'd spied Rowan at the door and had begun swimming through the crowd, wondering if he'd missed his shot with the redhead.

As he made his way across the gallery toward his sibling, however, he did feel a hint of pleasure. He and Rowan were close, but their busy schedules meant they didn't see each other often. Since the house fire two months ago, Reece had moved into a rental place up in the hills—very private, very secluded. He wasn't doing a lot of traveling, so he didn't have to leave Cecil B. with Rowan. Normally, he'd like this reunion. But his seventeen-minutes-younger twin definitely had bad timing.

She'll be waiting. She had to be. Their chemistry was too strong for her to resist. And if she wasn't? Well, he'd just have to entice her all over again. Despite what he'd told her about regret, he wasn't going to let her go without taking another shot.

"Reece, wait."

He paused as someone snagged his sleeve. Surprised,

he turned around and saw a middle-aged woman with coarse, gray-streaked hair scooped up on one side and secured with a flower. She looked familiar, and wore a dreamy expression he'd seen on the faces of many women before her. He inwardly flinched, steeling himself for what he knew was coming.

"It's been a long time," she said, her voice barely above a whisper.

"Uh...yes."

"I've missed you."

Missed him? Did she even *know* him? "Look, I..."

"You don't remember me."

He racked his brain, to no avail. "I'm sorry, I'm afraid I don't."

Her hopeful smile tightened. "Of course, why would you remember? We only met twice. Anyway, I need to talk to you. I was hoping we could slip away for a minute. Maybe upstairs?"

Her suggestion was too much like what he'd asked of Jess a few minutes ago for his comfort. Had she been eavesdropping? Damn, couldn't he get a single night out without his privacy being invaded?

"Hey, bro, how's it going?" Rowan came in to save the day, as he often did when he knew Reece had been cornered by some determined, hopeful fan. "I don't mean to be rude," Rowan continued with a friendly smile, "but I haven't seen my brother in ages, and we have a lot to catch up on. Family stuff. You understand."

The stranger's eyes narrowed, and Reece noticed her fists curling at her sides. So. She was *that* type of fan. His stomach clenched and he stiffened, knowing she didn't want an autograph. She had personalized their relationship in her mind. She thought he returned her feelings.

He knew from experience he couldn't give her the slightest hint of encouragement. He hated to play the role of shitty ex–movie star, but he knew it was for the best. "If you'd like an autographed photo, you're welcome to contact my office. We're online."

"I have one," she snapped before whirling around and stalking away.

"Gee," said Rowan. "Was it something I said?"

"No. I think it was the fact that I have no clue who she is."

"Stalker fan?"

"I sincerely hope not."

"You're just a chick magnet ... *Eddie*."

Shaking his head, Reece resisted the impulse to punch his fraternal twin in the jaw.

"You gonna say thanks for my timely arrival?"

"It might have been timely in one regard, but definitely not in another."

He didn't mention he'd been about to take a stunning redhead up to the private viewing room. This crowd was filled with people he didn't know and had no interest in talking to, and people he *did* know—who interested him even less. He'd wanted to get away, to be with her, and the invitation to come upstairs had seemed like the perfect way to do it.

Then his brother had come in. No way could he have whisked Jessica out of the gallery and up the elevator without Rowan seeing. And following. Rowan would have enjoyed being the kink in the hose.

"I told Aunt Sharon I'd be here," Rowan replied, apparently not noticing he didn't have Reece's full attention.

"She'll be pleased," he murmured.

"Don't think Raine's gonna make it, though."

Reece wasn't surprised. Their baby brother, Raine, an ex-soldier and current security company owner, was bodyguarding a dimpled darling of the cinema. Not only was Raine not the art gallery type, but this exhibit wasn't suitable for an eight-year-old movie starlet. Then again, Rowan, a police detective, wasn't exactly the art gallery type either. Yet here he was. That said something about how much they loved Aunt Sharon.

"So, how's it going, *Georgie*?" he replied, getting his brother back for calling him Eddie.

Rowan held up both hands in surrender. "Okay, keep your voice down, we're even."

"We'll never be even. Georgie is far worse than Eddie."

Their birth names had been a dreaded family secret since the kids were old enough to start school and understand firsthand what the word *bully* meant. Fortunately, with the two of them sticking together, they'd usually managed to come out on top. Until they'd moved to Hollywood, become child actors, and learned the real meaning of the word *bully*.

He shook his head, not wanting to think those thoughts. That they weren't usually on his mind said a lot about how far he'd come. He only wondered if his brothers had, too.

"Tell me about it," Rowan said with a heavy sigh. "I

guess that's one thing we'll always have to thank Mom for…even if Dad will call us by our given names from now until eternity."

That was understandable since he was never happy she had them legally changed.

Reece smiled faintly as he thought of their dad, a hardworking electrician. Reece had stayed with him for a week after the fire, enjoying the time alone with the happy retiree.

The fact that all the brothers had kept the names their manager/mother had sued to give them when they were kids said a lot about how much they'd disliked the ones they'd been given at birth: Edward, George, and Thomas. Few people knew their birth names. For decades, the world had known them as Reece, Rowan, and Raine Winchester, having watched them grow up on the small screen, and the big one, from the time the twins were seven and Raine just a baby.

And Rachel, of course. Their older sister, destined for stardom, the teenage drama queen.

Long gone, but not forgotten. At least not by her younger brothers.

Although none of them were actors any longer, the names still worked. *Rowan* sounded like the kind of guy who bloodhounded his way through crime investigations, as his brother did in the police department. *Raine* was pretty good for a man who rained down holy hell on potential kidnappers or stalkers as the owner of a private security company specializing in child-actor protection.

Reece? Well, it probably didn't matter if the world

knew his birth name was Edward, but he'd gotten used to it. Though, considering his real name was so average it might have gotten him off the damn cover of *People* magazine several years ago, he probably should've changed it back. *Eddie* didn't sound like the "Sexiest Man Alive," an honor he would gladly have done without.

"So, truce?" Rowan asked, flashing a grin.

"Truce," Reece said, forgiving him for the name bit, even if he hadn't quite forgiven him for interrupting his time with Jessica. He gave his sibling a quick backslap.

"How's everything going?" Rowan asked. "Your latest project coming along well?"

"Actually, yes. It's even under budget."

"No way. Nice." Rowan stepped closer and lowered his voice. "And any news about the house?"

Reece took a deep breath. "No, nothing yet."

"The lead detective who's working on it is good. He'll crack it."

"Before the new place is burned to the ground, too?" Reece had hired security to keep an eye on the construction of what would be his new house, but still...

"Just be thankful you weren't in it."

"Huh. Maybe if I had been, I could have caught the asshole in the act."

"Or you might have died in your bed." His usually cheerful brother sounded concerned.

"I'm a light sleeper."

"Not if you're breathing smoke. Besides, if you *had* woken up and found somebody in your house, you probably would have beaten the crap out of him and gotten yourself sued."

It sounded crazy, considering he'd been the victim, but he knew his brother was right.

Although the harassment had begun when he was a kid, he'd never gotten used to it or been very patient about it. This time, it wasn't merely tearstained letters, intrusive photographs, pleas for kisses, or phone calls that kept requiring him to change his number. His home had been destroyed. Someone could have been killed. He wasn't about to take that lightly.

Reece fucking hated feeling stalked. The sooner they caught the arsonist, the saner he would feel. Knowing somebody out there was living only to mess with him was enough to drive him out of his mind.

"Okay, enough about the fire. Seeing anyone?"

"No." *Not yet, anyway.* Raising a brow, he added, "Speaking of which, you still owe me one for introducing you to Miss People's Choice Award last month."

His brother, broader and darker than Reece, smirked. "How about I pay you back by not making a play for the redhead you were chatting up when I got here?"

Reece's good humor faded. He and Rowan had always enjoyed a friendly rivalry when it came to women, though never for long. Reece had an unfair advantage here in Hollywood, and he knew it, so if he and Rowan had their eyes on the same female, he usually bowed out.

But not this time. Oh, hell no. "Hands off."

"You didn't just call dibs on a woman. What are we, middle schoolers?"

"Don't even think about it. Not her." She'd been his object of fascination for two months, since the day he'd seen her through the security system. He wasn't about to let his competitive brother interfere, which Rowan might, if only for a prank. He had that younger twin humor thing down pat. Some might consider it strange, given his career choice, but Reece would bet few at the LAPD knew about Rowan's mischievous side.

"You're serious."

"Yes I am. I've gone to a lot of trouble to get to know her."

Getting Aunt Sharon to set up this showing had been challenging. Yes, she loved the art Liza Shepherd had created, as did Sid. But the artist had no reputation, no name recognition, no guaranteed high price point, nothing to bring wealthy people in to spend a lot of money on her work. It had been a gamble.

By the looks of things, the gamble had paid off exponentially. The show was a great success. He'd seen several people handing over gold cards to the cashier. Sharon would be happy, Sid would be thrilled with his commission, Liza would be suitably proud.

It was all thanks to the redhead, who'd jogged in off the beach and pitched for her sister. Jessica Jensen. The woman he hoped was waiting for him by the elevator.

"Oh, shit, I can't believe it," Rowan muttered, dropping the subject completely. His whole body stiffening, he stared past Reece's shoulder, toward the gallery entrance. "It's Steve Baker. When did he get back in town?"

It was Reece's turn to stiffen as tension wired through his body. He hadn't seen Steve in years. Like Rowan, he'd had no idea the man was back.

Why he was at the gallery was anybody's guess. Maybe he was trying to rekindle old friendships, if you could call them that. They'd known the guy as kids, when his star had been on the rise playing a wisecracking teen. But considering how the friendship had ended, he and Rowan could have done without the reunion tonight. Or ever.

"If it isn't the Winchester twins," Steve said, his face breaking into a grin as he walked up to them. Steve had always been tall; now he was a little overweight and a very big guy. "Long time no see."

While Reece's guts twisted, Rowan managed to look normal. Who ever knew the cop would be the better actor? "How's it going, Steve?"

"Pretty good. I've been working a lot in Italy."

Reece had heard the man, once a teen idol—part of the Frat Pack, as Steve and several other teens, including Rachel, had been dubbed all those years ago—had been making B movies in Europe. Too bad he hadn't stayed there.

"Nice," said Rowan.

When are you going back? Reece thought the words but didn't say them.

All he wanted to do was get away, to forget the ugly past. He wanted to focus on the future—namely, the immediate future involving Jessica Jensen. But some dark history hung like a storm cloud, always threatening to peal thunder and to lightning bolt his life straight to hell.

Steve Baker was a stark reminder of all the things Reece wanted to forget: loss, grief, anger, rage, violence.

Worse. But Reece couldn't reveal his true reaction. He could show nothing, let nothing slip. He and Rowan had worked too hard to forget those dark days.

The last thing they could allow was for his late sister's boyfriend to dig up the ugly past all the Winchesters wanted to remain buried.

* * *

Jess waited for nine and a half minutes before heading toward the back hallway. She had made the decision to go upstairs with Reece Winchester as soon as he'd issued the invitation, and then had changed her mind a dozen and a half times. She'd been playing the pluck-petals-off-a-daisy game in her mind. *I will go, I will not.*

She'd ended on *I will go.* Maybe by cheating. Probably by cheating.

She didn't question her final decision. It might be the best one of her life, or the worst. She didn't think she'd care either way. Jess had always been one to take chances. Coming out here to pursue her writing dreams had been taking a chance. Walking into the gallery that day had been another. Without risk, there could never be reward.

What reward Reece Winchester might have in store for her upstairs, she didn't know. But she was going to find out.

Casually moving through the crowd, Jess offered the faintest of discouraging smiles to anyone who tried to approach her. She was also taken aback to see a couple of hard stares from women, perhaps jealous because she'd been engaged in a private conversation with Mr. Superstar. A platinum blonde—perfect for a role as the evil ex—huffed and rolled her eyes as Jess walked by. One older woman with long salt-and-pepper hair, wearing an ill-fitting, though expensive, black dress, glared at her pointedly, muttering what sounded like a slur under her breath.

The dislike wafting off complete strangers was palpable. If a simple conversation garnered such anger, she felt sorry for anybody who actually got involved with the famous movie star/director. Which she would not. Ever. Period.

As she meandered through the gallery, she avoided making eye contact with Liza, who was surrounded by admirers. She headed toward the back hallway, where, she recalled, there were small studios, a conference room, and an elevator leading to what she assumed were upstairs offices. But before she even got close to it, she felt a light touch of warm fingers on the small of her back. A quick inhalation brought the unmistakable scent of his cologne, and his presence was confirmed when he moved beside her, his breath warm on her temple.

"You've decided?"

"How do you know I'm not going to the bathroom?" *Smart, Jess, talk about bodily functions with Mr. Hollywood, why don't you?* "Umm, to touch up my makeup."

"You don't need to. Plus, the ladies' room is in the other direction."

Defeat made her sigh. "Okay then, yes, I was heading toward the elevator."

"I know. You couldn't resist."

Damn, he was holding on to his advantage. "No, I suppose I couldn't. I do want to see it, if you still want to show it to me."

Good lord, from bad to worse. Jess was flirtatious, but she'd put her hand on a Bible and swear she hadn't been going for sexy, saucy innuendo. The man just screwed up her thoughts and left her brains scrambled.

"I mean, your piece."

Wondering if he was laughing at her idiocy, she quickly glanced over, noting his serious expression. She also noticed the tension in his strong body, and a faint frown he couldn't entirely erase. Something had bothered him during the ten minutes they'd been apart, but he was obviously trying to put it aside.

"My piece?"

"The piece of art you bought previously and are having delivered to your house," she spelled out, feeling ridiculous.

"I know what you meant."

Of course he did. "I've been trying to figure out which one it is," she admitted. "But I couldn't get close to any of the ones still on the floor."

"You'll know everything shortly."

Everything? Well, maybe. Every bit of him was launching an attack on her senses. Thought had no place in this. Twenty minutes ago, she was a rational, slightly stubborn, more than a little snarky woman in a blue dress. Now she was a walking nerve ending, exposed, jangled, and raw.

He was stared at, and a few people tried to speak

to him, but he had that Hollywood-bad-boy aloofness down to an art form. Jess, too, was gawked at by men and women. Yet the crowd melted out of their way, letting him take her off like a tribal leader ushering a virgin toward a rumbling volcano. Did that make her a human sacrifice? How funny that, right now, she truly didn't care. She wouldn't be able to protest if she wanted to.

They reached the back hallway, and he stopped before the elevator. Reece punched in four digits, ushering her inside when the door swished open, and followed her into the mirrored interior. As the door closed, leaving her alone in a small space with the man, tension roared again. Not fear, God no, but the most visceral awareness she'd ever experienced with another human being. She saw each individual golden-brown hair on his head, the flecks of light and dark swirling in his pupils, the smoothness of his masculine jaw, and the breadth of the powerful shoulders straining against the perfectly tailored fabric of his jacket.

Jess found it hard to breathe. She'd never had a panic attack in her life, had been accused of not having a fear gene, but she was well on the way to freaking out here. So she looked for something to say—anything— to make this moment normal, and less sacrificial-virgin-heading-toward-the-volcano.

Unfortunately, stupid fangirl came out. "Did you ever regret not doing James Bond?"

One brow went up.

Swallowing, feeling dumb, she went on. "I mean, when they wanted you to do the James Bond as a kid movie. Every young actor in the world wanted it, but you walked away."

In fact, he'd walked away from Hollywood completely for several years. She'd heard stories about a dispute between his parents—his mother in California wanting to keep her kids in the spotlight, versus the father who lived on the East Coast and wanted his children away from the movie scene. There had also been a lot of speculation about the death of their sister, the golden-girl Rachel, a TV star. Many had assumed the family tragedy was what had driven the boys out of the business.

Reece had left acting as a still-cute kid with a dimple, but he'd come back as a drop-dead gorgeous eighteen-year-old with an attitude and table-broad shoulders.

His jaw stiffened a tiny bit. "I take it *you* were disappointed by my decision?"

"I was eight years old at the time. Of course I was disappointed. The world revolved around me, don't you know?"

"I'm sure it did."

Had his eyes twinkled there?

"The truth is, I didn't like the director."

A thirteen-year-old backing out of a potential blockbuster because he didn't like the director. What a world he must have grown up in. "I see."

As if realizing how that might have sounded, he went further, his mouth twisting into a grimace. "I *really* didn't like him." He grunted.

She sensed a story, judging by his audible disgust. "Oh?"

"Let's say he's no longer in the business. I might have helped him get that way."

Wow. Definitely a story. Jess was dying to know more, but a quick shake of his head told her he'd pushed the subject out of bounds.

"Plus I was burned out."

Burned out. At thirteen. Maybe her childhood wasn't the absolute worst in the world.

He wasn't finished. "When you were thirteen were you certain you were doing exactly what you wanted to do for the rest of your life?"

"I was just happy I had a roof over my head," she admitted with an unamused laugh.

The elevator reached its destination and the door swished open with a soft ding. But rather than stepping out, or gesturing for her to, Reece pushed a button to keep the door open, and focused his attention on her. "Are you being facetious?"

She shook her head. "Nope. Add orphanages and foster care to the typical zits and angst and you'll have a good picture of me as a tween."

A frown pulled at his strong brow. "You were an orphan?"

"I'm not little and my name's not Annie, so don't go feeling sorry for me."

"You're perfect, and as I recall, *her* story had a happy ending."

The *You're perfect* part almost went right past her, but since the words were accompanied by a quick, appreciative stare, she grabbed them and clutched them to her heart like a pair of lost Jimmy Choos. "My story had a happy ending, too," she said, managing to keep her tone conversational. "No Daddy Warbucks, but Liza's mom found me and adopted me."

"Found you? Did you run away?"

"A few times, but that's not what I meant. Liza and I were best friends in elementary school," she explained. "But she moved to another town and we lost touch. Then my mother died and I ended up in foster care. Liza's mom later heard about it and got me out after two years."

"Two years," he murmured, appearing thoughtful. "At such a difficult age."

"That's when I met you," she admitted, offering him a cheeky smile. "Whenever I lived anywhere near a movie theater, I'd go there to escape. I got really good at slipping in with big families. I would park myself in a theater and stay all day to avoid going to wherever home was."

"Good for you."

"You didn't say any of the things people usually say when they hear my history."

"Such as?"

"Such as, 'I'm sorry,' or 'You poor thing.' Or," she added with an eye roll and a grunt, "my personal favorite, 'What doesn't kill you makes you stronger.'"

"What an awful saying," he said, sharp, almost angry. "No child needs to be *that* strong."

"I agree. And something tells me you have reason to know that, too. Don't you?"

His stare met hers, those strange eyes laced with mystery. She suddenly realized she'd told him a lot about herself, and he'd revealed nothing more than she could have discovered in a copy of the *National Enquirer*. Damn, she really needed to learn the art of being mysterious and circumspect.

Seeing how stiff he'd become, and feeling his tension, she cursed herself for her words. He probably thought she was groping for details about his famous, tragic sister. She really hadn't been. Honestly, Rachel Winchester's story was far too common in Hollywood. Young teen gets famous, makes a lot of money, falls in with the wrong crowd, starts doing drugs. She gets so strung out one night she falls—or, some say jumps—off the balcony of a high-rise hotel in Atlanta. So sad. But not exactly uncommon.

No, her real object of curiosity was Reece himself. She wanted to know why he'd come back to Hollywood like a young man on a mission, driven and laser-focused, making a half-dozen movies before practically flipping the bird at everyone and quitting acting to move behind the camera when he was in his prime. A mystery lurked there, which was why she'd made the comment. "I'm sorry, I wasn't..."

"Forget it." Finally letting go of the open-door button, he added, "Come and see my latest obsession."

She followed him out. "You're obsessed with a statue?"

"I like perfection," he admitted, walking down a hallway lit with soft, recessed lights.

Everything about the gallery below was tasteful. Up here, it verged on opulent. The fixtures were ornate, the hallway lined with art by masters she'd actually heard of.

She followed, noting the silence as her high heels sank into the plush carpet, until they reached the last door in the hall. Unlocking the door, he remained back for her to enter ahead of him. She did so, stepping into blackness, and then waited for him to turn on the overhead light.

He didn't. Instead, he reached around her to push the door shut, enclosing them in the private room. His hand brushed her arm as he moved. The connection was brief and light, but it came from out of the darkness, surprising her. She managed to keep her moan behind her lips, knowing if those fingertips had again found her hot spot and lingered there, she would have dropped to the floor on hands and knees and begged him to kiss his way down her spine.

One floor below, two hundred people were talking, chatting, buying art, and selling themselves. But she felt cocooned, wrapped in a silky layer of secrecy. His low exhalations were barely audible above the raging thud of her own heartbeat, and she waited for another touch.

The tension rose, becoming almost unbearable. His breath warmed her temple as he moved around her. God, was he going to kiss her? She didn't want him to do that in the dark. She wanted it to be bright, with lights, music, cymbals clashing, if only so she could make herself believe it was really happening, and imprint the memory on all of her senses.

He moved past her toward a dais. One of Liza's statues stood on it. She saw the faint outline, the gleam of soft grayish white, but couldn't distinguish which piece it was.

The air was somehow expectant, and she had the

strangest feeling she was acting out a script someone just shoved into her hand. She didn't understand the story, or the characters, or the motivations. He was totally in control—the director. He knew who she was. He'd sought her out. He'd gotten her alone.

What was he planning? What would happen next? Would someone yell, "That's a wrap," and cut the scene? Most importantly—what, exactly, was the rating on this film of her life?

There was a clicking sound, and then tiny lights on the base of the platform shone up, illuminating the piece from below. Jess saw it, recognized it, and sighed.

Touch Me.

She was not surprised. It seemed impossible, yet somehow inevitable, that this would be the sculpture he bought, the one he wanted to show her. Fate seemed to be playing tricks on her, setting her up but not cluing her in to the fact that she was being carried on a random current or drawn onto a twisty path by forces she never knew existed.

"*This* is my favorite," he said, watching her, speculation in his gaze.

Swallowing hard, she tried to find her voice. Could this be deliberate, and not fate?

Reece Winchester's favorite piece of Liza's art happened to be *Touch Me*. And she was in it. Jess was the one touching herself.

No, there was no way he knew, not when Liza made sure to change the features and shape of the face, with only the barest hint of her real lips and jaw. The eyes, nose, cheeks, forehead, and hair were not hers. From the neck down, she looked just like any other curvy young woman. He had no idea she'd been the model; he'd just gotten her alone and was trying to get a rise out of her for some reason.

If so, wow, had his plan backfired. All she could think when she looked at the statue was that she needed to hit the StairMaster, because her thighs were getting a wee bit thick.

"I imagine you can see why I wanted to keep it all for myself," he said. "It's remarkable."

Jess couldn't help warming under the admiration, even if he was just admiring Liza's skill. "And you've already bought it?"

"Yes. I knew the moment I saw her I had to have her."

Whoa. His expression was covetous, his voice thick and heavy. She again caught a double meaning. Did he mean the *her* sculpted out of clay, or the *her* standing nearby?

No. It was the damn statue. He had no idea who she was. It needed to stay that way.

Remaining cool, she asked, "Do you always get what you want?"

"Always, Jessica."

Her heart skipped a beat. His voice throbbed with intensity. The words weren't a boast; they were a promise.

"Lucky you," she said, feigning nonchalance, wondering if he could sense her blood was racing through her veins. Seeing the way he eyed the statue, knowing she was the one whose naked form he was appreciating—even if he didn't realize it—gave her a wicked, secret thrill. What, she wondered, would he say if he knew she was the one shown, naked, half reclining, her hand between her legs?

One thing was for sure—nobody who knew the truth would call her Cinderella again.

He leaned against the back of a nearby sofa, crossed his arms in front of his broad chest, and stared at her. The pose was utterly masculine, the attention unnerving, as if he was waiting for something. Finally, she realized he was expecting her to react to the statue.

"Uh, well, congratulations on getting to it first. It's nice."

"You think so?" he asked, his tone casual, his body powerful. She was again reminded of a lion trying to figure out whether he'd prefer a tasty gazelle or a yummy zebra.

"Sure."

*Tsk*ing, he shook his head. "No, it's not."

"It's not?" she whispered through dry lips.

"*Nice* isn't the word. She's magnificent."

Straightening, he glided toward her, moving silently. *Predator and prey.* She didn't even think about it and took a quick, involuntary step back.

He followed. Crowding her. He was close, so very close. He radiated heat, making her sway a little. Reece obviously had no concept of personal space, and she had to tilt her head back to look up at him, a rarity for her, especially in heels.

"I am curious about one thing," he murmured, searching her eyes.

"What would that be?" she managed to whisper.

"I'm wondering," he said, lifting a hand and brushing

his fingertips against her jaw, his thumb rubbing against her bottom lip. "Why did she disguise your beautiful face?"

Completely shocked, she couldn't reply for a moment. Her jaw fell open, and she stared up at him, wondering how he could be so certain. He wasn't trying to tease the truth out of her; he sounded like he was absolutely sure she'd modeled for the piece, when in truth, there was no way he could know. She had no tattoos, no distinguishing marks—nothing made her body any different from any other woman's. He *had* to be guessing.

But she knew he was not.

"Who told you?"

Liza wouldn't. She just *wouldn't*. But maybe she needed to show Sharon the model release forms, one of which Jess had signed. Might Reece have seen it?

"Nobody told me."

"Then how could you know?"

He raked a hot gaze down her body. "How could I not?"

"You...you recognized me?"

He nodded. "The minute I saw the statue."

She gulped. "No one else ever has."

"Well, then apparently no one else sees you as clearly as I do."

Wow. Great line. Only she didn't think it was a line. He sounded totally serious.

"I'll repeat the question," he said. "Why the secrecy? Why did she hide your face?"

Licking her lips, Jess wished she had brought a drink

with her. Her mouth was so dry, and it was so darned hot in here. Well, it wasn't hot in the room, but the heat he put off was melting her like she was a Hershey's bar left on a dashboard.

"She didn't need my face." Trying to lighten the moment and cover her embarrassment, she forced a laugh and looked away. "Wanted only for my body. Story of my life."

"Don't do that," he said. "Don't mock yourself." He took her chin in his hand and tilted her face up to look directly into her eyes. She quickly fell back into wild, hypnotic Reece land where thought didn't exist and there was only action and reaction, motion and emotion. "She wanted your face. Didn't she."

It wasn't a question. And Jessica didn't try to deny it.

"Why did you say no?" he asked, dropping his hand. She immediately missed its warmth, which was crazy since she'd just been mentally whining over how freaking hot it was in here.

"I guess I didn't want the notoriety. I'm trying to be taken seriously as..." Realizing if she said she wanted to be a screenwriter he might assume she was about to go all Hollywood on him and launch into a script pitch, she changed direction. "I mean, I work at a bar and already have to fend off grubby men with grabby hands. The last thing I'd want is for any of them to see that piece, recognize me, and decide to be more persistent with their attention."

His jaw flexed, as if he was gritting his teeth, and his eyes narrowed. "They *touch* you?"

"Perils of working in a place called Hot Buns."

Seeing his confusion, she added dryly, "We don't sell burgers, and we wear short shorts."

He got it now, and the jaw-tightening thing got worse. "Why?"

"Why do I work there?"

A nod.

"Girl's gotta eat." She gestured toward the statue. "Look at those thighs. I've obviously gotta eat a lot."

His eyes narrowed. "I told you not to do that anymore."

She gulped. He was deadly serious, as if he had the right to give her orders. It was caveman. It was unacceptable.

It was kind of hot.

"Self-deprecation doesn't suit you. You have to know you're beautiful."

Good lord. Reece Winchester was telling her she was beautiful? And he sounded like he really meant it? She knew she was sexy. She had assets and knew how to flaunt them. But nobody had ever called her beautiful.

Now, Liza? Oh yeah. Her sister was soft, fragile. Any guy would look at her and think, "She's so lovely." Jess? They'd think, "I'd do her."

First off, she wasn't much short of an Amazon. While her dark red hair was eye-catching and she had a decent body, her eyes were a muddy brown and her nose had a bump from a long-ago break earned in a foster-care fistfight. Freckles tended to attack her pale skin when she was in the sun, and the cleft in her chin was absolutely mannish. So, no, she'd never considered herself beautiful, or even very pretty. Just hot.

"Oh, crap, the chin!" she groaned, realizing how Reece must have recognized her. She darted over to the statue and looked, honestly unable to remember whether Liza had used her real chin. The cleft she'd hated since toddlerhood was pretty distinctive.

But it wasn't there. Liza had smoothed out her jaw and closed up the little space with something more rounded and feminine.

"It wasn't the chin," he told her. For the first time, she heard what may have been genuine amusement in his voice.

Swinging around to confront him, she saw he was not smiling, but those amazing eyes finally held a hint of a twinkle. "Then what?"

He shrugged. "Everything. It was everything."

"It couldn't have been *everything*," she snapped. "You've never seen me naked."

Another of those not-quite-a-smiles tugged at one side of his perfect mouth. "Not yet."

Holy shit. He'd said it as if he expected to see her naked. He could probably pick up the phone and have whoever was on this month's cover of *Cosmo* in his bed by the time he got home tonight. So why on earth would he want her?

"Wait a minute, you said you recognized me as soon as you saw the statue."

"Yes."

"But you bought the statue before the opening. You had already seen me. The real me."

He nodded once.

"How? When?"

"Through the security cameras."

Yes, of course. She'd noticed the cameras all over the gallery floor downstairs. Security would have to be tight considering the value of some of the artwork the business dealt with, so naturally they would have video monitoring.

"I saw you the day you came in off the beach and talked to Sid," he admitted. "I was here to meet with Sharon and watched you through the monitor."

His voice thickened as he said *watched you*. He made something simple sound so intimate, as if he'd been studying her. Considering he saw that statue and realized it was her right away, perhaps he had been.

"And only from seeing me through a camera, you recognized me as the model for the statue when you saw it?"

He shook his head.

"Please tell me you didn't Facebook stalk me."

A tiny, real smile. *Glorious*. Not the full frontal she'd been seeking, but close enough to get her bells ringing. "I don't do Facebook."

"You have a page. I follow it."

"Have *you* been Facebook stalking *me*?"

Heat flooded into her cheeks. "No, of course not, I..." God, this was embarrassing. "I like to keep up with Hollywood stuff, okay?"

He relented and didn't push it further. "Somebody handles the official page for me."

Of course. His *people*.

"And the acting one is fan based."

Ahh. The acting one was the one she'd "Liked."

Along with about two million other people. But she didn't say so. She suspected Reece was touchy about his early years in Hollywood and preferred to be thought of only as a writer and director. Which was really sad, because, to her, he was always gonna be Runner Fleet, intergalactic space pirate. Inspiration for her first erotic dream. And, to be honest, many more.

"I made a point of being here when you came back with Liza to meet with Sharon."

She scrunched her brow. "Are you the reason Sharon asked Liza to bring me that day?"

He didn't even try to deny it. "I wanted to see you again."

"But why? Please tell me it wasn't because you're a perv like Sid."

"I wasn't fascinated only by your body." He paused. "Wait, Sid is a perv?"

"World class."

"He made you feel uncomfortable?"

"Hell, *you* made me feel uncomfortable earlier, the way you were staring at me."

"That wasn't my intention." He wasn't exactly apologetic, but he did sound sincere. "I couldn't take my eyes off you."

She lifted a hand to her throat, brushing the tips of her fingers in its hollows. "Oh."

He stepped closer, until she felt the brush of his pants against her bare leg. "And now?"

She couldn't reply at first, caught in the web of magnetic power surrounding the man. Having to tilt her head back to look up into his face, losing herself in that intense stare, she couldn't even remember the question. "Huh?"

"Are you uncomfortable now, Jessica?"

"Jess. Uh, everybody calls me Jess. Or sometimes JJ."

"I don't."

Okeydoke. "No, I'm not uncomfortable now." *Liar.* "I suppose I'm confused."

"About?"

"About why you're so interested in me." It couldn't be personal, could it? But what else would he want? What else did men ever want?

He reached up and cupped her cheek in his hand. "You have a face made for the camera."

Realizing he was explaining why he'd been watching her, she shoved away a hint of disappointment that it *wasn't* because of any sexual attraction. Was he scouting for talent, looking for some young, fresh face to put in his next film? Well, the famous director was definitely doomed to disappointment.

Snorting, she tossed her head. "Sorry to tell you this, but I have the acting ability of a pig on steroids."

His hand fell, his eyes widened, and his mouth creased into that big, white, devastating smile. *There it is. God help me, there it is.*

She fell. Immediately. Instinctively. Fell into something she'd never experienced in her life and couldn't yet identify. But it was potent.

She shivered, unable to help herself, both excited out of her mind, and for some reason, utterly terrified. When laughter—real, genuine laughter—emerged from his lips, she lost her last coherent thought. He was gorgeous when still and serious. Laughing and smiling? Lord, the man was simply intoxicating. She couldn't resist him if she wanted to. Oh, how she hoped he didn't want her to.

"Crap," she whispered, knowing any walls she might have wanted to build between her and this so-far-out-of-her-league man had crumbled into dust, whether he wanted her just for her nonexistent acting ability or for something more... personal.

"Do you always say the first thing that comes to your mind?" he asked.

"I'd much prefer to say the last thing, but those comebacks often occur to me hours after the original conversation, when there's nobody to say them to."

His laughter deepened. "Happens to the best of us."

"Oh, right. I find it hard to believe you don't always get the last word."

"Very rarely."

"With your job? Come on, Director Winchester. *That's a wrap*—were there ever three more glorious words in creation?"

His tone dry, he replied, "Some women might choose another three."

"You're not pregnant?"

"I want you."

"Those are pretty good, too," she snapped off, before she realized he was being serious. Very serious. There was no laughter now, only pure intensity. And heat. Oh, heavens, the heat.

He wanted her. This remarkable, incredibly sensual man, wanted *her*. It wasn't about a love affair between her face and a camera; he was suggesting a far more intimate relationship.

He stepped toward her. She tried once again to step away from him but realized she was blocked by a broad, highly polished mahogany table and could go no farther. But he could come forward, and he did, moving so close she could feel his body heat, though he wasn't touching her at all.

She glanced toward the large window overlooking the dark beach and the churning blackness of the sea. Someone could be standing out there, watching them in the softly lit room. But honestly, she didn't much care. How could she when this gorgeous, perfect man was about to touch her?

He lifted a hand to her face, cupping her cheek, sliding his fingertips into her hair. Moving again, until one leg slid between hers, he dropped his other hand to her hip and pulled her close. He didn't stop at her hip. Reaching around her body, he scraped his fingertips down the vulnerable vertebrae, to the base of her spine.

Shuddering, Jess closed her eyes and dropped her head back. "How did you know?" she whispered, moaning through the words.

"Know what?" he asked as he leaned closer, close enough for his breaths to fall soft upon her skin. Close enough for her to lose all sanity, all clarity.

Focus. She stared up at him. "How did you know if you touched me there I'd melt?"

He didn't even hesitate. "Because you quivered and arched your back when I was staring at you from across the room earlier."

Just like that, with a glance across a crowded room, he had discovered something about her no lover ever had. This man saw things others did not, visualized the world in strange, sharp, and perceptive ways. He had recognized her in the statue, had seen through the casual, quippy chatter and zoned right in on the woman who had been thinking about his hands and his mouth and his body since the minute she'd felt his attention on her in the gallery.

His fingers dipped lower, caressing her skin, teasing the curves of her rear, even as he pulled her hard against his body. She sucked in a gasp, shocked at the strength of him, every bit of him hard and powerful.

And then he was kissing her. That warm, wonderful mouth was covering hers, and she had one second to believe it before her entire world went up in flames.

CHAPTER 4

Jess had gotten her first kiss when she was eleven. Early bloomer, one might say, though one would be wrong. It wasn't exactly her choice, but rather the forceful demands of an older foster sibling. Thank God he hadn't gone any further.

Since then, she'd decided kissing was one of those skills you really had to work on because not everyone could do it right. In her experience, most men actually did it badly, all thrust and no precision, all brute demand and no subtle seduction. Reece, though...Reece was again the exception to the rule. Because, oh, dear lord, he was the world champion of kissing.

Jess forgot she was being kissed by a Hollywood legend. All she knew was that in the arms of a sensual, seductive man, every other thought was pulled from her head except that this must be what heaven felt like.

His perfect mouth, a mix of strength and softness, melted against hers, both asking for and demanding her surrender. His lips were soft and supple for a man who seemed so rigid, and she whimpered as he coaxed his way inside. Sweeping his tongue against hers, he teased her, tasted her, and she loved the warm, wet, give-and-take. Then he grew more serious, more demanding, hungrily exploring every corner and crevice of her mouth.

He tasted of fire and scotch. She was burned and intoxicated.

If she were in a regular world—in her normal persona, not surrounded by erotic art, not wearing a designer gown, not a little tipsy from one strong drink—she might have been able to keep this whole thing in perspective. But perspective was the last thing she wanted right now. This didn't need to make sense, and she didn't have to know what would happen next or what it meant. For once, she was simply going to enjoy herself.

He pulled her closer, until they were glued together from chest to thigh, all her softest parts meeting his oh-so-very-hard ones. He was a tall man, but not a brawny one, and every inch of him was firm and rippling with muscles she could feel pressing against her. His hand still cupped her jaw, and he tilted her head to the side, demanding more—as much as she could give. She welcomed him, meeting each rapacious plunge of his tongue with a thrust of her own.

Jess was reborn, coming to life in his arms, his kiss awakening something inside her she hadn't even realized had fallen dormant. Or had never flowered at all. She'd always been sure of herself, where she stood, what she liked, what it took to reach her on a deep, intimate level. It was a place no man had ever *really* found his way to or even cared enough to try.

Reece did. He plumbed into her, discovering her like an adventurer on expedition to a new, uncharted land. She lost herself in him completely; there was no man other than this one, no other world outside this room. His kiss was magnetic, the fingers on her back stroking her to an insane level of excitement. Her sighs of pleasure turned into helpless whimpers when he let go of her face and traced his knuckles down her throat, the thumb brushing against the hollow. He stopped at the deep V of her dress, and she arched toward his touch.

"Please," she whispered into his mouth, letting him know he didn't have to stop at all.

"Please what?"

He was going to make her beg, wasn't he? Always in control, leading her to the precipice but insisting she be the one to jump off. He wouldn't push her or pull her. She was on her own.

"Please keep touching me," was as far as she would leap.

It was enough. He caressed the inner curves of her breasts, revealed by the low-cut dress, and she made no effort to stop him when he began to kiss his way down, following the path his hand had taken. Dropping her head back, keeping her fingers twined in his hair, she let the table support her. She arched toward him, dying as his hot mouth pressed kiss after wet kiss down her throat, until his smooth jaw brushed against her breasts. Then he was nudging the fabric over.

She remembered one second too late what she was wearing beneath the dress.

"What in the hell is *that*?" he asked.

Realizing immediately what had shocked him—and

it wasn't the, if-she-did-say-so-herself, nice breast he'd just revealed, she groaned. "Oh, crap."

"What have you done to yourself?" he growled, his jaw as hard and rigid as the plaster used in Liza's artwork.

"Whoops. Sorry. I forgot," she said, trying to sound light and unconcerned, though embarrassment clawed at her. "It's the first time in my life I've ever worn these dumb things. I never imagined somebody else would be undressing me tonight."

Or that she'd be so disappointed he'd stopped.

Yeesh, so much for out of her league and not gonna happen. She'd been ready for the full-court press and some bits of gluey plastic had interrupted the play and blocked the hoop.

He straightened and pulled away. Swallowing hard, she couldn't decide if she was furious or glad this was ending as quickly as it began. Maybe both. She was furious she'd let herself go so fast and so far, but was glad it hadn't gone so far she'd have to do the walk of shame through her best friend's big art opening.

Or maybe she was furious it had stopped at all, and glad she got to be in this man's arms at least once.

She quickly discovered, though, that it was not over. Her unfortunate choice of undergarments hadn't entirely killed the moment. Because, without saying a word, Reece reached for the thin straps of her dress, which draped over each shoulder, and pushed them off. She gasped as both sleeves dropped down her arms, taking the front of her dress with them. The blue silk was stopped from falling all the way off her only by the curves of her hips. The cool, air-conditioned room brought goose bumps to her nearly bare, very vulnerable, upper half.

And then his warm fingers were on her, tugging at the fabric, and the dress hit the floor.

Too surprised to react, she could only stand there as he studied her. His stare was frank and deliberate, raking across her, top to bottom, in long, slow strips, his expression not only approving but covetous. Goose bumps? Ha. She suddenly feel incinerated where she stood. Jess instinctively wanted to cross an arm over her breasts and another down between her legs, in an Eve-old pose of modesty.

But she didn't. No. She stood there and let him look at her, let the warm hunger rolling off him wash over her. His obvious appreciation was arousing, thrilling. Never in her life had she been more thankful the cut of her dress hadn't allowed her to wear Spanx, and that her panties were jet black, lacy, and sexy as sin.

Unfortunately, she was not as sexily clad up top.

His attention returned to her chest. "Those are the most appalling things I've ever seen."

Tossing her hair, she arched a brow, trying not to think about being naked but for her high heels, a few triangles of lace, and a couple of angled pieces of rubbery tape—in front of a man she'd met an hour ago but had fantasized about for a decade. "Actually, I've been told I have pretty nice breasts."

"They're gorgeous," he snapped. "But *those*"—he gestured toward the two coverings, through which her dark nipples were easily visible—"are an abomination."

"Have you seriously never seen a woman wearing these?"

"No. Never. Why in God's name would you?"

"This dress couldn't be worn with a bra, and I can't very well go braless."

"Yes, you can. And the next time you wear something like that, you will."

All because he said so? Yeah, right. As if he'd know, or care. "I'm too busty."

"Trust me, there's no such thing," he said, the voice as dry as dust.

"As my mom used to say, gravity will inevitably defeat perkiness."

"Enough," he said, ignoring the basic truth. "Tell me you can get them off. I want to touch you."

Her heart jackhammered at his demand. The feminist within her rebelled. She should protest. She'd never had a one-night stand, hadn't had sex in a year, and she'd had absolutely no intention of sleeping with the man when she came up here with him. Who the hell did he think he was, making such an assumption?

But the devil on her other shoulder reminded her of another truth: She'd been fascinated by Reece Winchester for a long time. Now, having met him, she wanted him like a junkie wanted her next high, and she might never have a chance like this again. Jess felt as if she were being torn in half, want warring with wisdom. She couldn't say if the smart feminist was going to win this internal struggle . . . or the little devil was.

"You feel it, too. I know you do," he growled.

"Feel what?"

"This...connection."

He was right. She did feel it. This wasn't a movie star infatuation or being flattered by a good-looking guy or any kind of seduction.

There was something powerful between them. She didn't know the word for it, because attraction simply wouldn't do. So his own choice of word—connection— seemed right.

That wasn't easy to admit, however. "I barely know you."

"Your body knows everything it needs to."

"You know my body so well, do you?"

He gestured toward the statue, reminding her he did, indeed, know her body very well.

"This is crazy, Mr. Winchester," she insisted, trying to be strong, even though she knew she was close to consenting to a life-altering interlude. But it might also be something she would regret tomorrow, when she was not under the influence of one Flaming Orgasm and desperate for another, of a very different kind. "I'm not one of your Hollywood bimbos who will bend over when you say you want to insert tab A into slot B."

"I never said anything about tabs and slots, Miss Jensen," he said, edging closer. He looked as if he was holding back a storm of raging want. "I've been thinking about you for weeks. I thought I could wait for you, get to know you, figure out why you affect me so powerfully. But the truth is, I can't even conceive of walking out of this room without having touched every inch of you."

"Wow," she whispered, believing him. This visit

upstairs might not have been an impromptu one, but she believed him when he said he hadn't brought her up here to ravish her, to put it in old-fashioned terms.

He glanced over his shoulder at something in the far corner of the room and muttered, "Believe me, I know this isn't an ideal time and place." She couldn't see what he was looking at. *Whatever.* She wasn't sure her brain would process anything except that tall, sexy body standing right in front of her. Especially since she kept hearing *thinking about you for weeks*.

He'd really been wanting her for so long?

Yes, she really thought he had. The desperation was unmistakable. She had the feeling if she refused him, he'd walk over and toss the statue out the second-story window.

That would be a darn shame. Someone walking on the beach below could be hurt. She wouldn't want someone's injury on her conscience.

She still knew this was a bad idea, and that she should at least try to resist. "Um, taking these things off would be easier said than done," she said, gesturing toward the stick-on bra. She hadn't exactly said yes. But she hadn't said no, either.

He apparently viewed her words as a plea for help. Without another word, he reached for the sheer tape, tugging at the top corner. The stupid glue was incredibly strong, and in his efforts, he pulled at her skin. When she winced, he immediately stopped.

"Did I hurt you?" Although his voice was gruff, she heard concern in it.

"A little. I think NASA invented that glue—it's

superstrength. And, to be honest, I can't remember how to get them off. I might have to use baby oil or something. The directions are on the package at home." She was not exaggerating. If he wanted her as much as he said he did, he might have to live with the boob tape.

"I don't know about you, but I certainly don't carry baby oil in my pocket."

A saucy inner voice almost asked if he had lube—he certainly seemed to jump at sexual opportunity pretty quickly. But she stayed quiet. Especially because she didn't like the thought. Was he always this fast with seduction, or was she a rare exception?

Doubts intruded. He might not have brought her up here to have sex-with-a-stranger, but he'd probably be feeling the same way about any woman who'd attracted him as much as she apparently had. There was nothing terribly unique about her. "Maybe this was a bad idea," she said.

"Jesus, I'm thwarted by a sticky chastity belt."

She couldn't help snickering. "I mean, it could be worse. It's not *literally* a chastity belt." She shuddered, picturing the sticky stuff on her more sensitive parts.

He shook his head slowly. "You've got a strange sense of humor, Jessica."

"At least one of us has one," she mumbled, feeling like she was baiting a bear.

The bear reacted, grabbing her by the waist and lifting her onto the table she'd been leaning against. Although he was manhandling her, and frustration made his eyes darken to near brown, he was careful not to hurt her. "Apparently I don't when it comes to you."

He drew in a deep, audible breath, pulling back, dropping his hands. She almost saw the cogs turning in his brain as he regretted the quick lapse into emotion and reined himself in. It was fascinating to suddenly be able to read someone who been so enigmatic a short time ago.

Their breaths were the only sounds in the room. She saw his jaw flex as he gritted his teeth, and the way his body tensed and tightened. Nothing about his mood or his body language frightened her. She knew the battle being waged was purely inside him. He hated to lose control. She had gotten under his skin, taunted him into reacting without thinking, and he didn't like it.

The tension was unnerving, and she wondered if she'd pushed him too far. Perhaps he'd decided she and her sticky breasts were not worth the effort, and he was about to storm out of here, go downstairs, and pick up one of those Hollywood bimbos she mentioned. One whose nipples weren't superglued to a rubber covering.

Finally, though, a long, low exhalation eased from his mouth. He rubbed a hand over his jaw and rolled his shoulders back in a slow stretch. He'd gotten back the control he'd so briefly lost. He didn't head for the door; he merely offered her the slightest smile.

She almost sighed in relief, at least until he licked his lips, and she saw his smile was the half-quirked, dangerous kind. The gleam in his eyes as he stared down at her was all the warning she needed. *Predator.*

This prey again regretted baiting him. But she was also more excited than she'd ever been.

He lifted his hand and ran his fingertip across the

slope of her breast. Though it was only the faintest scrape of skin on skin, and much of his touch was blocked by the tape, she quivered in response.

"Still think it's funny?" he asked, bending down to lick along the same path. His tongue was hot and wet, and she wanted to cry as he slid it over her nipples, covered by the hateful barrier, just thick enough to prevent her nerve endings from soaking up the sensation. "Because I, for one, am not amused that I can't suck you and leave my mark on you."

Jess forgot how to breathe.

Stepping between her parted legs, he pushed her back until she was lying on the table, braced by her elbows. She was quaking now. Unable to say a word, she watched and felt him kiss his way down her front.

"What about now, Jessica? Still laughing?" he whispered against her midriff.

"No," she managed to choke out.

Oh, no. She was not laughing. And neither was he.

His warm, strong hands dropped onto her thighs, his thumbs stroking the inside. They began to move up. And up. Meanwhile his hot mouth continued to move down. And down.

She arched toward what she wanted. Everything within her not already soft and wet got that way at once. She groaned as he dipped his tongue into her belly button, and his thumbs moved under the elastic of her skimpy panties to tangle in the curls between her legs.

Close. Oh, God, he was so close. She almost screamed with the need for him to move his hand the teeny, tiniest bit. The faintest brush of his fingertips was going to send her into the stratosphere, and she wanted that touch more than she wanted to live until the sun rose.

As for his mouth...she wasn't sure she could even take it.

"*Please*, Reece."

"I like hearing you say my name."

She'd repeat it a hundred times if necessary. Pride was long gone. She didn't even care that she was nearly naked while he wore a perfect, unmussed suit. It might look wicked to anyone who walked in on them, but she truly didn't care, she just needed him to...

As if her own imaginings had brought calamity on them, the door to the room suddenly swung open. Jess had just enough time to gasp and leap off the table. Reece stepped smoothly in front of her, blocking *most* of her from view, before the overhead light switched on, flooding the interior with bright illumination.

She peeked around Reece's broad shoulders. Two men stood in the doorway. One of them was Sid Loman. The gallery manager met her eye, and she swore for a second she saw a smirk on his face. That was probably because of the second man, who held a professional-looking camera. A camera he was using.

Son of a bitch. This intrusion was intentional—a complete setup.

"What do you think you're doing?" Reece barked.

"M-Mr. Winchester," Sid stammered. "Uh, I had no idea anyone was in here. I was giving a private tour of the gallery to a member of the press."

The guy wasn't merely a perv; he was also a crappy liar. The interruption was for his own amusement or financial gain. If the creep hadn't set this up to try to embarrass Reece, and her—who'd barely given him the time of day when he'd made a few fumbling come-ons—and to make a fast buck from a guy who looked like pure paparazzi, she'd eat her boob tape.

"The *press*." The very word sneered. "Miller, I thought you and I had an agreement."

The photographer clicked away, trying to edge around to get a better shot at naked little old her. Jess glued herself to Reece's back, clinging more tenaciously than the stick-on bra.

"I had no idea you'd be in here, Winchester," the intruder said, still photographing.

"Take another step and you're going to have to sue me again."

The tone was so calm, so reasonable, it took a second for the words to sink in. The photographer had sued him? Why would he *have* to...Oh. She got it. The two men had tangled before. Physically, she suspected.

"Don't do anything you might regret," Miller said.

"I never have regrets." Reece's calm voice was belied by the rigid tension of his body. He was ready to fight, she could feel it in the flex of his muscles, and hear it in the seething anger disguised by the rational-man conversation. "How much did you pay for your camera?"

"A lot," the guy said.

"I'd like to have one. Maybe I could buy it from you. Would thirty thousand cover it?"

Jess was so shocked she lurched back, forgetting she was naked but for some tape on her breasts, skimpy panties, and spiked heels. Unfortunately, her legs were still shaky from what they'd been doing before the interruption, and she stumbled. Before she could land on her ass and make this situation go from bad to abso-fucking-lutely mortifying by landing spread eagle on the floor in front of three men, Reece saved her. He swung around, turning his back to the men, and put his steadying hands on her hips. "Are you okay?"

"Don't you dare let that man extort you!" she snapped.

"I don't like my privacy invaded." He kept his voice low, intimate, and his eyes softened as he looked down into hers.

"Seems to me mine is the privacy being invaded." She glared over Reece's shoulder. "And, buddy, if you even *think* about selling naked pictures of me to the tabloids, I will sue your ass so hard you won't even have time to say the words *peddling pornography*."

"Let me handle this."

"He can't sell naked pictures of people, not if I don't sign a model release or something."

"Do you think female stars who make the mistake of going out without underwear sign releases before their crotch shots spread all over the internet?"

Oh. Right. Though she never kept up with such gossipy garbage, even she had heard of a few A-listers whose privacy had been so brutally invaded.

"You're disgusting," she said to the cameraman. He was young—early twenties, maybe. She memorized his face for her hit list in case she ever decided to become an assassin.

"Guy's gotta earn a living."

"Do we have a deal, Miller?" Reece asked, his back still to the other men.

"I think I could part with this equipment for thirty grand."

Reece still didn't turn around; he was focused only on Jessica. "Done. Put the camera on the table and get out. My office will take care of the payment."

Although infuriated by this blatant extortion, Jess didn't interfere. She also, however, didn't take her eyes off the photographer as he unlooped his camera from around his neck and placed it down as directed. No way would she trust him not to try to slip out a memory card.

"If those pictures turn up, I'll know where they came from," Reece said, continuing to shield her bare body from anyone else's view. He sounded calmer, but his arms, to which she clung, continued to flex and bulge with tension and protective anger.

"They won't," the guy said. He nodded at her and smiled. "Nice to, uh, meet you?"

"Go to hell," she snapped.

Offering Sid a shrug, he headed out the door. The manager started to follow, but Reece, his sixth sense apparently in overdrive, barked, "Don't *you* move."

"Me?" she asked.

He shook his head. "Pull your dress up," he murmured, "while I deal with *this*."

He turned slowly, shifting on his heel, providing a concealing barrier for her as he pivoted around to face his employee. His body was broad enough for her to quickly bend down, grab her dress, and yank it up into place. She had the willies just thinking of creepy Sid seeing any more of her than he already had.

Focusing on shoving herself back into her clothes, she missed the first few words of the conversation, but there was no mistaking it when Reece said, "You're fired."

Sid's eyes bulged. "You wouldn't . . ."

"I just did."

"But you can't!"

"Of course I can. You'll get a month's severance. Sharon is more soft-hearted than I am, so I suspect you'll also get whatever commissions are owed to you from tonight. But I want you out of here immediately."

Heat washed the older man red, right down to the too-tight collar of his dress shirt. "I'll sue you for wrongful termination."

"You signed a privacy contract," Reece retorted. "Bringing a photographer up here, to the staff-only part of the gallery, violated it. That's sufficient grounds for termination."

The other man's mouth opened and closed, then Sid visibly deflated as he realized his catastrophic error. "Look, it was a mistake. You can't hold me responsible. How was I supposed to know what you were up to in here?"

Oh, she had no doubt the creep had known exactly what they were up to. Jess's skin crawled thinking about it.

Reece, as if knowing she was now covered, walked away from her, stalking toward the other man, punctuating each angry step with an equally angry word. "It wasn't a mistake."

Sid lurched back, but Reece was in his face now, towering over him, so physically intimidating that Jess felt nervous for the perv. But only a little.

"You were trying to set us up. You hoped to make some quick cash and humiliate a woman who didn't want anything to do with you."

The man's eyes darted toward her, narrowing in anger. "What has she said to you?"

"Only enough to make me wonder what other women you've harassed."

"You need me," the other man pleaded.

"I need you like I need a rodent infestation in this building. Frankly, I wonder if there already was one. Were you actually watching us like some filthy rat, waiting for the right moment to walk in?"

If flames could spew out of someone's eyes, Reece would be in need of an asbestos jacket. Sid looked enraged as he sputtered. But suddenly, his attention shifted. He cast a quick glance toward the rear corner of the room and visibly calmed down. It was like watching a switch flip as he retreated back into the role of smarmy manager. "I'll go collect my things."

Reece grunted and turned away from the older, smaller man. "Your things will be held for you. You can come back for them tomorrow. Put your keys on the table and go."

"But I need..."

"Do you think I'm stupid?" He swung around again, his anger reigniting. Now it was an almost tangible, electric presence in the room. She suddenly realized Reece had turned his back on Sid to try to let the man get away before his rage could completely engulf him. "Do you think I'm going to leave you free to wander around and worm your way into Sharon's office so you can download a copy of the security tape from this room?"

Gasping, she realized what, exactly, Sid might have been looking at before the little smirk. Spinning around, she confirmed her worst fears, noting the small security camera in the back corner, hugging the ceiling. It was just like the ones downstairs that monitored every inch of the gallery floor. She hadn't even noticed this one when they'd come in. It would have a clear view of every part of the room. Including the table on which she'd been lying, spread out and nearly naked, like a pagan sacrifice.

The whole truth washed over her. The comment Reece had made about a rodent watching them hadn't been rhetorical. The disgusting manager and his paparazzi cohort might have borne witness, through the lens, to everything they'd done.

A cry rose in her throat and threatened to choke her. She had to lift her fist to her lips to hold it in. Jess was not entirely successful. Because, suddenly, something else popped into her mind, and her sob erupted from her mouth in a low, harsh whimper.

There'd been a moment earlier when Reece had glanced behind him, toward that corner of this room. He'd known the security camera was there. He'd looked at it and had to know it was recording. And he'd still gone ahead and...and...oh, *God.*

Humiliation poured into her as she remembered how

blatant and erotic the interlude had been. She'd been utterly exposed, not only to him, but to the prying eyes of an electronic spy, one to which Sid, Sharon, and who knew who else—maybe the security guy—had access.

"I didn't even remember there was a camera in here." The man smirked. "And I wonder if your guest knew there was one," Sid said, sounding smug as he lobbed the verbal grenade.

He had reason to. It had definitely exploded, erupting in the middle of the room and destroying the moment. Exactly as the pig had wanted.

He left. Reece didn't try to stop him, didn't say anything. Neither did Jess.

She couldn't speak, could barely think. All she knew was she was standing alone with a man she'd been about to have sex with...the complete stranger she'd fantasized into something he obviously was not. Far from being a hero, a character from one of his movies, the famous director was apparently as much of a creep as Sid. He'd planned to videotape them having sex, and she would never have known. He could have done anything with that tape—kept it, shared it, posted it on the internet. Her life could have been ruined, her career here in Hollywood definitely so. In some respects, she supposed she should thank Sid. He'd stopped her from making the worst mistake of her life.

Now there was just one thing to do. Walk away from Reece Winchester and pray to God she never set eyes on him again.

* * *

For a long moment, Reece stared at the door through which Sid had departed, calling himself ten kinds of fool. He'd handled this whole thing so badly—made mistake after mistake, from the moment he'd laid eyes on her through the security system. The very first day, two months ago, he should have gone downstairs and introduced himself. Looking back, it seemed so logical, so easy, and he would hate himself for a long time for not doing that. It was his own arrogance—his desire to set the stage, to put her in a gown, in the rich setting she deserved—that had fucked all this up. He'd been going for the long scene, the payoff moment, not just taking things as they came, putting out his hand and saying hello.

His brothers said he thought too much. Planned too much.

Right now, he'd have to say he agreed with them.

He finally turned to face her. "Jessica, I'm—"

She responded by slapping him right across the face. Hard. So hard his ears rang. He didn't react, knowing he'd deserved it.

"How *could* you? Is this your typical seduction routine?"

"It wasn't like that."

"I should have known. You can have any woman who catches your eye...and do just about anything to her. Including secretly recording her, humiliating her, ruining her."

"I didn't do it intentionally."

"Are you going to try to tell me you didn't remember the camera was on?" She sounded the tiniest bit hopeful, but then frowned. "But I saw you look back there."

"I hadn't planned on bringing you up here and tearing your clothes off."

"So you said."

"And it's true."

"But the camera..."

"The camera. Yes, I knew it was there, and that it was on."

She lifted a hand to slap him again. He remained still, ready to let her do it.

The hand dropped. Instead of lashing out physically, she took a deep breath, lifted her chin, and turned toward the door. She was going to walk out of here without another word.

He put a hand on her shoulder. "I intended to erase the file."

"Oh, sure you did." She swung around and glared. "You were carried away, huh?"

"I swear it. I remembered it was there after it was too late and made a mental note to delete it later."

"Don't bother lying, Mr. Great Director," she snapped. "I should have realized this was a setup as soon as you admitted you lured me in here after seeing me through the security camera."

That sounded bad. Really bad. Sid-the-Creep bad.

Reece thrust a hand into his hair, frustration making him shake. "Look, those two didn't see anything except you ducking behind me," he insisted. "The overhead lights were off when they came in. As for the camera, they *couldn't* have seen anything. The video monitors are in Sharon's office, which was shut and locked. An alarm rings when it's opened with anybody's key but hers and mine. Sid gambled on walking in here and catching us."

"Doing exactly what we were doing? As if he knew because you do this all the time?"

"Absolutely not." He stared at her, silently urging her to believe him. "The point is, nobody was watching, and nobody else would ever have seen that recording."

"Until when? Were you going to have a party and invite friends over for a viewing?"

"Damn it, Jessica, how many times do I have to say it? I never meant for this to happen. I would have erased the recording the minute I could." He grabbed her arms, gripping her tightly, feeling as though something important was about to slip through his fingers for good. And it was entirely his own fault.

"You're hurting me."

He immediately loosened his grip. "Stay. Let's talk. Get a drink. We can talk about the weather, or movies, or politics. I don't care. Just...stay."

Her eyes were so big, luminous, and her lips—plain, all lipstick kissed off—were trembling. For a second, he let himself hope he hadn't screwed this up beyond repair.

"Please leave me alone," she finally whispered, blinking rapidly as angry tears formed in her eyes. "I'm not used to this world you live in, and I don't want to be a part of it. You've humiliated me enough for one night."

Reece always knew what to do. Always. He made his plans, he acted on them, he didn't veer in unforeseen directions, never got off course, and he never apologized.

So he was completely out of his depth here. "It was never my intention to hurt you."

"I don't know or care what you meant to do, Reece. All I know is I'm embarrassed, and I'm angry, and I want to forget any of this happened. Now, I'm going downstairs to spend the rest of the evening celebrating my sister's big night."

He waited one more long moment, searching her face, looking for an opening, some hint of softening. She ground her teeth, jutting out her jaw, completely determined. He'd blown it completely.

"I handled this all wrong," he finally said, dropping his hands and stepping away. "Tonight wasn't supposed to be like this."

"Oh, you had it all planned out, how it was *supposed* to go?" When he didn't deny it, she barked a humorless laugh. "Bravo, the great director. Jesus, you're as bad as Sid."

He flinched. The insult had been about as low as she could go.

"It's been...interesting getting to know you, Mr. Winchester, though frankly I hope to God I never lay eyes on you again."

It was an exit line if he'd ever heard one, and he'd heard plenty. But although she turned to the door and reached for the knob, she didn't open it, and she didn't go through it. She stood there in the silence for a moment, finally whispering, "Maybe I'll wait a minute."

His pulse sped up. But she didn't turn back toward him. Instead, she let go of the knob and walked over to the large window overlooking the beach. The sand below was dark and shadowy, the ocean beyond it a vast blackness, visible only by the gleams of moonlight dancing lightly on the surf.

"Do you think they're gone yet?" Her voice was low and shaky. "Sid and that guy? I don't want to run into them downstairs."

Reece knew he was the last person she wanted comfort from right now, but nobody else was available. He hated to see her hurting so badly. Her anger had faded; now she was sad and humiliated. And alone. So he went to her, wrapping his arms around her. She stiffened, resisted for a second, and then allowed him to pull her close. She buried her face in his neck. He felt moisture there as she silently wept.

"I'm sorry," he whispered, the words unfamiliar in his mouth. But he meant them like he'd never meant it before. He gently stroked her hair, wanting her to believe him. "So damned sorry, Jessica."

She drew in a long, hitchy breath, and he wondered if she'd calmed down enough to realize he had been telling the truth about his intention to erase the tape. He hoped that was what she was about to say, anyway.

Before she could say anything, though, the world exploded.

A crack ripped the night, and even as the noise reached his ears, the large window erupted inward, showering them with glass.

It took less than a second for his brain to place the sound he'd heard right before the window shattered. It had been a shot. Someone had fired a bullet at them through the window.

He had one reaction, only one thought. *Jessica!*

Reece didn't plan, didn't fear, didn't worry a gun might be aimed at his head. All he could do was dive on her, taking them both down to the floor, up against the front wall of the room. They were under the window; the cement block construction would protect them as the glass had not.

But shards from the window still rained down, landing on his back and littering the carpet all around them. She was so soft, so exposed in her sexy dress, and his brain screamed as he thought about thousands of tiny bites being taken out of her skin. So he wrapped himself around her. He grabbed her head, tucked it into his neck, and lifted her up off the floor into his arms, pulling her frantically against his chest, covering her, shielding her.

Reece didn't know who fired or what might come next. He only knew he would keep her safe until his last breath.

He had put her in this situation, and he'd make damn sure she came out of it unscathed.

CHAPTER 5

The sound of a gunshot blowing out a massive window *should* have been enough to bring a halt to the most crowded of parties. That hadn't been the case at the gallery showing, however. In fact, nobody in the noisy downstairs section of Venice on the Beach Fine Arts had even realized what had happened Friday. Reece had raced down an emergency staircase, dragging Jessica with him, to warn everyone. His—definitely sexy—brother, a cop, had taken over. All the patrons were quickly ushered into windowless bathrooms and conference rooms to wait for emergency responders.

It had been a long night. She'd been interviewed by the police. There were worried patrons and, to everyone's surprise, a quick sellout of Liza's art.

Well, maybe it wasn't so surprising. Word of the drive-by shooting—or run-by, since the shot had to have come from the beach, from someone on foot—had, of course, hit the news. Celebrities were involved, after all. Everybody knew curiosity got people talking; in this town scandal steeped like Earl Grey. Buying a piece of art on display at the same time somebody had shot at Reece Winchester seemed like a sound investment.

Unfortunately, all the press coverage brought people she'd rather not hear from crawling out of the woodwork. Like the one whose number had shown up as *Unknown* on her phone screen Tuesday morning as she walked across campus. God, she wished she hadn't answered it.

As soon as she heard his voice, she snapped, "How did you get this number?" *And how soon can I change it? Again.*

Johnny, her ex, ignored the question. "Are you all right, baby doll? You weren't hurt?"

Cringing at the endearment she'd hated but endured, she said, "I'm fine."

"I literally died when I saw the pictures and read about the shooting. You could have been killed!"

Did you? Literally? "I wasn't. And it's not your concern, anyway."

"Of course it is," he said, a hint of a whine in his voice. She'd always hated that whine, which didn't match his big ex–football player's body. "You know how much I care about you."

"Well, stop it. I don't want you caring about me, Johnny. I want you out of my life."

As usual, he ignored what she wanted. "Why were you alone with that guy?"

Of course. They'd arrived at the real reason for his call. Not because she might have been shot, but because she'd been alone with a handsome man when it happened. He hadn't changed a bit. She was tempted to hang up, but cutting off communication and trying to keep out of his reach, verbal or otherwise, hadn't worked during the past year. Why would it now?

She swallowed, not sure if what she wanted to say was going to inflame him or get him to finally realize they were *finished*. But she had to try. "I was alone with him because we're involved," she said, crossing her fingers behind her back.

"You're screwing that spoiled Hollywood prick?" He'd yelled so loudly she had to pull the phone away from her ear.

"I'm hanging up now."

In his rage, he didn't even hear her. "Did he fuck you right in the building while that slut sister of yours was showing off the garbage she calls art?"

Ahh, there was the good ol' boy she remembered. "I've moved on. You need to, too."

"You bitch!"

Jess was trying hard to remain calm and strong, but the fury in his voice made her shudder. It brought back so many memories of his verbal and emotional abuse. He hadn't ever hit her, though she knew he'd wanted to a couple of times. He'd screamed at her often, and had done what he could to mess with her head. Things like attacking her self-confidence about her writing, her looks, and her femininity.

After the breakup, he'd followed her, not caring if she spotted him. There'd been endless heavy-breathing calls and notes slipped under her door. The worst was when he'd smashed the windows in her car. He'd found her books and papers and burned them. Blackened pieces of a script she'd been working on were strewn on the floor with the glass. Although she had backups, she'd felt utterly assaulted. Invaded.

Fortunately for her sanity, everything had calmed down over the past couple of months.

Then the phone rang. If the harassment and threats started up again, she might lose her mind.

"Reece is very protective. He won't like you calling me, so you'd better back off."

Letting out a loud laugh, he said, "You think I'm scared of some pussy actor?"

"Not only is he incredibly strong, he's also wealthy."

"Oh, sure, you're after him for his money. I wasn't rich enough for you, huh?"

"I said that to make sure you understand he has connections. He can hire security." She scrambled for more. "His own brother is a cop."

Johnny fell silent, and Jess hoped he was reevaluating his actions. She'd never called the police on him before, afraid it would escalate things. Maybe this ruse with Reece would do the trick, and her ex would actually be smart for a change.

His snarl said he was still completely stupid. "He'll dump you. He'll use you and throw you away. You'll be begging me to take you back."

She ran a weary hand through her hair, knocking her ponytail holder loose. "If he does, it will be my business, Johnny. Not yours."

"JJ, listen…"

"No. I'm done listening. As for begging you to take

me back?" She laughed, knowing she sounded a little hysterical. "I wouldn't beg you to throw water on me if I were on fire."

Then she hung up. Johnny Dixon had already consumed far too much of her time and energy.

"Do your worst, you son of a bitch," she muttered, sensing a resolve in herself that might not have been there a year ago. Glancing at the time, she realized she was late for her appointment with her academic advisor. She shook off the worry her life was about to detour back into Crazypants land, and raced across campus, knocking on Professor Alan Bent's door at exactly four minutes past her scheduled time. Bent was a former Hollywood staple whose successful screenwriting career had grown old, as had he.

"I'm so sorry," she said, out of breath, after he'd ushered her in.

"Please, sit down," he said, smiling. "Take a few breaths. I looked out the window and saw you running across the lawn."

She dropped to the chair, heaved a few times, and then nodded her readiness.

Apparently, he had something other than academics in mind. "So, has there been any word on the investigation into the shooting?"

"No."

The older man, *tsk*ed. "I still can't believe you were caught in the crossfire."

"There *was* no crossfire, Professor. It was one shot. Mr. Winchester protected me. We alerted everyone else. And the police didn't find anyone."

He still looked curious, as everyone had in the few days since the incident. Good thing Reece had bought the camera from the photographer; the pictures would have been much more popular with the news coverage. The story about the attack had gone national.

Unfortunately, a reporter had found out who she was and where she worked, and came into the restaurant for an ambush interview. He'd been less interested in the shooting than in why she had been alone with Reece at the time. More reporters had followed, and her boss ordered her to stay home until this all blew over. She hoped it would soon. She couldn't afford the unpaid time off. Liza could cover the bills for a while, given her success at the showing, but Jess liked to pay her own way.

Remembering Johnny's phone call, though, she acknowledged there might be a silver lining. If she wasn't at work, he couldn't come in and harass her, as he had a couple of times last winter before her boss banned him.

"Frankly, my dear, I'm glad there was too much traffic for me to get to the gallery in time," Alan said. "These old bones can't handle that much excitement."

"I'm glad, too." She had invited him, sensing he was lonely. The Hollywood elite weren't always kind to those who aged out of usefulness—in *their* view. Alan had hit the skids, career-wise, and, judging by the shabbiness of the tweed jacket he always wore, financially. Jess wouldn't want to think about any harm befalling him physically.

Fortunately, nobody else had been hurt at the gallery. Only her and Reece. She had tiny cuts on her face, arms, and shoulders, and a few on her legs, but nothing else. Reece had lifted her off the glass on the carpet with one powerful arm, and shielded her from the shards tinkling onto them from above. His head, broad shoulders, and back took the brunt of it.

He'd refused to let anyone look at his injuries. But the flecks all over his suit and the gleams of glass twinkling in his hair hinted he hadn't escaped unscathed.

He'd put himself in danger for her. She still didn't know how to feel about his heroic actions, given how devastated she'd been in the minutes leading up to the potentially deadly shot.

"Have you got any thoughts about who might have done it? Or why?"

"No. The police questioned me that night and called me again yesterday to follow up, but didn't give me any more information."

"I suppose they're focusing on Mr. Winchester, since he was most likely the target."

"Most likely."

Alan frowned. "He's not the charmer the world thinks he is."

Disdain dripped from his words, which surprised her. There was some bad blood here. "He could have been killed," she pointed out.

The shooter almost certainly hadn't been aiming at her. Famous movie stars were often targeted by stalkers.

Or maybe Sid Loman had been pissed off about being fired. According to police, his car was still in the gallery lot, and he hadn't returned to his apartment.

One more possibility whispered in her brain. She

dropped her gaze to her own hands, not even listening to what Alan was saying. *What if it was Johnny?*

"Are you all right?" her professor asked.

"Fine," she said, knowing she sounded breathy.

He got up and went to a small refrigerator, getting her a bottle of water. Twisting off the cap, he put the bottle in her hand and ordered her to drink.

She gulped the water down, trying to douse the heat of her own imagination. It was impossible. Wasn't it? Johnny couldn't have been spying on her Friday night. He couldn't have seen her in the arms of another man, the first she'd even kissed since the breakup. He *couldn't* have fired at them. Could he?

"Feeling better?"

She nodded, finding it hard to focus on this meeting. But she had to think about her degree, so close she could almost taste it. Johnny couldn't be allowed to cost her that, not on top of robbing her of her peace of mind for so long. "I'm fine. Thank you for the water."

"Certainly." He sat down again. "Are there any leads at all?"

Back to the subject she didn't want to discuss. But he'd been kind, and she couldn't brush him off. "There are cameras all over the building, including one facing the beach. The police think the shooter stood in the surf, in the darkness, just out of range."

"It sounds like a long distance."

"Which could be why he missed."

Johnny's father had put a hunting rifle in his hands at age nine, and he continued to do so whenever he went home to visit.

"Well, I do hope you are being careful," the professor said, clearing his throat.

"I am, thank you."

"Now, about why I called you in today..."

"Have you read *A Child in the Street*?"

She had finished the script she'd been required to write as her final project weeks ago and had been sweating about his reaction since. She'd clawed the script from a dark, private place that dwelled deep inside her. It wasn't easy to let somebody else visit there.

"Actually, no."

Well, shit was her first reaction. Her second was *Thank God.*

"You seem relieved." He peered at her over a file. "Are you concerned about it?"

"You remember how nervous I was in my first class with you."

He chuckled. "I had to pry your papers out of your hands."

"This project. It's especially..."

"Intimate, I'm aware."

"I thought you hadn't read it."

"I might have peeked at the first few pages." His unruly gray brows furrowed, and she suspected she wasn't going to like what he was about to say. "They're...a bit self-indulgent."

Jess felt herself deflate, knowing what he meant. Although Alan didn't ask what she'd based the story on, he would probably soon realize it was about her. Sooner or later, every writer wrote autobiographically. She was no different. So the main character was an eleven-year-old foster kid, sassy, smart-mouthed, streetwise. Bad things happened to her, but she didn't get a happily ever after. It was a might-have-been tale, and she didn't need a shrink to tell her why she'd written it.

"I'm sorry to hear that," she said. She'd been stupid to pour so much of herself into it, opening herself up to not only criticism of her writing, but judgment on her own life.

"Don't be discouraged. As I said, I've only read part of it."

"Well, hopefully it will improve for you."

"You're certainly talented, Jessica. I've always seen you writing comedy, however. This dark angst might not be exactly right for you."

She managed not to laugh in his face. Dark angst was why she reverted to comedy much of the time, verbally and in her writing. Getting herself out of bad situations with caustic humor had become second nature. That didn't mean, however, that the darkness wasn't still there, lurking beneath the wisecracks. She didn't dwell on the things that had happened in her past—the loss, the heartache, the fear—and she had mostly good memories, thanks to her mothers, biological and adoptive. Memories had a tendency to lurk, however. She'd felt the need to exorcise those demons through her fingers on the keys.

Maybe she would throw the whole thing out, hit delete on her laptop file and consign it to the recycle bin. And then empty that bin. Even if she failed, even if she never pitched it, at least she'd gotten the words out, and could, she hoped, move on to new things.

Alan reached across the desk and patted her hand

with his pale, wrinkled one. She knew he didn't like to give harsh criticism, and he usually tempered it with praise. "You're an excellent student. I have no doubt you will go far."

"Thank you. That means a lot."

He moved a pile of papers on his desk—scripts from other students who were probably going to get better grades—his expression growing serious. "As for the reason I asked you to stop by today, you've been offered an internship."

She gasped. "Really?"

"A well-paying one."

Her jaw fell. She'd been prepared to work like a dog for pennies. That was how things went in Hollywood. Everybody was interested in cheap labor; any student wanting to break into the industry prepared for indentured servitude as part of the dues-paying process.

"Where?"

His mouth twisted. "The offer is from Win or Lose."

"Son of a bitch," she snapped, immediately throwing herself back in her chair.

"So you're not interested in working with Mr. Winchester?"

Right now she'd like to give Mr. Winchester the same treatment she gave to handsy, grabby customers at the bar. Anything from a drink in the face to a knee in the crotch. Because the man she most wanted to avoid was the owner of Win or Lose Studios.

It was a small outfit, but there was nothing small about its films. The company had a great reputation, winning a lot of prestigious awards. If anybody else in the world owned it, she'd leap at the chance. But how could she work with Reece Winchester, given what had happened between them? How could she trust him with her career when she didn't trust him with her body? *Get real. You don't trust yourself around him.*

"I'm not interested in him at all," she mumbled.

Alan's brow went up in skepticism, but she told herself she meant it. Reece had humiliated her in front of paparazzi. He'd sucked her into his stalker drama, as if she didn't have enough of her own in the past year. He'd put the police in her life and the media on her tail. He'd caused her to lose her much-needed hours at Hot Buns. Now he thought he could make it up to her with a job?

She didn't wonder how he'd found out she was in need of an internship. Judging by the things he'd said Friday night, he'd been interested enough in her to research her background. Her status as college senior wouldn't have been too hard to find out for someone with his contacts.

"I can't do it," she said.

"I concur."

"You do?"

Her advisor nodded. "You don't want to get further entangled with the man. The world might think he's the golden child of the industry, but his life is riddled with secrets and scandals. Believe me, I know. I worked with him."

Jessica gaped.

"Oh, yes," he said, seeing her reaction. "Without my writing and direction on *Walk Along with Me*, Reece Winchester would never have become so famous."

When she'd learned during her first class with him that Bent had written and directed one of her all-time favorite childhood movies, she'd been surprised. Alan was fussy, staid, highly literary, and old-school. "That was such a popular film."

"It wasn't in my regular line. Honestly, I was in a financial bind." He wrinkled his nose. "I did it for the money."

That was *not* a surprise. As a teacher, Alan was about the art. Everything they studied in his classes involved scripts with deep themes. A hit kids' movie didn't qualify.

"Well, no matter why you made it, I want to thank you for it. I loved that film. It got me through some rough days as a kid."

He nodded to acknowledge the compliment, then returned to his point. "The whole Winchester family was bad news. The boys were wild, and the poor sister wasted on drugs. Their mother was obsessed with fame. The ultimate stage mom. I had her banned from my set."

Jess suspected he wanted her to prompt him for details about the whole family. But she knew better than to indulge in backstabbing and gossip. Here, words were repeated and embellished, often creating feuds and scandals. She didn't need to start her career that way.

"What if I don't get another job offer in time?"

"You might get something, or you could pick up a job in the fall." He cleared his throat, straightening and appearing a bit pompous. "Perhaps I could help. I do still have some connections in this town."

Connections like an Oscar-winning writer and director who created hit movie after hit movie? Hmm. The more she thought about this, the more she realized she might have to do what was right for her future, no matter why she'd been offered the position.

"God, this is confusing. The trouble is, with work and classes in the fall, summer is really the only time I can do an internship. I need something to happen *now*."

"Don't decide yet. Let me make a few calls."

"I appreciate that. But I have to admit, a recommendation from him *would* open doors."

He nodded curtly. She hadn't meant to hurt Alan's feelings, but she had to wonder if he really had any connections left in this fickle town.

"It is, of course, your decision."

Jess had come too far in her life to lose an opportunity just because she questioned why she'd gotten it. Besides, if Reece Winchester was hiring her to get in her pants, he was in for a big disappointment. *Zipper up, buttons buttoned, buddy.*

"I think I should do it."

"With your *personal* connection to him?"

She couldn't even respond. Yes, she'd let herself get caught up in the glamour, the excitement, the atmosphere, and the stupid Flaming Orgasm the bartender had made for her. Heavy on the orgasm. All of that might have made her a little reckless with Reece Winchester, but should it affect an important decision about her future?

Reece had hurt and embarrassed her, yes. He'd also protected her, however. When the shot rang out, and the glass burst inward, he'd thought only of *her* safety, not his own. He'd covered her, wrapped himself around her, physically sheltering her as no one ever had in her life. Like she was precious. Like she mattered to him.

She'd tried to block out those memories. Late at night, though, when she was alone and could no longer believe the lies she'd been telling herself, his tenderness was what she remembered. Even more than the kisses, than the touch of his hands on her naked skin. It was the way he'd held her. The way he'd protected her. *That* she couldn't get over.

Jess slowly let a deep breath ease out of her mouth. Emotion couldn't overwhelm logic. Too much was at stake. Her heartbeat slowed from its rapid rhythm, and a calm settled over her. She might be disappointed—in fact, she probably would be, since he was a man, and a spoiled one. But that dive, that embrace, those soft whispers and the brush of his hand through her glass-strewn hair, meant she had to give him a chance.

Maybe he just wanted to get her into bed. Maybe he thought she owed him.

But maybe it was something else.

"I'm going to say yes."

Alan nodded, his mouth pinched. Reaching for a piece of paper, he jotted down an address. "They'd like you to come in today at two." When she lifted her hand to take the paper, he added, "I assume I don't have to warn you about how cutthroat this business can be."

"No, you don't."

"I'm going to anyway. Watch yourself. There are

rogues and thieves who live to take advantage of the young and vulnerable."

Rogues? He really was Errol Flynn–era Hollywood.

"Don't trust. Don't share your ideas. *Definitely* don't share your script, especially not with your new boss. It would be the worst mistake you've ever made."

"Are you kidding? I haven't even told my sister what it's about. I'm paranoid about leaving my laptop at home because I'm so worried she or my roommate will snoop."

Not that they would. She knew that logically. Emotionally, the fear was always there.

"You're in good company then," Alan said with a chuckle. "No one has neuroses like a writer. I'm afraid it never gets better."

Wonderful.

"You have to be determined and must truly want to succeed in order to make it in this industry."

She was. She did.

He wagged his index finger and warned her one more time. "Remember, trust *no* one."

She had dreams of Hollywood success—on her own terms, not on the coattails of a man who'd gotten her naked within an hour of meeting her. *Ugh.* But she wasn't stupid. She'd been around the block a time or two, and had been burned. She was taking enough of a risk by agreeing to accept Reece Winchester's job; she wasn't about to trust him enough to hand over her guts, soul, history, and dreams in written form. Since she was soon going to be working with the man, probably closely, considering the trouble he'd gone through to make this happen, she only hoped she didn't live to regret trusting him with her body.

One thing was sure. She would never—ever—trust him with her heart.

* * *

After his brightest pupil walked out, Alan Bent listened to the door close and the click of Jess's footsteps fading down the hallway. He sat in silence for a long moment, evaluating everything that had just happened. Once it sank in, he let his anger loose and swept a shaking hand across his desk. Papers flew, rubber bands snapped, sending pages of scripts flying. Seeing his dreams slip out of his grasp, he couldn't bring himself to care about the mess.

"Damn that man. Damn that girl. And damn this town."

Everything had been going so well. He'd laid out a clear path for his triumphant return to mainstream moviemaking, and had begun taking the first few steps down it. He'd worked hard to rebuild connections, calling in favors, putting out feelers. He wasn't remembered as he should've been, which infuriated him. Cashing in on his least favorite but most successful film, *Walk Along with Me*, at least got him through the doors of lower-level studio executives.

They were interested. All of them, interested. He was once again fielding calls and taking lunches, part of the world he loved that had been denied to him for so long.

He'd envisioned studios competing for rights, giving in to his demand to direct and offering full creative control. His return would be covered by *Variety*. He would cast Farrah Allen, the hottest child-actor in the country, in the lead role. He foresaw a record-breaking box office, awards, and smooth sailing right into a new future.

Then Reece Winchester hired his prized pupil, threatening to rip away everything he'd dreamed of. Again.

Isn't ten years long enough? He looked at the awards on the bookshelf, proof he belonged here, that he deserved a spot at Hollywood's table. "I did my time in purgatory."

Plus, he had changed. He wasn't the man he'd been during his heyday, when drugs had been so easy to get and dark cravings so simple to indulge. If given a chance, he would prove that to everyone. Even Mr. High-and-Mighty Winchester. No, *especially* him.

But not if Winchester found out what he was up to and ruined everything.

"They should never have met," he mumbled. "I should have gone to that gallery and prevented them from ever speaking."

It was too late, though.

How long would it be before the intern asked her boss, the extremely successful writer/director, to read her screenplay?

She can't do that.

Not if Alan wanted to sell it under his own name.

Opening a desk drawer, he reached inside and withdrew his working copy of *A Child in the Street*, which he'd renamed *Street Girl*. Although he'd had the original in his possession for only a couple of weeks, the copy he had made was worn and crumpled from rereading. Penciled notes filled the margins. Yellow highlights emphasized turning points and edited dialogue. He'd jotted in more detailed character descriptions and ideas for additional scenes.

Street Girl was the best screenplay he had ever read. It represented his future, his comeback, and the answers to his financial problems. As for taking it? Well, everyone in Hollywood lifted something from time to time. It was the price of being in the business.

The story was not that unique, but the way she presented it certainly was. Every turning point was perfectly placed, the beats laid out with precision. The dialogue sparkled, and the ending killed. Audiences would fall in love with a precocious little girl, only to have their hearts ripped out at her fate.

Until Jessica had met Reece, Alan hadn't worried about what would happen when she found out about his movie deal. She might learn what it was about and grow suspicious. But who would believe her? Besides, movies took years to get off the ground. It would have to get backing, financing, then get made and released before she would ever know for sure.

This was a rough town. She might have given up by then.

Maybe she wouldn't even be alive. Accidents happened, after all. Hadn't she learned that just the other night?

Even if she put up a fuss, it would be his word—the

word of a respected, experienced moviemaker—against a nobody. She'd said many times that she'd never even told her family what she was writing about. She had handed him what she claimed was her only printed copy. As for her laptop, which she carried to school and where she kept the file . . . well, something could be done about that. He already had a few ideas . . .

It was the perfect plan. She was young and talented. She'd have other chances. But this was his *last* one.

"Unless Reece Winchester ruins everything for me again."

There *had* to be a way to stop that from happening. He couldn't give this up without a fight.

Alan leaned back in his chair, his fingers entwined on his chest.

He had some thinking to do.

CHAPTER 6

M r. Winchester? Ms. Jensen is here."

Reece jerked his gaze up from the pile of crew reports he'd been shifting around on his desk. He'd kept his eye on the clock more than the paperwork, knowing his new intern was scheduled to come in today and wondering which Jessica he was about to see.

The sultry beauty who'd been in his arms in the gallery?

The enraged wronged woman who'd slapped him across the face?

The college student? The faithful sister? The terrified victim covered with glass?

She walked in.

Ahh. The prim professional.

She wore a blouse buttoned to her throat and a plain knee-length gray skirt. With her hair twisted into a tight bun on the back of her head and a pair of glasses perched on her nose, she could have come out of central casting as a secretary from a 1950s period piece.

He had to laugh.

"What?" she snapped.

"Nothing, Jessica. Absolutely nothing." Rising from his desk, he walked around to greet her. "Thank you for coming in."

She extended her arm straight out from her body for their handshake. "Mr. Winchester."

Hiding a smile, he shook, and then stepped closer, reached for her chin, and tilted her face up. He studied her, looking for the cuts he'd seen on her cheeks last week, seeing redness and one or two tiny scabs. God, how they enraged him.

"How are you?"

She licked her lips and stepped away. "Never better. What about you?"

"Totally fine."

"Did you ever see a doctor?" she asked.

"Not necessary."

Her head swung toward him and her eyes narrowed. "Yes it was. You had blood on the back of your neck and your hands, and shards of glass on your clothes and your head."

"Paying pretty close attention, were you?"

As he'd been paying close attention to her. They'd both apparently worried about the other more than themselves.

"Only because of the glass," she insisted. So stubborn. So sexy in a buttoned-up schoolteacher way. He could come to *like* this woman even more than he *wanted* her.

"I was fine. No real damage done."

Except to his mood. He'd walked around for days in a state of rage that someone with an ax to grind against him had endangered a completely innocent woman. Whether it had been Sid, the ex-gallery manager, or the psycho who'd burned down his house, or someone else entirely, he hoped he got to them before the cops did. He ached for payback for every tiny mark on her face.

He didn't doubt the shooter would be caught. After the fire, he'd hired a private investigator recommended by his brother Raine. Now the man had more work to do. He trusted the police, but it seemed clear Reece was in somebody's crosshairs. While he could take care of himself, he wasn't about to let anybody else be endangered.

"Have you heard anything more about the investigation?"

"Not really. Whoever did it was smart enough to stay out of range of the security cameras covering the exterior of the building."

"I heard."

"As for any other clues, well, footprints on a popular beach in June won't help. They did say judging by the bullet they recovered in the gallery wall, the gun was a nine millimeter."

According to his brother, that was a good thing. Since the shot had probably come from down by the water, it had been a long-distance gamble to take with a handgun. Rowan had told him if a rifle with a scope had been involved, it could have been a lot worse. The shooter could have hit his target. Or worse, missed his target and hit this woman.

"So whoever did it probably didn't plan ahead, or he'd have brought a better weapon," Jessica mused. "This was more... passionate. Spur of the moment."

Wondering what she was thinking, he said, "Sounds likely. Why?"

She paused for half a second, and then quickly shook her head. "Just playing detective."

"Don't. Please, let the professionals handle it."

"Of course. I was merely thinking, not acting."

"Good. No way do I want you to confront a deranged person."

"Yeah," she mumbled. "I've had enough of those in my life."

"What?"

"Nothing."

He didn't pry, knowing he had to respect her boundaries—though thinking about her rough childhood, her years in the foster-care system, sent his imagination to dark places. He hoped one day she would trust him again and open up about her thoughts and feelings.

"Have they been able to find Sid?"

Reece's eyes narrowed as he thought of the weasely man. The longer the former gallery manager stayed out of sight, the more Reece suspected him. "There's been no sign of him."

"I know you think he might have done it, but I'm not convinced he did," she said. "I mean, he'd just left the building. He would've had to have a gun on him."

"Given the value of the merchandise at the gallery, he might have qualified for a license to carry." Rowan would undoubtedly find out.

Wanting to distract her from what had happened the other night, he said, "Please, have a seat." He gestured toward a trio of chairs fronting the window of the office. It looked out onto Santa Monica Boulevard, so there was no great view, but it was a sunny day, and he liked the way the beams brought out the gold highlights in her hair.

She smoothed her skirt as she sat down, and he took the chair opposite her.

"This isn't an interview," he explained. "You already have the job."

"Why?"

"Because I thought you had spirit and imagination, and I need an intern."

Her sneer was accompanied by an eye roll. "I figure it's more likely either you wanted to get me into bed or you felt guilty about almost getting me killed. Maybe both."

This was a battle he'd anticipated. He grabbed a folder from his desk and gave it to her. "Look."

"What is this?"

"Lists of other student interns we've hired in the past. Dozens of them. All with your experience level, all with appropriate salaries."

Opening the folder, she thumbed through the documents. She reached a page and stopped. "This is my application from *last* summer."

"Yes."

She shoved the glasses up onto her head and lifted the page to read without them. Jessica had either put them on as a costume piece or usually wore contacts only for distance. He almost laughed. Damn, he'd laughed more around this woman in the couple of times he'd met her than he had in the past month.

"There's a notation here in the top corner, with 'Next year' written beside it."

He didn't have to read over her shoulder. "It means you were evaluated last year, came close, and were earmarked for consideration again this summer."

Her brow furrowed as she considered what he was saying, and then she finally slipped the paper back into the folder. "You mean I was already on a list for this job? Before we, uh...met?"

"Before I ever even laid eyes on you through the security camera."

A slight flush rose in her cheeks. "Don't remind me. I'd like to forget all about it."

She might. He never would. "My staff keeps track of the best people. We usually don't hire until a student is close to finishing school and might consider taking a full-time position if things work out. That's why you weren't interviewed sooner."

She sucked her lips into her mouth, probably remembering what she'd just said about his motives for hiring her. He waited for an apology, already knowing he probably wouldn't get it.

"I guess that makes sense," she finally said.

No *I'm sorry for thinking the worst of you*. As expected. Considering what he'd put her through, he didn't blame her one bit.

She lifted the folder to hand it back, but despite her calm tone, her fingers were shaking, and several pages slid out. They both moved to catch them, his hand brushing hers, her slim calf sliding between his pant legs. The connection was electric, as it had been the night they'd met, and they both froze as tension and attraction flared between them.

She pulled away first.

He retrieved the papers, slipped them back into the folder, and put it back on the desk. "So why did you tell me you work as a waitress rather than admit you're studying screenwriting?"

"Because screenwriting doesn't pay the bills."

Maybe. Or she didn't want him to know for fear he'd think she was about to make an elevator pitch. Literally, considering how long they'd been in the gallery elevator. He hoped so, anyway. He liked her independent streak, and he already knew she wanted to get where she was going on her own merits. Which meant finding her name in a personnel record, with a note from someone in HR, had been more than a stroke of luck. It had seemed almost fated.

"Is it typical for the CEO of a production company to interview the new intern?"

"No. But this isn't an interview. As I said, you've already got the job."

"Why did you bring me in, rather than someone in HR?"

"Because I know you'd think I found out what you were studying and set this whole thing up to get you into my clutches."

"You clutched me plenty the other night," she grumbled.

There she was wrong. He definitely had not. He hoped there would be a lot more clutching in their immediate future. But not until he got her to trust him. "You would have been chosen even if we hadn't met Friday night."

She licked her lips and lowered her gaze, averting those brown eyes. "Really?"

"Really, Jessica."

She finally relaxed, settling deeper into her chair. He knew she'd come in here wearing pounds of mental armor, to go along with the physical armor she'd donned in choosing her prissy outfit. The woman had pride.

"So, do you trust me again?"

"Who said I did before?"

Direct hit. "Ouch."

"You didn't give me much reason to."

"Yet you chose to meet me at the elevator Friday night."

"That required *some* trust. This requires more." She crossed her arms, eyeing him. "You've gone to a lot of trouble over me, Mr. Winchester. You saw me on camera and arranged Liza's showing. You had her bring me back for the meeting so you could watch me again."

He didn't reply. How could he defend himself? Could anyone understand the camera lens was his security guard—his weapon against invasions into his thoughts and his private life—and he was armed at all times? Putting something between himself and the rest of the world had been natural to him for years...ever since his fucked-up childhood. He'd had his fill of being watched, and now he preferred to be the watcher. That had been one reason he'd left his adult acting career as soon as he'd had the clout and the money to switch solely to directing. But it did sound pretty bad when she put it that way. "I wasn't..."

"You also bought the statue and lured me up there to see it."

"It was an invitation," he pointed out, knowing his defense sounded weak.

"And then stripped me naked and put me on a table."

"I didn't strip you *all* the way. Speaking of which, did the baby oil work?"

He'd swear a flush of color rose from her throat, up her neck, and into her face. She was trying to sound cut-and-dried as she raked him over the coals. Instead, as she dissected his actions and his motives, she looked pretty damned adorable.

"It was fine."

"Did you throw those horrible things away?"

She tossed her head, making the one silky strand of hair bounce against her cheek, and brushed it back impatiently. "That's none of your business."

"Actually, I am still holding a grudge against them."

"Don't distract me. I wasn't finished telling you off."

"Oh, please, do continue," he said, settling back in his chair.

She sucked in a deep breath, and then slowly blew it out. "You obviously had somebody spying on me because you found out where I went to school."

"It wasn't hard to find out," Reece said with a shrug. "My twin's a cop. My other brother owns a security company. Family benefits."

Her eyes rounding, she finally left off the verbal barrage. "Raine is in security?"

Startled, he quickly realized that of course she would know his youngest brother's name. Raine had been the cheeky, smiling star of a bunch of commercials when he was a toddler. Hell, they still ran them sometimes on an old cartoon network.

"His company's called Hollywood Guardians."

That was how his brother saw himself, as a guardian of the young and vulnerable. No surprise, given what their family had endured. The youngest Winchester had seen the worst of the worst, which was why there was nothing his older brothers wouldn't do—hadn't done—to protect him. Hell, maybe they should all be called guardians. Not angels, though. Oh, no. Unless they were fallen ones.

"Raine sparkled from a young age. I thought he might follow in your superstar footsteps, as a kid, and as an adult. Why didn't he?"

Reece didn't like the way this conversation was going. In fact, it had already gone further than he ever allowed with people who weren't related to him by blood. Considering he'd almost gotten her shot the other night, however, the least he could do was admit a few of his secrets.

"He grew out of it. Now he runs a business protecting children."

"Sounds pretty specialized."

"But necessary in this town," he replied in an even tone. He didn't want to elaborate, however, and admitted something else. "We were all pretty burned out when we left. As you can imagine, we were targets of the press before Rachel died. Afterward, the media attention was brutal. Dangerous, even."

Jessica's curious expression shifted into sadness. She didn't say it, though. Didn't say those words. *What doesn't kill you makes you stronger.* Of course she didn't.

Not sure why, he went even further. "My dad and Aunt Sharon came from the East Coast. They offered to stay and let us continue in the business, if we wanted to."

"But it wasn't what you wanted. Not after what had happened to Rachel."

Not after what had happened to Rachel.

Not after what had happened to their mother.

Not after he and his twin had done things that should *never* be asked of a kid in order to protect the family they had left.

"Exactly," he said, hiding the darkness that gnawed at him every day of his life. "So we went. Tried to have a normal life."

A tiny smile. "How did that work out for you?"

"Let's just say middle school wasn't my favorite time." Or high school. Or any place where he was treated like either a movie star or an entitled prick.

"I'll bet. Then you grew up and all of you came back to the left coast."

"Right. Rowan started law school but dropped out to become a cop." His twin had said his hypocrisy only went so far. "Raine left for the army the day of his eighteenth birthday." Reece's jaw might have tightened, but he kept his fists from clenching on the armrests of his chair as he thought about the night right before his kid brother had left. "When he got out, he started his business here."

"Starting up is never easy, especially in this zip code."

Reece shrugged. "He had some investors."

She understood. "The same ones who helped your aunt with the gallery?"

"Maybe. It turned out to be a *very* sound investment."

"Aren't there a lot of security companies out here?"

"Yes." Justifiably so, as the fire at his house had

proved a couple of months ago. "But Raine's company is specialized. The studios hire him a lot. He focuses only on protecting child stars; he has some army buddies working for him, and they take their jobs seriously."

They had to. God knew Hollywood was full of predators and psychos. He didn't just mean the sicko fans who saw kids in movies or on TV and formed disgusting obsessions. There were also the monsters who lurked in plain sight. The ones who'd found their way into the business and indulged their darkest proclivities. Those were the ones every show-biz parent should be worried about, and they were the particular ones Raine protected children against.

If only somebody had done the same for the Winchesters all those years ago, their lives might be very different now. More of them might be alive, anyway.

She remained silent. He wondered if she had any idea he'd just told her more about himself, and his family, than he'd revealed to anyone in years. Maybe it was because he owed her, considering what had happened at the gallery. The sight of her covered in broken glass wasn't something he'd soon forget. But he also knew it was because he wanted her to trust him. Wanted to make up for the admittedly controlling way he'd *directed* her into his arms.

"I wouldn't have guessed it," she finally said. "Raine seemed as comfortable in front of the camera as you were. Rowan doesn't surprise me. He was never as good as the rest of you."

He had to grin. "I'll be sure to tell him."

"Oh, no, please don't! I meant, he didn't seem as into

it as the rest of you, whereas he appears to be the perfect cop. He was so thoughtful Friday night. He even called to keep me posted on the investigation."

"He called you?" Reece stiffened. "The case isn't even in his jurisdiction."

"Oh." She licked her lips. "Well, I guess he was just being nice."

He knew exactly why Rowan had stayed in touch with Jessica: to piss Reece off. Oh, yeah, and he was good at his job. But his call had been about needling more than anything else. Reece would lay money on it.

"He's also very handsome," she said, looking at her own hands.

He heard a note of mischief in her voice. She was trying to make him jealous. *Progress.*

"Remind me to kill my brother."

A giggle slipped out from between those pink lips. His tension eased. He let the dark memories fade away as he focused on sitting in the sunshine with this woman who utterly fascinated him.

She crossed her long legs, her skirt rising above her knee. Reece let himself look for a moment, and then turned his attention back to the reaming out she was giving him.

"So, are you finished?"

"Finished what?"

"Prying into my history."

She gasped in indignation. "I did no such thing. You're the one who kept talking."

Yes. How strange. "Well, are you at least finished calling me a creeper like Sid?"

Her shudder preceded her words. "Creepy Sid."

Glass in her hair, on her skin, tearing her dress.

God, how Reece would like to get his hands around the man's throat.

"But you're not a creeper."

"So what was that character assassination all about?"

"That wasn't character assassination," she said, her voice softer than it had been. "I was just laying out the reasons I might find you untrustworthy."

She fell silent, as if wondering if she'd gone too far. Considering Reece felt like utter shit, he probably should tell her she hadn't. After all, she'd said nothing but the truth.

"I really would have deleted the footage. But you're right."

Her brow shot up.

"I should have stopped as soon as I remembered the security camera. It *was* pretty fucking creepy."

If he'd been thinking more about her feelings, and less about his hunger for her, he never would have continued. He would always regret it.

"I apologize, Jessica. You are right about everything. I was completely out of line, and I'm truly sorry," he said. He fell silent. What more was there to say?

She looked directly at him. Reece didn't offer justifications or try to couch his apology with self-righteousness, or do a politician's cop-out: *I'm sorry if you were offended*. She had called him on his bullshit. He'd deserved it. He regretted it. He just hoped she saw it that way, too, and was willing to move past the bad beginning he'd inflicted on them both.

Finally, after she'd studied his face for so long he wondered if she was a mind reader, she nodded. "Apology accepted."

A beat. A moment of acceptance. The faintest realization that they were starting over.

His heart pumped hard, his blood surging. This was his second chance to really get to know her, with no preconceived ideas or plans. They were on even footing now. He was going to have to give up control over where and when they saw each other and see what happened, not an easy thing for him.

Everything he'd thought he knew about her before faded as he came to recognize something else about her. Not many people in this town were as forgiving, as open, including him. She'd just revealed a kindness, a generosity of spirit she usually hid beneath her sassy mouth and ridiculously sexy curves.

The woman was likable. Not only to-die-for fuckable, but *nice*.

She offered him a tentative smile, her wide mouth tugging up at one side. A dimple appeared in her cheek, one he'd never seen before. It went straight to his heart.

Reece had to smile back, broadly, completely charmed and knowing they'd turned a corner. Seeing his reaction, she gasped. Her cheeks heated up, and he had to wonder why she seemed more affected by a simple smile than she had by a sincere apology.

He didn't understand her, not yet. But he was going to. He would just do it up front, out in the open from here on out.

Her face flushed, she got back to business. "So, I'm your intern. What does that mean?"

"It means you're at my beck and call."

"During work hours," she pointed out.

He didn't try to soften the truth. "Sure. Plus after hours. Late nights. Weekends. It all depends on how busy I am. And believe me, I'm always busy."

"Oh," she whispered.

"As you probably noticed, the office is small, mostly for administrative functions. I travel a lot and am usually on set at one of the studios I'm working with or renting. Or I'm filming out of town. I have to go to Colorado next month to check out some locations my scout is recommending. You'll come with me."

A suspicious furrow appeared between her brows.

"It's part of the job, Jessica. Don't go doubting me now. You can call my last intern, Walter, if you want a reference—he'll tell you I'm an asshole and a perfectionist. He'll also tell you he worked sixty hours a week, traveled everywhere, and had no personal life." He smiled. "And that he landed a job with Miramax right after graduation."

Her relieved smile said she found the thought of being worked to death comforting. "We will have separate rooms during all these trips?"

"Of course." At least unless she decided she didn't want to.

"With all these hours and the travel, I guess it's just as well I lost my other job."

Reece frowned. He suspected he knew why—the publicity might have been good for business, but it was probably also a distraction. He had to be honest, at least with himself, and admit he wasn't unhappy she wouldn't be working there anymore. He hated that men might sometimes put their hands on *buns* other than those on their plates. But he also hated that her association with him had cost her something more than a dress and her peace of mind.

"I'm sorry."

She shrugged, reaching for her purse. "You're paying me more."

Then she couldn't have been making much. He wondered how she supported herself and went to school in Southern California on a waitress's salary. That had to require some serious dedication and work ethic. "It's not enough. I'm giving you a raise."

She rolled her eyes. "You can't."

"Actually, I'm the owner, and I can."

"Absolutely not. I'm not going to start out here as the teacher's pet, or be thought of as the bimbo who got her job because the boss wants to jump her bones."

She was right. He didn't want her viewed that way by any of his staff. Even though he did, very much, want to jump her bones. "All right. We'll start you where we start all interns, and reevaluate in a month, based on performance. Fair?"

"Fair. So, boss"—she dug in her purse until she found a pad of paper and a pen—"reminding you to kill your brother is the first thing on my to-do list. Anything else?"

Damn, she was sharp. He'd never had a smart-ass for an assistant, and he suspected he was going to like it.

Most employees—as well as rising actors and Hollywood wannabes—treated him with head-down respect. This gorgeous, red-haired, aspiring screenwriter would give as good as she got. He could hardly wait to get started.

"Thanks for the reminder. Your second task will be to write a speech for me for a dinner being held one week from tonight. I'll also need you to attend with me as my date." Seeing her mouth drop open on the word *date*, he explained. "It's part of the job."

"Did Walter go last year?" she asked, sounding suspicious.

"He would have, if I'd attended. Besides, we *should* appear in public. I have to introduce you as my new intern. It will help with the rumors."

"Yeah, right."

"I know this town. It will dampen the whispers about why we were alone in the gallery." He couldn't lie to her, adding, "That doesn't mean all the talk will stop, but it could help."

"Do you always show up at big events with your intern?"

"Call Walter and ask him."

"You expect me to believe he was your arm candy last year?"

"I guess you didn't see the tabloid articles," he said with a sigh.

"Oh, I saw them," she admitted. "But nobody in the world could convince me you were gay. And that was *before* you got me naked on the table."

Jessica. Naked on the table. Christ.

He had to shift in his seat to relieve the sudden

tightness in his pants. How was he going to keep this professional, at least long enough for her to trust him again? The only way he'd have another chance with her was to wait until she decided she wanted to give him a second shot. He'd consigned himself to a special kind of hell and a devilish torment.

"Are you going to tell me what this speech of yours is for?"

He wasn't comfortable talking about his philanthropic work. "I'll have my administrative assistant, Abigail, email you the details as soon as we're finished."

"Thanks."

"It's a formal event."

Nibbling her lip, she nodded slowly. "Got it."

He thought about her blue dress, torn by glass and stained with flecks of blood. Hers *and* his. Did she have anything else to wear? Well, he'd make sure she did. He didn't say anything, not wanting to argue about it, and knowing she would.

"Anything else?"

"When can you start?"

"My last final is tomorrow morning."

"Perfect. You're mine full-time after that."

She considered his remark. "As long as we both remember it's just for work."

"Oh, of course." At least until she dropped the pretense that she didn't want him as much as he wanted her. He rose from his chair. "Now, if you're finished telling me off, and I've groveled sufficiently..."

"You didn't grovel," she pointed out, rising as well. "You simply apologized."

"I'm not good at groveling."

"Color me shocked."

The woman was hard on the ego. "Come on, let me show you the building and introduce you around so you can hit the ground running."

She followed quickly, as if pleased at the prospect. Jessica had already met his administrative assistant, and they seemed to like each other. They talked for a few more minutes, the older woman advising her to bring a sweater since the building could get cold.

They hit the break room for fresh-brewed coffee, and then he showed her where she'd be working—in a small cubicle appropriate for an intern. Afterward, he walked her around the technical spaces. The building contained a green room where he sometimes did touch-up shots, and a small cutting room, which he seldom used in favor of a larger one they rented from time to time. There was also a soundproofed studio where he held readings, plus a storage room filled with original prints of past projects.

She asked pertinent questions, showing she knew her stuff. And she was friendly and professional with his other staff members: two people in HR, one in accounting, four in media, and one in legal. If any of them had seen the news reports and wondered why he'd hired her, they were professional and loyal enough not to show it. He knew she'd had the same worry, but he could feel Jessica relaxing with every introduction.

"Do you have any questions?" he asked when they'd finished the tour.

"No, I think I've got it, and I'm raring to go."

He nodded, agreeing with her. She had already shown him she had energy, ideas, and talent. If he had never laid eyes on her before today, he would still have been impressed as hell.

Knowing himself, he also suspected he'd have been asking himself if it would be totally out of line to kiss her. Kind of like he'd been doing all afternoon.

If he didn't, he might just lose his mind.

Yes, he was putting the decision into her hands, and he wasn't going to push her. That didn't mean the smallest nudge would be totally wrong, did it?

They were in the building's lobby. Because the entrance was key coded, with an intercom outside, they didn't use security. The entire first level housed the technical and storage rooms, no offices. That meant it was completely empty. They were alone.

"So, after today, you will officially be my intern," he said, looking down at her. Her brown eyes sparkled with excitement.

"Yes, and I can't wait to start."

"Meaning today, you're not working for me."

She tilted her head in confusion. "I guess so."

"Good."

He didn't say anything else, merely sinking his hands into her hair, wrapping the one loose strand around his fingers, and pulling down all the rest from its bun. He leaned toward her, waiting for her to realize his intent and pull back if she wanted to.

She didn't pull back.

Those luscious lips parted for him, her tongue welcoming his as the kiss became hotter, wetter. Carnal.

She wrapped her arms around his neck, and he tilted her head so he could explore her deeper. With her soft body pressed against his, he couldn't help remembering how it had felt to watch that dress fall to the floor Friday night. The images had haunted him every night since. He'd gone to sleep thinking about her long legs, curvy hips, slim waist, and full breasts...even if they had been covered with tape.

They weren't now. He felt the erect points pressing against her blouse. God, how he wanted to unbutton it and touch her, skin to skin. He wanted to stroke her nipples, draw them into his mouth and suck them while she tangled her fingers in his hair and pulled him even closer.

He dropped one hand to her hip, and then cupped her perfect ass. She groaned, arching into him. His rock-hard cock nestled into the warmth at the top of her thighs, and he couldn't stop himself from thrusting. His heart thudded when she shifted her legs apart to let him.

A car honked from outside. She stiffened, snapping out of the spell that had enveloped them both. With one last hungry exploration of her mouth, he ended the kiss and stepped away.

Jessica's heavy breaths matched his, and he suspected her heart was pounding, too. Her cheeks were flushed, her lips red and swollen.

Her eyes, of course, held fire.

"What was that, Mr. Winchester?"

"A kiss, Miss Jensen. Just a kiss."

"Bosses aren't supposed to kiss their employees."

"Which means that starting tomorrow it can't happen again. I respect you and want others to as well."

She pushed her loose hair back and tucked it behind her ears. He'd made a mess of it but couldn't say he was sorry. "So that was a goodbye kiss?"

"If you want to call it that. Personally, I'd call it 'See you later.'"

"You really are a cocky bastard."

He laughed out loud, liking that someone finally had the nerve to tell him what they thought of him, especially here, in the building he owned. "Yes, I am a cocky bastard. Admit it, though. You like that about me."

"Keep telling yourself that."

"All joking aside, Jessica, whatever happened Friday night, whatever mistakes I've made since the day I first saw you . . . " He leaned close enough to brush his cheek against her hair, inhaling to capture the tropical scent. "You want me just as much as I want you."

* * *

Jessica arrived at work even earlier than she'd promised. Knowing she had kicked ass on her last exam that morning, she couldn't stop smiling. Now she got to start her new job, really becoming a part of the industry she'd been so passionate about for years.

The thought of working side by side with Reece Winchester didn't hurt her mood any, either. Even if she hadn't entirely forgiven him for that hot kiss he'd laid on her yesterday, which had left her confused, achy, and horny as hell.

Nope, nope, nope, she reminded herself.

Bopping her head to some cheerful music playing on the radio, she pulled her dilapidated PT Cruiser into the parking lot, seeing Reece sitting in the driver's seat of a nearby sedan. Its engine was running, and Reece was drumming his fingers on the steering wheel, watching her closely as he talked into his phone. His frown said his mood wasn't quite as upbeat as hers.

He lowered his phone. "Come on, we have to go over to Sunset Bronson," he called.

She took his command in stride, actually pleased he was all business right from the first minute. That kiss yesterday had been amazing—mind-altering—however, it had also worried her. Yes, he'd promised to step back to within appropriate boundaries, but she hadn't been entirely sure that he would do it.

She grabbed her laptop bag, hurried as quickly as was possible in heels to the other side of his car, and slid into the passenger seat. "Good morning."

"I've been waiting."

She pointed toward his dashboard clock. "It's seven minutes before eleven."

"I didn't say you were late," he said, his mind obviously elsewhere. Gesturing toward two foam cups in the center console, he added, "The one in back is yours."

"Oh, thanks. The coffee on campus is horrible." She took a sip and sighed. "How'd you know how I take it?"

"I made you some in the break room yesterday."

"I'm surprised you noticed. Or remembered."

"I have a pretty good memory."

"So what's up? Why are we going to the studio?"

"I hire space there. My editing team discovered a problem with something we filmed in New Mexico a couple of months ago."

"The new Reynolds film?"

"Yes. I really don't want to call the cast and crew back there to reshoot, so I'm going to see if we can do some creative cutting or rewriting and salvage what we've got."

"Sounds great," she said, enthused at the prospect.

"That's not how I'd describe it."

"Sorry, I didn't mean it's great that you have to fix a problem like that." What a way to start her job—being happy about her boss having difficulties with his work.

"Forget it, I understand. Is this your first time in a big studio?"

"I went on some backstage visits for school, and obviously there's a nice setup on campus. But almost all of my experience has been on student films. I've never been involved with detailed editing of a major motion picture."

"Well, welcome to your crash course."

"I can't wait. Did you just direct or did you write the screenplay?"

"Both."

"What's it about?"

He gave her a quick synopsis of the film, a sexy thriller with a romantic triangle and lots of twists. It was the kind of movie he was perfect in, and she wished he were starring in it, too. But she had the feeling his acting days were over.

"Sounds awesome. I can't wait to see it. What happened that you have to fix?"

Shaking his head ruefully, he replied, "Same old story—some local screwed up the shot. The crew didn't even notice him hamming it up on the roof of the building next door."

These days, everyone tried to be famous by mugging for the camera whenever one was around. "Oh dear. I guess that's the danger of filming outside the studio."

"Definitely. Anywhere that's harder to control increases the chances for a screw-up. There are some infamous ones that slipped through editing and made it on screen. They're almost legends now."

"I remember the modern truck driving by in the background of a John Wayne Western."

"Not to mention the magical moving duffel bag in *Stripes*."

"The white van in the battle scene of *Braveheart*. The kid covering his ears in *North by Northwest*."

He looked impressed. "You do know your movie trivia."

"I could play this game all day. I told you, movies were my escape as a kid. I was an addict even before my mother died. When she was in hospice, I'd curl up with her on her bed and we'd watch old classics on TCM."

Seeing the way he looked at her, with warmth and sympathy, she wished she hadn't said anything. To prevent him from trying to come up with a suitable reply, she quickly asked, "Has anything like that ever happened with one of your other movies?"

"Twice," he said, following her lead. "Neither error

made it all the way through the editing process into the final product."

"Are you certain?"

"With today's critics and audiences? If there's a mistake, you can guaran-damn-tee it'll be pointed out on Rotten Tomatoes before it even goes wide."

She had to nod, conceding the point. The consumer had gained a lot of power in this business, which, as a movie lover, she considered a positive change. But it did seem a shame that some films got shoved into streaming services or secondary channels because early word of mouth was negative. Not any of Reece's, certainly, but it happened to others.

"I'm sure you'll figure out a way to fix it."

"I hope so," he said, his jaw tight. "Because the film certainly won't make much sense without the main murder."

"That is a problem in a mystery."

"The editor has tried everything from tightening to overlaying, but there's a key close-up where the guy looks like he's coming right out of the killer's ear."

"From every camera angle?"

"Sounds like."

"Bad luck. If you can't find a workaround, will you have to go back on location?"

"Possibly. Unfortunately, three of the leads were in the scene. I know from experience that none of them are fond of reshoots, and I think Reynolds is actually out of the country."

He shook his head slowly, probably thinking of the cost and scheduling nightmare of trying to grab three major stars, who'd most likely moved on to other projects. While she was thinking that, as the newbie, the whole mess might be left in her lap to work out.

She could hardly wait to get started.

"So, if you have to go back to New Mexico, I assume I'll be going with you."

"Yes. Like I told you yesterday, this job does include travel."

"I don't imagine there are any location scouting trips to Paris on the schedule, huh?"

"I'm afraid not."

"Bummer. It's number one on mine and Liza's bucket lists. She wants to go for the art. I want to go for the macarons, éclairs, bread, chocolate, and champagne."

He barked a laugh.

"You think I'm kidding? I'm a total foodie. That's why I need to hit the StairMaster. It's also why I was out jogging the first time you saw me."

"In spandex with that high, bouncy ponytail," he said, sounding like he was enjoying a particularly good memory. "That was a very bad day for me. You were like a beam of light."

She thought back, wondering about the timing. She knew roughly when she had gone into the gallery—it had been about eight weeks before Liza's showing.

Now she remembered something else that happened about eight weeks before the showing. "Oh, my God, the fire."

He hesitated, then admitted, "Yes. Believe it or not, me having to come back to deal with the fire was why the problem happened on the set."

Double bad luck. He must have been walking under a little black cloud in April. She wondered what to say, but not for long. Reece was generally reluctant to talk about the past. He focused on the here and now, and on the future. *Such a planner.* So she said, "Anyway, about my thighs..." She quickly snapped her mouth closed, realizing how that sounded. Seeing his half grin, she knew he'd finished the sentence in his head. Probably with something like: *About my thighs wrapped around your hips? About my thighs opening in welcome?*

"I meant, um, about the sculpture, and my food issues. Liza not only disguised my chin, I think she thinned out my thighs, too."

His glance at her legs wasn't exactly surreptitious. She was wearing a pretty suit, a light blue one. The skirt length was modern yet still professional. Which meant a few inches of thigh were revealed when she was sitting.

"She didn't change a damn thing," he said, putting his eyes back on the road. "Nor did she need to."

Jess closed her eyes at the audible appreciation; he'd practically growled his words. The car suddenly felt very hot, despite the air-conditioning blowing toward her face. Lord, how was she supposed to maintain the distance she'd demanded, both before and after that crazy kiss yesterday, when he made his attraction to her so obvious?

Reece had said he wouldn't make a move on her again until she made it clear she wanted him to. As much as she'd told herself that day wasn't going to come until Satan's palace was buried in snow, she'd already started thinking maybe she'd be ready at the end of the summer, when her internship was over.

Who the hell are you kidding? You'll be ready by the time the day is over.

She was doomed. So totally doomed.

"You know, we shoot a lot in Canada," he said.

The comment yanked her out of mental lust land, and she replied, with such eloquence. "Huh?"

"We've shot in Montreal before. They speak French there, too, though I don't know if the food is as good."

Her brain finally caught up. "I guess it'll have to do." To her embarrassment, her stomach grumbled audibly. "Darn, now I made myself hungry. I stayed up so late studying last night I overslept and didn't eat breakfast."

"Don't worry about it. You will soon be introduced to the joys of studio food. Not to mention the insane, fast-paced studio life."

She settled deeper into her seat, able to shove all other worries out of her mind. This was the first day of her new life. She'd worked long and hard for this opportunity, and she wasn't about to let her attraction to her new boss screw it up. He had done the right thing, backing off and putting everything in her hands, and she would be able to stay strong and resist him.

But as she cast a quick, surreptitious glance at him, at the strong hands gripping the wheel, the thick arms, the broad shoulders, and oh, all the rest of him, she had to concede one thing.

Maybe she wasn't as strong as she thought she was.

CHAPTER 7

They thought he'd tried to kill Reece Winchester.

Sid might not care if the prick dropped dead, but he *hadn't* been the one who shot at the famous director. True, he had a gun and usually carried it. But he'd left it at home the night of the gallery showing. He was an innocent man.

"Jesus, you really blew it," he muttered, rubbing one hand over his bleary eyes and lifting a bottle to his mouth with the other. He'd been drunk for several days, while he tried to figure out how to get himself out of this mess. "You shoulda gone to the police right away, dummy."

Nobody answered. He was alone in a dirty, stained-sheet hotel room, where he'd been holed up since last Friday. The place catered to poor surfers who stayed four to a room, but it was all he could afford, and the rent was still enough to suck him almost completely dry of cash.

"Shoulda told 'em," he groaned, queasiness warring with fear in his gut.

Friday night, when the shot rang out, he'd been stomping up the beach, fuming and wondering how to get Sharon alone to tell his side before she got it from her nephew. Maybe somebody saw him there and could give him an alibi. Maybe a security camera picked him up. Maybe they'd believe him when he swore he'd seen somebody else—a figure all in black and wrapped in night—shooting from the edge of the shoreline.

Sid had stood frozen with shock for a solid ten seconds after the crack of gunfire. He hadn't thought about his own safety at first, and might even have been visible to the shooter.

The realization had finally put some haul into his ass. He'd run toward the street, frantic to get far away from a crazy person with a gun.

Good thing he'd followed his instincts. Because it hadn't taken long to figure out who the real target was: *him*.

"Why didn't you stick around and tell 'em who was being shot at?" he said, hearing his own self-pity but knowing it was justified. "The cops woulda believed you."

Sure they would have. He was a fuckin' art dealer, well known and respected.

Mostly. Yeah, he was an art dealer, but art wasn't all he dealt. Heroin had a better markup, and more people could afford it.

It all came down to money. Sid's gambling addiction was a ravenous monster. He had to feed it, which meant dealing drugs, as well as skimming off the top at his legit jobs.

If he went to the police, they'd dig and probe, wanting to know why he thought he was the target. Sid couldn't tell them. If he revealed his theory of why the shooting had happened, he'd get himself deeper into trouble with people a lot more dangerous than the LAPD.

"Fuckin' horses," he muttered. "Fuckin' craps. Fuckin' Vegas."

He owed more than fifteen grand to one of the toughest private bookrunners in Sin City. Little Joey was not one to forget a debt. So there were fifteen thousand reasons why that bullet had been monogrammed with Sid's name, not Winchester's.

It hadn't been hard to figure out, given the warnings. They'd started with phone calls from guys with deep voices, and then his tires were slashed. A jackboot-wearing thug had come into the gallery last week, threatening to torch the place if Sid didn't come up with what he owed.

Message received. The bookie didn't want him dead, just terrified. It had been a warning shot. He'd been seen walking in front of the window that night, and somebody shot it out. So he'd been reminded of the stakes of this game: Fifteen grand or his life. He thanked his lucky stars the shooter sent by Little Joe hadn't seen him on the beach before he'd run away. At least, he didn't *think* he'd been spotted. That he wasn't wearing casts on every limb said he probably wasn't.

The very possibility, though, had made him bolt like an animal rather than thinking things through. He'd literally run in terror, fleeing through town, until his heart felt like it was gonna blow a valve. People out partying got out of his way, staring after him like he was a crazy man, and he was pretty sure he'd knocked one rich bitch right outta her Donatella Versace platform shoes.

A few minutes later, his brain had kicked back on and he called himself an idiot. He'd stopped, gasped for breath, and realized he was running when he should be making *tire* tracks. He'd returned for his car, hoping he hadn't lost his chance to drive away. Unfortunately, he was too late. Cops were swarming. One bullet fired at a former movie star and all of Southern California showed up.

Watching from up the block, he'd lurked in the shadows. His tension grew, nerves straining, until he'd finally left. He had no friends to call, no car to drive away in, and no courage to steal one. *Hide!* It was all he could do, knowing he couldn't go home with thugs looking for him.

The longer he stayed at this hotel—almost a week now—the more terrified he became. The shooter had probably already figured out Sid was lying low somewhere not too far from the gallery. He rarely slept, fearing he would awaken to the sound of his own arms being broken.

"Coulda taken a cab. Gone to the airport. The bus station." He swigged some more bourbon, tipping the bottle back, draining the last few gulps. "Too late now. No money to get there. No cash to pay for a ticket." He had a stack of twenties in his safe at home; in his line of work, banks were a no-go. But he couldn't *get* home, even if he weren't scared to death to try because it was surely being staked out.

He'd thought about making a try for his car again, but hadn't seriously considered it. Joey's goons, or the cops, would have his leased Mercedes guarded. He had no wheels, was down to his last twenty bucks, and was scared to risk even poking his head out of the crappy hotel room.

"How the fuck am I supposed to pay them back without my job?" he muttered, hating Reece Winchester even more.

All his problems would have been solved with one clear digital image. If only the rich bastard hadn't been able to convince the paparazzi dude to give up his camera. Full-color pictures of the reclusive director and the bombshell in blue would have brought in a *lot* of money from the tabloids. Sid, having provided access to the photographer, could have claimed half of it. He'd tried demanding half of the thirty thousand Reece was "paying" for the camera. That would have cleared up his entire debt. But the photographer was a dick and wouldn't play ball. Now, Sid had not only lost out on a windfall; he didn't even have a job.

"Thanks to that son of a bitch."

He wanted to get even with the stuck-up director almost as much as he wanted to get out of this mess alive. *Not to mention outta this room.* He was cracking up. He'd eaten only junk from the dusty vending machine in the lobby for the last six days. He wanted food—real food. Right now, a rare steak and a baked potato dripping with sour cream sounded like the closest to heaven he'd ever get. Glancing at his empty bottle, he realized he needed something else, too.

Over the next hours, as the blissful bourbon high began to wear off, visions of a tasty meal loomed larger in his mind. Joey, meanwhile, shrunk. He'd hidden for a long time; nobody could know for sure that Sid was still in the area. Even if they suspected it, what were the chances he'd be spotted?

"Nil," he mumbled, trying to convince himself. "It's a sure bet."

Besides, starving to death sounded worse than getting beaten up. A man had to eat.

He caught a glimpse of himself in the mirror. *Can't go out looking like this.*

He dampened his hair, ran his fingers through it, then shook out his shirt and pants. He'd had nothing else to put on for days, and had been rinsing stuff in the tub. Another glance at his reflection said he wasn't exactly respectable, but not *too* bad. Besides, the scruffier he looked, the less likely he was to be recognized—or identified by a waitress after he dined and dashed on a pricey meal.

Finally, he made his move. Opening the door slowly, he stuck his head out and sniffed the California night, surprised at how quiet it was. The world had seemed much louder from inside the shithole where he'd been hiding. Now, though, there were no voices, no car horns, nothing. It was eleven p.m. on a weeknight, and the neighborhood had settled down.

Knowing there were late-hour restaurants and bars down on Speedway, he crept out of his hole. He stayed behind cars as he walked across the gravel parking lot, his confidence growing with every step he took. Sure, somebody mighta watched the neighborhood for a day. Even two. But more than that? No way. He'd been totally paranoid.

Being out in the world, his rational self was coming

back. There was a way out of this, sure there was. Reaching the sidewalk, he even started to picture it. He knew things about the artwork in the gallery where he'd worked until last week. There were pieces upstairs worth far more than he owed Little Joe. Sid had been there throughout the construction of the place, including the security system. He knew the position of every camera. He could figure out a way to get inside without getting caught. He *had* to.

With a plan developing, he began to smile. His steps grew more sure and steady. His car was probably still in the parking lot. He could get in it, go home, and get word to Joey about his solution to their little problem. No sweat. Everything was gonna be A-okay.

He was whistling, knowing the grumble in his stomach was about to be answered by a massive meal, when he heard a sound. A soft click. It came from behind him.

Panic returning like a gunshot to his gut, he swung around. There was nothing.

"You're losing it."

His brain tried to calm his body, but his heart had started thudding and his skin felt limp on his bones. Taking deep breaths, he cursed his imagination. He was jumping at the slightest noise, at the touch of a cat's foot on a porch, or a lock being flipped on a front door nearby.

Nobody was looking for him.

Besides, if the worst really did happen, if somebody really did find him, all he had to do was tell them he had a great idea and ask to get on the phone with Joey.

The bookie was a businessman. When he found out he could get a shitload more than fifteen grand by lifting a few paintings from a rich Hollywood bastard, he'd probably thank him.

Turning around again to keep walking, he immediately let out a tiny squeal when he saw someone standing right in front of him. Someone dressed all in black, their face concealed by a hood, and by the mimosa tree overhead that blocked the streetlight. If danger were a physical thing, he'd have been knocked over. It wafted off this person who'd crept up on him so easily and eerily.

All thoughts of negotiating fled his mind. He couldn't talk his way out of this one.

Turn. Run!

Before he could move, he saw the hand rise. It held something. "No, don't, I can—"

Electric shock hit Sid in the chest. Running was no longer an option, because every one of his muscles exploded with pain.

He collapsed backward, hitting the sidewalk with such force he felt his head split open. His mouth slammed shut, his teeth plunging into his own tongue. Blood gushed from lips that wanted to form cries of agony but could find no air with which to do it.

Sid twisted, thrust, and arched, not in control over a single movement. *Pain.* It was like nothing he'd ever felt. His body was completely beyond his control and he jerked and writhed, his muscles quivering, contracting, and spasming. Agony saturated each of his nerve endings.

The enforcer who'd come to collect on his debt

moved above him. Tall and concealed in shadow, hard to see through Sid's teary eyes, the person clicked a button, and the electricity ceased. There was no relief, though. Sid still twitched on the ground, his pants wet with his own piss, his body not obeying any of his brain's comments.

"I've been waiting for you. Thank you for finally coming out." The voice was soft, floating down to his ears on the evening air, barely audible. "You've made this a lot easier."

"Ahh..." Trying to talk. Trying to think. Unable to do either.

Sid blinked, making out the dark figure through his twitching eyes. His attacker reached into a pocket. Pulled out a... "N-n-noo. Puh-please."

The weapon rose, the muzzle pointing down. Toward his head.

"I'll p-pay."

"Yes, you will."

"Money...can get..."

"Who cares about your money?"

What the hell? No money? No self-respecting bookie would say such a thing. "Not...from Joey?"

The head tilted, a glimmer of light shining on a pale chin. "Who's Joey?"

If every inch of him weren't hurting, Sid might be able to figure this out. Right now, only one thing sank in. This was not hired muscle here to collect on his debt. "Who...are..."

"I saw you last Friday night on the beach. I assume you saw me, too."

"Didn't see...swear."

"I'm sorry, I can't take that chance."

A pop. A quiet puff from the silenced weapon. Sid heard it but didn't feel anything.

Sid Loman was never going to feel anything again.

* * *

Although he'd warned her that the hours would be long, Reece had watched for any sign that Jessica was getting tired of working her ass off. They had both been in the office more than out of it since Wednesday, and so far, not one complaint had come out of her mouth. She'd just put in a full thirteen hours, on a Saturday no less, and insisted she was fine to come in early the next morning.

It seemed the more he piled on her, treating her exactly as he would any intern, the more she thrived. She'd sucked up everything she could learn, starting with sitting in the cutting room with him on her first day, listening to him curse, and offering suggestions that, while not workable, were worth considering. And when he'd realized there really was no help for it but to redo the screwed-up scene, she'd taken on the task of pulling the reshoot together like a pro.

He knew she was looking forward to her first location shoot in New Mexico, scheduled for three weeks from now. He only wondered if, by that point, she would still be pretending she didn't want a personal relationship with him. No matter what, they would have separate rooms—he didn't want her treated with disrespect.

That didn't mean, however, that the rooms couldn't adjoin.

So far, she was being amazingly resistant, even though he caught her watching him closely when she thought he wouldn't notice. Once, after he'd whipped off his jacket and rolled up his sleeves, he caught her staring at his hands, and had to repeat a question three times just to get her attention.

She wanted him. But her stubbornness was keeping her from doing anything about it.

"Are you sure you're okay to drive home?" he asked as they walked out of the building a little after ten p.m. Saturday night.

"Why wouldn't I be?"

"We've been working a lot of hours."

"I'm fine. As long as the duct tape holding my car together holds up, I can come in as much as you need me to."

He eyed her tired gray PT Cruiser convertible, the only other vehicle parked in the lot, aside from his. He always heard the thing from his office when she arrived. It rattled. It squealed. It groaned. With its rust spots and faded top, he pegged the car as more than a decade old. "You're putting a lot of wear and tear on that car. Maybe you should use..."

"Forget it, I'm not using a company car," she said, throwing a hand up to silence him.

"How do you know I wasn't going to say city bus?"

Gasping, she drew that hand to her chest. "Was that a joke, Mr. Winchester?"

His own lips quirked. "Maybe."

*Tsk*ing and shaking her head, she replied, "I must be a bad influence on you."

She could be. Or maybe she could be a good one.

Working with her so closely over the past four days, he'd realized Jessica brought out something youthful and fresh from inside him. Those were things he barely remembered being. It caught him by surprise. He hadn't needed anyone except his family since he was a kid. But he had found he needed her around, if only to bring a smile out of him every once in a while.

"You really don't have to walk me to my car," she said.

"It's late," he said, noticing the streetlights weren't bright enough to banish all the shadows.

When they reached her convertible, he waited for her to unlock the door, then opened it for her. Before she got in, he caught the faintest whiff of smoke. Reece reacted to the scent reflexively, his muscles tensing. He'd been that way since the day he'd come home to find his house in ashes.

"What happened?"

"What do you mean?"

Crouching down to look inside, he saw a black spot on the passenger-side carpet. He gestured toward it. "Did you have an electrical fire?"

"Not exactly," she replied before catching her bottom lip between her teeth.

He knew the gesture, having seen it a few times before. She was uncomfortable, or she was hiding something. While he'd been ready to say goodbye, he couldn't until he found out the rest of the story about the smoky smell. So he slammed the door shut.

"What are you doing?"

"Let's go to the diner across the street and have coffee."

"It's ten o'clock at night."

"They have decaf."

"Does any self-respecting person in Hollywood really drink decaf?"

Ahh, she was catching on. "Come on, you need to build up your tolerance anyway."

"But I thought we were finished for the day," she said, looking puzzled.

"We've been working so hard, I don't think you've even had a chance to go out for lunch this week. I need to introduce you to the local cuisine."

"I brown-bag it," she said. Her chin was up, and she sounded proud of herself. He only wondered when she'd had time to eat anything from that brown bag, considering he'd kept her on the run every day since she'd started.

"One day you might forget. You'll need to know where to grab a sandwich to bring back to the office. I'm such a workaholic, you'll rarely get to take a full lunch break."

"Did Walter?"

"Never."

"Okay. I only hope they make their tuna salad with mustard."

Grimacing, he could only shake his head. "Disgusting."

Entering the empty shop, he greeted the owner, Charlie, with a nod. "We're just going to have coffee. We don't intend to keep you late."

"Ha, keep me as late as you want. It's better than going home to snotty teenagers and a perpetually pissed-off wife."

Jessica's brow went up as they walked to an empty table in the back. "So are his kids really snotty?" she asked, taking a seat across the booth from him.

"Yes. I think that's why his wife is perpetually pissed off."

"Or it could be because her husband spends all his time here and isn't home to help with them."

"Good point."

After they ordered their coffee—fully leaded for both of them—he got around to the reason he'd brought her here. He couldn't stop thinking about the burned interior of her car. Arson was his trigger lately, and he wanted to know what had really happened.

"Now, tell me about the fire."

She tilted her head in confusion.

"In your car."

Charlie, working alone tonight, set down cups of coffee in front of each of them. Jessica smiled her thanks, and then took time to add cream and sugar to hers. She stirred, blew on the surface, and then sipped. "Mm. Great coffee."

"The coffee sucks. Now quit stalling."

He saw her brain working to figure out what to say, and finally she answered in her typical blunt manner. "You're not the only one who's had to deal with a stalker."

Reece stiffened. "Oh?"

With a humorless laugh, she said, "We ought to

form a club. Stalkers 'R' Us. We could show up at our meetings in wigs and trench coats, waving our matching restraining orders."

"Not funny, Jessica," he said, fearing the worst. If she'd been so reluctant to talk about this, especially after what happened last weekend, it must have been pretty bad. "Tell me."

Her explanation came grudgingly. "I was dating a guy. His name was Johnny."

He blew out a breath. "That's a child's name."

"He has a child's maturity level. Anyway, I ended it a year ago. He, uh, didn't take it well."

His hands clenched together in one large fist under the table. "How badly did he take it?"

"He became angry. Violently so." She gazed out the window, her expression pained. "To be honest, he put me through hell."

Funny how the air in a room could turn red. At least, that's what color it appeared to be through his furious eyes. "Did he hurt you?"

"No. Not really."

She swallowed, which told him she might not have been entirely forthcoming. Reece used all of his acting ability to not let her see his desire to throw furniture, punch walls, and find the miserable coward who'd dared to lay a hand on her. Which he knew that piece of shit had done.

"He took away my sense of security. I never knew if he was watching, if he would call, or show up at work." She sighed. "Or break into my car and burn all my stuff."

There it was. The answer to his question. Judging by

the smell still lingering inside the convertible, the crime couldn't have taken place very long ago. Considering the breakup had been last year, the ex was not getting better with time.

"That spineless bastard," he snapped, bending forward over the table.

Ignoring their boss/intern boundaries, he reached for her hand. Their fingers entwined, and he squeezed, offering support and commiseration. Reece understood the destruction of fire, and how it felt to know your possessions had been sent up in smoke. He'd been relieved no one had been hurt in the flames at his house, but that didn't mean he hadn't regretted the loss of some irreplaceable things. He hadn't cared about the financial cost of anything he'd lost. The emotional one, however, had been painful.

Fire wasn't just dangerous physically. It destroyed memory.

"I guess if anyone understands, it's you. I lost some books; you lost your entire house."

"It was just a house," he mumbled. "I had insurance. My dog was okay, and nobody was hurt. That was all that really mattered."

"But what about the things in it?" Her eyes widened. "Oh, my God, your Oscars!"

"The statue's not as important as the credit on a résumé. Not a big deal. Other things were a lot more important."

"Such as?"

He had brought her here to talk about her problem, not his. But he admitted, "Some personal stuff that was hard to lose. My sister and I did one movie to-gether..."

"*Together at Last!*"

Not surprised she knew, he smiled faintly. "After filming ended, she asked me to sign her script. Then she signed it, too, and wrote something about the wonder-ful Winchester stars." He shrugged. "Silly, just a pile of bound papers with some signatures."

"That must have broken your heart." It was her turn to squeeze his hands, offering kindness and understand-ing. She had grasped right away why he'd been more upset about a memoir of a special time he'd shared with his lost sister than a gold statue. Not a lot of people would...but she had.

Charlie came back to refill their coffee, and Jessica slid her hands from his, curling them around her cup as she declined a top off.

Reece had gone back to sad-memory land quite enough for one night. He'd been distracted from the real issue, but he wasn't anymore. "So, this Johnny pile of shit. Did you get a restraining order?"

She shook her head, suddenly looking embarrassed. "I was afraid it would escalate things and set him off even more."

Which this Johnny had probably counted on. That's what *all* abusive pricks hoped for when they harassed their victims. A vulnerable woman could wave a piece of paper with legalese on it saying he had to stay away, but it was a gamble that he'd obey. Considering that piece of paper was often the match that lit his violent flame, the odds on that bet weren't great.

"It's a catch-22."

"Exactly," she said. "He backed off a couple of months ago, after I threatened to turn him in for the vandalism of my car. I'd reached my breaking point."

She sipped her coffee, looking out the window again, intentionally avoiding his eyes. There was no telling lip nibble, but he knew there was more she wasn't saying. He also knew what it was.

"And now he's back."

She lowered her cup and gave him her full attention. "How did you know?"

"Are you forgetting I am a watcher? I pay attention to things. It became pretty obvious when you were talking about him. So what happened?"

"I got a call from him earlier this week. The same day I was coming in to talk to you, in fact. He saw the news coverage and claimed he wanted to see if I was all right."

He knew better than to think that was all Johnny the Big Baby had said. "What else?"

She hesitated before admitting, "He wanted to know about you."

"What did you tell him?"

She looked into her half-empty cup. "Um, I told him you and I were...involved." Jerking her head up, she quickly added, "I'm so sorry, I know I shouldn't have. I was hoping if he believed I'd moved on, he might leave me alone."

He didn't tease her about the confession because he knew men like this Johnny. Telling him there was someone else had probably only made her more desirable in his eyes. "Has he been in contact again?"

Her deep sigh and lowered lashes said he had. "I've spotted his car around."

"What's his full name?"

She peered at him intently. "Why?"

Because I want to break his arms for hurting you, and kill him for making you feel unsafe. "As certain as I am that it was the person harassing me who took the shot last Friday night, we have to at least consider the possibility it was this Johnny."

If he'd known the words were going to bring tears to her eyes and make her mouth tremble, he wouldn't have said them.

"Oh, please no."

"It's a long shot, Jessica. A thousand-to-one chance. I'm the one with the enemies and unhinged fans. Still, the police should know."

"I know." She sniffed. "I'll die if it was him, if I was the one who put you in danger."

"If I was the target, would you blame *me* for what happened to you?"

"Of course not!"

Shrugging, he simply replied, "Then how could I possibly blame you?"

They fell silent, and he relived that moment, that shot, the glass, and her ragged dress. No, she might not blame him, but he would forever blame himself.

"So what's his full name?" he asked. "I'll call the detectives and let them know."

No-go. "I'll call them myself. I don't want you to get dragged into it."

As if he wasn't already? But despite how much he

asked, she would not give him the rest of the details and said she would not give them to Rowan either. Apparently she'd realized there wasn't much the brothers didn't share. She instead insisted on calling the detectives in Venice.

Fortunately, Rowan and the guy were friends. He'd get the name. And then Reece would figure out a way to make sure that prick Johnny-whatever never set another fire. He did, after all, have experience doing whatever it took to keep sick bastards away from their victims. It had been his life's work when he'd first come back here at eighteen.

After they finished their coffee, they headed back across the street to the parking lot. She would have a company vehicle by next week, like it or not. Before getting into her car, she turned to face him, lifted a hand, and straightened the collar of his shirt.

The brush of her knuckles on his neck sent electricity straight through his body. It thrummed and sizzled, probably because he'd been thinking about her touch every time he'd been with her at work. And when he hadn't been with her at home.

"Thanks for the coffee, and the conversation," she murmured.

Reece lifted a hand and caught hers, holding it against his chest. He stared down at her, and she gazed up at him, her dark eyes catching a gleam of moonlight. Despite the car horns and the rumble of traffic, they fell into a strange silence. The night felt hotter than it had before. Steamy. Sticky. He'd touched her in the diner, when she'd needed support and strength. But this was different. Very different.

Their stares locked, and he was back to last Friday night—before the shot. How it had felt to kiss her, to touch her. How much he'd wanted her. She let out a tiny sigh, and he knew she was thinking the same thoughts.

"I think I'm soon going to have to apologize to you again," he said.

"Why?"

"Because I know I'm going to kiss you sooner rather than later."

Her expression something between a smile and a glare, she jabbed a finger at him. "You said you'd back off, that we'd be entirely professional."

"We will be," he insisted. "Except for one kiss."

"Did you kiss Walter?"

"Would it help if I said yes?"

She wagged her brows. "Depends on if there are pictures. Could be kinda hot."

"Not funny." Realizing he never should have threatened to kiss her, he said, "Forget I said anything. It's your call whether anything else happens between us."

She was close, so close. So beautiful with her sassy grin and her shining hair. He couldn't stop himself from stepping toward her, putting a hand on her hip.

"Don't think that means I'll find it easy to wait," he whispered. He leaned forward, inhaling deeply the scent of her hair, and her warm, fragrant body. "Or that I won't try to tempt you to *make* that call."

She licked her lips, breathing deeply. He saw the way her heart fluttered in her throat, just above the collar of her prim blouse. Her pretty nipples pressed against her blouse, and a flush rose into her face.

She still wanted him. There was no denying it.

"Jesus, Jessica, you working here might kill me."

Putting her hand on his forearm, she leaned up on tiptoe until her kissable mouth was all he could focus on. "Reece?"

The parking lot spun. Or his head did. "Yes?"

"The ball's in my court, isn't it?"

He lifted her hand to his mouth, kissing her fingertips, sliding one in his mouth and sucking gently. "Mm-hmm."

She pulled her hand away, but she didn't flounce off. Instead, she came even closer; he felt her warm breaths on his neck. Then she whispered, "I'm not going to change my mind."

He blew out a slow breath.

Her lashes fell to half-mast, hiding her eyes. "At least not in week one."

His heart stopped, and then roared to a start again as he took her meaning. Grinning, he watched her get into her car and drive away. She never looked back, leaving him standing there in his own damn parking lot. He remained there for a long time, shaking his head, trying to cool off and answer the questions swirling in his brain.

Questions like: How was he going to maintain a professional relationship with this woman? Had he really agreed to that until she changed her mind?

And most importantly, would week two be soon enough?

CHAPTER 8

O_h, my God!"

Jess looked up from her toes as Emily walked into the bedroom, holding a sheath of what looked like scarlet fabric in her arms. Her expression was vague, a little stunned.

"What's wrong?"

Her new roommate gently placed the material on the bed, careful to avoid the nail polish tray. Jess had been sitting here painting her toenails, grumbling about tonight's event. She really wasn't interested in attending the gala, though she was impressed with the award Reece was getting for his work with a children's charity. Despite his claim that introducing her as his intern would explain why they'd been alone when they were shot at, she had her doubts. It might look like he was sleeping with his new intern. Even though he wasn't.

You could change that any time you wanted to.

But she wouldn't.

It's week two.

"Shut up," she mumbled to the devil on her shoulder.

"Huh?"

"Talking to myself."

"Well stop it and look. A courier brought this," Emily said, her tone almost reverent. "I'm sorry, I opened it, thinking it was a costume for *Hamlet*." Em performed regularly with a local theater. Like just about everybody else around here, she wanted to break into show business, and was doing it via the familiar waiting-tables route. "There's some other stuff, too, but I didn't open it once I realized this wasn't for me."

Jess continued to eye the slithery red material. "That had better not be a gown."

"Of course it's a gown, dummy. The most gorgeous gown I've ever seen!"

"Damn it."

"Oh, right, exactly the reaction any woman would have when her fairy godmother drops a red ball of wonderful onto her lap."

"You don't get it," she grumbled.

Reece had been bossy and in control since day one. She wished she could say she didn't like her new job. In truth, the past several days had been thrilling. Being with him—going from soundstage to cutting room to office to food cart on the back lot—had introduced her to the world she wanted to inhabit. A world she already loved.

Reece Winchester was a brilliant man. She'd known that, of course, but seeing him in action—the way he thought, the imagination and the vision—was stunning. He grew more attractive by the second, and it was agony to spend hours at a time with him. Their attraction was visceral, but she knew nothing was going to happen between them unless she made "the call."

She couldn't. How could she get involved with some-one she didn't fully trust? Someone she worked for?

Well, *maybe* she could do it while she worked for him, as long as he didn't treat her differently at work. And as long as nobody else knew about it. But *definitely* not too soon.

Week two. Knowing Emily would think her crazy if she talked to herself again, she didn't snap at the inner voice.

"He's my boss, not my fairy godmother. He has no right to send me clothes."

Before Emily could respond, Liza burst into the room, her eyes as round as dinner plates. In one hand, she held a pair of red jeweled shoes. In the other was a shoebox bearing a name every shoe hound in the world would recognize.

"Ho-ly shit," Liza said when she saw the dress on the bed, almost the exact shade as the shoes. "I think Santa came early by way of Rodeo Drive."

"Don't get excited. I'm giving it all back." She saw their crafty expressions. "Unworn."

Emily and Liza looked like they wanted to beat her on the head with the spiked heels of the shoes. Liza whisked the tray away, and the two of them plopped down on either side of her.

"There's no harm in trying them on," Liza said, bending to slip a shoe onto Jess's foot. Jess yanked her foot back, remembering her wet nails. Polish stains would make them impossible to wear.

Not wear, return!

"Whoops, guess I'll have to model them for you."

Liza stuck her own feet in. She was petite, so the shoes were a good two inches too long, yet she still cooed in delight as she stood to display them. "If I stuff cotton in the heels and toes..."

"You'd still be four sizes too small," Emily said, hopping up, too. "But I'm just the stepsister to fit into them. Pretty please, Cinderella, can I try them on?"

Jess merely sighed, watching as her roommates swapped shoes. She couldn't blame them. They were glorious. Dream shoes. Princess shoes.

The heels looked less enormous on Em than they had on Liza. Preening, she lifted the dress by the shoulders, held it up against her body, and let the soft drapes hit the floor in front of her. Jess spied the label and gasped, unable to imagine what it had cost. More important than the name, though, was the simple beauty of the dress. Classy, but also sexy, with a V-neckline that would skim her curves, and glimmering crystals set carefully to accentuate the hips.

The man certainly knew what appealed to a woman... almost as much as he himself did.

Emily spun it around, displaying a flare in the bottom folds. Jess could muster no surprise when she saw the deep V in the back. She didn't doubt Reece remembered her weakness for having the small of her back caressed. It would provide him the perfect access.

Wait, what was she thinking? She couldn't wear this, couldn't let him dress her like she was an adult Barbie doll. She had her own clothes, including a perfectly respectable cocktail dress. Wasn't a little black dress acceptable for any Hollywood event?

"Nope," she said, tearing her eyes away from the dress. And those *shoes*. "I can't..."

"You can, sister, and you will," Liza said in a tone Jess remembered their mom using. "It's his fault your blue one was ruined. The least he can do is replace it. And damn, girl, he replaced it right! This was almost worth the hours it took to get the glass out of your hair."

She shuddered. "No outfit is worth that."

"You haven't seen the jewelry yet."

"No way!"

"I knew you would freak if you saw that first." Liza hurried out of the room and came back with a velvet box and an embossed envelope. She shoved both into Jess's shaking hands. Jess ignored the box and opened the letter.

Dear Miss Jensen:

I know you will try to refuse, but I suspect your blue gown is unwearable, for which I am responsible. Consider this a deserved replacement and just put it on.

Oh, and wear your hair down.

Reece

PS: Calm down. The jewelry is borrowed from a local store famed for loaning items for Hollywood events.

"Oh, bummer, you don't get to keep the rubies?" Liza said, reading over her shoulder.

Her mouth went dry. Rubies? Breathing became impossible, so she simply held her breath. Flipping open the box and seeing what was inside, she nearly dropped it onto the floor.

Definitely rubies. Not lab-created stuff, either. These were real, deep red, and flawless. There were drop earrings with large, crimson stones surrounded by diamonds, and a stunning tennis bracelet. The necklace was what really caught her eye. Good lord, the single ruby hanging at the end of the chain was the size of a walnut. It would rest perfectly in her cleavage.

The ensemble probably cost more than she'd make in the next decade.

Her roommates sighed in appreciation, but she could only say, "Oh, crap."

Jewelry, dress, shoes... this was too much. Reece had done exactly what she'd asked him not to. He'd stepped from the boss-employee relationship she'd told him she wanted into something more personal. He'd sworn tonight's gala was about business, and insisted any other intern in her position would have been required to attend, too. Somehow, though, she wasn't convinced.

Did you send rubies to Walter last year? She seriously doubted it.

"Everything is perfect for you," Liza said, tempting Jess into doing something she knew she probably shouldn't. Like the two of them always had to each other. "Most men would have been scared to send red to a redhead, but he obviously has a good eye."

She *did* look good in red, strangely enough. "I don't know. How can I do this?"

Liza turned on the bed and took Jess's hands. "Something *awful* happened to you. Something traumatic. For that alone you deserve an *I'm sorry* gift from the dude. Plus, you scrimped and saved to afford your blue dress, only to have it end up in tatters."

"It's not exactly tattered," she grumbled. "I could probably sew it up."

Emily looked scandalized. "Darling, you do not *mend* a Dior!"

"Definitely not," Liza said.

"You bury it with full military honors," Emily added, still appearing shocked at the idea.

Liza huffed, giving Emily a *Shut up* glare. "The point is, he *should* replace it."

Jess glanced at the jewelry box. "And all the rest?"

"It's borrowed, remember?" Liza cajoled. "No crime in wearing it for a few hours."

"What about the shoes? I mean, I could always wear my black ones."

"Don't you dare!" Liza grimaced at the thought. "Girl, if you don't keep them so I can drool over them, I'm going to add your face to every nude woman I ever sculpt."

"Plus, if you try to send all this back, I'll steal that dress and wear it on stage," Emily said. "I'd probably get makeup all over it. Not to mention sweat. Those spotlights are pretty hot."

"Like you won't borrow it if I keep it," she grumbled. Emily was notorious for that.

"It doesn't matter; you *are* keeping it," said Liza. "Well, except the jewelry."

She was surrounded, outnumbered, every argument answered and outweighed. Jess had never been ganged up on before by her sister and her friend, and even though she knew they were making sense, she didn't like it. "He has me in a corner."

Liza hid a grin. "I know. What a horrible man. He should be ashamed of himself." Even as she spoke, she was pulling Jess to her feet and tugging her ratty bathrobe off her shoulders.

Jess harrumphed as she stood there in nothing but a basic black bra and her regular boy's cut underwear. She hadn't intended to wear the old undies, not really. Well, okay, that was a lie. Maybe she'd *thought about* it. If she were so unappealingly clothed under her little black cocktail dress, she'd be less tempted to let Reece Winchester take it off her.

No taking off dresses. He was her boss. She might have considered being a number on his scorecard the night they met. No more. She now knew what kind of field he played on, where paparazzi snuck in on private moments, and stalkers or ex-employees took potshots at you. Attraction be damned, she wasn't going to play in his league, other than professionally.

And you didn't for a whoooole week. You've made your point. Now it's week two.

She harrumphed, wishing the naughty voice in her brain would shut the hell up and stop tempting her to do dumb things. Her roommates probably thought she was still griping about the gifts.

"Oh, man, there's one more box," Liza squealed. "I can't believe I forgot it."

She hurried out. Jess watched her, flutters in her stomach. If her sister came back with fur, Jess would go for the can of spray paint under the sink. If it was just about anything else...

"You have to put these on first!" Liza said as she raced back in. She dropped a box onto the bed and tore it open. Under a pile of tissue paper was more red silk, though not a lot of it.

Jess's heart skipped a beat as warmth surged to all her softest places at the sight of such sultry lingerie. There were lacy, wicked underpants with thin straps that would ride high on her hips, plus a contraption that looked kind of like a bra, but not exactly. It had cups, but no straps, and the back and hooks were very low, probably fitting around the waist. "What *is* this?"

"It's a backless bra," Emily said. "For when you wear dresses cut low in the back."

Jeez. If only she'd asked her roomie before taping herself up the last time. Of course, if she'd done that, Sid and his slimy photographer cohort might have seen even more of her.

"All right, no more arguing," Liza said. "We'll give you one hour to fix your hair and your face, and put on every single thing he sent. Otherwise, we'll hold you down and dress you."

Emily tapped her phone screen. "Timer set. One hour."

Liza wagged her index finger in Jess's direction as the two women left the room. As the door slammed shut, her sister called out, "And don't you dare come out in your black dress!"

Although she groused, Jess did as she was told. She did her hair. *Down.* She applied her makeup. *Heavy.*

Then she drew on every silky, sensuous thing Reece had sent to her. *Amazing.*

She didn't think she was ever going to be able to take this dress off. She could hardly tear her eyes away from the mirror, wondering how Reece could have known exactly what size she wore, in lingerie, in dresses, in shoes. It was as if she'd stood on a dressing room platform and had obsequious salespeople cutting and stitching just for her.

He'd been high-handed, yes. But it was also thoughtful. He planned for everything.

Like he did the night we met.

She didn't feel the familiar anger about it, however. Not after his simple but sincere apology, and the way he'd treated her at work since her first day on the job. He didn't favor her; he was just as hard on her as he was on everybody else. But he taught her, encouraged her, and made her feel like she really belonged.

Although demanding, he was a good boss, which wasn't surprising since she suspected he was a natural leader and excelled when in control. Shivering, she couldn't help wondering exactly how much control he had to have in his most intimate interactions.

"It's been an hour," a voice called. "Get out here."

When she came out of the bedroom, Liza shrieked. Loudly. "Holy shit! You look like Jessica Freakin' Rabbit. The sexiest man of the year is gonna fall to his knees when he sees the hottest woman of the century."

Liza's loyalty was unquestionable, and Jess knew she'd have said all these things to build up her confidence. Emily, though, always told it like it was. She walked in a circle, studying Jess from wavy-haired head to designer-shoe-clad feet. She smoothed a sleeve, straightened the crystals hugging her hips. She licked her index finger, then wrapped a strand of Jess's hair around it to fix a curl hanging by her cheek.

"Eww."

"Hush, the genius is at work."

Emily designed and sewed costumes for the theater company, so she did know what she was talking about. Finally, she stepped away and eyed her handiwork. A smile crossed her face.

"So?"

"So, you look like Jessica Freaking *Jensen*, a woman who deserves to be on the arm of a Hollywood superstar."

Both her roommates beamed, their excitement for her energizing the air. It leapt into her body, making her heart shudder and her stomach roll. Which only made her more nervous as she tried to remind herself to keep her expectations where they belonged. "This is a business dinner."

"Uh-huh."

Jess glared at Emily. "It is. I'm his employee."

"Well, considering the way he was looking at you after the shooting at the gallery—hovering over you like you were the most precious thing in the world—I suspect he views you as more than that," Liza said. "When he sees you tonight, the boy is gonna be wrecked."

He might be. That didn't mean he was going to get what he wanted.

What *did* he want? She wasn't sure. She assumed he still

wanted to have sex with her, but he'd gone further than most men would to get her. Another man might have sent her apology jewelry. This one had given her something she needed more: a job. He'd said he would leave control of their personal relationship to her, and other than that toe-curling moment when he'd sucked her fingertip the other night—*God*—that's what he'd done.

Jess liked making her own decisions and was glad he intended to let her do so. But that did make it harder. It had been easy to let herself get swept away by his charisma. Now, if anything happened between them, it wouldn't be because of any sweeping; it would be because she chose to let it. No excuses. No moonlit seductions. No sexy sculpture. It was all on her.

Before she could stew more, a knock sounded on the door. It was crisp and confident, two hard taps saying the visitor demanded to be allowed entry. God, had any woman ever tried to deny entry to Reece? Through a door, or, um, other entrances?

"Seriously? He's picking you up at the door like a prom date?" Liza whispered.

"My prom date met me at Denny's, remember?" she shot back, keeping her voice low, too. Their door was as thick as paper. The many locks on it wouldn't stop one strong kick. Hopefully now that they were all doing better financially—including Emily, who had made some money from a TV commercial—they would soon be able to afford a better place.

"I thought he'd send someone up to get you," Emily said.

"Maybe he did," Jess said, wondering why they all

assumed it was him. Two hard knocks equaled Hollywood god?

Emily hurried to the door, took a deep breath, peered through the peephole, and let out a tiny giggle. Mental note: two hard knocks *did* equal Hollywood god.

Schooling her expression, her roommate opened the door. And there he stood. All six foot two of him, tuxedo-clad, with his golden-brown hair, those amazing amber eyes, and lean, handsome, unsmiling face. Jess melted as his gaze moved immediately to her, those lion's eyes gleaming with appreciation. What rational woman wouldn't?

"Please come in," Emily said, playing the role of elegant hostess. She was a natural.

Jessica focused her attention on Reece as he entered the small, dingy apartment. He should have looked out of place, like a prince in a fast-food joint. Instead, his expression was easy, relaxed, and pleasant as he shook Emily's extended hand.

"I'm Emily. I don't think we had the chance to meet the other night," she said. "I got there late. Right before the, uh...excitement."

"Good thing you weren't out on the beach when that nutso fired," Liza said as she, too, walked over to Reece, and shook his hand. "You know you'd better take care of my sister tonight, right? If any more bullets come flying her way, I'll retract my blessing."

Jessica groaned. This was *worse* than prom night. Well, the prom part at least. She and Liza had bailed on their mouth-breather dates and gone to a movie. A Reece Winchester one.

"I mean, my blessing for her to work for you, of course."

"Of course," he replied, his voice low and smooth.

Then he gave her his full attention. No more introductions or handshakes with her roomies—he was full-throttle, intense male, and was totally focused on her. He examined her, looking down at her feet, where the tips of the to-die-for shoes peeped out from the dress, and then his stare rolled up, studying every inch of her.

By the time he reached her face, Jess was shaking. She tried to disguise her reaction. "Hey, boss, the clothes were totally unnecessary."

"They were entirely necessary. That dress should be ashamed to ever have hung on a hanger when it was so obviously meant to be on you."

She saw Liza relax, and would swear Emily sighed. Jess rolled her eyes. "Good line."

His eyes gleamed. "I'm no longer an actor; I don't deliver lines. It's merely the truth."

Quivering on jelly legs, Jess tried to focus. "Did you get the speech I emailed you?"

"I did, thank you."

"It's okay?"

"Perfect. The tone is exactly right."

"Good. I've never heard of this award you're getting, so I had to do some research."

Her research had revealed a lot about him. Reece donated profits from every one of his movies to a local organization that helped troubled youth, which was why he was getting an award tonight. The email from his administrative assistant had been professional but a bit gushy, so obviously those closest to him knew about his generosity to his favorite cause.

"Tonight's going to be yet another let's-pat-ourselves-on-the-back-and-pretend-we're-all-the-best-people-in-the-world one," he replied, sounding weary.

"I got that much." She'd been wondering why he was going. It didn't seem his style.

"I normally wouldn't attend in person—I'm not interested in the preening. But I want the attention for the charity and hope my fundraising efforts will be matched by donations tonight."

"Ahh." That would be a lot of matching. She wondered who else was going to be attending this event. Whoever they were, they must have deep pockets. Feeling butterflies in her stomach, she hoped nobody there had seen the media images of bloody her in the torn dress.

"Are you ready?"

"Yes." She spun around and reached for her purse, which sat on the table.

The moment she touched the bag, Emily shrieked. "Don't you *dare!*"

"What?" She threw the shoulder straps of the big leather satchel over one arm.

"You are not carrying that monstrosity," Liza said.

Reece frowned. "I apparently forgot something."

"Wait!" Emily darted toward her room. They heard things bouncing around, being thrown, and in seconds, she was back with a small silver clutch in hand. "From when I did *Hello, Dolly!*. It's not red like the shoes, but it's close enough to the beadwork to look all right."

Jess couldn't even get a word out as her sister and their roomie yanked her floppy purse away and dug out the few things that would fit in the useless evening bag. Lipstick, a comb, her ID. The two of them worked independently of her. Although her initial reaction was irritation, she finally had to laugh out loud.

"What's funny?" Emily asked.

"Two evil stepsisters you're not. You are, however, both out of your minds."

"He's the one who's out of his mind, Cinderella," said Liza, jerking a thumb toward Reece. "For forgetting the damn purse."

Reece's let out a dramatic sigh. "I suck."

Jess gaped, surprised to see this lighter side of him. She liked it. A lot. Of course, who could be dour and stern when surrounded by the wonderful warmth and solidarity of her besties?

"You've lost your acting chops, Mr. Academy Award Winner. That was not convincing."

"True. But remember, I never won for acting."

"You were robbed." Liza's indignation was audible. "Jess and I threw popcorn at the TV the year you didn't win for Best Actor."

Jessica glared at her sister, not feeling the need to give Reece any more proof of her youthful crush on him. She'd gushed enough the night they'd met, thankyouverymuch.

He didn't acknowledge the comment other than with a tiny shoulder lift that probably accompanied a silent laugh. "I *am* sorry I didn't think about a purse."

"It's fine," she insisted, straightening a slipping

shoulder strap of her gown. "I still can't believe you went to all this trouble."

"It was the least I could do considering what happened to your blue dress."

Emily flicked the ruby Jess wore. "I think she could forgive you if she got to keep this."

Jess gasped, mortified. "Emily! That is not funny."

Reece didn't hide the chuckle this time. "To quote someone I know, it was *kinda* funny."

Remembering their conversation, right in the middle of their make-out session, she felt her cheeks heat with embarrassment. She'd been so nervous when they met, the smart-ass street kid within her had taken over her vocal cords. It was like she had a split personality.

Although she'd been trying to focus only on the here and now, the details about their near-miss sexual encounter tried to fill her brain. Memories pounded against her temples, her thoughts scattered and confusing. *The laughter. The attraction. His kiss. Their torrid encounter. The photographer. The crack of a gun. Her torn dress. The glass showering on her.*

His protectiveness as he shielded her body with his own.

Jess's amusement faded as she acknowledged that they were attending a big public event together tonight. It worried her, especially if Johnny had been the attacker.

She didn't worry so much about being in the line of fire herself. Her real worry was Reece. If Johnny had erupted into violence because he saw them kissing, then she was responsible for Reece's injuries. Conversely, if someone were gunning for him, would they give up after taking a risk like that? Shooting into a public building packed with people, in a trendy area, indicated desperation and rage.

The more she'd thought about it, the more she worried about Reece's safety. She cared about him far too much to even consider him being the target of someone's rage, and she was determined to be his secret bodyguard, no matter what.

"Okay," Liza said, "I think you're ready."

Emily hurried to the door and held it open. "Be good, kiddos. No splashy headlines, unless they're titillating ones."

Liza nodded, but then offered Reece a last warning look. "And definitely none involving guns, stalkers, or shattered windows. You put my sister in harm's way again, and I'm gonna take my hammer and chisel and put a hurting on you."

* * *

If Jessica was impressed by the stretch limo, she didn't show it. Instead, as they rode in the back, a tinted window separating them from the driver, she insisted on tweaking his speech. It wasn't necessary. She'd nailed it. Honest, blunt, funny—the words were just like her. There was also a poignancy to it, intended to pull at heartstrings and loosen purse strings. She'd obviously done her homework, and the words felt as natural as if she'd been the one involved with California Dreams for Kids—the charity helping underprivileged locals.

The speech had been *so* good, he'd become curious about her scriptwriting. He'd never produced anything from a student before, but he'd certainly read raw scripts and given advice.

"Are you even listening to me?" she snapped.

"I *do* have a bit of experience with public speaking."

She tossed her head, which made her glorious red hair catch highlights in the early evening sunlight shining in through the open sunroof. She'd worn it down, as he'd asked her to, and it draped beautifully over her pale shoulders. He hadn't been able to stop himself from wondering if she was wearing the matching lingerie beneath the wicked red dress.

Not going to find out. Tonight was about regaining her trust. He had to keep reminding himself of that, and not think about stripping her bare and getting back to where they'd been before they'd gained a fucking audience. Not to mention a fucking attempted murder.

"Acting in a movie is not the same as giving a speech to a bunch of other rich, spoiled Hollywood types, you know."

"You're calling me a rich, spoiled Hollywood type?"

Funny. Anyone who knew the whole story—his siblings—knew he had never been spoiled or indulged as a kid. He'd grown up way faster than anyone should have to, as had his brothers. Especially in the months after Rachel's death, before his mother had been hospitalized.

She'd been mad with grief, hungry for revenge, and high most of the time. When she started skipping her medication, the mental illness she had long kept in check took over, turning her into a person they barely knew. Her illness had left Reece and Rowan to be the adults, to take care of Raine. They'd also been the ones who'd had to cover up the things their mother was doing. Dark things. Potentially deadly ones.

No. Nobody died. He felt sure of it, as did Rowan. His twin had, years later, as a cop, searched endlessly for any mention of an unsolved hit-and-run in Beverly Hills or anywhere nearby that night. He'd found nothing. Still, the memory of how the two of them had spent their thirteenth birthday continued to haunt him. It always would.

"I'm sorry. That was rude."

"Thank you," he said, boxing up the traumatic memory and shoving it into a slot in his mind where he put all the dark stuff from the past.

"Now, let me hear it. Pretend I'm your audience."

He groaned. The woman was as tenacious as a pit bull. "I swear, Jessica. I can handle making a few remarks without a fifth dress rehearsal."

"But there are lines I think you should deliver..."

He put a hand up. "Employee? This is employer. Enough."

"Fine," she grumbled, crossing her arms over her chest. He didn't see a pout on those lips, but he'd swear one was nearby.

"You're such a sore loser," he said, trying not to laugh.

"I didn't lose."

"Yes, I think you did."

"Do we always have to revert to childish games?"

He grew entirely serious, wondering if she'd loaded the question intentionally. "No. I'd prefer not to. But you're the one who has to call the play, remember?"

She understood. He could tell by the flare in her eyes and the way she licked her lips. He'd meant what he'd said about backing off and not trying to lead her through any scene he had set up. He only hoped she would soon decide to step forward.

Swallowing, looking nervous—so unlike her—she fell silent. A minute passed. He wondered if she was thinking she should never have come...or should never leave.

"Can I ask you a question?"

"It depends on the question." Was there a purr in his voice? Maybe. He could hardly wait to find out what she wanted to know.

"What made you come back to Hollywood? You'd left the limelight and it sounds like you had a good life with your family back East. I'm curious about what motivated you to try to recapture your childhood acting career when you turned eighteen."

He didn't have to think about it. The memory of the moment he'd made his decision was imprinted on his psyche. "A tabloid headline."

She didn't respond, waiting for him to explain.

"It was a week after I graduated from high school. I was working at a car wash."

"*Seriously?*"

"Nothing wrong with honest labor. I needed to earn college tuition."

"But didn't you have money left from your earlier years in the industry?"

He stiffened, not wanting to discuss where he and his brothers had spent all their movie earnings. Their mother had lived her final years in a very exclusive, private mental hospital, where she got the kind of treatment she needed. It hadn't been cheap. "No."

"Residuals?"

"For a twelve-year-old kid? Please." Especially difficult when your inexperienced, high-strung mother was your manager, and your agent was a slimy piece of shit. "Anyway, I was on my break and went inside the gas station to get a beef burrito."

"Brave man."

He managed a smile before continuing. "I saw a tabloid with a cover article about Caleb Blankenship's death. First and only time in my life I ever bought one of those things."

"Caleb...his death was so sad. He was with you in *Walk Along with Me*. That movie was practically a part of my childhood."

"I hear that a lot."

"It's strange, I recently found out my professor directed it."

He froze, his teeth slamming together in his jaw, every cell going on alert. "Alan Bent?"

She nodded.

Although Reece's stomach heaved, many years of hiding what he was thinking enabled him to not puke, or punch out the car window. "So, he's back in town."

"Yes. I've had him for a few classes. He's my academic advisor."

Jesus fucking Christ. He'd thought the dirt he and

Rowan had dug up on the man had driven Bent out of California for good. They might not have been able to get enough evidence to convict him, but they could easily have ruined him and destroyed his legacy. Reece couldn't believe the former director, who'd sworn he would retire to Arizona, had slunk back.

Jessica had continued speaking. He hadn't even heard her. "After I discovered it, I must have watched that movie once a month when I was a kid. I even managed to hide the tape at every new foster home. I probably still have it somewhere."

He hadn't forgotten she'd been in the system; he just didn't like to think about it.

"Is it one of your favorites, too?"

"It was fun to make."

Despite the way the experience was colored now, through a veil of adult knowledge, the shoot had been one of the best of his childhood. He and the other two leads had been cast as a group of twelve-year-old boys on the run. They'd spent the summer playing in the woods. They'd gotten so close, it was like he gained two more brothers. The three of them—him, Caleb, and Jamal Stone—had decided to be friends forever, owning Hollywood when they grew up.

Reece was now a director.

Jamal was a surgeon in Chicago.

Caleb had died in the street of a heroin overdose when he was eighteen years old.

"So you found out about Caleb's death when you saw the tabloid?"

"Yes. We hadn't been in touch for years. Not after

what happened with my sister." So Reece hadn't known what had happened to drive his friend to make his destructive choices. He wished he had; God, he wished he'd known and could have helped him. But he was so fucked up about his own family trauma he hadn't even wanted to remember the people from his old life.

Jessica licked her lips and shifted her gaze. He knew what she was going to say next.

"Um...were the stories true? About what happened to him?"

Reece's hands clenched into fists. "Yes."

Like other vulnerable kids, Caleb had fallen prey to one of the monsters who lurked in Hollywood. Right after Reece read the article, he'd tracked Jamal down. His old friend had confirmed everything, saying Caleb had called him a few months before he died. On the edge, strung out, and in pain, he had named the man who'd molested him. Jamal had tried to get him to come to Chicago, even sent him a ticket. But Caleb never showed up.

There was no doubt in Reece's mind that the molestation led to Caleb's eventual suicide, or accidental overdose. Frankly, he didn't think either of those were correct. He considered it murder. It had just taken years for Caleb to die.

"I'm sorry." Her voice lowered. "I've heard rumors it's a serious problem in this town."

"No," he said, anticipating her next question.

"No, it's not?"

"No, it didn't happen to me or my brothers. That's not why we left."

He didn't claim it hadn't happened to Rachel. There were some things he wouldn't share with anyone other than his immediate family. Some secrets were too dark, too dangerous, too loaded with potential repercussions, even all these years later.

"I'm glad. I guess this town really does need the kind of service your brother provides."

"Oh, absolutely."

Raine had seen more, known more, than either Reece or Rowan. The things the youngest Winchester knew— but couldn't entirely remember—about their sister's death had haunted him, damaged him, making him angry and rebellious. So much so a judge had given him a choice to go into the military or go to jail for stealing a car when he was seventeen years old. He'd chosen the military, leaving on his eighteenth birthday, immediately after one last fateful visit with his big brothers in California. *That night. God, let me forget that night.*

"Why did Caleb's death make you want to come back? I would have thought it would have cemented your disgust with the whole industry."

A hard smile, devoid of humor, pulled at his mouth. "It did. Which *is* why I came back. Getting high enough on the ladder enabled me to bring down some justice when I could."

He didn't continue, not wanting to discuss it further. If they went on, he might tell her what he thought about her professor. Bent, that monstrous, twisted piece of garbage, had been the first person Reece went after when he came back to LA. After Jamal had started him down the path, Reece had used every connection he had left to confirm it. What he learned made him feel worse about all the things he *hadn't* noticed while they'd been making that long-ago movie. When he'd landed in California, he'd painted a target on the man who'd ruined Caleb's life. And, judging by what he'd found out, other kids' lives.

Hearing Alan Bent was now back, and teaching students, made him sick. He'd have to do something about that.

"Sir? We'll be arriving in ten minutes," said the driver over the car's intercom.

Jessica stiffened. Her eyes darted around, as if looking for an escape. She'd been just as nervous when he'd picked her up. For a few minutes, she'd been distracted by their conversation. Now her nerves were apparently stirring up trouble again.

"It will be fine. Relax and try to enjoy yourself." He shrugged. "If nothing else, you'll get fodder for your stories. I certainly do whenever I'm around this crowd."

She gulped. "What if people look at me and think I'm your mistress? They'll say you hired me because we slept together."

"But you're not." *She could never be called anything as sordid as mistress.* "And I didn't." *She earned her job.* "And we haven't." *Shit.*

"They'll *think* I am."

"No, they'll think I'm a damned lucky man."

Her glare said he hadn't helped matters. "I thought the point was to throw some water on the gossip, not gasoline. Aren't we going as boss and intern so people will believe that's why we were alone together the other night?"

He couldn't prevent a tiny smile at her optimism. Jessica had high expectations for herself, and, apparently, for others. It was something else he liked about her. He only hoped she wouldn't be too disappointed if those expectations were crushed beneath the Brunello Cucinelli loafers and the Manolo Blahnik slingbacks.

"I will introduce you as a promising screenwriter, my new intern, replacing Walter, who a lot of them knew last year." Whether they believed it was another matter.

They won't. Not when she looked like *that*.

"I have to admit, though, I might have overestimated how effective it will be."

Her eyes narrowed. "Explain."

He let his gaze travel over her, from soft waves of lush red hair draped over smooth, milky-pale shoulders. Her soft breasts pushed up to create tantalizing cleavage. The rest of her was equally perfect, straight down to her painted toenails peeping out from the bottom of the gown that hugged every generous curve of her body. "Look at you."

"There's no mirror," she snapped, her anger rising.

"You're stunning."

The compliment did not appear to help. "I'm hot. There's a difference."

A loud laugh burst from his mouth—he simply couldn't contain it. "Sure. Totally different thing. Do you really not know you make men weak in the knees?"

"Don't make me punch you."

She certainly knew how to take a compliment. "Look, I'm known as someone who's dated a few attractive women."

Her lips pursing, she blew out a raspberry sound.

"So mature."

She blew another one, louder this time. His laughter deepened. "I'm not bragging, believe me. I'm single, I'm watched, and you're an amazingly gorgeous woman. Come on, did you really believe us being seen in public together was going to *stop* the gossip?"

She punched him. Literally *punched* him. Hard. "You lying jerk."

"Maybe I deserved that." Rubbing his upper arm, he added, "All right, I admit it. I didn't want to come here alone tonight."

"Why didn't you call the latest *Playboy* Playmate?" She hopped to the opposite side of the car and rapped on the glass partition. "Is this soundproof? Tell him to stop. I'm getting out."

Reece followed her, shifting to the other leather bench seat and sitting close. Their legs were pressed together, as were their hips. He felt the heated, angry breaths leaving her mouth. Her eyes glittered in the soft interior lights of the car, and her cheek flexed as she clenched her jaw. No way was anyone going to believe he didn't want her.

"I know I should say I'm sorry. But I can't regret spending more time with you."

Slowly shaking her head, she replied, "I thought you weren't going to arrange and direct things anymore. Not going to decide what happened between us."

The words hit a lot harder than the punch. He hadn't considered it that way, because he had, indeed, brought Walter to various events last year, especially when he had to speak.

But she was right. He'd manipulated her without even intending to. Was it his go-to response? Had he been acting this way for so long it was second nature? "Damn."

Silence stretched between them. She wasn't banging on the partition to try to get the driver to stop the car. Nor was she relaxing against him. She merely studied him, staring into his face, as if trying to crawl inside his head, to the dark places he concealed from the world. If she'd actually seen them, she probably would have leapt out of the moving car to get away from him.

"You weren't trying to manipulate me this time," she finally whispered.

Had he been? Even he didn't know. He did know one thing, though. "Not intentionally."

"I guess it's your default reaction."

He suspected she was right. Being in control, preparing for what might come at him, and doing whatever was necessary to get the resolution he wanted was the way he'd lived his life since his mother checked out of reality.

He'd told Jessica he was going to back off and let things go where they would. Minutes ago, he'd said it was her play. Now he realized he'd loaded the dice before he'd handed them to her, not even realizing he was doing it. "I'm an ass."

"Finally something we agree on."

"I'm sorry." He closed his eyes and sighed, rubbing at the corners. Self-examination was pretty damn wearying, which could be why he generally avoided it. "It seems I always have to apologize to you." Which he rarely did to anyone.

"You wouldn't have to if you'd stop doing stupid things."

Easier said than done, considering he often didn't even realize he was doing them. How did you break the habit of most of a lifetime? "I'll try."

The intercom buzzed. "Five minutes, sir."

Five minutes until he dragged her into a place she didn't want to be, with people who might not treat her the way she deserved to be treated. *No.*

"Let's skip this and go out for pizza." He pushed the intercom button to tell the driver to take them somewhere else—anywhere else.

"Stop." Feeling a touch as soft as air, he looked down.

Her fingers rested on his hand, and she gently stroked until he loosened his clenched fingers. It suddenly hit him: *She* was comforting *him.* The woman could be as tough as nails, as sarcastic as a comic, as alluring as a siren. But there was softness in her, such kindness. Even vulnerability, though she didn't like to let people see it.

"Oh yes, we are going," she said. "You deserve recognition for the good you've done."

"They can mail me the plaque."

"Forget it, mister. I spent a lot of time on your speech, and it deserves to be heard."

He found a smile. "Please don't make me practice it for you again."

Her laughter cut through the last of the tension hanging over them, and he could only look at her—the sparkle in her eyes, the curve of her lips.

God, she was beautiful. More, she was *lovely*, inside and out. The gleam of the woman he'd seen through the camera of the gallery all those weeks ago was nothing beside the brilliant light of the real Jessica. The hours he'd spent with her had taken the self-protective layers off her. The further down under her shell he got, the more fascinated he'd become.

He didn't think about games, or directing the action, or setting up the scene, or even his promise to let her make the call. Everything other than a deep need for her flew out of his mind. So he leaned over to twine his fingers in her lush hair, pulling her toward him for a kiss.

Her eyes flaring in surprise, she drew in a shocked breath, but didn't pull away. Their mouths came together, and they had no breath except that which they shared.

A half second later, her lips parted, and her body melted against him. He remembered this mouth. The taste of her. The feel of her. But everything about the night they met had been deliberate, a planned seduction. She would probably accuse him of being clinical about it, and he would deserve the accusation. Now, however, there was nothing beyond the need to explore her, to swallow her laughter, to draw her close, to blow away artificial barriers. To *know* her.

She tilted her head, inviting him deeper, and their tongues stroked and slid, all heat and hunger. Lifting her arms, she twined them around his neck, arching into him. Reece groaned at the press of the body that haunted his dreams. He reached around her waist and lifted her onto his lap. She didn't straddle him—not in that dress—but she did immediately moan and writhe against him when she felt how hard he was for her.

No time. Fuck my life.

"Reece," she groaned against his lips, "we can't..."

"Just a kiss."

They stopped talking, stopped thinking, taking what they had for all it was worth.

A kiss. Simple and sexy and hot, but not leading to anything else. Not when they were at most three and a half minutes away from the hotel where the banquet was to be held.

He intended to spend three of those minutes in her mouth.

She was strawberry-sweet, and the tiny sighs coming from her throat made him want to kiss his way down it. He instead focused on the moment, what he *could* have—her lips, her tongue, her warm exhalations, and the softness of her curvy ass on his lap. They gave and took, languorous and slow, savoring the journey, for lack of a final sexual destination.

And then the car pulled up to the glitzy hotel and stopped. They had arrived. Loaded with regret, he dragged his mouth away from hers, watching her slowly open her eyes and blink a few times. They looked at each other, and he watched for her reaction. He didn't know what to expect. Resentment? Anger? Hunger? Maybe she would acknowledge they were heading down this path despite their own spoken intentions?

"Thank you," she whispered, her eyes dreamy, soft and luminous.

Gratitude? Hell, that he had *not* expected. "Only you," he said, shaking his head.

She stiffened. "Only me what?"

"Only you would thank a man for a kiss, when the truth is, every guy here tonight is going to wonder what it would be like to have you in his arms."

She wriggled off his lap. "I wasn't thanking you for the kiss." The shift of her eyes said she was lying. "I was thanking you for distracting me. Picking a fight, and then apologizing."

Was that what he'd done? If so, he had to remember how to do it again.

"In case you hadn't noticed, I've been nervous about tonight. You helped me forget about it for a while, that's all." Her voice trembled on the word *all*. "So, thanks again."

As her chin went up, and she lifted her gaze to meet his, Reece smiled. He leaned toward her and kissed the little bump on her nose—the perfectly imperfect one. "Liar."

Her jaw fell, but before she could respond, the door was pulled open from the outside. Reece exited, glad he'd gotten the last word.

Or…maybe not. Because as he bent in to offer her his hand, she snapped, "I should have bitten your tongue."

This time, he didn't smile. He threw his head back

and laughed as she stepped from the car to stand before him.

Flashbulbs turned twilight into noon. Voices yelled questions. The moment—his laugh and her striking face as she emerged from the limo—would be on every tabloid next week.

She realized it, too, and stiffened. "Oh, my God, there are cameras everywhere."

"It's all right," he said, moving close and putting a hand on the small of her back.

He hadn't done it consciously, but when he felt her quiver beneath his fingertips, and remembered why he'd bought her this dress, he couldn't regret it. He'd meant to lend her support as she walked her first paparazzi gauntlet. Again, though, he'd managed to distract her, and could hear her tiny moan of pleasure as he stroked the delicate bones of her spine.

Christ, how long was it going to be until he could taste that sweet spot?

"I'm ready." Her head went up as they walked the red carpet to the hotel entrance. She painted on a pleasant expression and straightened to her full height. In those shoes, she was almost eye level with him. They would be well matched for tonight's obligatory dancing. They also lined up pretty damned spectacularly in other ways, in more private settings.

Tight pants. Shit. *Get it together.*

Velvet ropes held back fans and photographers, and although Jessica managed to make herself look used to the attention, he stayed close, knowing nobody was prepared for this carnival atmosphere their first time out. He'd had to deal with it as a kid, and only because he'd usually had his family with him had he been able to get through it.

"Almost there," he said as they reached the entrance and were greeted by a doorman. The shouts for autographs faded behind them as they got inside. "You okay?"

"Nope," she said as they followed elegantly scrolled signs directing them toward the gala.

"You're doing fine."

"Frankly, I'd rather be slinging beers at the beach."

"Frankly, I'd rather be there with you."

Following signs to the ballroom, they went slowly. From the corridor, he could hear the roar of conversation, the swell of laughter, and the tink of glasses. He already knew the room was filled with the same people, who attended the same parties, playing the same roles. They were hoping to be noticed, make the right connection, charm the right director.

They thought he was one of them. Maybe he was, in a way, considering he was here under pretenses as false as their own—looking only for their money, not their company. Maybe they all deserved each other. Him included.

Jessica, though, was an innocent. He hoped he didn't live to regret this. Bringing her here and introducing her as an employee had been the excuse. Wanting her on his arm had been the reason. But how it would affect her hadn't been part of the thought process until minutes ago, and he'd felt like crap about it since she'd called him on his bullshit excuses.

"So many people," she whispered.

"Keep telling yourself it's a performance," he said.

"Everyone here is acting their part. All you have to do is the same."

"Pig on steroids, remember?" she said.

"It's exactly like Liza's opening night. Just people wanting to be part of the next big thing." Feeling her tension, he continued, putting it in terms she would quickly grasp. "You're writing a scene in your script, and it's not working. The characters aren't doing what you want. You have to figure out what's wrong."

"Okaaaaay. Your point?"

"Getting there." Patience was not this woman's strong suit. "To really get into their skin, to make them come alive on the page, and, later, on the screen, you have to walk in their shoes until you are absolutely certain what they would do next. You have to act it out."

She stilled, watching him closely.

"Is the room dark, or is it bright? What do you hear?"

"I hear rich people."

He ignored the dry quip. "Would she walk down the steps, or would she run? Does he hand her the money or throw it at her feet?"

She was getting the point. "Does she slap him across the face or kick him in the nuts?"

He hid the horror every man felt at such a threat, not doubting this woman could—and probably had, given her background—made good on it a time or two. "I think you've got it."

"So...they're all characters acting out their own individual scenes."

"Every one of us is. You watch them, remember it's all fiction, and play your own role."

"You *are* a director. So who are you playing?"

"Spoiled, rich jerk?"

A twinkle in her eye, she replied, "I thought this was fictional."

He shook his head. "Jesus, woman, direct hit. Who do *you* think I should play?"

"Spoiled, rich asshole?"

Man, she was good. "A double whammy. Three times and I'll be lying dead on the floor."

Jessica giggled, a light, musical sound at odds with her husky speaking voice. It was pretty damned cute. He'd seen her aroused, seen her snarky—a lot. He'd seen her sexy, funny, a little tipsy, and scared to death. But what he saw now was pure enjoyment.

She was having fun. She'd begun to lower her guard and trust him to get her through the night. Physically? Yes. She'd allowed her defenses to fall more than once around him. But this light, relaxed flirtation, when they both knew it couldn't go anywhere, given the place, was something new. He liked it.

"Okay, one more chance to figure you out, huh?" She thought about it some more. "Liza and Em have been calling me Cinderella for days."

Meaning she considered him Prince Charming? Nice.

"So how about you be the stern king, sitting high above everyone, all judgy, watching the ladies competing for your son at the ball."

He should have known. "You are *so* hard on the ego."

"I think yours gets stroked enough."

Her eyes shifted, and he knew she was thinking about how her words sounded. About what she might stroke for him. He didn't call her on it. Since his dick was already rock hard, and probably pushing out the hem of his tuxedo jacket, he would be risking fire.

"You'd better take care if you're playing the girl who loses her shoe. If one of those falls off, your roommates will lock you out of your place until you find it."

She tossed her head. "No, as Liza discovered earlier, I'm Jessica Rabbit."

Of course she would never choose a sweet, innocent princess. "Naturally."

Plucking at her red dress, she added, "Or maybe a she-devil?"

"Always with the jokes."

"That's me. All big mouth and enormous ass. Men always want one but not the other."

Somehow refraining from admiring that ass, he took her by the shoulders and made her focus on him. She needed to hear what he had to say. "You're so full of it."

"What?" she said, her jaw falling open.

"Do you think I don't recognize a defense mechanism when I see one? I grew up in this town. I learned before my tenth birthday how to hide my feelings by shooting off my mouth."

She licked her lips. "I don't know what you—"

"Yes you do." His hands tightened. "The smart aleck is funny. The sexpot is amazing. But the real woman was just here, and she's the one I want to spend the night with."

He heard her suck in a breath and hold it.

"Let me see her. Let me be with her. *Trust* me, Jessica."

She lifted a trembling hand, smoothing her hair, considering his request. He knew why she had a hard time trusting, especially after the missteps he'd made. He only hoped she'd gotten to know him well enough to finally take a chance and lower those defenses.

Finally, she spoke. "What about you, Reece Winchester? Who are you really? The controlling man who pursued me relentlessly the other night? The one who threw himself on top of me to protect me? The one who gave me a job?" She smiled. "Or this flirtatious guy who laughs and jokes. Am I seeing the real *you* tonight at last?"

The real him? Who was he? Honestly, he wasn't sure anymore. He'd played a lot of roles in his life, and he didn't mean in front of the camera. He'd been a twin, a son, a sibling. A star. Those were the positives, for the most part. But he'd also been a rotten bastard. A vigilante. An accomplice. A criminal. That he'd gotten away with his crimes—and helped others do the same—didn't make that truth about himself any easier to acknowledge.

Funny, he had long ago accepted who he was. But for a little while at least, Jessica made him wonder if he could actually be somebody else.

His silence probably answered more than he'd like it to.

"Now who's being secretive?" She placed a hand on his chest, as if she could feel the waves of the past hitting him and pulling him under, away from the frothy surf where he'd been playing with her. He wanted to swim back, to let go of the dark currents swirling in his heart and his mind. What would it be like to be the kind of man she thought he was?

"Let me see him," she ordered. "Let me know him."

Their stares met and locked. It was a big thing they were asking of each other. A monumental thing on his part, and, he suspected by a few things she'd said, on hers.

He wished he could do it, let go of the past and become the man he might have been, if not for his dark, twisted history. He didn't want to be the cold, arrogant son of a bitch. Not with her.

If he didn't have others to worry about—their lives, their memories, their freedom—maybe he'd say to hell with it. What wouldn't he give to stop worrying that the past would catch up with them all? He couldn't imagine how it might feel to stop doing what all those people in the ballroom were doing: playing a part.

She waited for his answer, her eyes sparkling, her expression entreating. While he knew it was impossible, something in him had to relent, to at least accept the possibility of change.

"I'll try." It was as far as he could go, and it was further than he'd gone in many years.

With a slow nod, she met the challenge, too. "So will I."

They shared one more intimate look, and then a few people walked out of the ballroom, chatting as they crossed the marble-tiled floor, away from them. Knowing they had been lucky to have escaped notice for this long, he turned toward the banquet. She fell in beside him, letting him take her arm. Her body was no longer tense. She seemed ready to face the night.

As they stood in the doorway and the roar of the crowd flew directly at them, she mumbled, "Maybe I'm not playing a screenwriter. I feel more like a zookeeper about to throw raw meat at the lions and hyenas."

"Funny. That's *exactly* what you're about to do."

"Only *I'm* the raw meat. And the lions and hyenas walk on two legs."

He slid an arm around her waist. "Don't worry, Jessica. I won't let anybody bite you. I promise."

CHAPTER 9

Maisy Cullinan's night had started perfectly. She'd stared in rapt attention as Reece Winchester delivered his speech, looking so handsome under the lights, his warm expression obviously focused only on her.

Then everything had gone to hell.

As she watched tonight's most talked-about couple mingle in the crowded ballroom, nausea turned her stomach into a volcano. While they moved around the room, her stare followed, at least until rage blurred her vision. She could almost feel herself ripping out fistfuls of red hair by the roots, scratching those cheeks, tearing off the slutty dress.

She couldn't believe Reece had brought the tramp here. This was supposed to be *their* special night. Only the who's who of Hollywood should have been allowed—movie stars and rich philanthropists, like her. Maisy had the *right* to be here, bought and paid for. Maybe she hadn't grown up with a silver spoon in her mouth, but her lottery winnings could be spent just as well as movie money. So she deserved to be among these people. She fit in. The slut in the red dress did not.

"She looks like she belongs in *Penthouse*, not at a charity dinner."

"What did you say, darling?"

Maisy flinched, knowing the blonde seated beside her had heard. She couldn't remember the woman's name—Candace? Carla?—but knew her husband produced crappy films.

"Oh, nothing," she said with a bored smile, one she'd seen on other woman and practiced daily in front of the mirror. Hers was probably fine, considering everybody's looked as fake as their tits and their tans. "I was talking to myself. Don't you ever talk to yourself?"

"No, I don't," the producer's wife said with a smirk, so condescending. As if Maisy hadn't paid every bit as much for her plate of food as this spoiled bitch. "But if you were talking about the woman with Reece Winchester, I hear she's his new, uh, *assistant*."

"Assistant, my ass. Abigail's his administrative assistant," Maisy snapped. She knew all about Reece's employees, just as she knew all about his life.

"Abigail?"

Realizing she'd sounded more interested than she should, she said, "I, uh, met her once, when I stopped by Reece's office." He had been out of town, on location. But she'd needed to be near him, at least to smell his unique scent, be close to the desk where he worked.

"I see," the woman said, so pleasant, so phony.

It was so hard to know what to say, and who to say it to. People here weren't like the ones in Scranton. They were better at hiding what they meant, disguising their meanness behind polite talk. Not that there weren't mean people in Pennsylvania. Everybody had been mean to her back in the day. Crazy Maisy, they'd called her. She'd slaved at the grocery store six days a week, ringing up their melons and their cucumbers, but she wasn't even worth saying hello to.

Then she'd won a record-breaking lottery jackpot. She'd suddenly had more friends than Miss Congeniality in a beauty pageant. But she hadn't given a penny to any of them, and had traded her small life in Pennsylvania for a big one in Los Angeles.

Her windfall had obviously been fated. She'd always known she would end up with Reece, ever since he'd smiled at her from a giant screen. She'd waited, and she knew he had, too. It was why neither of them had ever married, and why his relationships never lasted. They were meant to be together. He was the man she was going to spend the rest of her life with.

"Well, not assistant, I suppose. He's introducing this one as his new summer intern."

So he really had hired her, the cheap piece who'd lured him upstairs the other night? She was going to be around him constantly, flaunting herself? Her anger boiled. "No, no, she can't be."

"Who can't?"

She couldn't even pretend to be friendly. "I'm talking to myself again. Do you mind?"

The woman stood up, so graceful, like she was rising from a couch where some man had been dropping grapes into her entitled mouth. No matter how she practiced, Maisy hadn't yet been able to copy that languid LA style, and envy made her bitter.

"Darling, you shouldn't let people know you talk to yourself. You can't possibly know how wicked gossip can be in this town." She patted Maisy's shoulder in pretend concern. "After all, you wouldn't want anyone to think you're crazy."

A roar of denial came to her mouth. *I'm not Crazy Maisy! Nobody better ever call me that again. I'm rich, and rich people don't get put in hospitals and drugged with pills and tied up to bed rails.* But she didn't say anything at all as the woman walked away. Her focus was elsewhere: on her primary enemy.

Whether it was the showy clothes or the hair, the devil who'd caught Reece's eye now caught hers. The dress was too low, the shoes too high, the jewelry too big and obviously fake. Everything about the woman screamed cheap and poor. How Reece could have been sucked in, she didn't know. Maybe he was just being protective because of the gunshot.

That gunshot. She gulped, glad Reece hadn't been hit. At least the timing of that had been good. It had made them stop the hanky-panky they'd been doing upstairs in that private gallery.

It had almost killed her to see them kissing up there. Maisy had left the gallery, needing to stomp and rant because he'd gone upstairs with the woman. So looking up and seeing them in the window had just about made her head fly off.

She pushed the memory back into the darkest part of her brain, where ugly things lived, and focused only on the future. On her and Reece. Miss Red Dress would give him what he wanted—what all men wanted—and then he'd get bored and pull away. He would settle down only with someone who was his equal. Someone like Maisy Cullinan.

Unfortunately, that didn't ease the sting of the thought of the redhead sharing his bed.

"How would you like her if she wasn't pretty?" she mused, her stare clawing at the woman's back from across the ballroom. "If her hair was chopped off, and her skin was scarred, and her fancy dress was ragged and torn, would you still want her then?"

Maisy relished the thought. She imagined the scene, thinking like a film director. And suddenly, one of her excellent ideas popped into her head. She could *make* it happen.

She'd have to find a place—*the bathroom*—and would need supplies—*from a maintenance closet*. It could work, if she could only find a way to get the little tart alone. It might not be easy in this crowd; she would have to think carefully. Even with the best plan, however, she would need some real luck to pull it off.

Then again, everybody knew Maisy was lucky. She was the one-in-three-hundred-million woman, and had the bank account to prove it. If that luck held, by tomorrow the redhead would look entirely different. After that, men wouldn't stare at her with lust. Only with pity.

* * *

Reece did a beautiful job on his speech, as Jess had known he would. The rest of the evening, however, was definitely not something she had ever expected.

She had pictured a lovely charity event with people focused on good causes acknowledging those who went above and beyond in supporting them. Reading about the three awards being given out tonight—to Reece and two others—she'd envisioned a boatload of tender hearts, floating on a sea of compassion, on a planet of goodwill.

Uh...no. Philanthropy might live in the checkbooks of these members of the LA elite, but their charity ended at their lips.

She'd never been around a cattier bunch in her life. This crowd could give lessons in snottiness to contestants in a reality TV matchmaking show. Considering one such former contestant was here tonight, maybe they actually did.

"You know, I kind of hate you right now," she murmured as she sipped her champagne.

Reece lowered his own glass, which held sparkling water. Not surprising. Drinking could lead to a loss of control, and publicly losing control was one thing he wouldn't do. He barely did it privately, judging by how in-check he'd kept himself their first night. She'd been quivering with need. Reece had merely directed the scene. At least until a bullet came through the glass.

Nothing could have prepared either of them for that action sequence.

As for what had happened in the car, well, he'd lost control for a while, as had she. She'd been tempted to tell the chauffeur to keep driving forever. But she wanted tonight for Reece, wanted him to get recognition for something other than his incredible looks, his acting, or his films.

"I thought we'd moved past your hatred of me."

"I said kind of."

"Moderately better. Didn't the shoes at least bump me up to more than dislike?"

The kiss in the limo had. She wasn't going to admit that, however, not when they were in the middle of a crowd and couldn't do anything about it. "The shoes put you on the pie list."

"Pie list?"

"I mean, I love cake. But I'll eat pie. It's okay. You're now pie. I only hate certain kinds of it, while I love any kind of cake."

He shook his head, his eyes twinkling. "Oh, to be smothered in cream cheese icing."

Yum. Her favorite. How delicious it would be to lick it off his powerful body.

Annoyed at her own vivid imagination, she forced herself to remember she was scolding him for not warning her about this dumb gala. It had ruined all her illusions. "I can't believe I actually expected an evening of kindness and shared philanthropy. These people are awful."

He threw back his head and laughed. Two hundred heads swung and four hundred eyes stared. Jess caught her lip in her teeth, and she could almost hear the whispers from the rich and nosy, people dying to know what had caused his amusement.

"Did you really expect anything else?"

"Actually, yes, I did."

"Sorry to tear off your blinders, but if you want to work in this business, you should see it as it is. Brutal, cutthroat, seething with ambition and jealousy."

"Gee, you make it sound so appealing."

She couldn't help wondering how old he had been when he'd learned that lesson. Being raised in this world might explain why he was so closed in, so mistrustful. Why he always had to maintain a distance and control his interactions with others. Including women. Including *her*.

Taking her empty glass away and putting it on the tray of a passing server, he said, "Come on before somebody interrupts to ask what was so funny, and oh, by the way, is dying to tell me all about his new raunchy comedy about a bunch of groomsmen."

"I think that was called *The Hangover*. Or *Bachelor Party*. A classic."

"Movie fanatic."

"Guilty."

As amusement swirled between them, other things came with it. Liking. Even, she thought, the beginnings of trust. So she didn't ask where they were going and simply went with him when he took her hand. She hoped they were headed for the exit.

Unfortunately, he instead steered her toward the crowded dance floor. Jess tried to change direction, but he was quick to block her path. He swung her into his arms and pulled her along to the music before she could even protest: *But I can't dance!*

Only, apparently, she could, at least with the right partner.

They fit together. With this man, her height was not a negative. Their bodies melded, angle to curve, hardness to softness. They were two pieces of a puzzle that snapped together to form a perfect picture. She relaxed in his arms and let him lead her, knowing they were being stared at, but not caring. Besides, it was him they were staring at. Him they always stared at. Women imagined being with him, men just imagined *being* him.

He was so tall, straight, and masculine. Even wearing a tuxedo, with his thick hair perfectly combed and his jaw closely shaven, he gave off an aura of utter masculinity. Although the clothes were perfect for Mr. Hollywood, she knew he would have looked equally sexy in jeans and a T-shirt. Or an intergalactic space pilot's uniform.

"I really have to stop thinking of you as Runner Fleet," she muttered.

"My favorite role."

"Really? I would have thought he was too funny for you." Realizing she might sound insulting, she quickly added, "Not that you're not funny. Well, you're not." *Bad to worse.* "I mean, you play funny well, even though you didn't do it very often." She never understood why. He'd been really good. "I just can't picture it now that I've gotten to know you."

He tilted his head quizzically. "Was there a compliment in there? Or a question? Or are you just calling me humorless?"

"Oh, lord," she muttered, not wanting to admit her brains were scrambling just being in his arms, smelling the spicy cologne blended with his own unique scent. He was hard and strong, and...and...she wanted him. She just wanted him. She'd been unable to think of anything else except how amazing it would have been to remain in the limousine, exchanging more of those long, hungry kisses, stripping off their clothes, and making love for hours.

Despite everything she'd been telling herself about him, she was caught. Even knowing he had set up their meeting like a puppet master, knowing exactly what was going to happen when he lured her up to the gallery, she would say yes all over again. He'd tempted her with a job, but she didn't regret taking it. Maybe he'd done the same thing to get her here tonight.

Whatever. It didn't change a thing. She craved the man.

It wasn't smart. It definitely wasn't professional. It probably wasn't safe for her heart. Or, judging by the icy stares and invisible knives being thrown at her from other women, her body. Nobody had ever accused her of doing the safe, easy thing, however.

He had to know what she was thinking. Only a whisper of fabric separated their bodies, so he must feel her rapid, shallow breaths brushing his neck, and the thudding of her heart against his chest. At the very least, he must have noticed her nipples were hard and her legs weak enough to make her lean into him more than was strictly necessary for the dance.

"Jessica?" he murmured. "Look at me."

She swallowed hard and lifted her eyes.

"What do you want?"

Everything? Anything? To go back in time to earlier this evening, or to that night he'd kissed her in the lobby? The private gallery where he'd stripped off her dress? Or maybe to the day when she'd first come in and he'd seen her through the security camera?

"Why do you have to be so difficult?" she whispered. "This would have been so much easier if you'd simply come downstairs and introduced yourself on day one."

He didn't ask her to explain, knowing exactly what she meant. "Yes, it would have. Believe me, I'll regret that decision for the rest of my life. So what do we do about it?"

Breathless, nervous, and hopeful, she said, "I think we—"

"Can I cut in?"

Shocked, Jessica swung her head around as a man's voice spoke from beside them. She felt Reece's body tense against hers. He went very quiet and very still. Well, more quiet and more still than he usually was. "I didn't know you were here."

"I've contributed to programs fighting teen drug addiction for years."

Good lord, if Reece grew any stiffer, he'd be a board. "Oh."

"It can't compare to what you've done. Congratulations. Sounds like you've made a real difference in the lives of needy kids. Your speech was great."

"The organization does the great work. I just throw some money at it," he said.

He still hadn't let her go, one arm around her waist, a hand holding hers. If anything, he pulled her closer. It didn't look like he was going to allow the stranger to cut in.

But more, she wasn't about to step out of Reece's arms and into somebody else's. "I'm happy where I am, thank you."

The stranger laughed. "Touché."

Reece didn't relax, eyeing the other man with some unidentifiable emotion. She couldn't call it dislike, precisely. She'd seen Reece interact with people he didn't like; despite his acting ability, he could rarely hide it. With this man, it was something else. Something more subtle.

"So, old friend, are you going to introduce us?"

Reece let out a long, slow breath. "Of course. Jessica Jensen, meet Steve Baker."

He extended a hand, as did she, managing to hide her reaction to his identity. *Steve Baker.* Childhood actor. Half of the Steve-and-Rachel teen supercouple.

Steve Baker and Rachel Winchester had been the king and queen of every tweenage girl's heart, their "pure" romance unique in Hollywood. Then Rachel had wound up dead in the street. The public had turned on the boyfriend who had supposedly led her down the powdery-white Cocaine Road.

Although still handsome, he'd aged a lot. Redness in his cheeks and on his nose, and deep lines in his forehead, hinted he'd lived hard since his fall from grace. He was also heavy, not the wiry teen he'd been. She couldn't help wondering what his life had been like in recent years.

"Uh, I remember your TV show, of course," she mumbled to fill the silence. Baker had played the middle son in a sitcom called *Dear Family*. She'd never liked it, though much of America had ... at least until the scandal. It had gone off the air shortly after Rachel's death.

Baker, who was probably about five years Reece's senior, though he looked even older, groaned. "*Please* don't ask me to say the line."

She knew what he meant. His character was famous for asking if he'd been adopted by his wacky family. The line had been repeated verbatim in almost every episode. She'd always considered it lazy writing. "I promise, I won't."

"So, Reece, if you won't let me steal her away for a dance, how about a drink? My treat."

"It's an open bar," he replied.

"Okay then, I'll treat you both."

His joke landed on the floor between them, the silence thickening like a dry sponge tossed in water. It was noticeable, uncomfortable, and completely understandable. If she were to come face-to-face with someone who might have contributed to *her* sister's spiral into addiction and death, she wouldn't be able to even look at him, either.

"So, uh, are you still acting, Steve?" she asked when the two men stopped talking.

"Yes, I do, overseas. I hope to get back into the spotlight in the US." He cast a quick glance at Reece. "Maybe you could toss me a bone?"

Reece remained silent.

"Sorry, not the place. I'll have my agent get in touch."

She squeezed Reece's hip to get him to say something. Finally he muttered, "Do that."

Steve beamed. "Thanks. But seriously, I'm not in town to audition. I have to settle some issues regarding my late father's estate."

"Your late father? I'm so sorry," Jess said.

Reece's turn to pinch. He squeezed her waist in warning, telling her to be quiet.

She understood why when Steve responded, "My father was Harry Baker."

It took her one second and then she put it together. "Oh, God," she whispered, recognizing the name, of course. How had she never heard the famous Hollywood agent had been actor Steve Baker's father? She felt like the most insensitive person in the world to have brought up the conversation. "I'm so sorry, I had no idea."

"Not a lot of people put us together. He and my mother divorced when I was young. I'd been out of the public eye here, living in Europe for many years by the time he...died."

The common surname had probably helped, too. Still, it surprised her that someone embroiled in the Rachel Winchester scandal wouldn't have been of interest to those seeking answers about his father's death.

She didn't know what to say. What *could* she say? "Sorry somebody murdered your famous dad in his Beverly Hills home six years ago." Or "Sorry the killer got away with it." God, no wonder the son had stayed away. He'd probably never been able to escape the shadows of his past. And she'd just dragged them out and shone a spotlight on them.

"Please forgive me, Mr. Baker. I shouldn't have been so nosy."

"It's okay," he said, rescuing her from her own embarrassment.

She doubted the murder of a parent could ever be okay. How could a son live with knowing his father had been found, shot dead, in a pool of blood in his own home? The news coverage had been relentless, the details salacious. It was like a film plot—a murder mystery about a movie insider whose client list read like a who's who of the industry. The unsolved case had never been far from the public's mind, kept there by tabloids, or salacious revisits on the murder channels. Nobody had forgotten the story, and she doubted anyone would. It was Hollywood legend.

"I'm in town to deal with the last details of the whole business. My father's house was tied up in legalities for years. When I was finally cleared to take possession again, I knew it wouldn't be easy to sell. I think it's been on the murder tour since the day after it happened."

She winced at his matter-of-fact tone, wondering how people could be so dark and twisted as to want to visit sites of such horror.

"I've finally got a buyer, though. Property values triumph over blood spatter."

Morbid, though she knew black humor could help. "I'm glad it worked out for you."

"Me too. God knows I was never going to move into that house again."

"I can't imagine what it must be like," she said, reaching out to put a hand on his arm.

He covered it with his own, and squeezed. "Thank you. I miss him every day."

She'd lost a parent. More than one, really, since both the mothers in her life were now gone. So she understood his pain and empathized with it. "I'm sure you do."

"Jessica, it's time to go."

Okay, he didn't like being around the guy, but Reece could have picked a better moment, or at least a slightly warmer tone. The man had been grieving over his father, for heaven's sake.

Steve immediately dropped her hand. "So soon?"

"Yes, I'm afraid my intern and I were about to leave. Good seeing you, Baker," Reece said, taking her arm in a firm grip. "We're going."

"Nice to have met you," the man said as Reece ushered her off the dance floor.

He practically dragged her toward their table. "What's wrong?"

"Other than the bloody scab you just ripped off?"

"I know. I feel like such an idiot," she mumbled. "I was caught off guard. I didn't mean to be insensitive or to pry. I had no idea who his father was."

"Don't say another word about *him*," he bit out from a jaw cut from marble.

Jessica sucked in a shocked breath as he turned into a stranger, an icy man whose entire body was rigid with what she immediately recognized as fury. "Reece, I didn't mean to—"

"Get your things."

Her irritation rose. "I'm trying to explain."

"Don't," he snapped, his tension alive and sparking, a live wire on a deadly circuit.

"But—"

"Enough. You're meddling in things that are none of your business." When she gaped at him, he thrust a hand through his hair, as if realizing suddenly who he was barking at. He closed his eyes and put a hand over them, rubbing at the corners.

"What's going on, Reece?"

"I...you..." His hand fell. He stared at her. Without another word, he spun around and strode across the banquet room, ignoring the people who put hands on his sleeve or tried to step in his path. He wasn't running, merely walking purposefully, like a man on a mission. But something in her knew: He *was* running from something. Maybe her. More likely the past.

"Oh, God," she mumbled, knowing it was her fault. By foolishly opening up an entry into Steve Baker's history, she had also thrust sharp daggers into his own.

It all came back to Reece's sister. He *had* to associate Steve with Rachel, and when he saw the man, all those memories flooded in. Steve was a living reminder of the life Rachel had been denied. He'd had years to grow up, to laugh, to love, and to have relationships. While Reece's sister was remembered only for the swan dive she'd taken in her last moments on this earth.

"Way to go, dumbass," she told herself, grabbing her purse and going after him.

"Lovers' quarrel?" a bitchy-looking woman asked as she strode by.

Jess kept walking. Her only response was to lift one hand and flip the woman the finger over her shoulder. Hearing a gasp of indignation, she suspected the message had been received.

Now she had to deliver one to Reece. At least, as long as she could find him.

* * *

Watching Reece ignore everyone and stride toward the exit as the crowd parted like a god was passing through, Steve Baker couldn't prevent a frown. The stunning red-head hurried after him, trailing like a lackey, when, in truth, Winchester was damn lucky to have the beautiful woman on his arm. But, like all golden boys, he never appreciated anything, never even noticed that he had it all while others had nothing.

"All hail the king of Hollywood," he muttered, realizing he probably sounded bitter. But if anybody had a right to, he did.

He could have had that life. He *should* have had it.

Once upon a time, his star had been on the rise, just like Winchester's. No, he hadn't landed any movie deals, but he would have. He and Rachel were in talks to star in a remake of an old teen beach romance. With their popularity, there's no doubt it would have been a major summer hit. More, it would have been his chance to break out of the TV sitcom middle-son role and really make something of himself.

"Gone," he muttered, walking off the dance floor and heading toward the bar. A few people eyed him, trying to place his face. Nobody did. Just another Hollywood has-been hanging around to try to recapture some glory.

He ordered a scotch and lifted it in a toast. *To you, Rachel.*

God, how he'd loved her.

Everyone had called theirs the teenybopper romance of the decade. It had never felt small or juvenile to him. Rachel had been his whole world. They'd planned to marry, to have kids, to blend their Hollywood dynasty families and produce a new one such as this town had never seen before. She'd wanted all those things as much as he had.

Right up until the moment she hadn't.

She'd stomped on the dreams, not to mention his heart. While he'd worshipped her as an angel, she'd chosen some new, exciting friends over him, and they'd pulled her into a life of drugs and partying. He never knew who they were. He just knew she'd rejected him, shattered him, and crushed all his dreams, personal and professional. He hadn't been sure he could survive it.

Then she died. He'd been free of her and the pain. Or so he'd thought. Because he'd suddenly found himself the one blamed. His career disappeared along with his friendships. He'd had to practically flee the country to get any work at all.

He swallowed the alcohol, letting the heat wash down his throat to warm his stomach. Not much warmed him these days, not since he'd been back here, on a quest and learning the truth about all the mysteries that had haunted him for so long.

He knew most of the story now, after speaking to the one person who could tell it to him. He'd been digging to find the rest, unearthing secrets and planning what to do with them.

Funny how the Winchesters were always tied up in those dark secrets.

Funny how they didn't even realize how much he knew.

Funny they had no idea he intended to expose them and bring their world crashing down.

Funny.

But not.

* * *

As Jessica exited the ballroom, she saw Reece disappear through a set of double doors leading deeper into the hotel. She hurried after him, dodging men who tried to talk to her and women who probably wanted to trip her. Reaching the doors, she shoved through them and found herself in another hallway, much like the last one, with rooms all down the sides. Meaning there were two hallways, exactly alike, separated by double doors right down the middle. Weird.

Ahead of her, she heard a click as one of those unmarked doors closed. Taking a guess on where the sound had come from, she hurried to it. A twist of the knob and she stepped into a supply room with shelves stacked with tablecloths, napkins, centerpieces, candles, and other regular banquet supplies. A tall, shadowy form stood a few feet away. Even in the low lighting, she could see the gleam of his eyes as he watched her come in after him.

"I can't believe they left this thing unlocked. Somebody shady could steal the silver."

Nothing.

"Reece, are you okay?"

"You shouldn't have followed me." His voice was low, a growl from the darkness. "I needed a minute alone."

She supposed she should be grateful he'd taken that

minute alone in a supply closet and not in his limo. Given his tension, he might have ridden away, stranding her. She didn't think he would be that rude. Then again, he'd obviously been desperate to get away from Steve Baker.

"I'm so sorry."

He crossed his arms and leaned a shoulder against the wall. "Forget it. I overreacted."

"No, I don't think you did. I didn't understand. Now I believe I do."

"I doubt it," he said, sounding dry and almost amused in a jaded way. "Go back to the party, Jessica. I'll be there in a minute."

"No thanks. I'll wait for you." Crossing her arms, she leaned against the wall, too, intentionally matching his pose.

But not for long. He straightened and stepped closer to her, all tension and heat. "Do you ever do what somebody asks you to do?"

Taking a step of her own, she went right back at him, "You didn't ask me. You told me. I've never responded well to orders."

His jaw flexed; she could almost hear his teeth grind. "Will you *please* go back?"

She tossed her head. "Look, dude, I am not walking back into that vipers' den alone. Those people are toxic."

"Yes. I suppose we are," Reece replied with a bitter laugh.

His own character assassination really pissed her off. "Stop comparing yourself to them!"

"You're right. I'm worse."

Now hers were the teeth clenching. Frustrated, angry he'd even consider putting himself on the level of the assholes who thought they lived in a world one level higher than everyone else, she grabbed two fistfuls of his jacket collar. "Shut up, Winchester."

He stilled.

"Shut up and let me apologize. I'm sorry about what happened back there. But I am not going to let you stay in here and fume by yourself. If you want to fume, you're going to have to do it with me."

A long pause. Then, out of the darkness, his hand lifted, and he sank his fingers into her hair. He stroked it, stepping closer, and she immediately felt a change in the air. The angry tension had shifted. It had become something...else. Still tense, and maybe a little angry. But oh, there was so much more.

"There are many things I'd like to do with you," he said, his voice smooth and seductive. He moved again, until his powerful body pressed against hers. "Fuming isn't one of them."

She arched toward him instinctively, her hips thrusting against his, and she shivered when she realized he was fully erect, rock hard and massive, beneath those fine tailored clothes.

The passion of their argument had turned into another kind of passion altogether.

Her heart danced, and her blood became a river rushing through her veins to deliver all the cells carrying *excitement* to her organs. A lot of it went right between her thighs. With nothing but a touch of her hair and his sexy voice whispering seduction, she was wet and swollen, aching with need.

"Oh really?" she asked, trying for light, knowing she'd failed. How could she not? A strong, sexy, angry man was pressing her back into a wall, his dick hard, his hand in her hair, another suddenly landing on her hip, strong and solid. "What, exactly, would you like to do?"

"Your turn to shut up, Jensen," he said.

She just barely had time to suck in a deep breath before he pulled her toward him and slammed his mouth on hers. She gasped, she groaned, she burned, she flew. Most importantly, she opened her mouth and plunged her tongue against his, hot and demanding. She met his anger and frustration, giving them back to him as pure desire. It wasn't like the languorous kisses they'd shared in the car earlier tonight. It was powerful and wild, all thrust, sound, and fury. A mind-blown, I-think-I'm-gonna-die, soul-shattering kiss.

Somewhere outside of their small closet, which had grown hot with their passion, a voice called out. They ignored it.

He still held her by the hip and by the head as they continued the hard, completely unfiltered kiss. He wasn't hurting her, but he *was* keeping her exactly where he wanted her. She couldn't have moved if she'd tried.

Jess had never known how she would feel about being dominated, but the hint of it now thrilled her. She trusted him. Despite his occasionally gruff exterior, inside Reece was a protector. He would never hurt a woman. Besides, she had nowhere else she wanted to be, and she didn't want him going anywhere, either. To ensure he didn't, she reached around and grabbed his fine, taut ass, tugging him toward her, moving her feet apart to make room for him.

"Oh, Reece," she groaned into his mouth when she felt how perfectly he fit there, in the warm space at the top of her thighs. He thrust against her, and she cried out as his powerful erection hit her in the perfect spot to make her even more crazy and wet.

"Say it," he ordered as he moved his mouth down to press a hot, wet kiss on the nape of her neck. He scraped his teeth across her pulse point, and she shivered with the need to have his mouth in other places. "Say it, Jessica."

She knew what he wanted. What he was waiting for. The ball was in her court, and she had to call the play. She didn't even have to think about it.

"Game on."

That was all it took. Reece came back to her mouth for another hot kiss as he reached for her dress and yanked it up to her waist. This wasn't going to be slow and sexy, all strokes and slides. It would be hot and hard, fast and illicit. A wild fuck to slake the desperate hunger for the time being. Jesus, she was out of her mind with excitement.

He reached up and hooked his fingers in the lacy panties, yanking them down until they puddled around her ankles. Kicking them out of the way, she cried out at the feel of his hand between her legs, his fingers dipping between her swollen folds to test how ready she was.

"So wet. So hot," he grunted, burying his face in her neck as his body shook.

He stroked her clit, firmly, expertly, and Jess came so fast and so hard her legs went weak. He didn't slow down at all, plunging a finger into her vagina, hard and deep. She gasped, clinging to his shoulders as she arched toward his hand.

"More," she groaned, cooing as he gave her what she wanted—another finger, another plunge, a bite on her neck as he lifted a hand to tug her breast out of the strapless bra.

As he tweaked her nipple, she reached for his groin. He wasn't, thankfully, wearing a belt, and she went right for the top button. Her hands shook when she realized his damn pants were designer and had a long row of buttons, rather than a zipper.

He worked them open like a pro, flicking them with one hand while he continued to finger fuck her with the other. Then he shoved the trousers down, and he was free, his big, steely cock springing into her palm.

Jess gasped at the power, squeezing it, wanting it. Wanting it *now*. No more fooling around, no foreplay necessary. They'd been building up to this since the minute she'd felt his eyes on her from across the crowded gallery. She was just patient enough to watch as he yanked a condom from his jacket pocket—*jacket pocket? Seriously?* This was one confident guy. Not that she gave a damn at this particular moment.

Gripping her waist, her dress bunched around it, he lifted her high. Jess leaned back against the wall, opening her legs and wrapping them around his lean hips. "Now, damn it."

He came into her with one hard, powerful thrust,

groaning with pleasure as all her softest, silkiest parts opened in welcome. Jess wasn't quite as discreet, and the scream she let out wasn't a bit quiet. He reacted quickly, covering her mouth with his, kissing her hungrily.

She wished she'd yanked his shirt off. She wanted to scratch him, bite him, and writhe so hard against him they would meld together as one being. But she had to settle for cries and whimpers as he pulled out and then slammed into her again, driving himself up into her core, where no one had ever reached her before. Another orgasm exploded from her sex to her soul, rollicking and roaring in a jubilant dance through her entire body.

"God, Jessica, how I've wanted you," he muttered as he watched her come, obviously feeling her clench and squeeze him deep inside. "Since the minute I saw you."

She didn't so much float back from the orgasm as slam down to meet another delicious thrust. "If only you'd bothered to come downstairs and say hello, we could have been doing this every day for weeks."

"Don't torture me, woman." He groaned. "Even my cock could weep at the thought."

"So let it."

Naughty whispers faded away as his thrusts got faster and more frantic. It didn't take long before he let out a guttural groan, buried his face in her neck, and went still. She felt him pulsing deep inside her and sagged in his arms, exhausted, thrilled, sated, and wondering when they could do it again.

"Hate to tell you this…"

He instantly tensed, looking into her eyes.

"I'm going to have to insist you do that to me again soon."

His hard laughter was louder than her sob of disappointment as he drew out of her and let her down. "Can we get into a bed first?"

She leaned up to kiss him softly. "Maybe the back seat of a limo?"

Just like that, he began to harden again. She almost collapsed. "Let's get the hell out of here."

They quickly straightened themselves up as much as possible in a closet, giggling like teens who'd gone at it right below the noses of the adults. Finally, they emerged from the closet into the dark hallway. They paused to look at each other to make sure there were no telltale signs of what they'd been up to. Ha. Fat chance.

His tux was wrinkled, one of the buttons on his shirt missing. His hair looked like he'd stuck his finger in a socket, and she smoothed it as best she could.

Her own hair was tangled—her little comb useless against the twist of his fingers. Plus her dress hung crookedly. She suspected the hem had torn. Emily would kill her, but she might have to do a bit of sewing repair on it.

"Worth it," he said, brushing his lips against hers.

"So worth it," she replied.

As they began walking, hand in hand, she had to make sure he got the message she had followed him to deliver before they'd been so deliciously distracted. It mattered that he didn't think he couldn't trust her to know when to say something and when to remain silent.

"I don't want to rip off any scabs, but I really do want you to know how sorry I am about what happened earlier."

"I shouldn't have taken it out on you." He sighed. "I react badly when I see Steve Baker."

"I assume it's because of your sister?"

His next step might have had a hitch, but he ignored it and kept walking. "Haven't you figured it out yet? Everything goes back to my sister."

His entire life was tied to that night in the Atlanta hotel. Everything before it had been lost. That which came after had made him the man he was now. She wondered if his brothers were the same way, and imagined they were. Reece was the only one who'd gone back into show business, however. It was probably harder on him than the others.

"In case I've never said it, I'm so sorry about what happened to her."

"So am I." He fell silent for a second, and then admitted, in a low voice, "Despite the stories, Steve didn't get her hooked on drugs. It wasn't his fault, and he got a bad rap for it."

Her turn to miss a step. Reece paused to steady her and they stopped dead in the middle of the hall. "I thought that was why there was bad blood between you."

"No bad blood. I don't blame Steve. He's just a reminder I could live without."

Of course he was, as she'd suspected earlier. Now, hearing Reece didn't hate the man, she felt better. She wished the wound wasn't still so raw he couldn't even stand to be in the room with Baker, but she knew people reacted to loss in different ways.

"Do me a favor. If we run into him again, don't bring up the past."

There was no *please*. He didn't say the word. But he'd uttered a plea all the same. Her heart twisted. She knew this man better than she'd ever expected to. There was a vulnerability to Reece Winchester, one he almost never showed the world. She'd caught a glimpse of that man in the car earlier. Still, she'd never imagined hearing such loss-inspired pain from him.

"I won't," she said, hating his anguish, yet understanding it, too. *Rachel. Poor damaged, lost Rachel.* God, if she ever lost Liza, she didn't know what she'd do.

"Thank you."

"But, Reece, I have to say this. Holding on to this agony isn't doing you any favors."

A long, slow breath eased out from between his lips. "I know."

"Maybe you could think about letting it go, or even extending an olive branch to Steve. It's probably what Rachel would have wanted."

They reached the double doors leading from hallway B back into hallway A. Right before he opened them, he answered, "Maybe. Better yet, maybe he'll go back to Europe soon and I won't have to do anything at all."

As they entered the front hallway, a loud rumble of chatter, champagne-inspired laughter, and music assaulted them. Nobody appeared to notice as they slipped back into the crowd, which was a good thing. She'd drawn enough jealous stares tonight. Now that she actually deserved them, having spent an amazing interlude with the sexiest freaking man she'd ever known, they might sting more. Especially since she *looked* like she deserved them.

Stepping close to him, she whispered, "By the way, I have a headache."

"What?"

"Use me as an excuse. I have a headache and we can't stay for long goodbyes."

Nodding and putting a warm hand on the small of her back—instantly arousing her again—he led her toward the atrium that served as the hotel lobby. As she'd expected, once they were spotted, he was stopped every few feet. Her imaginary headache might have been a brain tumor, considering how gushingly sympathetic people were once they heard the excuse. If she'd had to stay five minutes more, and be offered any more sure-fire homeopathic remedies, she'd probably have gotten a migraine for real. Fortunately, they finally did get past the crowd, nearing the exit.

"I'll have the car brought around," he said, appearing as relieved as she felt.

"Okay." Thinking about how long it might be before they got to wherever they were going tonight—even if just for a long, *long* drive, she said, "You know, while you do that, I think I'll go to the ladies' room."

He brushed a strand of hair off her cheek, his finger-tips gliding gently across her temple. "While you're there, you might want to put a cold cloth on your fore-head. I suspect you'll want to get rid of your headache quickly. Before we get into the car."

A glimmer of sensual knowledge appeared in his eyes, and she sighed, knowing exactly what was going to happen there: everything they had done in the closet. Plus many more deliciously wicked things they had not.

Quivering thinking about it, Jessica began to walk back the way they'd come. They'd been close to the ladies' room, and she should have used it then. She'd just been distracted.

Long before she got near the facilities, however, she saw a line winding out the door and down the hall. There was no corresponding line of men. Typical.

Noticing the woman she'd flipped off earlier, and not wanting to deal with any nonsense, or with the line, she considered whether she really needed the pit stop.

"There's another one down the hall of the east wing," a passing woman said, apparently noticing her less-than-enthused expression. "It's empty—no one waiting at all."

About to voice her thanks, realizing there was at least one nice, helpful person around, she saw she couldn't. The woman had melted into the crowd. Jess had gotten only a glimpse of long, coarse, dark hair with gray streaks.

Heading back the way she'd come, Jess stopped to let Reece know where she was going. Of course, in the ninety seconds she'd been gone, he'd been cornered by a famous actor. Even from several feet away, she could hear the man angling for a role.

"I'm sorry to interrupt," she said, lifting a shaky hand to her temple. "Is the car here yet? I think this headache is turning into a migraine."

Taking the hint, the actor asked Reece to call him

to schedule lunch, looked at her and suggested the best homeopathic guy downtown, and then left them alone.

"Thanks for the rescue. I didn't expect you back so quickly."

"I never made it to the ladies' room. The line was too long with catty women I wouldn't call ladies. I'm going to go to the other side of the hotel where I hear it's much less crowded."

"I'm glad you stopped on the way. Your timing was impeccable. That guy never lets up."

She smirked. "And that's different from everyone else here...how? These people are so pushy they might as well be on construction sites moving dirt around."

Chuckling, he said, "Now go. And I swear I'll get the car here this time."

Before they parted again, however, she heard a man's voice say, "Congratulations, Reece."

Good grief, were they ever going to get out of here?

About to go into full-on migraine tears mode, she hesitated when a broad smile broke over Reece's face. Wondering who'd inspired the warm look, she saw an older man, probably in his early sixties, tall and handsome, with thick, graying brown hair.

"Dad," Reece said, and she almost fell over. "What are you doing here?"

Of course he had a father. Everyone had a father. But his father was *here*? Now? And, judging by his surprised expression, Reece hadn't even known?

"Why don't you tell a guy you're getting an award?"

"It's not a big deal, really. Why didn't *you* let me know you were coming?"

"Not a big deal, says my kid the philanthropist," the older man said as he opened his arms and drew Reece in for a bear hug.

The embrace was so affectionate, a living example of parental love reciprocated. Given what Reece had told her about the way his father and aunt had taken the boys away from the darkness and scandal of their childhoods, she'd been prepared to admire his dad. Now that she'd seen the happiness in Reece's face, she could easily love him.

"Your speech was great. Brought tears to my eyes."

"I can't believe you didn't come up and sit with us for the whole thing."

"Ahh, I didn't have a ticket. I snuck in the back to watch your speech. Been waiting for you to leave—I knew you wouldn't stay long. I was afraid somebody'd kick me out if I let on I was there without an invite." His brow furrowed. "Then you disappeared for a while and I was afraid you'd snuck out the back. Not that I'd've blamed you."

Feeling her cheeks warm, Jess waited to see how Reece would respond to his unexplained disappearance.

He merely gaped. "You snuck in? Are you kidding? I could have gotten you a ticket."

"If you'd bothered to tell me about it, Eddie, I would have asked you to!" The old man cuffed Reece's shoulder, and she almost giggled.

Then she realized what he had said. "Eddie?"

"Don't you dare," he muttered.

"Ahh, this must be the pretty girl who was with you when some lunatic shot at you," his father said, turning to face her. He examined her carefully, head to toe, not revealing much. Then, slowly, he nodded, and extended his hand. "Edward Winchester. I'm very pleased to meet you. Especially since my lughead son hasn't told me anything about you."

Lughead. Eddie. There was almost too much to grasp, and she wanted to both laugh and hug the older man. A smile on her lips, she shook his calloused, working-man's hand. "I'm Jessica Jensen, Mr. Winchester. It's *so* nice to meet you."

"Call me Edward."

They talked for a few minutes, some father-son banter the *National Enquirer* would probably love to hear. She listened, and then realized the men might want a moment alone.

"I was about to go to the ladies' room."

Reece nodded. "While I was supposed to call for the car. Dad, join us."

"In the ladies'?"

Reece sighed as his father wagged his brows.

"No way," the older man added. "I met a nice hostess at the restaurant upstairs where I waited out this shindig. I think I'll go back up there for some pie."

Jessica and Reece looked at each other at the same instant, and she felt a giggle rise to her lips. "You know, we were just talking about pie a little while ago."

"Well, why don't you two join me then?"

"Thanks, Dad, but we don't want to cramp your style." Reece's eyes—those eyes that had once seemed predatory to her and now looked warm—twinkled, and his devastatingly sexy smile flashed. "Besides, Jessica doesn't really like pie."

"I didn't say that."

"Oh, have you discovered a liking for pie all of a sudden?"

She licked her lips. "Actually, pie might just have become my favorite dessert. I'm looking forward to trying all sorts of varieties."

"Well, then, you'd better get busy tasting."

Mr. Winchester—*call me Edward*—looked back and forth between them, not understanding, but not asking what they were talking about. Nor did he ask again if they wanted to join him; the man could obviously read the signals. His smile said he approved.

"It was lovely meeting you, Edward," she said.

He put his hands on her shoulders and drew her in to kiss her cheek. While close, he whispered, "I like seeing my son smile. He doesn't do it often enough. So thank you."

Squeezing his arm, and promising Reece she'd only be a minute, she took another peek at the line coming out of the nearest restroom and immediately headed for the other one. The hotel lobby was massive, with enormous potted plants, flowers, and fountains. But it wasn't hard to navigate. The building was shaped like a squared-off U, with the elegant entrance at the bottom, and hallways forming the sides.

As she passed the main doors, she could hear voices rising like a giant swarm of bees from outside. They would once again have to run a gauntlet to get to the car. She wondered how many paparazzi would take pictures of her mussed hair and uneven dress. Fortunately, she had a few minutes to prepare herself.

Reaching the other wing, and turning up the hall, she realized the woman who'd given her the tip had been right. It was deserted, and actually a little creepy, considering the other side of the hotel was a zoo. There were many conference rooms, none of them in use at this time of night. Spying a sign toward the back of the corridor, she headed toward it and pushed inside, immediately seeing the outer vestibule area was empty, too. No gossipy women sat together in front of the makeup mirror whispering as they touched up their lipstick. So she didn't have to worry one of them had a nail file with which they intended to stab her in the eye.

The interior, functional part of the ladies' room appeared to be empty, too. No attendant was on duty, so she stood at the sink and carefully splashed cold water on her cheeks. Not wanting to keep Reece—and their limo rendezvous—waiting, she went into one of the private wood-slat-framed stalls. If only she hadn't had sparkling water with dinner and champagne afterward. The dress was formfitting and a challenge to get out of. *Probably why Reece just tossed it up rather than taking it off.*

Mmm.

The downside was that designers never thought about women needing to pee in tiny cubicles.

Though she'd expected to be alone, a click came from next door. She hadn't heard anyone enter the bathroom or walk across it. The other person had caught her off guard. Worse, she had ignored bathroom etiquette by taking the stall right beside Jess's, rather than one of the several other unoccupied ones.

Well, maybe the other woman hadn't realized somebody else was in here. The cubicles were made for privacy, the doors and partitions going almost all the way to the floor. So she couldn't have seen Jess's feet or the hem of her dress.

"Bitch."

Jess stiffened, not sure she'd actually heard the word. Had someone called her a name, or was the other occupant talking to herself? Or had she merely imagined it?

Confused, she strained to hear. But it wasn't another whisper that caught her attention. It was a smell. A powerful, chemical scent wafted into the compartment. She noticed it with one deep inhalation. Her dress fell from her hands as she began to cough. Her throat and nose stung as if burned, and her eyes instantly filled with tears. Gagging, she covered her mouth with her hand even as the fumes started to make her feel lightheaded.

She could think of only one explanation. A hotel employee must have begun her nightly cleaning. The gala was taking place on the other side of the hotel; this side was totally empty. Of course she wouldn't expect anyone to be using this bathroom, and had apparently dumped a gallon of bleach or ammonia into the next toilet.

"Wait, I'm in here!" she called, risking opening her mouth again. She immediately regretted it as her tongue tasted chemicals. She also suddenly felt dizzy and confused, knowing she should be doing something—*getting out*—but her movements were sluggish.

She shook her head, hard, clearing it briefly, and

held her breath. Reaching for the lock, she twisted it, and pulled on the stall door.

It didn't move.

The door that had swung so freely a few moments ago was now stuck or jammed.

Before she could even wonder why, she heard a gurgle. Liquid suddenly streamed underneath the ribbon of space beneath the bottom slat of the partition. It glided toward her shoes and the hem of her dress. Yanking handfuls of fabric out of harm's way, she backed into the other wall.

"Stop, please. I'm stuck. I can't breathe!" Since she'd instinctively taken a breath before crying out, she quickly began to cough.

The employee didn't apologize or call out reassurances. There was more splashing, as if a huge bucket had been pushed over. Harsh, abrasive liquid streamed in even harder.

She had nowhere else to go; there was no retreat from the puddle now extending to the tips of her shoes. When it rose above the sole and touched her toes, her skin began to tingle, and then to burn. She let out a shocked cry, more surprised than pained, confused about why the woman wasn't responding. Was she wearing earbuds, listening to loud music while she worked?

Then the voice came again, a throaty whisper. "You deserve whatever you get."

Understanding slammed into her fume-muddled brain as fear assaulted her.

That wasn't a janitor. There was no misunderstanding by a cleaning crew about a bathroom still in use.

She'd been followed in here deliberately. She was being targeted by someone—the whisper was deep, but it sounded like a woman trying to disguise her voice.

Jess tried to escape again, pulling hard, and then pounding against the slatted door with her fists to try to break out. Although her hands hurt from the blows, nothing moved. Something was definitely holding the door closed. Someone had her right where they wanted her.

From next door came one more comment. "See if he thinks you're pretty now."

The malevolence in the voice chilled her blood, and she was momentarily frozen into utter immobility. Then something alerted her to movement above, and she jerked her head up.

A plastic jug. A rubber-gloved hand.

She knew what was coming.

Pure instinct made her fall to the floor and curl around the commode, covering her head, burying her face against porcelain. She drew in lungfuls of rank air— enough to scream for help with all her might, though she doubted anyone was close enough to hear.

Reece, oh God, please come!

Liquid began to dribble down—cold and shocking. She screamed again as the thick drops landed on her ankle. Then came more, and she tucked in tighter. Splashes soon reached her thigh—soaking quickly through the fabric of her dress.

Then the heavens opened up and a chemical rainstorm poured down on her like a poisonous, biblical flood.

CHAPTER 10

Although the sound of a woman's scream from somewhere nearby would always be shocking, this shrill cry of terror sent ice straight to Reece's heart. *Jessica. That's Jessica.*

He didn't know how he could be so sure of that, but he was. His feet were moving—running—before he'd even had time to evaluate why he was so certain the brief, horrified cry had come from her beautiful mouth.

"What was that?" his father called after him, as the hotel lobby began to buzz.

Someone else yelled, "Did somebody scream?"

God, yes, it was a scream. It was coming from the hallway down which Jessica had disappeared, looking for a restroom.

He raced around the corner, his feet pounding, his heart set on *Detonate*. Entering a shadowy corridor lined with unused conference and banquet rooms, as long and eerie as the one in the hotel from the fucking *Shining*, he heard another noise ahead of him. Far ahead.

It was an alarm. One of those emergency exit doors had been opened somewhere in the depths of this quiet wing. Someone was either escaping...or perhaps dragging another person out of the hotel.

"Stop!" he yelled, not knowing anything but fearing everything. After what had happened at the gallery, his mind went to dark places. An abduction? An assault?

Finally seeing the sign for the ladies' room, he noticed a strange, chemical smell. Although part of him leaned toward running down to the exit door, whose alarm still rang in a slow whine, he couldn't pass by the last place he'd known Jessica to be. He slammed against the door, bursting inside, and was immediately slapped in the face and the lungs with the acrid reek of bleach.

"Jessica!"

Hearing a faint, low groan, he crossed the lounge area in two long strides. As soon as he entered the main bathroom he began to cough—the bleach vapors were brutally strong in here. His lungs screamed, his eyes leaked water, and his mouth began to tingle.

He didn't know where the smell was coming from, but he immediately saw one of the wooden cubicle doors was barricaded. Someone had looped a rope around the outer handle, tying it to the next one. Whoever was inside wouldn't have been able to pull it open.

His heart thumped as he let himself imagine who was inside.

Reece didn't even mess with the rope; it was tied in knots that would take precious time to undo. Instead, he punched the center of the door, making a large hole.

And there she was.

Seeing Jessica curled like a comma around the

commode, he almost exploded in rage. Judging by the locked door, and the reeking fluid dripping down the wall, it had been poured down on her, leaving her with nowhere to go but the floor.

Someone was going to pay. Dearly.

He hammered the remaining slats out of his way and stepped through the hole, crouching beside her. "Jessica?" How the hell long had she been here breathing these vapors? Judging by the chlorine bleach splashing around his shoes and soaking the color out of her dress—*and her skin, all that exposed skin*—too fucking long. "I'm here."

She turned her head and looked up at him, her face splotchy, her eyes as red as her dress had once been. "Reece?" The word was barely a croak.

"I've got you," he said, scooping her into his arms. "Hang on, Jess."

He shouldered away more of the broken door and maneuvered her through it. He'd taken one step out when a uniformed hotel employee burst into the bathroom, accompanied by Reece's heaving father. The young clerk immediately put a hand to his mouth. "What's going—"

"Call 911," Reece snapped. "Do it now."

Not needing to be told twice to get away from the poisonous air, the young man raced out. Reece's father remained, his arm thrown over his mouth and nose, determined to help.

"Come on, we have to get her out of here."

His father nodded, going ahead of him to open the door. "Is she okay?"

"No." They hit the hallway, where the air was clearer. "Help me get this off her."

With his father bracing Jessica's limp, half-conscious body, Reece ripped the sopping dress off her and threw it aside. Seeing how reddened her skin was, from head to toe, he growled with rage. He wanted to commit murder.

"Take her in there, son. We need to wet her down."

Seeing his father open the men's room door, he carried her in. His dad went right to the nearest sink and turned on the tap, splashing water all over the marble countertop. Reece gently laid her on it, and got another tap going. As his father began to splash huge handfuls of water on Jessica's feet and legs, Reece reached around to unfasten her bra—once entirely red, now dotted with white—and pulled it off her. Every inch of skin revealed was splotchy; this fabric had been much tighter on her skin and had pressed bleach into her very pores.

"Bastard," he snarled as he also removed her underwear. His father averted his eyes but continued to soak her feet and calves.

Once she was wet from head to foot, Reece dispensed liquid soap into his hands and gently washed her face, her neck, her chest, and her arms. He struggled to remain calm as his hands shook with worry and with sheer mind-blackening rage.

She started to shiver. Her lips turned blue, and her teeth chattered. Jessica had been doused with chemicals, was being drowned in barely lukewarm water, and was lying naked on a cold countertop.

"I'm sorry, Jess. I know you're cold, but we have to get these chemicals off you."

"You...you..."

"Don't try to talk. An ambulance is on the way."

"But you..."

Knowing she wasn't going to rest until she'd had her say, he bent close so he could hear the words she was so determined to whisper. "What is it? What do you want to tell me?"

A cough, and then a faint, weak smile. "You...called me...Jess."

Torn between wanting to laugh and wanting to rip apart the person who'd hurt her, he heard shouts from down the hall. His father stopped what he was doing and hurried to the door to direct the rescue workers.

Although he didn't give a damn about anything except her well-being, he knew Jessica would prefer not to be laid out naked in front of a bunch of EMTs. He suspected when she was more aware, and remembered his dad had seen her that way, she'd be pretty mortified. The last thing he wanted to do was cause her more distress. Plus, knowing the place was crawling with paparazzi, and fully aware some of them had no morals or decency, he also feared she would be photographed as she was carried out of the hotel.

"Can you sit up, sweetheart?"

Nodding, she blinked and watched as he whipped off his tuxedo jacket. He lifted one of her arms and began to slide it in.

"Don't...ruin it," she mumbled.

"Jesus, woman," he said, unable to hold in a laugh, shocked and relieved she was already back to being her independent, bossy self.

She allowed him to wrap his jacket around her, and clenched it tight, some strength having returned to her limbs. Burrowing her face in the collar, she stopped shaking, as if finally warming up.

A second later, his father burst back in, accompanied by three emergency responders. After Reece quickly explained what happened, the one in charge, who introduced himself as Zack, said, "Juan, would you put a respirator on and check out the other bathroom? We need to know what chemicals were used, especially if it was a mix, like bleach and ammonia."

Reece felt his blood chill, knowing the combination could be deadly. At first, he'd thought someone had played a *really* ugly prank on Jessica. Now he had to wonder if they'd actually had murder in mind.

Since that night at the gallery, he'd assumed he had been the target of the shooter. He had barely considered her stalking ex to be a serious suspect. "Stupid," he muttered, angry at himself, wondering if the person who'd shot at them had taken another chance to kill her tonight.

Forcing his attention back on Jessica, he held her pale, cold hand as the lead paramedic, an older African American man with kind eyes and gentle hands, quickly examined her. He checked her breathing, pulse, and blood pressure, not revealing by word or expression what he was thinking.

By the time he was finished, Juan, who'd gone to investigate, came back in. He peeled a plastic mask off his face. "I found four jugs of bleach. Nothing else— including ammonia."

Thank God.

Zack began to pack up his blood pressure cuff. "You did a smart thing washing those chemicals off her right away," he said. "She's obviously got a redhead's skin— sensitive. It's why she's so blotchy. Getting splashed with household bleach doesn't even affect some people."

Lucky her.

Juan cleared his throat. "I should have said it wasn't just the household stuff. This was commercial-grade, industrial-strength chlorine bleach.

Zack's brow furrowed, his worry visibly increasing. "That increases the danger of burns in her throat, lungs, and nasal passages. We need to get her in right away. Let's get her loaded up."

"I'm going with you."

The man opened his mouth to argue. Reece's hard stare said he would not be denied.

"All right."

Jessica had already been moved onto a gurney for examination. Before strapping her in, Zack glanced down at her long legs, stained with bumpy rashes, against her pale skin and the stark white sheet. "Are you cold? Let's cover you up and keep you warm."

"Thanks," she mumbled. She smiled weakly. "Don't... want to give those jackals with cameras a-any cr-crotch shots."

The strength of the woman.

The paramedic chuckled as he pulled a concealing sheet over her, from toes to neck, and prepared to fasten the restraint straps.

"Wait," she whispered, her eyes flickering as she looked for Reece. "Take... all off."

He bent closer. "Take what, Jess?"

She reached a shaking hand up toward her neck. "Jewelry. Borrowed."

He smiled at her and pushed her hand down below the sheet. "No, gorgeous. It's not."

If she were well and had use of that powerful voice of hers, he knew she'd be giving him hell. But she was in pain, and confused, so she merely closed her eyes and let herself be fastened onto the restraint straps.

That scared the shit out of him, frankly.

"We'll keep you safe, ma'am," said Zack. "We'll protect your privacy as much as we can. You'll be at the hospital real soon."

Nodding his appreciation, Reece asked, "Where did you park?"

"Out front. I'm sorry, if we'd known who you were . . ."

"There's no help for it now. Let's go."

They headed down the corridor, his father hanging back, not wanting to be in the way. "Dad," Reece said over his shoulder, "my limo's outside. I'll have the driver take you home."

"You sure you don't want me to come to the hospital?"

"Thanks, but I think we're in for a long, rough night. Not just with her injuries, but with the press. I'd rather not give them anything else to report."

Although he'd worked as an electrician most of his life, his father knew this world. He'd seen his children living it. He'd saved them from it. So he didn't argue. "Call me with updates."

"I will."

Hotel security, and some uniformed police officers who'd responded with paramedics, surrounded them as they neared the lobby. Looking for a familiar face, he spotted a young officer he believed he'd met before. "Officer, uh…"

"Wilhelm, sir."

"Right, Wilhelm. Do you know who my brother is?"

The rookie nodded, looking nervous. "Uh, sure."

"He's in the Seventy-Seventh. Can you give him a call and tell him what's going on? I'd like him to look at this."

"Uh, the Seventy-Seventh is…"

Reece didn't want to hear about precincts and jurisdictions. "Just call him. Please."

"Okay. But, uh, I think one of our guys is gonna want to talk to you, too."

"I'll be at the hospital. He can find me there."

The young cop looked like he was about to protest. Reece ignored him, bending over to whisper to Jessica. "We're about to go outside. Stay strong, Jess. It'll be over in a minute."

Pinkish tears had been coming out of her red eyes since the moment he'd found her. But she blinked rapidly, as if fearing things were about to get worse.

He gripped her hand. "I've got you."

"Can you… pull the sheet over my head?"

Juan was pushing the gurney, someone else pulling it. But Zack, who walked by her side, ready to provide emergency services the moment they became necessary, heard her and promised, "Nobody's gonna bother you, miss." Looking around, he barked, "Form a wall!"

Three cops jogged over, taking up positions on either side of the gurney. Realizing they were providing a barrier to prevent anyone from getting close to Jessica, physically or with their cameras, he nodded his thanks. He took the fourth spot, by Jessica's right hip, and put a hand on her arm. Only a photographer on top of a van or a building could have gotten a clear shot at her.

When they reached the hospital, Jessica was taken for tests, including X-rays of her lungs. Reece was left alone in a waiting room making calls. After reaching her sister, the second call was to a doctor friend. He knew he was waking Jamal up in the middle of the night, but he needed somebody to talk him down off the ledge. Since reconnecting as young men, they'd remained in touch, and Reece considered him a real friend.

Jamal said words like *chemical pneumonia*, *chest pain*, *delirium*, and *neurological damage*.

Reece lost his shit.

After his friend gave him the names of the top doctors in Los Angeles, Reece started making demands. Sometimes it was good to have name recognition, especially when you wanted to get an internationally renowned internist from Cedars-Sinai out of bed in the middle of the night.

"What happened?" Liza burst into the room, a petite tornado wearing sweatpants, a long sleep shirt with a teddy bear on the front, and flip-flops. With wild hair and wilder eyes, she looked like she'd jumped out of bed and raced to the hospital ten seconds after Reece's call.

He didn't blame her one bit.

"Where's my sister?"

He quickly explained, not sparing any details. Reece had played this scene; he knew it by heart. When a sibling was hurt or in trouble, desperation and anguish replaced thought and rationality. So going over everything, step by step, was a way of keeping Liza focused and calm.

His technique wasn't entirely successful, however. When he told her about Jessica asking if her head could be covered by a sheet to avoid the photographers, Liza burst into tears. They streamed in rivulets down her cheeks; she didn't even try to wipe them off, instead putting her face in her hands and weeping quietly for a solid minute.

Eventually, not even looking up, she mumbled, "So you're saying somebody intentionally trapped her?"

He thought of the rope around the door handles. Jessica clutching a goddamn toilet. The red skin, the sopping clothes, the hoarse voice, and the confusion in her watering eyes.

You called me Jess.

"Yes."

She wrapped her arms around her middle and leaned forward, as if feeling sick, or in pain. Probably both. "Where is she now? Can I see her?"

He rubbed a weary hand over his face, wanting the doctors to hurry up and let him know how she was. The waiting was driving him crazy, and he knew it would do the same to her sister. "They're checking her out to see if the vapors caused any internal damage."

More tears. "Oh, Jess, baby. Why? How can this be happening?"

"I shouldn't have let her go anywhere alone." Never had he said truer words.

Her head snapped up. "No, you shouldn't have. She should never have gone out with you tonight in the first place. Why does she keep getting hurt around you? Who, exactly, have you pissed off, Mr. Winchester?"

Reece didn't reply, knowing he deserved her anger. This attack, like the first, had surely been directed at him. He'd wondered at first why someone with a grudge against him would go after Jessica, and came up with one possible reason. Maybe an enemy of his had realized he was involved with her—he was already falling for her like he'd never fallen for anyone—and wanted to punish him by hurting Jessica.

If so, their plan was working. He didn't think he would ever forgive himself.

"I don't know who did this, but I will keep her safe until whoever did is caught."

"No, *I'll* keep her safe. You stay away from her. Jess gets nothin' but pain when she's around you."

The accusation from the person closest to Jessica—who had already come to mean so much to *him*—stung. "Maybe you're right. But I have the resources to ensure no one gets near her again, and to be certain this case is worked on night and day until it's solved."

She blew out a slow breath, nodding. "I guess you do. But if you really want what's best for her, after this is taken care of and she's out of danger, you'll stop bringing your baggage into her life and go away."

Reece crossed the room to look out the window into the dark night. He knew Liza was right. People got hurt

around him. Most importantly, Jessica got hurt around
him. If there were any justice, he would be the one in
the hospital, and she would be fine. Looking at his history, at the crimes of his past and the secrets he'd kept,
Reece figured if anyone deserved some retribution, it
was him.

She most definitely did not.

You called me Jess.

"Do you have any idea who is doing this?" Liza asked.

He faced her. "Not really, though the police were
already chasing down leads from the shooting."

He hadn't seen Sid at tonight's event, and honestly, this
attack didn't seem like something that slimeball would
have done. He seemed more the take-a-wild-shot or club-
somebody-in-the-head-from-behind type. The trap set
for Jessica had been thought out, not to mention vicious.
Someone had stood on the toilet in the next cubicle,
looked down at her, and doused her with potentially
lethal chemicals. Such an act screamed personal.

There was another possibility, one he hadn't seriously
considered before he'd found her in that bathroom. "Tell
me what you know about this Johnny character."

"Johnny...you mean her ex? What does he have to
do with it? He's out of the picture."

"Not entirely," he said, realizing Jessica hadn't told
her sister about the obsessive man's recent phone call.
He didn't want to betray a confidence, but with Jessica
in danger, he needed to know everything. So he filled
her in, admitting Jessica herself had wondered if he had
been the person who shot at them last week.

Liza's hand went to her mouth and she staggered

back, collapsing into a chair. The fear mixed with anger on her face told him how serious a possibility this could be. "That bastard."

"She wouldn't tell me his full name," he bit out.

"Dixon. Johnny Dixon. Last I heard he was living in Anaheim."

He made a mental note, already trying to decide whether to ask Rowan or Raine to track this guy down. Rowan was a cop. He usually did things by the book.

Raine did not.

"Do you really think he could be the one after her?"

"It's possible. He stalked her. Is he really capable of hurting her?"

"Oh hell yes."

"What did she ever see in him?"

"Jessica met him and saw this big, good-looking country boy. Honest and open." Liza sneered. "I saw somebody I thought was playing a part and was probably a fucking racist."

He gripped the back of a chair, his fingers digging into the tired upholstery, wondering if Liza had been proved right. Judging by everything he'd heard about this Johnny Dixon, he suspected she had been. "What happened?"

"He wore the nice, considerate boyfriend mask for a while, maybe a year. But it started to slip. When she tried to pull away, he got really mean. Guilt-tripped her, beat her down."

Glowering, he came closer. "You mean he..."

Liza snorted. "No man'd dare smack Jessica around. If she didn't kill him, I would."

She eyed him steadily, asking a question he easily read. It was also easy for him to answer. "I'd cut my hand off before I'd harm a hair on her head."

As they continued the stare-off, he didn't say another word, wondering what it would take to get Liza to trust him. The more he talked to her, the more he respected her. He wanted that trust, though he doubted he'd ever get it.

Finally she nodded. "Okay then. We understand each other."

"I think so."

That didn't mean she liked him or would ever trust him with her sister again. At least she believed him when he said he wasn't an abusive pig. It was something, anyway.

"Johnny never understood anything except getting what he wanted. He worked on her emotions. She's got a vulnerable streak. Has she told you anything about her childhood?"

"Yes."

Jessica had mentioned it the night they met. Over the past couple of days at work, he'd gotten her to talk a little more. It hadn't been hard to get the picture. Spunky, feisty kid who thinks she's pretty tough gets put in the system and struggles to survive for two years while she's taught what toughness really is.

"So you probably know why she tries to be so strong. But she has a really soft heart, and he knew how to work on it. He made her feel guilty, threatened to hurt himself, or both of them. He also worked hard to steal her self-confidence."

"I think she found it again," he said, his tone dry.

Her sister might have smiled, reminding him of the one thing they did have in common: they both cared very much for Jessica Jensen.

"Yeah, she found it," Liza said. "But not until a while after she walked out on that piece of Kentucky-fried shit."

He actually smiled. Liza and Jessica might not look alike, but the sisters were similar in a lot of the best ways. "She told me he didn't take the breakup well."

"Huh-uh. We moved, we changed numbers. He came after her pretty hard." She rolled her eyes. "You can bet who he blamed. Every time he saw me, he let loose with all the N-words he'd been saving up while they were dating."

"The coward," he muttered. Jessica must have hated him for that, and hated herself for bringing such ugliness into her sister's life.

Before Liza could respond, the waiting room door was pushed open. Reece couldn't muster any surprise when he saw his two brothers stride in. His father had probably called them both before the ambulance even left the hotel driveway. A hint of relief hit him dead center when he saw Rowan's furious expression and Raine's serious one.

In times of crisis, Winchesters always stood together. They were a powerful, united wall, like the solid blue one that had blocked Jessica from the view of the press when she was being taken to the ambulance. They'd been that way since they were young and their world had erupted into death and insanity.

For a while, Reece and Rowan had protected their

baby brother, six years younger, from the darkest moments. Eventually they learned Raine had secrets of his own. And while there were still some things they had never talked about—nightmares he and his twin had hidden from the entire world—now the three of them trusted each other like no one else.

Rowan grabbed him for a quick hug. Raine, always more reserved, put a hand on his shoulder.

"How is she?" Rowan asked.

"Being checked out."

"Dad said she was awake and talking when they brought her in?"

"She was conscious."

She was also coughing like she was going to hack up a lung, and covered with rashes. Not to mention dizzy, confused, watery-eyed, terrified, and in pain. But sure, conscious.

You called me Jess.

Realizing Liza was watching from a few feet away, he introduced her to his brothers. He could tell by her expression she hadn't stopped thinking about Jessica's ex, wondering if he could really have done something so hateful to a woman he still insisted he loved. Reece had seen so much of the ugly side of people that he believed anything was possible.

"So what do you need us to do?" asked Raine, direct as usual.

"Keep her safe, first of all."

"No question."

His youngest brother was still all military—disciplined, powerful, strict, and relentless. He looked and carried himself like a soldier. Anyone who remembered the cute, cheeky little kid on a cereal commercial would *never* recognize him as the hard-ass standing before him in camo pants and a black T-shirt.

Rowan cleared his throat.

"What have you got?" Reece asked.

His twin looked back and forth between Reece and Liza. She got the message.

"Excuse me," she said. "I'm going to go get some coffee and try to reach Emily again. She had a show tonight. I know she'll want to be here." She offered to bring back coffee for everyone, but all three brothers declined, with thanks.

After she was gone, Reece asked, "What have you found out?"

"I just got off the phone with the lead detective, who's an old friend," Rowan said. "He's going to let me come in unofficially. He's already requested surveillance footage. Each hallway is completely covered, from several angles. Unless the person who did this is a five-year-old who got in and out through one of the small bathroom windows, we'll see them on the recording."

Raine barked, "How long will it take?"

"The night manager insists they have to get approval from their general manager, who's on vacation," Rowan said with a frown. "If he doesn't respond by morning, we'll get a court order to make them hand it over."

Great. Morning sounded like forever from now. Every minute Reece remained in the dark about Jessica's condition increased his tension. The clock on the wall seemed to be stuck...or moving backward. His famed patience and control both seemed to have deserted him; the longer the night dragged on, the more tense he became.

"I have one more piece of news," Rowan said. "Sid Loman is dead."

Reece's heart stopped beating. "What?"

"His body was found on a side street in Venice Beach a couple of days ago. They didn't identify him until last night. The guys who responded to the first report looked at missing persons cases, but didn't bother searching APBs." He looked and sounded disgusted at the beginner's mistake. "The medical examiner's office thought to do it and put it together right away."

"Cause of death?" asked Raine.

"GSW."

Reece had made enough cop movies to know that meant gunshot wound. "Any chance it was suicide?" *Guilty conscience?*

"Not unless he had a five-foot-long arm that bent backward. The angle of the entry wound says whoever did it was standing above him. Marks indicate he was tasered first."

Tasered and shot down in the street. Reece tried to feel something, but his mind was too focused on Jessica to have much of a reaction to the murder of a former employee. That would probably sound cold to most people; but for Reece, who controlled everything, including his emotions, it was reflex.

You called me Jess.

Swallowing as that control slipped again, he tried to give his full attention to his brother.

"The cops in Venice spent the day looking into this guy's background. He travels a lot to Vegas. Looks like he has a serious gambling habit."

"Any idea who killed him?" asked Raine.

Before he answered, Reece asked another question. "Could his murder have been connected to the gallery shooting?"

"Las Vegas police say they know him. He's in deep with a pretty dangerous bookie. So now Venice is wondering if *he* was the actual target, rather than you."

It was a reasonable assumption. If not for what had happened tonight at the hotel, Reece might even consider it a likely one. But tonight *had* happened. Jessica had been attacked, and it sure hadn't been by a man who'd been dead for days. Unless the two events were completely unrelated, which seemed unlikely, he didn't think the bullet that ruptured the gallery window had been intended for Sid. So why had he stopped one a few days later?

"Maybe he saw something," Reece murmured, rubbing his jaw.

"What do you mean?" asked Rowan.

Reece tried to pull his thoughts together, visualizing Friday night, seeing how it might have played out. *Directing it.* "I fired Sid and told him to get out of the building immediately."

Raine's eyes narrowed as he took in the information. Rowan already knew as much and merely nodded.

"He storms out of the gallery. Instead of going to his car and leaving, he goes out to the beach, needing to walk off the anger. He also needs to stay close because he wants to figure out a way to end run around me and get Sharon to give him his job back."

"Ahhh," said Rowan. Reece knew that his twin was starting to visualize the scene, too.

Raine cut to the chase. "You think Sid saw the shooter, ran and hid, and the guy waited him out and shot him down so he couldn't identify him."

Rowan smirked. "You never could let anybody finish a story."

"It was taking too long."

"You know our brother. He's always writes those long scene descriptions."

"Fuck off," he told them both, not truly annoyed by their badgering. As always, their presence lightened his mental load. That had probably been their intention.

Rowan opened his mouth to reply, but Reece's attention was immediately drawn to a gowned doctor who walked past a window overlooking the corridor, then turned and walked into the waiting room.

"How is she?"

"Are you Miss Jensen's family member?"

Liza, carrying a foam cup of coffee, arrived in time to hear the question. "I'm her sister."

From the beginning, the doctor had come off as unpleasant, especially when he learned Reece had called in someone else, who would be arriving shortly. At Liza's claim, he smirked, appearing skeptical. "*You're* her sister?"

"Don't *even*!" Liza snarled, looking ready to throw her coffee into his face. She was as intimidating as Jessica. "Now answer the question. How is my sister?"

"We've run several tests and are treating what we can. The skin rash is already clearing up, after several more washings. Her eyes have been flushed. The redness is still there, but the watering is slowing down."

"That doesn't sound too bad," said Liza, looking hopeful.

"Unfortunately, being exposed to so much industrial-strength bleach meant she ingested dangerous vapors. She has minor soft tissue damage to the nose, mouth, and throat."

Liza sniffled. "Oh, lord"

Reece put a hand on Liza's shoulder, bracing her. This time, she did not shrug it off.

"For *that*, she only needs rest, antibiotics, and pain medication."

The doctor's inflection told Reece the worst was yet to come. Liza must have realized it, too. She crossed an arm over her chest and put her hand on top of Reece's, gripping tightly.

"The most serious issue is her lung inflammation. In exposure cases like these, patients whose lungs are affected can develop chemical pneumonia, which can be quite serious, sometimes leading to the failure of other organs."

Reece closed his eyes, trying to maintain steady breaths. *In. Out. Stay calm.*

Hands landed on both his shoulders. Rowan and Raine stood behind him, and each one of them was offering the same thing he was providing Liza: a strong hand as a reminder of support.

"We will keep her here for a minimum of thirty-six

hours to watch for the onset of pneumonia." The doctor pursed his lips. "The throat injuries are unfortunate; we had to intubate her."

In. Out. Stay calm.

Hearing Liza sniff, Reece glanced over to see tears trailing down her cheeks. He held her hand tighter, and she gripped his like she was drowning and he was her lifeline.

The doctor was apparently used to ignoring the tears of family members. "She needs to be kept on oxygen, and on IV pain medication and steroids, for a minimum of twenty-four hours. I'm afraid with the throat irritation, the experience isn't going to be pleasant for her, especially when the tube is removed."

How doctors could describe torture as "unpleasant" boggled the mind.

"But it's better to be safe than sorry when dealing with something as tricky as this. We'll keep doing X-rays and breathing tests. As long as nothing more serious appears to be developing, she should be all right to go home in a day or two. She will have to continue checking in to make sure she doesn't develop bronchitis."

"*If* nothing more serious develops," Reece said.

Liza parroted him. "If."

As Liza thanked the doctor, Reece stood still, remaining calm.

At least on the outside.

Inside, he was a roiling, seething mass of anger, confusion...and fear. Though he was someone who prided himself on remaining rational and practically emotionless in most situations, he felt as though he had ingested a chainsaw and was being cut to ribbons inside. He couldn't stop wondering if he was to blame for Jessica's condition. It would have been bad if she had been hurt in an accident. But for it to possibly have been because someone was after *him* was something he wasn't sure he could get over.

He kept going over the doctor's warnings. *Soft tissue damage. Chemical pneumonia. Organ failure.* Below all of those fears, though, was a steady refrain that had been repeating in his mind, all night. The four words she'd whispered crept out of his memory to accuse him, console him, and challenge him.

Their echo had also made him face something, a truth that had been dancing around in his mind. He didn't just care about Jessica Jensen. He was falling in love with her. He'd never been in love before, which was probably why he hadn't even recognized it as it happened. But seeing her on the bathroom floor and hearing what she was going through had him ready to cut out his own lungs to give to her.

What he felt for her was hard, it was uncomfortable, and it was painful. It was also completely consuming, which was why he'd begun to suspect it was love. He had no idea how she felt about him, other than strong attraction, but it didn't matter, as long as she was all right.

You called me Jess.

Yes, he had, after being a stubborn ass from the minute he'd laid eyes on her.

He wouldn't make that mistake again, as long as she

pulled through. He'd call her whatever she wanted him to, and be glad to have the chance.

As long as she didn't hate his guts for putting her in danger.

* * *

Maisy sat alone in her mansion—close to where Reece's place was being rebuilt—waiting for news coverage about what had happened at the hotel. She hated waiting; she'd spent too much time doing it when she was young. She'd waited for visiting day, for bland meals, for medicine. Mostly she'd waited to *get out*.

She didn't like thinking about it, so she instead thought about her and Reece, living together in her beautiful house. Going room to room, she admired the shine of the gold plate she'd had put on every fixture, including the toilets. She loved the hand-painted tiles with adorable little puppies she'd used for all the kitchen counters.

Mostly she loved the colors. The interior decorator she'd hired when she bought the place had wanted everything to match. How stupid. What was the point of having a lot of rooms if they all looked alike?

No, she'd wanted something different every time she walked through a door, which was why her house was sorted by color. The white room was closest to the front door, with ultrabright carpet and walls. She had breakfast in the yellow room. The purple one was for dinner. The black one she used when she wanted to disappear. The red one was for when she was angry. Her bedroom was all green, with jungle wallpaper covering every surface, including the ceiling.

It was perfect, and all hers. She'd never had her own house before, but she'd bet this one would win awards for how beautiful—and expensive—it looked. After she and Reece were married, they would have big parties and invite people in for tours. For a fee, of course. Maisy might be rich, but she knew you only stayed rich if you watched the pennies and then the dollars would take care of themselves.

As she changed into her pajamas, Maisy let herself drift into happy memories from earlier tonight. She didn't think she'd ever seen anything better than the redhead kissing a disgusting, germ-ridden toilet bowl. Well, maybe the chemicals splashing all over her dress, turning it into a polka-dot nightmare. Everything had worked out perfectly.

Lucky Maisy. Lucky, lucky Maisy.

During the dancing, she'd gone looking for a place to set her trap. A few people had been walking down the other hallway, using the facilities, but she'd shut off the overhead lights, and they stopped coming. She'd found a maintenance closet, almost crying out with joy when she saw the big jugs of bleach. The hotel worried about their workers' safety: there were long rubber gloves and little single-use face masks on a shelf above the chemicals. It was like somebody up there was looking out for her.

She'd had a real scare when Reece and the woman had disappeared for a while, until she'd spotted them in the lobby. Getting close enough to eavesdrop, she'd

heard the woman say she was heading for the bathroom. Then it was just a matter of giving her some
friendly advice about avoiding the line, and getting over
there to wait for her to show up.

Lucky Maisy. Lucky, lucky Maisy.

Wondering if there were any news updates, Maisy
turned on the TV to one of those entertainment channels. They were talking about it, and she quickly turned
up the volume.

"Chemical *accident*?" she said, repeating the newscaster's
words.

Did they really think it had been an accident? Was
the girl too dumb to realize she hadn't been alone
in the bathroom? If they thought it was an accident,
nobody would be looking for her, would they? Reece
would think it was sad, then he would get a look at the
redhead's scarred face and bald head and would never
want to see her again. Everything had worked out the
way it should. And once again, Reece was all hers.

Maisy was the only woman he needed, and it was
about time she proved it. Her competition was out of
the picture, ugly and bald. Their house was all ready.

All she had to do now was bring him here, tell him
of her love, and everything would be perfect.

CHAPTER 11

Again and again, Jessica dreamed she was choking on something. Sometimes it was a lollipop, other times a hunk of meat. Always it terrified her. Always it hurt.

When not dreaming of that, she found herself floating on a cloud. Or swimming in a sea made of fog and brightly colored fish. She'd never used drugs, other than once trying a joint at a high school party, but she imagined this was what it felt like. She was weightless, dizzy, and unable to focus. She didn't like it, wanting her brain to stop spinning so she could think for more than a few minutes at a time.

The only time she felt safe and normal was when she heard a concerned male voice promising she was going to be all right. *Reece. That's Reece.*

She wanted to touch him back. Every time she started to feel more aware, though, a warmth would spread through her. It started at her wrist, traveling through her veins. Within seconds, she would disappear into cloud land again.

She didn't understand why it wouldn't stop. She wanted to ask him to *make* it, to let her come down to earth and be herself, but for some reason, she was unable to speak.

Because you're choking on a lollipop.

"Oh, honey, baby doll, can you hear me? I'm here with you now. You're gonna be okay."

She grimaced. *Whose voice?* Not Reece's deep, even tone. Not Liza's. Someone else. A voice that made the cloud she was riding on spin faster and faster, making her sicker and sicker.

"Nobody's ever gonna hurt you again, Jessie. I promise you."

Something heavy landed on her leg, above her knee, and squeezed. The touch made her skin crawl, like a huge bug had fallen on her. She realized it was a hand when it began to move up her thigh, possessive and intimate. Jess tried to shift away to escape his unwelcome touch but couldn't be sure she *was* moving, or if any of this was even real. *Find out!*

Pushing through the waves, swimming out of the cloud and the fog, away from the fish, the haze, and the lollipop, Jess forced her eyelids up. Little by little, she let in the light. It was harsh and artificial. Her eyes stung, and she had to blink a lot before she could keep them open.

Once she'd focused, she catalogued her surroundings.

Ceiling tiles. Fluorescent bulbs overhead. Cinderblock walls. Coarse sheets beneath her.

Johnny Dixon sitting beside her on a hospital bed.

Her heart pounded, her pulse raced, panic setting in. She didn't understand why he was here; she only knew she didn't want him to be. He shouldn't be anywhere near her. Shouldn't have his big meaty hand so *high* on her leg, as if he had the right to touch her, to claim her.

She tried to tell him to leave. No sound came out. She was choking, though air was still filling her lungs. But she could not say a word.

"Honey, baby, you're awake! You gave me such a scare."

She stared into his pale blue eyes as he hovered over her. He leaned too close, his breath hot on her face. She didn't remember much, but she knew Johnny had no business being here.

"I saw the story on the internet this morning. They showed a picture of you from the night of the gallery shooting and said you'd been attacked again. I just about lost my mind."

Pieces of the puzzle came together. The gala. The steamy stolen interlude.

Edward. His real name is Edward. How funny.

The man in the room, who was not the man she wanted to see, sneered, and tightened his grip on her leg. "Winchester left you alone, didn't he? The asshole dumped you here and ran out, only wanting to save his own skin. He better not show his face again."

Winchester. Reece. *Where are you?*

"Why didn't you call me?" That little-southern-boy whine. How she hated it. "You know I'm always here for you, baby doll. I would have come runnin'."

Thoughts and memories circled in her brain like ingredients in a mixing bowl. By sheer force of will, she plucked them out of the batter, one by one, and sorted out what was going on.

She'd been ambushed. It happened in the hotel bathroom. *Chemical rain pouring down.*

Now she was in a hospital. She was on heavy pain-killers that oozed in from an IV at her wrist, keeping her drugged and confused.

Her stalker ex-boyfriend was right beside her bed, and nobody else was in the room.

A tube was in her throat to help her breathe, so there was no way she could have called this fucking moron, if she ever would have, which she wouldn't.

He bent closer toward her face, as if he planned to kiss her cheek. She jerked away. Well, she thought she jerked. Her movements were sluggish and unclear, like moving underwater. At the very least, though, she got her cheek out from under his mouth.

"What's *wrong* with you?" he snapped, looking down at her with storms in his eyes. It was the way he always looked at her when she rejected him.

Where the hell were the nurses? Liza? Reece?

He cupped her face in his hands and bent down again, lips scraping her forehead. There was no way to escape this time, and she closed her eyes, praying she wouldn't vomit into the tube and choke to death.

"Get your hands off her, you son of a bitch!"

A shape ran across the room. Johnny went flying. A jolt of warmth hit her wrist.

No, not now! One surge of her pulse and heat traveled up her arm. Another and it hit her chest. Then her heart. And then it was off to the races, spreading through her body, and taking Jess to cloud-and-lollipop land.

When she came to full consciousness again—a minute or ten days later—Reece was there. He was sprawled on a chair beside the bed, asleep. He still wore his tuxedo shirt, unbuttoned, with the sleeves rolled up. It was dingy and had a smear of what looked like coffee on the front. His jacket was nowhere to be seen, and the pants were wrinkled. She looked over the side of the bed, seeing he'd kicked off his shoes and was wearing black socks.

Her brows pulled in a frown. Reece hadn't been taking care of himself. She wondered if it was because he'd been too busy taking care of her.

She shifted. He must have heard her, because his eyes flew open. Seeing she was awake, he burst from the chair, coming to her side. "Don't try to talk."

She shook her head, already having figured out that much.

"They have you on pain medication. You've been in and out of consciousness."

No kidding.

"The doctor said you'll need to be given oxygen like this until it's been at least twenty-four hours. Then they'll run some more tests."

She lifted her hands, putting them palms up to her side, shrugging a question.

"It's Wednesday evening. It's been twenty hours so far."

Twenty hours? She'd been lying here, rolling in and out of some weird psychedelic world for almost a whole day? Those must be some powerful pain drugs.

A storm falling on her. The reek of chemicals.

Oh. Right. The powerful bleach might be involved, too.

She suddenly remembered something else, unsure if

it had been real or a dream. Shivering to think that it had really happened, she had to ask now, not later. She held one hand out, palm up, and positioned her other over it, pantomiming writing with a pen and paper.

He shook his head. "You should rest."

She glared and pressed the imaginary pen harder, insistent.

Realizing she wasn't going to give up, Reece sighed, dug in his pants pocket, and got his phone. "It's the best I can do."

Good enough. She tapped the screen, trying to form letters, though her eyes stung and remained blurry. It was like looking at a screen through Vaseline-smeared glasses. But she believed he'd understand what she was asking.

Taking the phone back, he read aloud. *Jony hre.* His jaw tightened and she saw him grit his teeth. The flexing in his cheek said he might bite hard enough to break his own jaw.

God. Johnny *had* been here.

"Yes."

She waited, but he didn't say anything else, so she grabbed the phone back, scrawled a few letters, and held it up for him to see.

U hit hm? A slow smile creased the mouth that had done such amazing, wonderful things to her last night before everything had gone straight to hell.

"I might have." Reece looked as self-satisfied as a cat. "He won't be back. Ever."

Her eyes grew as wide as saucers as a possible meaning crossed her mind. Rather than take the time to tap the shocked question on the screen, she quickly drew her index finger across her throat in a slashing motion.

Reece gaped, and then threw his head back and laughed. And laughed. And laughed.

"You crazy, wonderful woman. You *are* going to be all right, aren't you?" Sliding on the bed next to her, he drew her into his arms. "No, I didn't kill him. I might have broken his arm, though, and definitely broke his nose."

Her expression must have revealed her surprise. Johnny might be a scumbag, but he was a *big* scumbag.

"Rowan and I fought our way through public school as teenagers. Now he's a cop. Raine's an ex–military bodyguard. We always have each other's backs. I have to work my ass off so I can keep up with them in case they need a wingman."

She liked that he always had backup. Being in the spotlight, he certainly needed it.

"Dixon won't bother you again. I dragged him into the parking lot and taught him a lesson, until my brother pulled me off him." He grinned. "Your sister showed up, too. When she heard he'd been in here, she almost ripped his guts out with a plastic spork from the cafeteria."

Love you, Liza.

"My brother took him to the detectives investigating what happened last night. They're going to question him." She could feel a rumble and realized he'd let out a small growl. "If he did this to you, he'd better *hope* they put him in prison."

Relief flooded through her. The nightmare with

Johnny might really end. If he'd attacked her, he would be put away. If he hadn't, he would probably leave her alone in the future anyway.

Johnny was a bully, but only to those he thought he could intimidate. If he'd gotten his ass handed to him, and had faced the prospect of going to jail, she knew he would steer clear of her. Deep down, he was a coward. He would not only be nervous about going up against someone who'd bested him in a fight; he'd also be too embarrassed to face anyone who might know about it. Like her and Liza.

She wished she could say thank you, and she didn't want to scrawl it. So instead, she curled into the crook of Reece's arm and reached for his hand. Their fingers entwined, she thanked him with her eyes. She knew she must look ridiculous—splotchy and tubed up—but he studied her face like she was the most beautiful thing in the world.

And then the pain medicine carried her away again. She drifted off in his arms.

By evening, when the rheumatologist Reece had brought in ran further tests, he said they had to keep the tube in overnight, just to be safe. Jessica wanted to cry.

The next afternoon, when they finally agreed to take it out, she wanted to cheer.

Either way would have hurt—the cheering more so—but her jaw ached from keeping her mouth open, her lips hurt from the pressure of the plastic, and her whole body rebelled against the foreign object inside it. The thing *had* to go.

"All right, sweetie, we're going to remove the breathing tube now. Relax, don't try to swallow or clench your throat, and it will be over in a jiff."

Jessica didn't entirely believe the chipper young nurse, and turned her attention to the other one, Alice, who was much older, and usually dour.

"It's gonna be nasty," the sixtyish woman said. "But we've given you a shot of analgesic. At least it will be over quickly. The aftermath will probably be worse."

Jessica knew what she meant. She'd been conscious enough to learn there were chemical burns in her esophagus. Pulling out the tube that had been breathing for her for the last day and a half would not be pleasant. As the nurse had said, though, the aftermath would be a lot worse as her throat healed from the tube and from the burns.

She'd had strep throat as a kid, and she remembered it felt like she was swallowing broken glass. This would feel like throwing that broken glass back up.

She wouldn't be able to sleep through it. Last night, she'd written a note to Reece, insisting they stop putting morphine in her IV drip. She'd been on a lighter pain reliever since. Already she felt more like herself, only a silent Jessica who couldn't cover her fear by cracking jokes. She hoped she wouldn't regret not having something strong to tide her over.

"Ready?" said the chipper nurse as they put some other doohickey on the end of the tube.

Closing her eyes so she didn't have to see some slimy, plastic, snakelike thing coming out of her mouth, she nodded. Although Alice was experienced, the tube apparently extended from her lips down to her toes, and its removal seemed to take forever.

She felt every inch. It hurt like hell.

At least it was out, though. They suctioned her throat, and then she was able to lick her lips and take a deep breath all on her own. *Heavenly.*

At least until she coughed. *Oh, God.*

"Take it easy," Alice said. "Your chest X-ray looked clear, but you might need to bring up a little fluid."

A little? Felt like an entire lung.

"You'll be fine," said the other nurse. "It wasn't so bad, was it?"

Jess didn't want her first words in almost two days to be a litany of curses against the young, energetic caregiver, so she remained silent. She also tried not to swallow. Amazing how quickly spit built up in your mouth when you were desperate not to let it slide down your throat.

Fortunately, the annoying nurse left, leaving only Alice, whose brusque manner suited Jess better. "Let's clean you up," she said.

The nurse took a warm cloth and washed around her mouth. Jess waited for the rash to sting at the contact with an abrasive, industrial facecloth, but didn't feel anything. Maybe the shot of painkiller had spread up into her cheeks. Or, hopefully, they had healed. Nobody had given her a mirror to check herself out while an alien probe was stuck in her face.

"There you go. Much better. Now your sister and boyfriend can come back in."

Boyfriend? If it wouldn't have hurt so much, she'd

have laughed to hear Reece Winchester described as a boyfriend. He was her lover—she fully remembered their wild sexual encounter. But boyfriend? Who could ever consider him a boy? Besides, for all she knew, they'd had a one-night stand. It might never go anywhere else.

The thought hurt more than her injuries. Not just the idea of never having sex with him again, like the limo sex they'd been denied. Plus sex in a bed. On a beach. On the kitchen table. More than anything, she hated the idea of losing the intimacy they'd begun to share.

Given that Johnny had shown up at her bedside soon after the attack, she suspected he'd been behind it. He'd probably even been the one who shot at them. She even knew why: he'd seen her moving on with someone else, and had decided to make her think somebody was after her, so he could swoop in and play hero, or loving boyfriend.

Nobody had ever accused Johnny Dixon of being too smart.

As much as it hurt to admit, Reece probably should steer clear of her. The idea that she really *had* been responsible for the near miss in the gallery crushed her. She cared for him too much to continue heaping trouble on him.

Cared for? Are you out of your mind?

She might be. Out of her mind, and out of her heart. As she'd feared, by lowering her guard and letting him into her body, she'd let him into her life.

She could love him. Maybe she already did. It had happened quickly, but Jess had always been in tune with her emotions. While it had been lust, and not love, at first sight, now that she'd gotten to know him—seeing his brilliance, his talent, and even his damage—she wanted the whole man, not just his amazing body.

"I swear, those two ought to go home and at least shower and change," Alice said as she tidied up the room, disposing of medical waste in one bin and the facecloth in another. "They've been here in the same clothes since you arrived.

Tears pricked her eyes; she would gulp if it wouldn't hurt so much. Of course Liza had stayed, just as they'd both stayed by their mom's bed day and night in her final days. But Reece? Why would he do it? Maybe he'd felt protective, guarding her until Johnny showed up. Johnny had been taken in by the cops, though. Why would he feel he needed to stay?

They'd had sex. That didn't mean he owed her anything, especially if she'd been the target all along, not him.

"Has anybody ever told you he looks like the actor who was in *Twisted*?"

Her lips quirked up on one side, and she nodded.

"I loved that movie." The nurse shivered. "My menopausal parts perked right up during some of those scenes."

Ha. At twenty-four, Reece had even been turning on middle-aged women, not just horny teenagers like Jess. She found some words and dug them out of her throat. "I'll...be sure...to tell him."

The woman looked down at her, at first puzzled, and then shocked. Her mouth fell open. It was the first time she'd appeared to be anything other than stoic. "You mean he's *him*?"

"Yeah," she croaked.

"Jeez, I can't believe it. I mean, we get stars in here sometimes. I changed Richard Burton's bedpan once."

TMI.

"But the young, handsome, healthy ones never show up in my ward." The woman straightened her pink uniform top. Her hand went to her hair, and she tucked it into place.

"Look nice," Jessica said with a weak smile.

"Do you mind if I flirt with your man? I haven't done that here since Richard Burton."

Jess chuckled, picturing the nurse coming on to a guy while cleaning his bedpan. That's when she noticed the shot of analgesic had started to wear off. *Now* it felt like she was throwing up that ground glass she'd swallowed earlier, and she grimaced.

Alice touched her wrist, glancing at her watch, checking her pulse the old-fashioned way. "It's okay. Try to relax. You sure you don't want some morphine?"

Huh-uh. She wanted to go home, not back to la-la land. "No."

"All right, we'll continue with the nonopioids."

Alice hadn't been out of the room for more than fifteen seconds before Liza burst in. She flew to the side of the bed, cupped Jess's face in her hands, and kissed her forehead and cheeks. "Oh, my God, I've been so scared. Are you okay?"

"Fine." *Ground glass.* "A spork?"

Her sister's head tilted in confusion. Then she grinned,

flashing a pair of dimples Jess had liked on their first day in kindergarten. "Good thing it was plastic. I tried to stick it in his ugly eyeball."

"Not...worth it."

"No, he isn't." She licked her lips. "That, uh, boss of yours sure took care of him, though. If his cop brother hadn't been here to pull him off, he mighta been the one who got arrested."

Reece. Where was he?

As if she'd called him with her thoughts, he burst into the room. Seeing her without the tube, he sighed so loudly she heard it from the bed. He took up position on the other side of her, gripping her hand, looking her over as if evaluating for damage.

"I'm fine," she said, cutting off his forthcoming question.

"I know you are. You're going to stay that way." His now warm eyes suddenly twinkled and the corner of his mouth lifted. "What did you tell that nurse? She planted herself in front of me to get an autograph and pinched my ass before I could get in here."

Jessica chuckled. *Ouch.* But worth it, given the mental picture. She opened her mouth to yank his chain about it, but then closed it, reserving her strength for an actual conversation.

"Don't talk, Jessie-girl," said Liza. She went to a side table, picked up a pitcher, and poured a glass of water into a paper cup. Bringing it over, she said, "Here. Drink some."

Jessica eyed the cup like it was a fat spider.

"You have to if you want to get out of here," Reece said.

"Yep," said Liza, lifting the cup to Jessica's lips. "If you don't pee, you gotta stay."

If she had an embarrassed bone left in her body, she might have blushed. But since Reece had found her hugging a toilet like a lover, maybe they were beyond such things.

"Not staying," she insisted. She took the cup. The first sip was agony. The second worse. By the third, though, she appreciated the coolness on her lips and in her so-dry mouth.

"Get out today?" she asked.

"Tonight," Liza added. "They found no chemical pneumonia, though you've gotta be really careful to keep getting checked out for a coupla weeks. Bronchitis is still a possibility."

What a cheerful thought. Especially on top of the hospital stay and expensive tests. More doctor visits added to the bills, which wasn't good for someone who had only the most basic medical insurance. If he was responsible, she would sue Johnny's ass off for every penny.

Now, though, she could only think about getting out of here. "Good. Need a shower." She wrinkled her nose at her sister. "So do you. You stink."

"There's gratitude for you." Liza looked happy that Jess was getting her snark on. She pointed at Reece. "Same goes for him. He hasn't been farther than the coffee shop since Tuesday night."

She studied him closely, from head to toe. Still in the rumpled tux shirt and pants, he did have shoes on now. He looked exhausted. Yet, with the hair standing on end, and the rough shadow on his unshaven jaw, he also looked sexy as hell. First-thing-in-the-morning-get-out-of-bed-after-a-long-night-of-sex sexy.

She beckoned for Liza to bend closer. "I kinda like it," she whispered in her sister's ear. Whispering was easier on the throat. Plus, she didn't want him to hear her say she liked his musky, hot, masculine scent. She was just telling Liza, with whom she shared all her secrets.

He chuckled. He'd heard. Crap.

Pretending she hadn't said anything at all, she continued to whisper. "This bed sucks. Wanna be home in my own."

Liza and Reece exchanged a look. At some point while she'd been lying in the hospital, the two of them had become coconspirators. They knew something she did not. "What?"

Liza stroked her arm. "We think it's best if you go stay with Reece for a couple of days."

Reece nodded his agreement, appearing as solemn as he did the night they met. This wasn't going to be a sexy-time sleepover, not that she was really up for one anyway. Something else was going on. A possibility came to mind. "Johnny. He was released?"

"It's not Johnny," said Reece, pulling up a chair so he could sit facing her. His gaze was steady, his expression worried. "The police got surveillance tapes from the hotel. It definitely wasn't Johnny who attacked you."

Not him? She'd been so sure after his unwanted visit here. "Who?"

Those eyes darkened to an angry amber. "A woman."

"Huh?"

He tapped his screen, pulling up an image. "Do you recognize her?"

She considered, suddenly remembering the woman who'd disappeared into the crowd at the hotel. She'd had long, dark, gray-streaked hair. "She told me I should use the other bathroom."

Reece muttered a curse. Liza said the same word loud and clear.

"She lured you right into a trap," he said.

The woman was a complete stranger to her. "Why?"

"Because of me." His hand swept through his hair. Judging by how messy it was, she figured he'd done it a lot lately. "It was my fault. I think she's the one who's been stalking me. She showed up at Liza's opening, and I got a bad vibe."

Jessica suddenly recalled seeing her there, too. She'd had hatred in her eyes. "Arrested?"

"Police don't know her identity yet. They're questioning the organizers and other people who were there the other night, and looking at photos on the state's driver's license database."

Needle, meet haystack.

"Once they have her ID, she will go to jail for what she did to you."

She licked her lips, thinking, putting things together. "And for...shooting?"

His hand tightened on hers. "Maybe. Probably."

So none of it had been Johnny. Reece hadn't been put in danger because of her. While she knew she should react with anger toward a woman who'd hurt her because she was so jealous of the attention Jess was getting from Reece, she wanted to weep with joy instead.

He, however, looked completely furious. "I'm so sorry she targeted you, Jess. I'll never be able to make it up to you."

She rolled her eyes. Yes, she'd felt the same way when she thought she'd been the one who'd brought darkness into his life. But him bringing it into hers? Well, hell, the man was a sexy superstar. Of course he'd have obsessive fans on his tail. It was part of the job. Whether they were personally involved or not, she could have come to the attention of a stalker just by working for Reece. Planning to work in Hollywood meant she knew all about the pros and cons, including the dangers. She accepted it.

His expression said he wasn't ready to believe that yet, and she didn't have the voice to argue it. Once she was better, however, she *would* argue, and she *would* make him believe it.

"Until they find her, Jessica, you are coming home with me."

He said it firmly, like she might not agree. *Ha.*

"I have a rental house up in the hills. It's secluded and secure. You'll be safe there. I'll make sure of it."

She didn't care where he lived, be it a house, a cabin, a condo, or a mobile home. Spending time alone with Reece, finding out what, exactly, she felt for him, whether he felt anything for her, and what they were going to do about it, sounded like heaven.

* * *

Hell. Her life had become a living hell with the ringing of a phone.

Maisy stared at Candace Waterstone, the snooty social climber who'd sat next to her at the charity gala, whose name she hadn't even remembered. The woman had been so phony the other night, pretending to give a crap about Maisy, patting her shoulder and offering her advice. What she was really doing was sucking up to her for her money, and at the same time looking down on her for getting it from the lottery. Like this fake blonde hadn't gotten hers by divorce.

"Believe me, nobody was more surprised than I when the police arrived at my door with your picture, asking if I could identify you."

Actually, Maisy would bet *she* was more surprised. In fact, she'd been in shock since Candace had called her this morning, saying she simply *had* to see her, and it was urgent. No way would she let such trash into her perfect house, of course, and she'd refused, wishing she'd never let the woman talk her into exchanging phone numbers. When Candace told her the police were trying to identify her, however, Maisy had agreed to come to her place.

It was much smaller. And boring—every room painted the same ivory, none of the furniture or carpet matching it. The producer's wife had no taste at all.

"I'm so scared for you, dear!"

"Of course you are," she mumbled.

She knew what was going to come next. Candace didn't have a genuine bone in her body.

She wanted money. She knew Maisy had it. She had something on Maisy. Therefore, she was about to blackmail her.

"The detective who came by said the police are interviewing people who were at the gala, trying to see if anyone can name the mystery woman. They're also looking at state records."

Maisy swallowed hard, glad—so very glad—she hadn't changed her driver's license from Pennsylvania to California yet. *Lucky, lucky Maisy.*

But if she was so lucky, how did they find out? She'd been so careful. There had been nobody around when she'd been stockpiling supplies in the ladies' room, and nobody when she'd run out of it after delivering the whole kit and caboodle onto that head of brassy-red hair. So how had they figured out she was the one who'd done it? Was she now Unlucky Maisy?

"The picture the officer showed me looked like it came from the hotel security system."

She jerked. "The hotel has a security system?"

"Well of course, silly. There are cameras everywhere. How on earth did you not notice them?"

Because I'm so stupid. That's what you think, isn't it?

She tried to bluff. "They have my picture from a camera. So what? I bet they have a lot of other people's pictures, too. I bet they have yours."

A hard, disbelieving, *Don't kid a kidder* smile made the woman look more genuine. "But not one of me carrying jugs of bleach into the bathroom where a woman was later attacked."

Oh, God. She *was* Stupid Maisy.

If only she hadn't paid attention to the jealous thoughts in her head. She knew she and Reece would end up together eventually. Of *course* he wasn't seriously interested in the red-haired woman, and Maisy should have pretended she didn't exist. She had let her anger overwhelm her, like it used to before she got better.

She wouldn't go back to being Crazy Maisy. She would never return to that place with people who screamed, people who drooled, people in white who shoved pills down her throat. She'd spent years in such a place, after the fire had killed her sister. *I didn't mean to kill her, but she made me so mad.* Those years meant she'd paid for what she did, and winning the lottery had been her reward for doing it. There was no way somebody so lucky would ever have to go back.

"Honestly, Maisy, if anyone can understand your frustration, it's me. I mean, I was just as shocked Reece would show up with someone like that."

"Why?" Maisy asked, suspicious. Why did Candace think it was any of her business? She had no personal connection to Reece, while Maisy did.

"She's not really our sort, is she? She's so obvious, with that red dress."

"You can't help but notice her." Poor Reece wouldn't have much of a chance if somebody so determined to get him put her mind to it. Well, the redhead's mind might have been put to it lately, but Maisy's had been for years and years. She had the greater claim.

"I don't know how many people you met at the gala..."

"None."

"Or how many of them already knew you."

"Only you."

"Good." Candace sipped her iced tea. Her glass had condensation on it. Delicately drying her fingers on a cloth napkin, she finally got to the point. "I am happy to help, but sooner or later, I have to be honest with the police. I'm sure people saw us talking at our table."

Here it comes.

"I do hate to spill the beans, but..."

"How much do you want?"

Maisy had brought her checkbook, knowing it would come to this. Candace had evidently anticipated it, too, which was probably why she'd seated them at the kitchen table, rather than in a more comfortable room. Easier for Maisy to write the check, or to count out cash. How considerate of her.

God, it made her blood boil. She hated the thought of giving her hard-earned winnings over to a black-mailer. But if the police were looking for her, and might take her back to that *place*, she needed time to get away and hide. She hated the thought of leaving her beautiful house and going far away. More than anything, she hated the thought of leaving Reece.

I just can't.

Maybe she didn't have to. What was the point of having tons of money if you couldn't use it to get out of scrapes like this one? She could lie low until all this died down and everybody forgot some dumb intern had splashed herself with bleach in a public bathroom.

"Wait," she whispered, suddenly thinking of something. If she changed how she looked, how would they identify her? She'd been wanting to update her look, cut her hair, and maybe dye it. Maisy had always been the type who blended in. There was nothing really unique about her, except her hair, which was why she'd kept the gray streaks. It was the only distinctive part of her. If she got rid of it, she'd be able to go on living in Los Angeles, right under the noses of the cops, though she would have to leave her beautiful house for a while.

There was one more way to make herself unrecognizable. "Who's your plastic surgeon?"

Candace lifted a hand to her heart, as if wounded. Maisy just raised an eyebrow.

"Oh, all right. He's in Phoenix. I'll get you his card. Now, are we agreed?"

"About what?"

"About the two hundred and fifty thousand, silly."

Hiding her growing rage, Maisy knew she had to go along with it, or else this evil woman could ruin everything. "Agreed."

"Excellent. That will be fine for the first payment," the woman said. "We'll talk about what comes next after the excitement dies down a bit."

Whatever the first payment was, even if Maisy doubled it, Candace didn't plan on it being the last. She would string this out, maybe forever. Filthy blackmailers always did, tormenting their victims by perpetually holding something over their heads.

It would never end. She would be imprisoned by this woman, like she'd been imprisoned in a place with soft walls.

She began to quiver, and then to shake.

"Are you cold, dear?"

Not cold. Furious.

When Maisy got angry, it was like someone stuck an electric wire inside her and she jerked and shook, needing to lash out, to do something to make the person angering her stop. She'd done it to her whining sister because the fifteen-year-old had borrowed her sweater and torn it. What *wouldn't* she do to someone who was trying to ruin her carefully planned, lucky life, and her future with Reece?

She opened her mouth, about to tell the woman she could shove her blackmail scheme. But she knew she couldn't. *Candace knows who you are, and she knows you're thinking about getting plastic surgery She could warn the cops you changed your appearance.*

That was a problem. A very big problem. Much bigger than a tear in a sweater.

"You really are shivering. Why don't I make you some warm tea," Candace said, still pretending to be a friend, even though she'd just extorted $250,000 from her.

She got up and went to the stove. Maisy rose and followed her, not entirely sure why.

Well, maybe a little sure.

On the counter there stood a lead-crystal pitcher from which Candace had poured the iced tea. Apparently plastic ones weren't good enough for her.

The pitcher looked heavy. *So* heavy.

Maisy wanted to know how heavy. She picked it up by the handle and felt her arm sag under the weight. The thing was like a cement block. Candace probably used it only to show off how much it had cost.

"I have Earl Grey and herbal. Which would you—"

"Nobody blackmails me." Caught up in the heat of rage, her whole body shaking, Maisy swung her arm at the woman, who'd just started to turn around.

She didn't know what to expect. Maybe she would miss. Maybe the pitcher would break, leaving a furious, injured Candace to call the police right away.

If that's what she expected, she'd been very wrong. When lead crystal came up against a human skull, crystal definitely won out.

The pitcher didn't even break. But Candace's head most definitely did.

CHAPTER 12

As promised, Jessica's doctor released her Thursday evening. Liza had left the hospital and come back with some clothes and personal items for her. After giving Reece a warning finger wag, she kissed her sister, and informed them she would be up to visit soon.

Liza had loosened up toward him after she'd found him beating the shit out of Johnny Dixon. But when she'd learned the person responsible for targeting Jessica had been his stalker, not Jess's ex, her guard had gone back up, though maybe not as high.

"Just relax," he told Jess as he helped her into the front seat of his car. "Take a nap. It's about a half-hour drive."

As he headed out of the city toward Hollywood Hills, she took him at his word, reclining her seat and closing her eyes. Her breaths became slow and even. Knowing she'd gotten a lot of sleep, but no real *rest* over the past couple of days, he didn't turn on the stereo for fear of waking her. He did, however, have to look over every so often to watch her sleep, unable to stop himself.

Awake, Jessica was fire, passion, and wit. Asleep she was the fairy-tale princess waiting for a kiss to awaken her.

He might have kissed her—a lot. But he was no

prince. In fact, Reece was so far away from a noble hero, he might as well be the villain of the story. He had no business being the one to take her home to play protective knight in shining armor. She deserved to be with someone better. Less fucked up, with a whole lot fewer secrets to keep and crimes hidden under his bed.

But someone better might not necessarily be someone safer. Right now, all he gave a shit about was keeping her protected. Until Maisy Cullinan was caught, he wanted Jessica behind the high fence surrounding his rental house, which backed onto a cliff nobody could climb. Finding out Maisy was a killer hadn't doubled the stakes; it had increased them exponentially.

"Stop frowning," she said from the other side of the car. "You'll get wrinkles. Then how will you pull a Clooney and be named the Sexiest Man Alive again when you're in your forties?"

"That was a long one."

She opened one eye—well, actually, she must have already had her eyes open a bit, since she'd seen him frowning. But she was no longer trying to hide it, and turned to look at him, a grin on her face. "What was a long one, Reece? I can't quite put my finger on what you're talking about."

Damn. The woman was hurt and hoarse, and she still managed to turn him on with a look and a smile. And though he hated that she'd been injured, her husky voice was sexy as fuck, too.

What kind of uncaring asshole would get turned on by a woman who'd almost been killed because of him? His kind, that was who.

"Hmm. What long thing have I come across recently?" She tapped her fingertips on her chin. "My memory is so unreliable."

"Stop talking. It's bad for you."

"But how can I get better if nobody helps me recover my memories?"

"I'm sure you remember everything you need to about Tuesday night."

God knows he did. The memories of everything they'd done together had cemented themselves in his brain. Although he'd slept only in bits and pieces the past few days, he'd definitely dreamed. When those dreams had not been about finding Jessica on the bathroom floor, they'd been about having her legs wrapped around him as he held her against the wall and pounded into her.

"Maybe I need to be reminded. I mean, I keep picturing something. It has to do with a closet. And me riding on this a great big…"

"Shut up," he said, his hands clenching the steering wheel. Never had his Mercedes felt so small. Not to mention his pants. *Uncaring asshole. Uncaring asshole. Uncaring asshole.*

"You just told a poor, injured woman to shut up?"

"You sound awful. Your voice is getting worse. Seriously, stop talking."

She crossed her arms and sank into her seat, her lush lower lip pudging out in the world's most obvious, intentional pout. The silence lasted for about a minute. He should have known she couldn't go longer. "So talk to me. About anything. Everything."

He sensed she wanted to hear something light, funny,

and breezy. Unfortunately, he knew he had to tell her something else. That afternoon, Reece had gone over to Rowan's house for a quick shower and to borrow some clean clothes. While he was there, the news had come in about a murder in Brentwood. A neighbor had seen someone going into the victim's house right before lunch; a rather plain woman with long, dark hair streaked with gray.

"Look, Jessica, there's something you need to know. The police have identified the woman who attacked you."

She remained silent. He could feel the increased tension in the car.

"Her name is Maisy Cullinan. After wasting a lot of time with interviews, some smart cop did a simple online search with the surveillance picture and found her. She won a multistate lottery jackpot eight months ago, and moved here from Pennsylvania."

Glancing over, he saw her roll her eyes, and he knew what she was thinking. *Why does somebody so dangerous to others win millions?*

"Do they know where she is?"

"Not yet. There's more." He took a deep breath and let it ease out. "The police think she murdered someone who could identify her from the gala."

She flinched, and then wrapped her arms around herself, as if cold. Reece didn't change the temperature in the car, knowing the chill had come from inside her. The realization that you'd been attacked by someone who had committed murder would freeze anyone.

"Wait, she killed someone who recognized her, even

though her face had been all over the internet after she won the lottery?"

He shrugged, not understanding it either. It made as little sense as the woman attacking Jessica in a place where she would be caught on visible security cameras. Maisy Cullinan was not a criminal mastermind. But she was a violent one. Meaning he intended to stick like glue to Jessica until she was caught.

"Imagine the good she could have done," Jessica whispered.

"I know. Instead, she moved to California." His temple began to throb. "Into a house that's within spitting distance of mine."

She sat up straighter. "Your house. The one that burned down?"

He nodded.

"Did she do it? Is she the arsonist?"

He thought about what else Rowan had told him about the deranged woman. When detectives found articles about her, including mentions of where she was from, they called the police in her Pennsylvania hometown. What they'd learned had been pretty damning.

"She killed her sister when she was a teenager." He cleared his throat, knowing how she would react to what came next. "She burned down their house with the sister in it."

"Oh, my God," she said, reaching over to put a hand on his leg. "So she's an arsonist. Of course she set the fire."

He dropped his hand on top of hers, entwining their fingers and steering with his left. "Rowan thinks so."

"I agree with your brother. Thank God you weren't there."

Maybe if he had been, he could have caught her, had her arrested, and she would not have been able to attack Jessica, or kill some other woman in her own home. He knew he couldn't think that way, but the self-recrimination still haunted him and would for a long time. Just one more piece of damage to add to his long list.

"If she murdered her sister, how come she's not in prison?"

"She was found mentally incompetent to stand trial and was institutionalized for decades. She was released a couple of years ago."

"All better, huh?" she said, sounding disgusted.

"Obviously not. Winning the lottery was probably the worst thing that could happen to her. Rather than staying in treatment, she had the money to go out into the world and do whatever she wanted."

"Like stalk her fantasy man."

Having seen his own mother struggle with mental illness, fighting against her need to do violence, he found a seed of pity inside himself for Maisy. But it didn't bloom—not after what she'd done to Jessica.

Still, he did understand the destructiveness of a tortured mind. Viv Winchester, his mother, might not have burned down houses or stalked people, but toward the end, her rage and illness had made her a danger to herself. And to others. If she'd found the person she was looking for, she might have committed murder, too.

Maybe she did.

Yes. Maybe she did.

He drove through the night, deep in thought. They were cocooned in silence, as if in their own world. Knowing Jessica was safe beside him gave him the most peace he'd had in days. Watching her struggle in the hospital to recover had been agonizing. And during that time, what he felt toward her had come into full focus.

He'd wanted her. He'd lusted after her. He'd liked her. He'd respected her.

Now he loved her.

There was no hiding from it. His feelings for her were unlike anything he'd ever experienced. Seeing her suffer had crushed him. Thinking she might die had nearly killed him.

If Jessica Jensen would have him, all he wanted was to keep her in his life. He didn't deserve her, he wasn't good enough for her, but he wanted her just the same.

"I want to keep you," he mumbled, admitting it out loud for the first time.

"Excuse me?" she yelped, her voice ending in a croak.

Christ, it wasn't the time or the place. The woman deserved romance, not to be claimed while she was still hoarse and weak. He'd acted impulsively; so unlike him. He needed a plan before he talked to her about their future . . . if they were going to have one.

"I want to keep you safe," he clarified. It sounded genuine, because he meant that, too.

"Oh," she whispered. "Thank you. I do feel safe with you."

Although he wasn't ready to talk about emotions, if there was any chance at all for the two of them, he would have to be honest with Jess about at least some of what he'd been hiding. No, he couldn't tell her everything. Some stories weren't his alone to tell. One thing, though, he could share. He *had* to.

He cleared his throat, wondering how to begin. With something like this, however, there was no easing into it. So he was completely blunt. "My mother was a paranoid schizophrenic. She was institutionalized for the final few years of her life."

She didn't gasp or act shocked. Jessica merely clenched his hand tighter. "Oh, Reece."

"We didn't know when we were kids. She was moody but kept it under control with therapy and medication."

Jessica whispered, "And then Rachel died."

"And then Rachel died."

She didn't ask any questions, falling back into a shared silence as he drove up the 101, maneuvering through some late evening traffic. He pulled his hand back, focusing on the road, not even looking at her. She was digesting his words. For all he knew, she wouldn't want to be with someone with so much fucked-upedness in his life. He had more baggage than any man, other than his brothers. Why would she want to hoist it, too?

Finally, she asked, "Was that the real reason you left Hollywood?"

It made perfect sense. He could leave it there. But he wasn't a liar, and he wasn't a coward. Although he had never told anyone, given what Jess was facing, with a mentally disturbed woman on her tail, he thought she deserved to know.

"Rowan and I were afraid she had killed someone." A chill went through him after he said the words, and for a split second, he remembered being that scared, confused kid who'd lost his sister, and then, in a different way, his mother.

"But... holy shit. Are you serious?"

"Yes. It was bad after Rachel died; my mom had a psychotic break. She was determined to find out who was responsible for my sister's death."

He glanced over and saw Jessica nibble on her bottom lip. Of course she was thinking nobody except Rachel had been responsible. She didn't know the truth. Moreover, she *couldn't* know the truth. Some secrets led to more questions, and more questions led to darker tales.

"Did she find them? I mean, find the person she thought was responsible?"

He turned onto Laurel Canyon Boulevard. They were almost back to the house, and he could focus on getting Jessica in bed and taking care of her. But he had opened this can of worms, and knew he had to shake it out completely. "She fell apart on our birthday. Mine and Rowan's. It was a few months after..."

Rachel's death. After Rachel died. After Rachel fell. After Rachel dove.

After Rachel was pushed?

"It was your thirteenth birthday, I would guess?"

"Yes. We blew out our candles, and she started screaming that Rachel would never have another birthday cake, that her sweet sixteen had been her last."

As he could have guessed, she immediately expressed pity. "I can't imagine the grief of losing a child."

"I know. My mother's illness made her reaction more...*extreme* than most."

"So what happened?"

"She threw the cake at us and took off." He didn't exaggerate, didn't emote, and didn't even have any feelings about what he was saying. That part was nothing, just another rough bump in the road you traveled with a parent who was seriously ill.

The rest of the night was where things got tough.

"Leaving you alone?"

"We grew up in Hollywood. Believe me, we were very mature thirteen-year-olds."

"School of hard knocks."

She again understood without an explanation. Knowing she had also been a pupil at such a school, he imagined she'd been just as mature at that age.

"We were used to taking care of Raine, so we put him to bed and stayed up late, playing video games." Here was where memory became cloudy. He'd tried so hard to forget that night, it wasn't easy to pull the thoughts back to the surface. "When she got home, we heard her screaming from the driveway. We went out and found she'd been in an accident. The front end of the car was banged up, and there was dirt and blood on the bumper."

"Oh, my God," she said, a hitch in her words.

He knew if he looked at her, he would see tears on her cheeks. He just wanted to finish so she could stop crying and he could go back to forgetting.

"What did you do?"

"We covered it up." He spoke matter-of-factly. There

wasn't even a tremor, not the least bit of hesitation in his voice. He had come to peace with what they'd done that night, even if he still haunted old news sites just in case something showed up.

"You were just boys..."

"Yes. Thirteen-year-old boys who'd lost their sister and were watching their mother go insane. So we got her into bed. Rowan pulled the car into the garage—he was always better at *Mario Kart* than I was."

She didn't laugh.

"Sorry. Bad joke." He cleared his throat. "We washed the blood off the fender, and, being stupid and thirteen, took hammers to try to pound out the dents. Not our best idea."

Jessica reached for his hand again and squeezed tightly. "What happened the next day?"

"She didn't remember a thing," he said with a shrug. "She accused us of taking the car for a joyride and wrecking it."

He didn't tell Jess what she'd done to punish them. She'd been ill, not the mother he'd once known. He didn't need to darken her memory further.

"That was the last straw for me and Rowan. We were too terrified to keep going the way we had been. We called our dad and let him know Mom was in a really bad way. He and Aunt Sharon had been out for Rachel's funeral, of course. They came back and took care of everything from there on out."

"Thank God for them." She lifted his hand in the darkness, pressing her soft lips to his knuckles. "You need to stop blaming yourself."

"What makes you think I do?"

"I know you."

Yes, he believed she did. He *had* blamed himself, for years, wondering if he'd allowed someone to get away with a hit-and-run murder. He knew he'd been a fucked-up kid in a fucked-up family in a fucked-up situation. That didn't mean he'd ever entirely forgiven himself.

"Did you tell your father about...everything?"

He shook his head. "We still had some loyalty to Mom. Bad enough she was going into a mental hospital; we didn't want her charged with killing someone."

"You can't be sure that's what happened, Reece."

"Maybe not. We watched the news for months. When Rowan became a cop, he dug deep into old records, looking for anything that happened in the region on our thirteenth birthday. He came up empty. He thinks it was a dog or a deer."

"He's smarter than he looks."

He jerked his head to look at her, seeing a tiny smile on her face. She was trying to lighten the mood, to bring him out of the darkness. Fiery, brilliant Jessica. How could she bring anything *but* light?

Arriving at the tall, metal exterior gate that blocked the long driveway up to the house, he stopped and punched in the security code, sharing it with her in case she needed it. He didn't imagine she would be driving anytime soon. Definitely not before she'd gone back for regular checkups to rule out bronchitis. But he did not want her to feel like she was being imprisoned here, not when all he wanted to do was keep her out of harm's— and deadly women's—way.

The driveway rose a hundred feet in elevation, in a very short time, with a sheer cutoff to the cliff on the passenger side. He'd gotten used to it, but he saw Jess grab her armrest, and she squeezed his hand so hard it felt like she was trying to crush it.

"Hold on, we're almost there."

They reached the final curve that swooped out onto the cliff, and then corkscrew-turned back toward the garage that was attached to the house. When they got out to the point, Jess threw both hands over her eyes and kept them there.

"You can look now, we're in," he said as he parked the car inside and cut the engine. She dropped her hands, revealing pale cheeks. Reece reached over and ran the back of his hand on her face. Her skin was cold, as if the blood had dropped out of it from fear. "Maybe I should have warned you about that."

"You think?"

"I didn't know you're afraid of heights."

"I'm not!"

He tweaked her chin, that cute, adorable, sexy-as-hell cleft. "You might want to rethink that."

"I'm not afraid of heights. I'm only afraid of falling from them."

"Huh, strong and mighty Jessica actually has a human weakness."

"You mean other than bleach?"

"Christ, don't even remind me," he said, his throat almost closing up. "If it matters, I did have the same reaction when I checked this place out. The remoteness is what I like best about it, though. Nobody can get to you here."

"As long as the woman who's after us is afraid of heights, too."

She was definitely getting back to her real self. "Nobody can come through the gate without the code or being buzzed in from the house. And there's no way anyone can climb up that cliff into the backyard. I can't think of a more secure location."

It was the perfect recuperation spot. She would be safe. She could sleep, swim in the enormous pool with the beautiful views of the valley, eat healthy food, and *heal*. Maybe while she was doing that, he would heal, too. Having shared one of the darkest memories of his life with her, he had begun to feel a little lighter. As if he'd finally put down one of piece of that baggage he'd been carrying.

"Just don't ever ask me if I'd like to go outside for a walk. I got vertigo inside the car."

"You can walk from the couch to the bed to the pool, but not another step."

She ducked her head to hide a grin, saying innocently, "You might want to add a stop in the bathroom to that list. Or else you might not want to swim in that pool after me."

"Gross, woman," he said, though he was inwardly laughing.

Jessica was fast becoming herself again, and he couldn't be happier. He wanted her nightmares to end and would do whatever it took to make sure they did.

He exited the car, then he went to her side to help her out. Knowing she hadn't eaten much in the hospital, and was still weak, he kept a hand on the small of her back as he led her to the door. She might have quaked just a bit. He still had yet to taste that spot on her body, but he intended to, just as soon as she was well again. "Let me help you in and then I'll get your bags."

Leading her through the kitchen to the living room, he flipped on some lights, including ones that brightened the back patio and the massive pool, with the lawn and cliff just beyond it.

"Oh, wow," she said, stopping to look out into the night. He knew she wasn't talking about the deck, but about the sharp drop-off behind it. The cliff fell away to reveal the beautiful valley, filled with the twinkling lights of the city, spread like a cloth of stars below them.

"Okay, maybe this location isn't so bad." Looking as if she'd just realized something, she said, "Wait, where's CB?"

Considering he'd told her about his dog, he wasn't surprised she'd asked. "My dad came and picked him up when I was staying at the hospital."

Her face fell. "I was looking forward to meeting him."

"I'll pick him up in a couple of days."

"Why not now?"

"Because Cecil B. is a big slobber machine."

"That's okay, I like dogs."

"Yeah, but this one will knock you on your ass. Let's wait until you're a little stronger."

She frowned but didn't argue any further. He slid an arm around her waist and led her to the couch. "Now, stay here and let me make us a late dinner."

She was hungry, he knew, but she'd also been on a lot of medication and was suffering from a sore throat.

Fortunately, he had some basics in stock. More fortunately, eggs were soft.

"Omelet okay? They're my specialty."

"Perfect."

Keeping watch through an opening over the counter, he heard her say, "No fungus!"

"Check," he said, putting aside the mushrooms he'd been about to wash.

Jess continued to spy on him. She was on her knees, looking over the back of the couch, watching every move he made.

"Don't you trust me?"

She shook her head.

"I know what I'm doing." He lifted an avocado.

Her whole face crinkled. "Eww. In eggs? Are you kidding?"

"Haven't you ever had a California breakfast?"

Lifting a hand, she ticked off her fingers. "Eggs. Ham. Cheese. The end."

"Boring."

"But...it's really all I think I can handle," she said, batting those eyelashes so blatantly he knew she was yanking his chain. "The doctor said I should really be careful for a few days."

"I thought you weren't an actress."

She flashed him a little grin, that dimple making his heart stop. "Okay. But you do know I'm not up to anything too...spicy." She licked her lips. "No matter how good it might taste."

Shit. She was not just teasing, she was flirting with him. As always, he reacted, but he didn't show it. Pale face, dark circles under her beautiful eyes, and lank hair reminded him he needed to be strong and not let it get to him.

But damn, that dimple.

"Give me ten minutes and it'll be ready," he said, stiffening his spine. And his will. Because, teasing or not, she was right. Simple food would be best for her as she recuperated. No excitement, nothing stressful, nothing too energetic.

That meant no sex. *Absolutely* no sex. *Definitely no sex* like they'd had Tuesday night at the hotel. *God help me.*

This was not going to be easy. Knowing she was injured and needed quiet and calm to recover, he'd told himself all day that he'd be fine. He'd expected his worry for her to outweigh the sheer hunger he felt every time he was around her. Yet here he was, a half hour after they'd arrived, holding an egg, watching as she batted those eyelashes. And his dick was hard.

He stopped looking toward the couch and tried to pretend she wasn't there. Getting a pan, he made a plain, nonspicy omelet that was exactly what she needed. Just like she needed a safe, plain, nonspicy night's sleep. Plus several more just like it.

He was a grown-ass man, and he had always been famed for his control. So no matter how much she smiled, or flirted, or batted her eyes, or flashed that dimple, he was going to make sure sleep and no excitement were exactly what she got.

* * *

It was amazing what good food, restful sleep, fresh air, cool breezes, warm sun, and a hot-as-sin man swimming laps in a crystal-blue pool could do for a woman's libido. Er, for a woman. Yeah, no. She meant libido.

Watching Reece's muscular body cut through the water, strong, even, and powerful, was so hot. Like, fry-an-egg-on-the-sidewalk hot. She couldn't take her eyes off him, though she hoped he didn't know it.

Lying on a lounge chair Sunday morning, wearing dark sunglasses, with a magazine in front of her face, she tried to keep her staring discreet. Fortunately, the way she was facing, and the glasses, enabled her to shift her gaze toward the pool without him even knowing he was being ogled by his houseguest.

A *houseguest*. She now hated that word. He'd treated her like one since they'd arrived at his home Thursday night. After assigning her a guest room—a damn *guest* room—he'd focused only on her health and well-being. He'd been the consummate host, refusing to let her lift a finger. He'd cooked for her, waited on her, steadied her when she walked, let her pick what music they listened to and what shows they watched on TV. He'd taken care of her every need.

It was really getting on her nerves.

Despite her insistence that she was fine, and that all the pampering had brought her back to full health, he ignored her protests. Mr. Ultimate Control had been so bossy, and so careful to treat her like a fragile doll, she was ready to deck him.

Which was why she had started to retaliate. Subtly.

The man was going to treat her like an invalid—

a sexless one? Well, she would just have to remind him she was all healthy woman. While he might have forgotten the wonderful, wild things they'd done together in the hotel closet Tuesday night, she most definitely had not.

Especially because she wanted to do all those things again.

They'd missed out on limo sex, but she thought deck sex might be just as nice, especially at night. They could fly over the city below like they were on a magic carpet. Only a magic carpet whose magic included wild sexual positions and lots of orgasms.

Aware her carefully voiced interest wasn't getting the result she wanted, she'd begun a plan of seduction. Friday afternoon, she complained it was too hot and began wearing as little as possible. First it was a T-shirt and short shorts. Reece had checked her temperature, wondering if she was having a delayed reaction to the exposure, saying the house was cold. It *was* cold. But she'd persevered.

Reece, she'd noticed, had spent a lot of the day drinking big glasses of iced water.

Yesterday morning, she'd replaced the shorts with the bottoms of her bikini. His water glass got even bigger.

When she picked the music for dinner last night, she'd made sure it suited her mood. She'd created a playlist on Pandora, leading it off with "I Want Your Sex." A little George Michael never hurt anyone. Reece hadn't said a word while they ate spaghetti, but he had definitely frowned. And drunk more cold water.

After dinner, she'd found a steamy old movie on demand. He'd sat there beside her as she watched it, pretending he had to work, reading scripts. Then, when he started paying attention to the TV, he began to pick apart the writing, the shooting, and the acting. So that part of her plan had been a bust. Directors were no fun to watch movies with.

She'd gone to bed last night so in need of sex, she'd considered taking a bath that included a hot date with her own hand. But she knew that wouldn't satisfy her. She wanted him. Only him. So before she fell asleep—after tossing and turning for at least two hours—she made up her mind that on Sunday she would have him.

"How's the temperature?" she asked when he stopped after fifty laps and stood in the shallow end of the pool. Water dripped off the tips of his golden-brown hair—more gold than brown under the brilliant sun—but it slid and glided from everywhere else. Glistening rivulets traveled down the lightly haired chest. Others made their way down the powerful six-pack of abdominals, rolling over each ridge. After taking a trip past the lean waist, each long stream fell straight into a happy trail that was making her so very sad by remaining out of reach.

"It's great." He swiped his hands through his hair, making those biceps bulge and his forearms flex.

Jess had to close her eyes, trying not to react. Could someone die of lust? Trying to constantly swallow it down could choke a person, couldn't it? If so, she was dead girl walking.

"Why don't you come in for a dip?"

She shifted on the lounge chair, lifting one leg and leaving it bent at the knee. He'd merely glanced at her when she came out wearing a fire engine–red bikini, not saying a word. So infuriating, especially because she knew he loved her body. "I don't know."

"Come on, you know you *want* to."

Hmm. Had there been the tiniest hint of suggestiveness in the comment, or was her horny brain imagining it?

"I guess," she said, lifting herself from the chair, her every movement languid. Although she had slathered herself with sunscreen when she'd come outside yesterday and Friday, she knew she had a little bit of color. At least she didn't look like a washed-out ghost as she had when she left the hospital.

Tossing her sunglasses on the chair, she sauntered over, dipped a toe in, and smiled.

He turned and dove under the water, swimming across the pool.

Damn it. Jessica had never had to actually seduce a man. Maybe she sucked at it. Maybe having seen her hugging a toilet bowl had grossed him out and he didn't want her anymore. Maybe he only felt guilty about what happened to her, and he'd brought her here for that reason, and not because he cared for her.

I want to keep you... safe.

The comment he'd made in the car on the way up here Thursday night kept coming to mind. She hadn't heard the word *safe* the first time he spoke, and for a few seconds, she'd let herself believe he really wanted to keep her in his life. Not just as his employee, not merely a lover. For a brief instant, she'd let herself think he wanted *her*. All of her.

Just as she wanted him. All of him. Body, mind, and...hell, yes, even his heart. Because, she feared, he'd already stolen hers. She had fallen in love with the stubborn man. He had been sexually frustrating her for the past two days, but, knowing he'd been doing it for her own good, she'd only fallen harder.

If he'd been trying to resist her for her own good, though, why would he barely look at her now that she was so much better? Especially when she was trying so hard to make him trip over his own drooling tongue?

"Stupid man," she grumbled.

Completely frustrated, she closed her eyes and jumped in. She bent her legs, dropped to the bottom, and then pushed back up. Hitting the surface, she winced at the coolness of the water. Then, strangely, her body grew warm—even *hot*. Her eyes flew open. Reece stood right in front of her and had set the water to boiling. He apparently had mad swimming skills, because she would have sworn he was all the way across the pool before she leapt. "Nice," he murmured.

"What's nice?"

His eyes narrowed. "The bikini."

She tossed her hair, which didn't toss at all because it was sopping wet and clinging to her head and shoulders. She hoped he got the point. "Oh? I didn't even realize you noticed."

His soft, sultry laugh clued her in to his mood. It held an edge, and she shivered, her heart starting to thud and her breaths getting raspy. "I realized you didn't realize."

"Tongue twister time?"

"What an *excellent* idea."

Without warning, he put his hands on her hips and pulled her hard against him. She barely managed to draw breath before his mouth captured hers, their tongues twisting in a way that was no rhyming game.

Jess wanted to sob with relief. He *did* still want her.

She threw her arms around his neck, turning her head to the side for a deeper, hotter connection. Despite the cool water dripping off them both, steam practically rose from their bodies. Their kiss was hungry, tongues giving and taking. He explored her mouth as if he needed to devour her, and he moaned as his hands skimmed from her hips, up her waist and midriff, to cup her breasts. Arching into his touch, she practically begged him to remove the bikini top, and with two tugs of each string, that's what he did.

Letting the top float away, he caught her breasts in each hand and stroked, making her moan against his lips. The water was a bit shocking against her vulnerable skin, but his hands were so big, so strong, so hot, she thought she'd die from the pleasure of it.

She'd ached for this. She wanted everything from him. And then she wanted it all again.

When Reece ended the kiss, he muttered, "You're such a cock tease."

"*What?*"

"You've been putting your hot body under me like

raw meat under a dog's nose, driving me out of my fucking mind."

"Oh, you noticed?" She leaned back, offering him more. She loved the way his hands felt on her, and the sun felt on her, and the water felt on her. Mostly she loved the way *Reece* felt on her. And she was dying to be reminded of the way he felt *in* her.

"Of course I did. I'm not blind. I wanted to do you right on the kitchen floor last night when you started dancing to that stupid old disco song."

Ahh. Donna Summer. A classic. How she did love to love him.

"I'm so glad you finally got the point."

"I got it the second you sashayed out of your bedroom Friday in those short shorts."

"So why didn't you do anything about it?"

He bent to bite her earlobe, making her hiss. "Despite the fact that a lot of people think I'm a selfish son of a bitch, I do know it's wrong to take advantage of a woman who's in pain."

She huffed. "It was just a little pain, and only in my throat."

He moved down that throat, tasting flecks of water, kissing, biting lightly. "Have I mentioned lately that you're pouty when you don't get your way?"

She stiffened. "I am no such thing."

"Yeah, you are." He licked her collarbone. "That mouth of yours was made for . . . pouting."

Oh, lord, did that ever put images in her head. Jess had a mental list of things she wanted to do with this man, and tasting every bit of him was high on it. She shivered remembering how big and hard he'd been last week, especially because he felt even bigger and harder now. While oral sex had never been high on her must-do list, it was with Reece. She wanted the intimacy of it, wanted to drive him crazy, wanted to pleasure him until he lost himself in her mouth.

"Admit you were pissed because you didn't get your way."

"If I admit it, will I get my way?" She groaned as he lifted her higher, his attention going lower.

"Oh yeah." His mouth was close, oh so close, to her breast. "Now admit it." He started rubbing his lips up the slope, his warm cheek brushing against her nipple for a brief, heart-stopping microsecond. "You've been sulking for two days."

"All right, I admit it." She groaned. "As long as you admit you've been a stubborn ass."

He laughed softly. "No, just a concerned one."

She lifted her head to stare at him. "I'm fine, Reece. My throat's fine, my body's fine. And I want you *so* much."

He kissed her, fast, hard, hot, and deep, then pulled away to rumble, "I want you, too, wild woman."

Pulling her legs around his hips, he continued a thorough, sensual exploration of her. Everywhere his mouth landed reacted with intense pleasure. Pushing her into a seat built into the side of the pool, he finally gave her what she'd been craving. He plumped her breast with his hand and moved his mouth over her nipple, pulling it between his lips and flicking it with his tongue.

She let out a low, satisfied cry and twined her fingers

in his wet hair. He sucked harder, and every nerve ending went on high alert. Each hungry suck sent fire surging between her legs. She needed it quenched more than she needed another lungful of air.

He seemed to know. Even as he moved to pleasure her other nipple, he slid a hand into the crotch of her bathing suit and stroked her clit. The heat of his fingertips and the chill of the water combined in a dizzying wave, and she gasped, thrusting against his touch.

Reece pushed her up out of the water, setting her on the edge of the deck, her feet still resting on the underwater seat. "Up," he ordered as he tugged at her bikini bottoms. She lifted, letting him pull them off her, holding her breath in anticipation of what was to come. She didn't know what he intended; she only knew it was going to be good.

He pushed her legs apart and kissed her right above the knee. Then those lips moved higher and higher, as if her thigh were a feast, until he reached her cleft.

"Beautiful," he muttered, his voice hoarse, before dipping in to taste her.

She threw back her head and cried out, captured by a deep, powerful orgasm that shattered her from end to end. Reece groaned with satisfaction, obviously realizing he'd brought her to climax within seconds, but he didn't stop tasting her, eating her into a frenzy.

"Oh, please," she begged, trying to pull him up. Orgasms were wonderful and all, but she wanted his body, wanted him covering her, filling her, *taking* her.

He stopped, looked up at her, and must have seen the need in her eyes. Without another word, he pushed himself up onto the step and rose to his feet in one smooth motion. Jessica gulped at his strength. Not to mention the massive bulge right in front of her face.

She lifted a hand, but he said, "Huh-uh."

Her bottom lip came out.

"God, I love that pout." He pulled her by the arms, stood her up, and stepped out of the water. Then, to her shock, he slowly walked around her, until he faced her back.

"What..."

"Shh. I've wanted to do this for weeks."

She knew what he intended one second before he kissed the nape of her neck and his hands went to her waist. His thumbs stroked the tiny bones at the base of her spine, and she lost her legs. She would have splatted face-first into the pool again if he hadn't held her steady.

"Oh, God," she groaned as he kissed his way down her back. Slowly. So slowly.

When he dropped to his knees and finally pressed his mouth against the deepest hollow of her back, she wanted to howl. It was so intense, so sensual, she had to arch forward, wondering how she had existed for twenty-five years without this man doing that to her.

But she needed him doing something else, and she slowly turned around. He smiled up at her. Reece Winchester's sexy, amazing smile, the one she'd longed to see up close and personal the night they met, was now all hers. It stayed on his face as he rose to his feet.

He reached for a towel and slowly rubbed it on her body, drying her, taking his damn sweet time. He had to know he was building the tension, the want. Part of her adored him for it. Part of her wanted to kill him.

After he'd dried himself, too, those muscles bulging and arms flexing, he tossed the towel to the side. Her hands went to the waistband of his trunks, slowly pulling the string to untie them. Before she managed it, he pushed her away, and then bent to sweep her into his arms, bride-style.

"What are you..."

"Inside. In a bed."

She shut up, letting him carry her through the house, to his bedroom. "This is where I should have been sleeping every night," she grumbled.

"Stick out that lip again," he said, his voice throaty. "I dare you."

She did. He caught it in his mouth and nipped her. She scratched his back. He twisted her hair. And then both of them fell onto the rumpled, unmade bed.

Although she wanted to pull his trunks off him, she wasn't sure she could, considering she was trembling like a leaf. So she settled for watching him do it. She shook when she saw him, all of him, masculine, massive, and proud. The closet had been too dark for her to really appreciate everything the man had to offer, and she had to clench her legs together, the wanting was so intense.

He grabbed a condom conveniently left on the bedside table, and sheathed himself. She was pleased to see that his hands trembled the tiniest bit—he was just as excited as she was.

Parting her legs in welcome, she smiled up at him. "I've been waiting for you."

"I know," he said, holding himself just above her on those powerful arms. "You're beautiful, Jessica Jensen."

She reached for him, cupping his face in her hand. "Do you think you want to keep me?"

There was no confusion in his eyes. He knew exactly what she meant. And he confirmed that she hadn't really misheard anything in the car the other night by saying, "Yes. I don't deserve you, but I do want to keep you."

She pulled him down and brushed her mouth across his. "That's good. Because I want to keep you, too."

Their lips parted and their tongues met. This time, their kiss was slow and sensual, and that was how he came into her. Slowly. Sensually.

Reece sank into her with exquisite restraint, a tender conquest this time, unlike the wild storm of last week. She closed her eyes, loving the feel of him as he dug a place for himself deep inside her, taking an inch, and then another, and then all of her body, and then her entire world.

Only when he thrust all the way home, wringing a cry of deep, guttural pleasure from her, did she again look up at him. She found him studying her face, his gaze intense, almost wondering.

"I *am* going to keep you, you know."

He said it as though there had been some doubt. Silly, silly man.

"Of course you are."

She arched up, meeting him as he began to slowly move in and out of her. Each movement was powerful, each thrust a claim. But even as they grew hotter, as the need increased, the intensity along with it, there was that same hint of wonder in his face.

It took her a while to figure out what it meant. When she finally did, she smiled and wrapped her arms and legs around him, whispering urgent demands in his ear.

He gave her what she wanted, hard strokes that broke her apart and put her back together again. When his whole body clenched, she clung to him as he came, hard and fast and forever. Only after he rolled over, dragging her onto him, did she allow herself to think about the realization she'd made when she had finally begun to understand the wonder she'd seen in his eyes.

Reece Winchester didn't just want to keep her.

He loved her.

CHAPTER 13

The phone rang early Monday morning, at around six thirty. Startled out of a sound sleep, for a second, Reece forgot where he was and what he'd been doing. Then he heard Jess mumble something in her sleep and glanced down to see her sweet, naked body curled around him.

Oh. Yeah. That's what he'd been doing. All night long.

He didn't know how he'd survived it. But, God, did he want to do it again.

He grabbed the phone. "Hello," he answered, keeping his voice low so he didn't wake her.

"Reece, it's me."

Rowan. He came to attention, hearing the seriousness in his brother's voice. Rolling away from Jess onto his side, he rose on his elbow. "What is it?"

"We've got her. Maisy Cullinan is in custody."

Relief flowed like a river, and he collapsed back on his pillow. "Thank God."

The woman who'd stalked him for months, who'd likely burned down his house, shot at him, and, most importantly, hurt the woman lying in his bed, had been caught. It was as if he'd awakened from a bad dream to face a sunny day.

With her history, and the damning evidence Maisy had left behind, he had no doubt she would be put away for a very long time. She would either go back to a mental hospital or go straight to prison. She might have enough money to hire the best lawyers, but she hadn't even tried to cover her tracks at the hotel; her face was all over the surveillance tape. Plus, according to Rowan, three neighbors of the murdered woman had now come forward as witnesses, and Cullinan's fingerprints had been found, not on the wiped-down murder weapon, but on a crystal glass holding watery iced tea in the victim's house.

It was over. Jessica was safe.

"There's more, bro. I don't think you're gonna like this."

"You've already made my day. Not much you can say that could ruin it."

"She wants to talk to you. She's insisting on it."

Reece inhaled slowly, and exhaled more slowly. Every muscle in his body tensed as anger roared through him. His head started to pound. The woman hadn't put him through enough hell? She was still trying to call the shots, to bend him to her will? Did she think she owned him?

"Why the hell would I agree to that?" he snapped.

Apparently he spoke too loudly. Jessica jerked awake. Her eyes flew open and she peered at him, asking a silent question. Feeling stupid for waking her, he forced himself to calm down. He grabbed her hand, shook his head, and returned his attention to the call.

"I know it's a lot to ask," his brother said. "And

normally I wouldn't. We've got her on attacking Jessica, and on the murder of Candace Waterstone."

"Okay, so what's the problem?"

"Sid Loman."

The gallery manager. The one he'd fired the night he and Jessica had met.

The one who'd turned up dead in the street.

"Did she kill him too?"

"She won't say. Nor will she say what she knows about the shooting at the gallery, or the fire at your house. Not unless she can talk to you."

"Jesus Christ." He put a hand over his eyes, knowing Jessica was growing more concerned. When he felt her hand on his chest, he grabbed it and squeezed.

"Maybe the other two cases will be enough to put her away, but you know she has a lot of money. She can hire the best of the best and drag this out."

Yes, she could, thanks to that stupid lottery jackpot.

"If she sees you, though, and gives us something on these other crimes, it adds more nails to her coffin. Hell, bro, she hinted that she might even confess and plead guilty, as long as she gets in a room with you."

If she didn't, the case would have to go to trial. With her many millions, the suspect could hire doctors, expert witnesses, and high-priced, unscrupulous attorneys. This nightmare might go on for years.

Jessica, the intended victim of one of Maisy Cullinan's murderous impulses, would have to testify, probably more than once. So would Reece, especially if she was charged with the arson and the shooting. It would be a Hollywood spectacle. There would be grand juries, hearings, trials, and appeals. Every time one of them came up, Jess would be dragged back through her worst nightmare, having to talk about what she'd gone through and relive it for years to come. Unless Maisy confessed and pled guilty.

"I'll do it," he said. "Where and when?"

"This afternoon," said Rowan. He sounded relieved. "She's being processed right now at Central, on Sixth Street."

"I'll be there."

"Thanks, man. For what it's worth, I think she'll do what she said. I know it's gonna be a bitch being in the same room with her, but, in the long run, it'll be the best thing for you, and for Jessica."

He disconnected the call, then waited for Jess to ask him who it had been or what had been said.

She wrapped an arm around his waist and entwined her legs with his, whispering, "You won't have to be alone in a room with her, will you?"

She'd heard, or she'd intuited. Jess was smart enough to know he had to do it. One more thing he loved about the woman—she had a lot of common sense.

"Definitely not."

Feeling moisture on his chest, and hearing the tiniest sniff, he wrapped his arms around her shoulders, knowing she was crying. He said nothing, aware she didn't like showing weakness. But it wasn't weakness. She was afraid only for *him*. That wasn't called weakness; it was called emotion.

They talked a little more, made slow love again, and fell back asleep. After only one night with her by his side, he wasn't sure he would ever be able to sleep well without her. His former relationships had never included nights like the last one, and he hadn't even realized what he was missing. Now he would know.

When he woke up again at nine, he watched her, wondering what single good thing he'd done in his life to find her. He also wondered when the bad ones would tear her away.

"Stop looking at me," she grumbled, pulling a pillow over her head. "Weirdo."

He got out of bed, taking his own pillow and tossing it on top of her. "I'm going to take a shower. The sooner I can get this day over with, the better."

The pillows came flying off. "Crap, I'd forgotten."

They exchanged a long look. He knew she wanted to ask him not to do it. She knew he would refuse. So neither of them said anything.

Once she was awake, she went into the kitchen to make them breakfast while he got ready for this afternoon's challenge. Knowing the woman in custody had invented some fantasy about them, and that she would read something into whatever he wore, he pulled on black pants and a black dress shirt. She could read into that whatever she wanted.

Going out to the kitchen, he heard Jess talking to someone. She was setting the table, her phone tucked against her shoulder, saying, "Okay, no, I'm fine. Of course I understand. I appreciate your candor. Goodbye."

He poured himself coffee, leaning against the counter. "Who was that?"

She sighed heavily as she began to butter toast. "My professor. He heard about what happened and knew I probably wouldn't be checking the school website, so he called to let me know about my final grade in his class."

"And?"

"B minus."

"That's not bad."

"It's the first B I've gotten in any of my major classes. Stupid final project got a D. I should just quit this business now."

He lowered his cup and went to her, taking her chin and lifting it up to stare at her. "Quitting is the one guaranteed way to fail out here. You never quit. Got it?"

She saluted. "Yes, sir."

That was Jess. Down for twenty-two seconds and right back to being confident and cocky. "So what was wrong with your final?"

"He said my writing wasn't mature enough to tackle the subject matter." She laughed. "Considering I was writing about my own life as a kid, I kinda wanted to argue that. But Alan knows what he's..."

"Alan?" he said, backing up a step. "Alan Bent? That's who you were just talking to?"

"Yes."

"Ignore him," he snapped, his stomach churning so much he didn't think he'd even be able to keep down a piece of that toast. "He's *nothing*."

Jess lowered the bread and the butter knife. Crossing her arms in front of her chest, she said, "When are you going to tell me what your problem with him is?"

He shook his head. Usually Jess was so sharp. Maybe her friendship with her advisor had blinded her in some ways. "I can't stand him," he admitted. "And if he says your work is bad, you should run out and copyright it because he's probably trying to steal it."

Her mouth fell open. "*What?*"

He knew better than to think he could leave it at that. He also knew that Jess had another semester to go, and she could end up in a classroom with that slimy SOB again. She wasn't a twelve-year-old boy, so he didn't worry about her physically. But there had been rumors about Alan's work in the past…and how he sometimes claimed credit for things he had not created.

"Think about it, Jess. Think about the one time I worked with him. I know you know what I'm talking about. Deep down, I *know* you do."

She hesitated, her head tilted as she puzzled it out. And then she straightened it.

"Caleb," she whispered.

"Caleb. And others."

Her hand on the counter, she staggered onto the nearest bar stool, shaking her head in disbelief. "Are you sure?"

"I'm sure." Whenever he heard Bent's name, he wanted to hurt someone, as the director had hurt several of the children in his power. "I found out after Caleb's death. Coming back here might have involved my need to get a little revenge. Rowan and I made it a pet project for several years. Bent was the first one we went after."

"You blackballed him."

"I wanted to get him put away but couldn't find enough evidence, or anybody willing to testify." He almost spit the words as he added, "This town likes its secrets."

She swiped both hands through her hair. He had no doubt she was mentally kicking herself for not having figured it out sooner. "He knows, and hates you for it. That's why he warned me off you."

Not a surprise. "What did he say?"

"He said I shouldn't trust you, shouldn't take the job, and *definitely* shouldn't let you read my screenplay."

"Did you believe him?"

She rolled her eyes. "Did you see me in the office last week? Have you noticed I'm here right now?"

"Smart ass."

"Jerk."

He leaned close and kissed her, both of them smiling.

Afterward, though, something began to nag at him. While killing time between Jessica's bouts of consciousness, Reece had dropped a few emails to friends in the business. He'd wanted to find out if anybody knew anything about Bent's return. He'd been surprised to hear the old reprobate was shopping a script, trying to make a comeback. It was about a . . . "A little girl?"

"Huh?"

The pulse in his temple began to throb. "What, exactly, is your story about?"

"Me. My childhood—dad gone, mom dies, kid ends up in foster care. Bad things happen."

"You're kidding."

"Come on, doesn't every writer put their own story on paper at some point?" she asked, looking a little hurt.

"No, that's not what I mean." He reached into his pocket for his phone, yanked it out, and pulled up a long list of emails, trying to find one in particular. He opened it, read the contents again, and then handed the phone to her.

"What am I looking at?"

"A response I got from a friend of mine at Miramax. Walter, actually. He did some checking and said his boss got that email from Bent, pitching a script."

"Okay. So?"

"Read the pitch, Jess."

She enlarged the print on the screen, then held the phone closer. He watched her as she read.

First, her brow furrowed in confusion. Then her mouth tightened.

The anger line appeared between her eyes.

And finally, she gasped. "Are you fucking kidding me?"

He plucked the phone out of her hand, knowing she was tempted to throw it across the room, not that he'd blame her.

"I can't believe it. Can this really be happening?" she asked, slamming her hand on the counter, her anger making her whole body shake.

Not even responding, he pulled up his contacts list, found a name, and dialed. "Shh," he told her as it began to ring.

She gaped. "Seriously? You're making a call now?"

"To a friend of mine, a literary attorney."

She started to say something, but he held a finger up to stop her as his friend answered. When she heard him tell the lawyer that he wanted him to file a copyright claim on a script immediately, now, this morning, and that Jess would email him the details within the next ten minutes, she let out a long breath and visibly relaxed.

As soon as he ended the call, she started talking again. "How could he do that? Does he really intend to just steal my story? The story I poured my heart into?"

"Yes, that's exactly what he intended to do." He held her closely, stroking her hair. "He won't try it now, though, I promise you that. This time when I take him down, he's going down for good."

* * *

After Reece left that afternoon, Jess sat for a long time, just worrying.

It wasn't like her. She was a doer, not a worrier. And part of her was feeling relieved, not concerned. She was glad that, for the first time since the night they'd met, she didn't have to fear for his physical safety. His stalker was in custody. On the other hand, she was also worried about him *because* his stalker was in custody, and he had agreed to meet with the evil, murderous witch.

It wasn't as though she feared Maisy Cullinan would have a shiv hidden on her, and would launch across a table and plunge it into his heart, screaming, "If I can't have you, nobody can."

No, that's ridiculous.

It was. Still, she wished she hadn't thought of it; now the picture was stuck in her mind.

Her more realistic concern, though, was about him being exposed to that kind of insanity. Everything he had told her about his mother, her mental illness, her breakdown, and her final years, had not only broken her heart; it had also made it clear he carried real scars from that time in his life. Now he was being put in a room with a mentally ill woman who was obsessed with him. She wasn't sure how he would respond.

He'll be fine, she told herself for the hundredth time, knowing it was silly to be worried about such a strong, capable man. He'd handled so much; he could certainly deal with this.

Maybe that was why the two of them were so drawn to each other. They'd each endured trials by fire at about the same age, and had come through them scarred but not completely burned. So logically, she knew there was nothing to worry about. But she wouldn't be completely at ease until she saw his car coming back up the long driveway.

Before he left, they'd sent all the documentation needed for his attorney to file a copyright claim on her script. Fortunately, Liza had brought her laptop to her at the hospital, so Jess had the file handy. She'd even let Reece talk her into sending a copy to him. It made her nervous as hell, but she couldn't deny that, if Alan proceeded with this scheme after he learned she was onto him, having someone of Reece's stature announcing that he'd read it might help. If it came to legal action, she would probably be able to prove her authorship with computer records and time stamps. Frankly, though, she'd rather cut the director off at the knees before it got that far.

Now, having nothing else to do other than wish she had an Alan Bent voodoo doll, she decided to go outside. It was yet another gorgeous California day, warm and breezy, with a brilliant blue sky. A dip, some lounging, and a good book seemed like the perfect way to put the done/over period on the story of Maisy Cullinan. When Reece got home, hot sex in that pool would be the exclamation point.

As always, she slathered her redhead's burn-prone skin with SPF 50 before grabbing a paperback off the shelf. It was the novelization of one of Reece's movies. She would bet he hated it, and she looked forward to teasing him about it when she finished. She could almost picture his expression when she claimed the book was always better than the movie.

Unfortunately, after reading only the first fifty pages of the thing, she had to toss it aside. It was so bad, she wouldn't even be able to pretend to argue with him about it later.

Hot after the brief time in the sun, she stepped into the shallow end, sighing as cool water enveloped her. She dove in and swam a couple of laps to get her blood pumping.

She was just about to switch her stroke when she heard a buzzer from inside the house, signaling someone was at the gate at the bottom of the driveway. Her heart lifted as she realized who it must be.

Liza had called earlier, saying she didn't think she

was going to be able to come up today after all, but
would try. Apparently her sister had worked it out. She
grabbed a towel and hurried to the sliding glass door.
The kitchen was tiled, and her feet were wet. Not wanting to make a mess, or slip and break her neck—Reece
would kill her if he came home to find her corpse in his
kitchen—she put one foot in and reached around the
wall to push the button for the gate. While she waited
for Liza to arrive, she dried off more thoroughly so she
wouldn't slip and slide her way through the house.

The doorbell rang. She hurried to answer it, prepared to ask Liza if she wanted her margarita on the
rocks or frozen. Spending the afternoon drinking fruity
drinks sounded like the ideal way to get her mind off
where Reece was and what he was doing.

She swung the door open, and the words died in
her mouth. It wasn't her petite, adorable sister. Instead,
standing on the covered porch was a tall, bulky man,
someone she would *never* have expected to show up on
Reece's doorstep.

"Steve?"

Steve Baker, former actor, a guy she knew Reece had
hoped to never see again, stood outside, a grin on his
face. "Hi, uh, Jessica, isn't it?"

"Yes."

He waited expectantly. She tilted her head in confusion.

"Oh, no, didn't Reece tell you I was coming up?"

She stopped her jaw from hitting her chest right as
it began to fall, snapping her mouth closed. "No, he
neglected to mention that."

"That guy," he said with a hearty laugh. He lifted a bulging satchel. "He's giving me a reading for a small part in his next film and told me to feel free to stop by so we could talk about it before the audition."

Part of her was thrilled Reece had done as she'd asked him to do. He'd put aside his old resentment and thrown a bone to an old friend. But she really wished he'd remembered to call the man to cancel, or at least let Jess know about the appointment. Especially because she was standing here in a skimpy bikini.

Although she felt awkward playing hostess in Reece's house, she felt bad that he'd come all the way up here because Reece hadn't called him to cancel. She also couldn't help noticing the sweat on Steve's brow and the redness of his face. It was a hot day, and courtesy demanded she at least let him come in to cool off before she sent him away again.

"He's not here, unfortunately. Something came up," she said, stepping back and opening the door wider. "But please, come in for a cold drink."

He followed her inside, closing his eyes and smiling as the cool air hit his face. "You're a lifesaver. My car's air conditioner isn't working right."

Leading him into the kitchen, she grabbed her beach towel off the counter and wrapped it around herself, sarong-style. She wished her shorts and shirt were here as well, but at least it was better than her bathing suit. No, she hadn't gotten any bad vibes off the man the first time they met, but given all her recent experiences, Jess couldn't help being on guard. The house was so secluded, and he was a stranger.

"Is iced tea okay? I brewed it this morning."

"Perfect," he said.

"Sugar and lemon?" Such a hostess. Emily would be proud.

"Please."

She prepared a glass, added a lemon wedge, and handed it to him. As he leaned to take it, she caught a whiff of something on his breath.

That's scotch. It was midafternoon, but Steve had already been drinking.

The first time she'd seen him, she had noticed his prematurely aged face and red nose, and suspected he had a drinking problem. Knowing he had driven up here after tossing one—or several—back irritated her. On these roads, even on the driveway—*especially* on the driveway—that was reckless.

"So do you have any idea when Reece will be back?"

Although she knew it might be hours, something made her say, "Could be any time."

"Oh, great. If you don't mind, I'll just stick around."

Crap. That strategy had backfired. Now, instead of keeping the man on his best behavior with the knowledge they could be interrupted at any second, she'd just given him an excuse to stay and wait. "Or it might take longer," she said, wondering if he heard the tremor in her voice.

"It's okay. Hey, I meant to say, I'm glad you're all right. I heard the sirens at the hotel last week, and saw Reece looking like a madman as you were carried out. When I read about it the next day, I understood why. How awful for you!"

"I'm fine, thank you," she said, sitting across from him at the tall breakfast bar. She sipped her own tea and wondered where her small-talk ability had gone. It was MIA, along with her peace of mind. *Why am I jittery?*

"I heard on the news this morning that they caught the woman who did it. And she killed somebody else? That's crazy, man."

Her hand tightened around her glass. Every time she thought about the murder, her thoughts darkened. Not just with sympathy for the victim, but with a hint of fear. It could so easily have been her, or Reece. Not just the night of the chemical attack, but with that shot at the gallery. No, the woman apparently hadn't confessed to it yet, but there seemed to be little doubt she was the one who'd done it.

"It was a rough couple of weeks. I'm glad it's over."

"Me too." That nonstop smile broadened even more, though his eyes seemed flat. Because she was studying them, she noticed immediately when he dropped his attention to her chest for a quick peek.

She straightened the towel.

He pretended he hadn't been looking.

"So it seems like you and Reece are pretty serious."

Jessica's tension built. Every woman knew to obey the little Spidey sense that said the words coming out of a man's mouth didn't match his mood or expression. This guy's didn't. His smile was too broad, his voice a little loud. He was trying to hide the fact that he'd been drinking. Maybe he'd just been fortifying himself for the meeting with Reece, knowing there was a lot riding on the audition, but she didn't think that was it.

Something strange was going on here. She didn't like it.

"I'm so...happy for him."

She heard the hesitation and saw his hand tighten around his glass. It was like he had a poker player's tell—a sign he unconsciously made when bluffing. She just didn't know what game he was playing or who was holding the better hand.

"You know, why don't I call him? Maybe he'll want you to come into the city and meet him at his office."

Not waiting for him to respond, she got up and headed for the door. She had left her cell phone outside. Good thing—she preferred to be out in the open rather than in the enclosed house. It felt a little safer, despite the fact that there were no close neighbors.

You're being paranoid. Steve was an old friend of Reece's family, and Reece himself admitted he'd been innocent in Rachel's descent. He had been maligned and practically ridden out of Hollywood. On top of that, his father had died a brutal death. He deserved her pity, not suspicion.

That was why she didn't react when Steve followed her out.

"God, what a view!" he said, staring out at the hills rising on either side of the yard, and the edge of the cliff that fell away across the back. "Can we sit out here for a while?"

Relief flooded her. That didn't sound like a man who was trying to keep her in an enclosed space. Of course, given the hills, the cliff, and the high metal fence running along the front of the property, they *were* in an enclosed space. It wasn't as confining at the house, at least.

"Sounds good. I was just enjoying the pool before you arrived."

"Don't let me stop you," he said, wagging his brows, giving off that creepy vibe again.

She smiled tightly. "Oh, I should stay covered up. You know redheads and sun."

Steve scooted another lounge chair close to the one she'd been using. Dropping his satchel onto it, he said, "Um, actually, mind if I use the restroom?"

"Of course not." She told him where to find it and watched him go inside. As soon as he was gone, she grabbed her shorts and T-shirt from the pool deck and yanked them on.

Why did men not realize women were primed to be suspicious of strangers? That it might not be cool to intrude when a woman was alone, to sneak uncomfortable glances and make suggestive comments? It was the twenty-first century. Every woman in the world had run into men who gave her the creeps. She didn't understand why the decent ones didn't grab a clue and follow some basic rules of conduct.

Maybe this isn't a decent one.

Remembering the reason she'd come out here in the first place, and suddenly wanting to hear Reece's voice, she glanced at the door, hoping to make the call before her visitor returned. She couldn't imagine Steve would tell such an easily disproven lie, but she wanted to be sure Reece really had been expecting him.

She only hoped she could reach him. He had been gone for about ninety minutes and might very well be sitting in a police interrogation room facing the woman who'd tried to kill Jess less than a week ago. Wanting something to ground her, however, she tried anyway.

Hoping to keep it dry, she had left her phone on a small table out of splashing range. She spun around to retrieve it, forgetting Steve had repositioned the other chair.

"Ow," she snapped as she banged right into it. That was going to bruise the heck out of her shin.

Her hard knock had not only injured her; it had also sent Steve's satchel flying off the seat. Pages of a scene-side, probably the one he was working on with Reece, had fallen on the wet cement, as had other documents, a notebook, and bound scripts. Embarrassed, and glad he was taking a while inside, she bent to scoop everything up. She'd have to lay the pages out on the chair and hope they would be legible when they dried.

Before she picked up a single one, though, something else caught her eye. It had fallen between the two lounges—a bound script, with all the typical proprietary warnings about not sharing it. ACTOR'S COPY was stamped on top, the title below.

And below that were two signatures, plus a hand-written sentence.

Her heart started to pound. Feeling like she was still in the water, moving through it slowly, she picked up the bound pages. She had left her sunglasses inside, and had to squint against the brilliant sunlight to make sure she was reading correctly.

ACTOR'S COPY: RACHEL WINCHESTER. *Together at Last.*

Below that, in a boyish scrawl, was Reece's signature; beside it, his sister's. The additional writing proclaimed the Winchesters as the world's biggest stars.

There was something else. Drawn in the bottom corner was a heart, with the initials RW and SB.

"Oh, my God," she whispered, recognizing what she held. There couldn't be two scripts like this; it was an irreplaceable piece of history. Reece's history, or at least one precious moment of it. He thought it had been lost forever in the fire that destroyed his home. But Steve Baker—Rachel's teenage boyfriend—had it in his possession.

This could mean only one thing.

"I wish you hadn't seen that."

She swung her head up. Steve stood a few feet behind her. Jess launched to her feet, clutching the script to her chest and backing away slowly between the chairs.

"You burned down Reece's house."

He stared at her for a long moment. "Please give that back."

She took another step back on the slippery deck. "Admit it."

He extended a hand, his whole face tense, a mixture of anger and what looked like sadness. "Please, Jessica, give it back to me. It's precious."

Not because of the signatures, she'd bet, but because of that heart. Rachel had doodled it on one happy day of her life, when all had been right with her world and cute TV star Steve Baker had been her boyfriend.

He started to walk toward her. Reacting instinctively, knowing she was in danger, Jess extended her arm, holding the script over the deep water. "One more step and she swims."

He froze, his stare focused on her hand. "You wouldn't. Reece..."

"Reece has already mourned the loss of this. Not to mention everything else he owns."

Steve's back stiffened. "That fire was an accident."

"Bullshit. They found accelerant."

Finally looking her in the eye, he insisted, "I didn't mean to burn the house down. I just..." He swept a hand over his red, sweaty brow. "I was looking for something."

"This?"

"No. Not that. But when I saw it...when I saw his room with all the awards, the pictures, the memories, I lost it."

The self-pitying tone really got on her nerves. "Poor you."

"Look, I was drunk. I went a little crazy seeing everything he had that I was supposed to. I dumped some booze on some of his stuff and threw a match. It just got out of control."

"So you let his house burn down because he was successful and you weren't." She glanced at the script in her hand. "All you gave a damn about was this."

He walked toward her again, reaching out. She leapt back, forgetting the other items that had spilled out of Steve's bag. Her feet hit wet paper, and she skidded like an old cartoon character slipping on a banana peel.

As her feet flew out from under her, she heard Steve cry out. He lunged forward, though whether he was trying to grab her or the script, she didn't know. It didn't matter. Her feet hit the water, the rest of her body starting in after them.

All except her head. That went straight down on the concrete lip of the pool before she fell all the way in. And brightest day descended into darkness.

CHAPTER 14

The ten minutes Reece spent with a deranged woman who thought he was going to marry her were eleven minutes too many. His only solace was that they'd paid off.

Sitting in his car as he left the city, he thought about the pool at the house. He wanted to get in it, needing to feel washed clean of the crazy that had rained down on him in that interview room. He wanted Jessica in there with him so he could hold her close and promise never to expose her to anyone like that again.

After a briefing with the detectives handling the case, Reece had gone into the interview room with three goals: getting Maisy Cullinan to confess to the shooting at the gallery, the murder of Sid Loman, and the fire at his house. He'd succeeded with two of those goals almost immediately. When she saw him, she'd begun to weep, begging him to forgive her for firing the shot at him through the gallery window.

Check. One down.

"I would never—ever hurt you, darling! I was just so mad," she'd exclaimed as she wiped her tears and her nose on her arm. "I can't control myself when I get mad. Why did you make me mad?"

She hadn't expressed any remorse at all when talking about Jessica, Sid Loman, or the woman she'd killed in Brentwood. She only feared he would believe she had intended to hurt *him*.

He had remained silent throughout most of the visit, letting her talk, plead, cry, and tell him all about her plans for their future. The recorded conversation had given the police enough details to charge her with a number of crimes.

Reece pitied her for her illness and her delusions. But maintaining that pity had been damned hard when she asked how much skin and hair Jess had lost because of the bleach attack.

"Her house. She wants to give me her house?" he muttered, shaking his head and drumming his fingers on the steering wheel. Her "gift" was the other reason she'd demanded to see him.

I bought it for us to live in together.

He'd remained silent throughout most of the visit, but at that, he hadn't been able to refrain from snapping, "Is that why you burned down mine?"

Her response had surprised him, and he couldn't help going over it in his mind. *I didn't do that. I would never do that! You lost all your things, all the awards and statues that would have looked so beautiful in our home.*

Her denial still bothered him. She'd confessed to everything else—including killing Sid Loman because she thought he had seen her shoot at the gallery window. So why not throw a little arson in the confession soup?

About to get off the highway, he suddenly remembered he had promised his dad he would come by to pick up Cecil B. today. He almost turned around to do it, but something made him keep heading toward home. He wanted—no, right now he *needed*—to see Jessica.

Reece had done what he had to do. Maisy had agreed to plead guilty to many of the charges, meaning Jessica wouldn't have to testify. Knowing what a relief it would be to her, he didn't want to delay telling her it was really over.

There was one more thing he needed to tell her ... that he loved her. Having realized it at some point during the past couple of days, he knew he had to say the words out loud.

He didn't deserve her, for any number of reasons. One was that he was still keeping secrets from her, for the sake of his brothers.

No. Not just them. You too. Coward. It was a bitter truth. He feared he would lose her if she found out what else he was guilty of.

"She could do so much better," he told himself as he reached the driveway and waited for the gate to open. But he was a selfish enough bastard that he wanted her anyway. He wanted her in his life, in his future, and he envisioned making her his wife.

That meant she had to know everything. She couldn't become part of his family without being told what that family was capable of.

For the first time in six years, he was going to have to revisit the memories of *that* night, and admit what he and his brothers had done. What happened between them afterward would be in her hands. He would have to hope she understood, and that she stayed.

Spotting a strange car parked in the driveway, he figured Liza had decided to pay her promised visit. Although glad Jess had company, he couldn't help being disappointed they wouldn't be alone for a while. Now that he was in the confession zone, he wanted to get it over with so he could proceed into the *I love you* scene, and then the black moment where he would wait and hope she wasn't so disgusted by him that she took off.

He wanted it over with, but he was also dreading it. He'd never been a procrastinator, but suddenly thought Liza's visit wasn't such a bad thing after all. *Delay of execution.*

Entering the house, he looked around and called, "Jess? Where are you guys?"

No answer. He headed for the kitchen. Figuring they were probably sitting by the pool, he dropped his keys and phone onto the counter and went to the sliding glass doors.

What he saw through them stopped his heart, until adrenaline surged and sent it racing. In a lifetime that passed in one endless second, he let what he was seeing soak in.

A large man was kneeling over a prone form on the far side of the pool. It was Jessica, limp and unmoving, the ends of her wet hair dangling in the pool.

Blood was running from her temple down into her hair.

Steve Baker's hands were on her shoulders, close to her neck.

"What the fuck did you do to her?" he shouted as

he threw the door open and ran outside, rage and fear warring to control him.

Steve jerked his head up, his eyes widening in shock. Looking terrified, he reacted in an instant, far faster than Reece ever imagined possible for such a big man. He yanked Jessica up, wrapping one beefy arm around her middle and one around her throat, clutching her back against his chest as if she were a rag doll.

"Stay back," he called. "She's barely breathing. She almost drowned. Come any closer and I'll finish her off."

Reece froze, wondering what in the name of God was going on here. This couldn't have been an accident; he wouldn't be threatening her if it were. Had Steve tried to assault her? Had he tried to cover up his crime by staging a drowning, leaving the woman Reece loved dead in the pool, a horrible gift for him to find when he came home?

Images of that scenario flooded his mind, but he forced them out. If he envisioned them too long, he would lose control. Jess needed him. Whatever he did now could mean the difference between her life and her death.

The thirty-meter-long pool separated him from Jess and Steve. He could run around it, or dive in and swim its length, but in the long seconds it would take to reach them, Steve might be able to tighten his grip and finish what he'd started.

He had to keep the man calm and wait for a better opportunity.

"You're sure she's alive?" he called, the words hard

to push out. Even as he asked the question, he saw her move, lifting a weak arm. He exhaled slowly. "It's okay, Jess. Everything's going to be okay."

"That depends on what you do, Reece."

"Baker, what the hell are you doing? Have you lost your mind?"

Steve was shaking, crying, his face red, his thick neck corded with straining muscles. He looked like a bull about to gore. "I know what you did. Admit what you did to my father."

The whole story changed in an instant, an unscripted moment striking the set like a lightning bolt.

A slow-motion shot.

Camera right.

Zoom in on the face.

Tight close-up to catch the director's expression as fear turns to remorse. Guilt.

And, cut!

"Steve," he called. He extended a supplicating hand and began to walk around the pool. "You don't want to do this."

"Stop right there!"

The arm tightened. Jessica whimpered. Reece froze.

The other man's eyes were wild; so was his voice. "You pick up the phone and call the cops to confess to what you did." He backed up, crossing the far end of the pool deck, closing the distance to the open space behind it.

"You don't understand," Reece said.

Steve took two more steps back. "How would you feel about losing someone you love?"

I already have. More than once.

He didn't say the words, not wanting to inflame the man further. Not when Steve had Jessica in his grasp. Not when he was backing slowly toward a sharp, rocky cliff, a mere fifty paces from the pool.

The jagged cliffs plunging to the valley below were stark, dramatic, and beautiful.

They were also deadly.

"She's got nothing to do with this. Please, let her go."

A step.

He threw a hand up, palm out. "I'll make the call. Just stay right there."

The crazed man kept going, dragging Jess through a rock-filled garden. Her heels scraped stone, but she put up no resistance. If she were fully conscious and coherent, he knew she would be struggling. But she was weak, probably finding it hard to breathe. He suspected powerful hands had been around her neck, choking her right before he arrived. Jesus. Once again, she was being robbed of oxygen because she'd been in the path of someone wanting to get at *him*.

"Steve, let's talk about this." He started walking again, slowly, as if approaching a wild animal. He had rounded the end of the pool and was moving up the long side, getting to within about twenty feet of them. Steve was perhaps another twenty-five feet from the edge of the sheer, rocky cliff. "I'll confess to everything. Just let her go. She's innocent, and she needs help."

The other man laughed, sounding almost happy. "You love her. You really do. The famous Reece Winchester, Mr. Cool, Mr. Aloof, has fallen in love at last."

"You're not thinking straight. You don't want to do this."

He took another cautious step. Steve seemed beyond noticing for the moment.

"Of course I do. My life is ruined. Why shouldn't yours be?" He laughed again, the laughter shifting into a crazed wounded animal sound.

Cursing the fact that he'd dropped his cell phone on the counter as he'd walked through the kitchen, Reece begged the man. "Bring her back. Please. I'll call the police right this minute and you can watch them take me into custody."

Another step for both of them. Knowing he wasn't getting through, he went over his options. He couldn't risk going for the phone to prove he meant what he said. Honestly, he wasn't sure a confession would stop the man. Now that Steve had realized how terrified Reece was for Jess, he might have only murderous revenge on his mind.

Reece moved again—*slow motion, drag the shot, zoom in on the upper body, don't show the feet. The actor draws closer, the audience barely noticing.*

He was playing a deadly game of chicken with the man, but he had no other choice.

Steve didn't take his eyes off Reece's face, too lost to anger and grief to notice he was getting closer. Not close enough to charge him, but almost. If they got to within ten feet of the edge, Reece would make a break for it. Now, it seemed wiser to continue to try to reason with him.

"Do you know why, Steve? Why your father died?"

"Because you and your brothers murdered him."

Jessica stiffened in Steve's arms. She was aware and listening. He hoped she was waiting for her chance to escape, and not so shocked by the ugly truths she was hearing that she hesitated.

"It wasn't murder, it was an accident. Raine was just a teenager. They fought."

"I know. I talked to the girl."

Reece sucked in a surprised breath. The girl...the missing girl?

"You didn't expect that, did you? She came to see me a couple of months ago, when I first got back. I gave her money, and she told me everything."

Not everything. They'd looked for her over the years, trying to find out what had gone on that night in Harry Baker's house. Raine's recollection was hazy. He'd been drunk, and a little insane, as all his repressed memories from childhood exploded into his brain like a bullet. All because of the nameless girl, who he hadn't even known was in the house until he heard her scream.

"If you found her, you know what really happened. You know why Raine snapped. Your father was raping her, Steve. He was raping a girl who looked no more than thirteen."

"That's a lie," he shouted.

"You know it's true." Another step. "I've heard the rumors about what was found on Harry's computer after he died...rumors you paid to keep quiet."

Steve's head swung back and forth violently, whether in denial, or in an effort to shake the memories out, Reece didn't know. He only knew the man was listening. More importantly, he'd stopped backing up.

"Your dad..." *Good old Uncle Harry, they'd called him throughout the years when he'd been their agent. Family friend. Jolly business partner. High-functioning alcoholic. Life of the party. Fucking sick rapist.* "He invited Raine over that night so they could say good-bye before my brother left for boot camp. He gave him alcohol."

Raine had been well under the legal age in California. That alone showed the kind of man "Uncle" Harry had been.

"They had a few drinks, and Raine was too drunk to drive home. He decided to crash at the house."

The youngest Winchester kid, cereal commercial star, had been seventeen years old, turning eighteen and leaving for the military the very next day. Before he got on the plane, he took a detour to hell.

"He woke up in the middle of the night hearing a girl crying for help and went out to investigate. He saw your father holding her down."

He didn't add that the moment had made all the horrific, repressed memories his kid brother had kept hidden from everyone—even himself—rupture inside his brain.

"He snapped, Steve. He went a little crazy, and the two of them fought. What happened was a fight. Raine wasn't trying to kill Harry."

Steve had been quietly listening, not appearing convinced, but at least paying attention. Now, though, his banked fury roared into flame again. "Liar—you liar! After the girl hid outside, she saw my father on the porch, screaming at Raine as he ran away. He was *fine*. And then she saw you and your other brother come

back a little while later. After you left, my father was
dead on the floor with a bullet in his head. You and
Rowan did it. Don't try to pass this off on Raine. It
was *you*."

Barcly listening to the man's slurred raving, Reece
shook his head. "You've got it wrong. Jesus, Steve, you
don't understand what happened. You don't get it."

"What don't I get? Cold-blooded murder?"

Reece swept both hands through his hair, feeling
weary and heartsick. He took a step forward, but Steve
warned him with a glare not to do it again. Still, they
were closer than they'd been since the standoff had
started. Close enough for Reece to lower his voice. He
wanted Steve to have to really pay attention to what he
was going to say next. He needed him to *hear*.

"Didn't you ever wonder?"

"Wonder what, why you killed my father?"

"About Rachel. Didn't you wonder why she changed
so much?"

Steve's suddenly grieved expression told him what he
needed to know. He still had feelings for Reece's sister.
They were the key to getting through to him.

"You must have asked yourself why she went from
a cheerful, happy girl into someone so moody and
depressed. Why she wanted to quit acting, why she
stopped wearing makeup and pretty clothes. Why she
broke up with you, why she started taking pills and
doing coke."

"Her new friends..."

"There *were* no new friends. I was there. I saw her
at home every night, saying nothing, turning into a pale

shadow, afraid to leave the house. Don't you think if she really was with a new crowd, pictures would have shown up in a tabloid, especially after she died?"

Steve looked as if someone had punched him in the gut. He groaned and leaned forward a little, though he didn't drop his hostage.

Reece suddenly realized Jess was watching him closely. Her eyes looked clearer, more focused. She stared into his, letting him know she was feeling better, able to help in her own rescue. But he didn't want to risk rushing them, not when they were so close to the cliff, and Steve was so strong. He much preferred to convince the man to let her go of his own free will, and believed he might be getting somewhere.

"Why are you telling me all this?" Steve mumbled. "She's been dead for eighteen years."

"Because you need to know the truth." He put into words something he'd never said out loud to anyone other than his two brothers. "She had all the classic signs of molestation."

Steve's turned apoplectic. "I never touched her! We never..."

"I know." He moved in—within ten feet now. "I know you didn't. She told me she wanted to wait until you two got married. You really were the sweetest teenagers in Hollywood."

They had been. Remembering the way his only sister had laughed at being called a prissy virgin, how she'd been proud of it, he wanted to scream at the injustice. She'd been too good for the world they'd grown up in. Much too good. And it had killed her.

Steve was heaving in deep breaths. His grip on Jessica might have loosened a bit, and his attention had definitely refocused. "You really think someone hurt her?"

"I know it. It started when she was fifteen and continued until the night she died."

Looking stunned, Steve stumbled backward, causing Reece's heart to lurch. But he quickly steadied himself, and Jess, barking, "Who? Who was it?"

Was it really so hard for him to understand? Couldn't he connect the dots?

Maybe not. Jess hadn't wanted to believe her teacher intended to steal her work. So a man refusing to accept his own father had raped his teenage girlfriend probably made sense.

Reece knew better than to just say it; he had to take Steve back in time. Right to the night when Reece's entire life had changed direction, setting him on a completely new course. "The night Rachel died..."

Steve flinched.

"You know she was in a hotel suite in Atlanta, baby-sitting Raine."

"She called me." His voice dropped to a whisper. "I was still mad at her for breaking up with me and I didn't answer."

Reece knew that. It was part of the legend, one of the reasons the fans had blamed him.

"She and Raine were watching a rerun of *Dear Family*—the episode she guest starred in."

"Season four, episode seven. That's when we met." His voice cracked. "She played the new girl in school who I was crazy about."

"I know. I think that's why she called."

"Oh, God...if I'd answered..."

"Don't do that to yourself. I really don't think it would have changed anything. Not once *he* showed up."

Steve stepped toward him, bringing Jess along. She stumbled, but he kept her against his chest. "Who? Who showed up?"

Reece moved in. *Eight steps.* "Raine was sick. He had caught a cold when they were on set. Rachel gave him cough medicine and put him to bed."

"Get on with it." Steve looked like a man possessed.

"You have to understand how I know what happened. Raine woke up later, wanting a glass of water. He heard Rachel crying out, saying the word *stop* over and over."

"Oh, God." Steve lifted a shoulder and bent his face to it, trying to wipe away tears.

"He went into the living room of the suite and saw her. Her clothes were torn, and she was being held down by a man. A man Raine recognized. A man he called Uncle."

Steve gasped, at last understanding. "No. Don't you dare say that."

"It was your father. Good old Uncle Harry. Life of every party."

"You're lying." Steve puffed up again, all anger, vengeance, and disbelief. "That's not true. My father was a great man."

"Don't you fucking *dare* defend him to me," Reece roared, his own fury rolling over him. Eighteen years' worth of it. "That man destroyed my family."

"It couldn't have been him. He wouldn't..."

"Raine *saw* him raping her. He was six years old. He didn't understand what he was seeing then, but he remembers now and understands everything."

Jessica tugged her bottom lip between her teeth, her eyes shining. She was probably seeing the scene as he did whenever his worst dreams taunted him, and it had brought her to tears. Not unexpectedly, she was focused on his drama, not on her own dangerous situation.

"When Rachel realized he was up, she hissed at Raine to go back to bed."

The brothers had wondered, over the years, what would have happened if Harry had been less focused on assault and more on her words. If he'd known Raine had seen him, might two of the Winchester siblings have gone over the railing that night?

"Go on, don't stop now," Steve snapped.

"Raine hid but watched from a dark hallway. She pushed Harry off her and ran to the balcony. Your father followed her, trying to get her to stop screaming. Only one of them came back in alive. *You* tell *me* why."

They stared at each other, both of them breathing heavily, both strained, tense, full of pain and anger. Both of them had loved the same lost girl. Both of them had once considered Harry Baker a good guy. Both of them had seen their lives, dreams, and families torn apart.

Both of them now knew the truth.

Steve's face crumpled. "Do you really think he...he killed her?"

Reece had wondered that same thing for years. "I don't know."

No one ever would.

Maybe his sister had turned the wrong way while trying to escape and fell by accident. Maybe she'd intentionally jumped, unable to stand another minute of what was happening to her. Or maybe the man who'd been attacking her pushed her over so he could keep her quiet.

Raine hadn't witnessed their sister's final seconds. A terrified, sick little boy, he had crawled back into his bed, certain he'd been dreaming. Even when he found out Rachel was gone, he didn't let himself remember, blocking the whole thing out of his mind for years.

Rachel's death would always remain an unknowable secret, a Hollywood mystery that would never be solved.

"Finish it, Reece. Please," said Steve.

Yes. Time to finish.

"Raine was traumatized. For his own sanity, his subconscious *made* him forget," he said, feeling completely exhausted and beaten down. "Six years ago, when he saw your father attacking that girl, he said it was like somebody had taken a big needle and injected all the memories back into his head. He lost it. He just went mad with grief and rage."

Steve slowly nodded. "Raine attacked him. The girl ran. They fought. That's why the house was all torn up but nothing was stolen."

"Yes."

Reece had come to the last moments of the story, the final confession. He had to admit to the part he had played on that awful night, when he at last learned the truth about his sister and had gone to confront the man responsible. Now was when Jessica would find out who he really was. He wondered if she would even be able to look at him again.

"Raine called me after he left the house. He was still half-drunk, beaten up, bloody, and wandering the streets. We went and found him and took him back to my place. He was just coherent enough to tell us everything, including his memories from the night Rachel...died."

"Rachel, oh God," Steve moaned, his mind clearly still on her more than everything else.

Reece plowed on, back in control of his emotions, wanting the telling over with. "Rowan and I went to Harry's house. I don't know what we were planning to do. Maybe kill him. Maybe continue to beat the shit out of him. Maybe call the cops. But it was too late. Whatever happened during the fight, Harry had been badly hurt. We found him dead on the living room floor."

Steve was still whispering Rachel's name, barely paying attention. He'd loosened his grip on Jess, almost enough for her to slip free. She hadn't done it, though. Instead, she was watching Reece, more interested in the ugly story than in dashing to safety. She appeared not only sad, but also a little puzzled, confused by something he had said.

"For what it's worth, I would have called 911 if he were still alive. He wasn't. You have to know, though, that Raine did not murder him. It was a fair fight. My brother was young and strong, but your dad was a big guy. It could have gone either way."

Steve whispered something. Then he repeated it. "Yes, he was. Very big. *So big.*"

At that moment, Reece wasn't entirely sure what Steve was thinking. About his father fighting with Raine...or attacking Rachel.

"She was so tiny, so vulnerable."

Rachel. The man was tormenting himself with visions of what his father had done. Reece knew from experience that he would do that for a long time to come. Reece and his brothers certainly had.

"What did you do after you found him?" asked Jess, more interested in old history than in her current situation.

"Well, we weren't about to let our kid brother get locked up for killing the man who destroyed our sister—and our entire family."

Silence. And then she softly gasped. "You cleaned it up." She shook her head, deep in thought. "Just like your mother's car."

Nodding, he set up the final scene and ran down the verbal storyboard quickly, moment by moment. "We made the bed in the guest room. Washed every dish. Wiped down every counter and every piece of furniture he might have touched. We deleted the call records on the house phone and took the cell with us. We removed every trace of Raine's presence—and ours—from the house. We even raked the gravel driveway so there was no evidence of my car being there. Then we left and never looked back."

Steve had finally started paying close attention again. He didn't say a word, but he did drop his arms, easily and without fanfare. After all that had happened, Jessica merely walked away from the man.

Reece started breathing normally again.

She didn't come to him, didn't fly into his arms. She had to know this wasn't over, so she went to the side, the three of them forming an odd, emotional triangle.

"I'd like to say I'm sorry, Steve. It isn't entirely a lie. I am sorry your life was ruined."

The other man, so still, so silent, just continued to stare.

"Reece," Jessica murmured.

Not wanting her to draw Steve's attention again, he didn't respond. "If it helps, Rowan and I never got over that night. Raine left town not even knowing Harry was dead, or that we'd covered it up. Soon after that, I quit acting. Rowan dropped out of law school and joined the LAPD. I think we were both doing penance, giving up something we had once wanted more than anything."

Small comfort, not much punishment, but it was all he had to offer.

The moment stretched on. He saw a dullness in Baker's eyes, as if he had accepted everything he'd been told but still couldn't wrap his brain around it. Well, that wasn't surprising. It wasn't every day you learned your father had been a monster and had died because he was trying to hurt another young girl.

"Reece, listen," she said.

"I'll confess," Reece said, meaning it. "I'll take the blame for everything. But please, leave my brothers out of it."

"Reece, please!"

He finally looked at her, seeing what looked like shock on her face. "Did you hear what he said before?"

"What?"

"The girl. That night. She saw Harry on the porch—*just fine*—yelling threats after Raine as he took off into the night."

Steve didn't react. In fact, he looked like he was in a daze, hearing only the echoes of long-dead voices in his head. But Jess's intensity caught Reece's attention. He tried to remember exactly what the other man had said.

"Everybody knows Harry Baker was shot in the head," she snapped. "Jesus, somebody leaked the crime scene pictures on the internet."

He swallowed hard. He hadn't needed to see the pictures. He'd seen the gruesome reality.

"Where did the gun come from? And if Raine shot him in the head, how the hell could Baker have gone out onto the porch and yelled at your brother as he ran away?"

"We didn't know he'd gone outside until today," he murmured as the dots tried to connect in his mind, a new picture trying to form where the old one had scarred his memories. "Raine remembered a gun. Harry pulled it on him. We thought they'd struggled over it and Harry had been shot in that struggle."

"Now you know that didn't happen. A man with a bullet in his head would not have been capable of walking, of going outside, of yelling threats. Come on, Reece. Think about it," she urged. "They fought. Raine staggered down the lawn. Harry was *fine*, up and yelling threats after him. And when you came back later..."

"He was dead. Shot in the head." Reece took a step back as the ground beneath his feet seemed to spin, his head along with it. Could this be true? God, had all of them been completely wrong about what had happened that night six years ago?

If Harry had been well enough to walk outside when Raine left, but so gruesomely shot dead when Reece and Rowan came back later, that meant something had happened in between. Something none of them had ever even suspected.

Someone else must have been there. That someone must have killed Harry Baker.

The implication made him stagger back two steps.

Jesus Christ. He and Rowan had cleaned up the scene to protect Raine. And in doing so, they'd helped a murderer escape justice.

"Steve, you have to give me the name," he urged. "Please, tell me how to find her."

Steve still looked almost catatonic, physically there, but his mind far, far away. Maybe he was envisioning an alternate timeline, where none of this had happened, and the teenage *Tiger Beat* supercouple had married and lived happily ever after, starring in their own TV show, bouncing babies on their knees. No drugs. No rape. No suicide...or murder.

It was a nice fantasy. God, how he wish they had gotten to live it.

"Please, Steve, help me. Rowan and I fucked this up, and we have to try to make it right."

The man finally reacted, sounding almost uninterested. "Maybe it was the father of one of the girls he raped."

Maybe. That didn't, however, stop the mental voice screaming, *You helped a murderer go free.*

"Suppose it was. Don't you think the truth needs to come out at last?"

Even if it meant Reece went to prison for accessory after the fact.

Steve shrugged. It was as if he'd already moved on from all of this and didn't really care about anything else. "The girl found *me*. She's a prostitute. I gave her cash. Don't even know her last name."

"What was her first one?"

His face twisted in concentration, and finally he said, "Marley. That was it. Marley."

"Do you remember anything else?"

His brow scrunched. "She was pale, had blond hair, and a long scar down her right cheek. I wonder if my father put it there."

Reece closed his eyes for a second, trying to focus. "Is that all?"

After a long moment, Steve nodded. "That's all."

Reece's hands fisted. It was a start, but he needed more to go on than a scarred, blond prostitute named Marley. So did his brothers. Damn it, now that he knew there might be another explanation for Harry's death, he *had* to know the truth. More: he had to make it right.

For six years, he and Rowan had believed their kid brother had killed a man, and that they'd helped cover it up. But they'd never actually *asked* him. Raine had been out of it, drunk, rambling, and confused that night. The next morning he'd left. He hadn't come back to California for several years. And the three of them, trapped in secrets of their own making, had never mentioned Harry Baker's name again.

If they had...might they have learned long ago that they'd all made some very wrong assumptions?

"Just don't know anything else," Steve mumbled. "I'm sorry."

"It's okay, Steve, never mind," said Jessica, her voice once again sounding husky, like it had last week. "You know the truth about what happened. You understand, and maybe you can even forgive. Can't we all let the secrets lie in the past and not drag everyone involved— dead and alive—through the mud?"

Reece frowned, staring at the dried blood on the side of her face. He might feel sympathy for the guy, but there was no way he would forgive and forget that he'd tried to kill Jessica.

She saw his reaction and quickly shook her head. "No, it wasn't him! I fell, I swear it. I slipped and hit my head on the concrete. Steve saved my life by pulling me out of the pool. If he hadn't, I would have drowned."

Although Steve didn't even respond, looking almost catatonic, Jessica's eyes convinced Reece she was telling the truth, not just trying to cover for the other man. Reece let out a slow breath, still angry she had been threatened and dragged out here, but a little more certain Baker wouldn't actually have hurt her.

Finally, Steve cleared his throat and lifted his head.

His eyes had gained some clarity, though there were still tears on his cheeks. But his voice was steady as he said, "No police. I don't want anyone to find out the truth."

He supposed it was natural not to want the world to know your father had been a monster.

"I don't want anybody to ever know what happened to her."

Rachel. Reece felt moisture prick his own eyes as understanding washed over him.

His sister's teenage sweetheart wanted to protect Rachel's legacy, not her attacker's. Steve wanted the world to remember her as a pretty, talented girl who'd made a serious mistake. Not a victim of her own boyfriend's father.

"All right," Reece said. "Thank you." He wasn't sure if he was thanking the man on behalf of his brothers, or his sister, or his father, or himself. Probably all of the above.

Steve shrugged, the same boyish, self-deprecating motion he used to make on *Dear Family*, when he'd been a goofy, wisecracking teenager who'd asked in every episode if he was adopted, and who had gone gaga over the cute new girl in school in season four, episode seven.

"Reece?"

"Yeah?"

"I loved her, you know. I never stopped."

A lump thickened in his throat. "I know, man."

Steve had one more thing to say. "I'm sorry I burned down your house."

Reece thought he'd misheard. He opened his mouth to ask Steve to repeat himself, but before he could say a word, he realized the other man was gone. He had disappeared in one blink of an eye.

Oh, God, Steve, no.

He knew where he had gone, what he had done. Having found out the truth about what had happened so many years ago, Steve Baker had left the scene for good.

Cut. That's a wrap.

"No!" Jessica cried, running to where he had been standing just seconds ago. She leaned over to look down, and Reece grabbed her around the waist to keep her from slipping on loose rocks and plunging a few hundred feet straight down.

Whatever she saw made her spin around and bury her face in his shirt. She cried and cried, probably for Steve, but, he suspected, also for Rachel.

They were who Reece cried for, too.

* * *

Aaaand...she was back in the hospital.

Jessica hadn't wanted to be taken to the emergency room by ambulance, but she knew she had to go. She'd been knocked unconscious and had nearly drowned. A lump the size of a duck egg was growing out of the side of her temple. She probably had a concussion. And Reece couldn't drive her in.

He was too busy explaining to the police why Steve Baker was lying dead far below them, unable to be reached until specialists came with rappelling equipment.

It was awful, so awful. She had hated being taken away, leaving him there to deal with everything, and was very glad when Rowan showed up. The brothers always stuck together, the twins especially. Rowan was a cop. He knew the entire history. He would help Reece through it.

"Don't you have a life?"

Jess managed a weak smile as Alice, the brassy nurse she'd liked when she was here last week, walked into her room to check on her. When the ER doctor found out she'd just been released after another incident last week, he had insisted on admitting her for observation. She was now lying in a room not far from the one she'd vacated on Thursday, being observed.

It was like the world's worst case of déjà vu.

"I guess I'm just accident prone."

The nurse turned her head to check the bulky bandage on her temple, and whistled. "Nobody did that with a bottle of bleach. I heard you almost drowned, too. You're just determined to fill your lungs with the wrong element—liquid instead of air!"

"Believe me, it's not intentional."

Alice nodded as she changed the bandage, whistling again when she saw the actual wound. "That's not a lump, it's a bowling ball."

"That could be why I have a headache the size of Wisconsin."

Worse, though, was the *heartache*. The look on Reece's face as he revealed what had to be the deepest, darkest secrets of his life, all to save hers, wouldn't leave her mind. Her heart had broken, bit by bit, as he'd bared himself, and his family, opening himself up to prosecution, scandal, and condemnation. For her, just to get her out of harm's way.

She'd known there were things in his past Reece had not told her about. She'd even known they probably had something to do with his sister. The rest had shocked her completely.

Alice checked her temperature, her pulse, and her blood pressure, working quickly and efficiently. When she finished, she glanced at the door. "So where's Mr. Hot Stuff? Why isn't he here with you?" She smoothed her hair. "Is he coming soon?"

Knowing that if she was going to be a part of Reece's life, she would have to get used to women always being interested in him, she shrugged. "He had some things to deal with. I'm sure he'll be here later."

"Great. I'll change into my blue scrubs. They flatter my eyes."

Winking, the woman exited, leaving Jess to go back to fretting and watching the door.

"Oh, baby, oh sweet, sad man," she whispered, desperate for news. She hadn't heard a word from him, and the paramedics hadn't let her bring her cell phone in the ambulance. So she had no idea what was going on up at the house.

There was only one thing she knew: Reece was going to have a hard time facing her.

It hadn't been difficult to see and understand the shame he felt about the secrets he'd been keeping. He had looked at her as if he thought she would judge him or be repulsed by what he'd done in his past. As if she could ever look at the man she adored and hate him for doing whatever it took to protect his loved ones.

She'd been shocked, yes. More than anything else, though, she had wanted to cry for him and his brothers, who had endured so much. *And for Rachel. Poor lost Rachel.*

The door opened. She sighed, wondering if Alice was back to ask about Reece's favorite color so she could find the right earrings.

"Can I come in?"

She swung her head around—*oh, God, that hurts*—and lurched up in the bed. "Reece, oh, my God, are you all right?"

He entered slowly, his steps almost tentative, a word she would never have used to describe him. "I'm fine. How are *you*? They admitted you?"

She shrugged and rolled her eyes. "They're overreacting. I'm fine. I think I'll check out against medical advice; this bed is so uncomfortable."

"Like hell you will." He strode over, his movements much more Reece-like, because she'd gotten him worked up. "You're staying here until the doctors say you are one hundred percent okay to leave."

"Oh, all right." She scooted over on the bed and patted the spot beside her. Reece looked down at it and frowned, but did not sit.

"What's wrong?" she whispered, suddenly afraid. "They're not going to arrest you, are they? They believe Steve committed suicide, right?" She pushed the covers off her legs, struggling to get out of the bed. "I'll tell them everything; they can't blame you."

He put his hands on her shoulders and gently pushed her back. "Would you stay still?" Tugging the covers up and tucking them around her, he added, "Everything is fine."

"The police..."

"You know the house has exterior security cameras. It was all right there on tape."

"Oh," she whispered. She thought of those last painful moments. "I hope they won't release the video of him taking me out there. Poor Steve...he doesn't deserve to be remembered as a monster." That was his late father's department.

Reece crossed his arms and leaned against the high back of an uncomfortable-looking wooden visitor's chair, remaining a few feet away. "They won't. Rowan has a lot of friends in the department. He'll call in every favor he can get to make sure the details are kept quiet."

"Good," she said, wondering what he *wasn't* saying. She knew there was more.

If that were all, if everything were really fine, he would be on the bed beside her, taking her in his arms, telling her how glad he was that she was okay, and that he never wanted anything bad to happen to her ever again. Or something along those lines. So why wasn't he?

"Talk to me," she demanded.

A beat. Then, "Jesus, Jess, I thought you were dead when I saw him kneeling over you." He dropped his head forward, covering his eyes with one hand. "I thought he'd killed you, and I wanted to die myself."

Her heart clenching, she murmured, "It was just a fall, sweetheart. Just me being clumsy and falling. I'm so sorry I scared you."

He lifted his head and looked at her face, his mouth tightening as his gaze rested on her bandaged temple, but softening when he finally stared directly into her eyes.

"What is it?" she asked.

He didn't hesitate this time.

"I love you."

She sucked in a shocked, pleased little breath, a warm, happy thrill coursing through her. He'd said the words as simply and easily as if saying hello. Like it was natural, something he could say every day for the rest of his life. That would be just fine with her.

"I love you, too."

He didn't smile. He didn't come over and take her in his arms. He stayed five feet away from the bed, his expression strained, his body tense.

"I can't believe you almost died because of me."

"I told you it was an accident."

"I don't mean just the pool. You were shot at. You were attacked with chemicals. You were dragged to a cliff…"

"Don't overreact. He wouldn't have thrown me off," she said, waving an airy hand.

"Damn it, Jess, it's not funny."

"I know," she murmured, chastened. "But I'm fine. I'm here, telling you I love you. Nothing really bad happened."

"Nothing bad?" He straightened, shoving the chair

back, and stalked across the room, pacing like a caged animal. "Nothing *bad*?"

She didn't say anything. She could almost feel his anger, a living presence in the room. But she already knew it wasn't directed at her. He was furious at himself.

"Nothing *but* bad things have happened to you since you met me. You've gone through hell for someone who isn't worth a hair on your head."

She was shaking her head before he even finished. "Don't say these things."

"I have to." He stopped pacing and looked down at her.

She saw the way he squared his shoulders, and his spine was as stiff as a board. Reece was steeling himself up for something. She had a dark suspicion about what it was.

"Everything you heard—everything I said out on that cliff—was entirely true."

"I know."

He didn't seem to hear her. "My life has been one nightmare after another. I've done awful things. Illegal, unforgivable things. I've lied about them. I've covered them up."

Swallowing, he came closer. His hand lifted slowly, reluctantly, as if he didn't want to touch her but could not help himself. He eased his fingers into her hair and slid them down a long strand. She suspected he thought he was touching it for the last time. But oh, did he have another think coming.

"I'm not a good man, Jessica. You deserve to be with a good man."

She grabbed his hand before he could remove his fingers from her hair. Her grip tight, she refused to let him budge. "Don't you ever say that to me again," she snapped, hearing her own anger. "You might not be the textbook definition of good, Reece Winchester, but you are *so* much more."

He eyed her cautiously, probably wondering if she was finished.

She wasn't.

"Okay, you say you can't call yourself good. So what? Who cares about good? Call yourself noble instead. How about loyal. Strong. What about decent—where does decency rate when it comes to a person's character?"

"Jess..."

"Frankly, given the choice between 'goodness' and any of those other things, I say goodness can take a flying leap."

"Don't make me into something I'm not."

Jess knew where this was coming from. She knew shame when she heard it.

Reece was haunted not only by what had happened to people he loved, but also by the things he'd done in response. His guilt had made him give up something he had really cared about—his acting career. His early retirement made so much sense now that she knew it had been about punishing himself.

Now he was trying to give up something else. But she wasn't a job. She would fight to hold on to what they had.

"You *are* decent, Reece. You *are* noble. You did things other people would never have the strength or courage to do. Maybe they weren't always the right things, but you did them because you need to protect the people you love. You don't need my approval, you don't need my forgiveness, but I'm telling you, I loved you before I heard what you said out there. *And I love you even more now.*"

He finally looked at her, studying her face, his golden eyes darkening to the amber shade she loved so much. His expression was filled with emotion—want, regret, tenderness. Maybe a little bit of hope.

And then, just when she thought she had gotten through, she saw self-recrimination.

"You get hurt around me," he said. "People have *hurt* you, and that's my fault."

Still holding his hand tightly, she shoved the bedding away, rising to her knees.

"Do you think I'm weak?"

"No, of course not."

"Then stop acting like I am." A jaded laugh escaped her lips. "My life hasn't much resembled a TV family sitcom either, in case you've forgotten. I'm not going to play a game of 'let's compare childhood trauma' with you, but you do realize you don't have a monopoly on shitty memories, right?"

"I didn't mean that."

She finally released his hand, only to slide her own up his arm. Lifting the other, she cupped his face, holding him still, and making him look at her. Making him listen.

"Bad things can happen. People can be hateful. Parents can die. Buildings can burn. Ex-boyfriends can terrorize. Madwomen can throw bleach."

She brushed her thumbs over his mouth and stroked his jaw, feeling the five o'clock shadow that emphasized his face, a face she now saw as so much more than just handsome. It was simply a cover, the surface of a man so deep, so wounded, but always able to rise.

God, she was crazy about that man. Head over heels for him. She never wanted to let him go.

"Nobody can ever predict when life will throw something awful at you—be it a disease or the death of someone you love. So all you can do is live it and trust that the happiness you find each and every day is worth the risk."

For an agonizingly long moment, he remained silent, looking at her, searching her eyes to make sure she meant what she said.

Silly man. Of course she did.

He was on the verge, but there was one more thing to say, and it didn't come as a surprise.

"I have to find out the truth."

"About Steve's father?"

He nodded.

"Of course you do."

"It might get ugly. I might be in legal trouble."

She didn't make light of it or toss off a joke. She had watched enough episodes of *Law & Order* to know he was probably right. He and his twin brother had broken the law. Perhaps it had been for reasons they had been able to justify to themselves, but the court rarely saw it that way. She didn't even want to think of the headlines, the speculation about his sister, and Harry Baker, and all the awful things that had happened to the Winchesters. She already ached for him, and for his family, knowing the pain they faced.

But he wouldn't be facing it alone.

"I'm there, Reece. Whatever happens, I am *there*."

"You're sure?"

"I'm sure. You're keeping me. And I'm keeping you. Even if I have to bake a file in a cake and go on the run with you, I am keeping you."

"So you'd break me out of jail?"

"Or I'll break in. As long as we're together, I won't be too picky."

Finally she saw it. It came slowly, but grew, that crooked, only-real-for-her smile.

She smiled back.

He leaned down, and she leaned up, and their mouths met in a kiss as soft and lovely as the brush of a cool breeze on a warm afternoon.

"Every day of my life," he murmured. "Every day I have you, I swear I will make you happy, Jess."

She drew him down to the bed, wanting to curl up beside him and hold him close until she could get out of this place and go home with him. Home...wherever that was.

"No, Reece. We will make each other happy."

For as long as life let them.

EPILOGUE

The Winchester brothers sat outside, drinking beer and looking at the sky. It was late, and lots of stars were shining, but they couldn't really compete with the lights of the city far below. Each had its own kind of beauty.

They didn't talk much. The silence wasn't uncomfortable, though.

Dinner had been good, a much-needed family gathering. It had been Jessica's idea to have everyone over. Since she'd been out of the hospital only for a few days, Reece tried to talk her out of it, but she had insisted. As soon as they were all together around the table—him, Rowan and Raine, plus their dad, Aunt Sharon, and, of course, Jess—he'd felt a strange sensation. It had taken him a second, but then he'd recognized it as contentment.

At that moment, he wasn't thinking about the past, or worrying if it would catch up to them. Looking around the table at his family, even if it was missing a few long-gone members, Reece was happy. More, he was looking forward to a future with the beautiful woman who had burst into his life with her bouncy ponytail all those weeks ago.

"Hold on to her," Rowan said, as if reading his mind. "She's special."

He smiled and lifted his beer. "You have no idea."

The three of them clinked bottles, the only sound in the quiet night. His dad and Aunt Sharon had left. Jessica had gone to bed. Now it was just the three of them.

It was time.

He hadn't stopped thinking about what Steve had said and what brilliant Jessica had recognized as so critically important. *He was on the porch, calling after him. He was fine.*

It had been six long years. All three of them had kept their secrets, not even sharing them with each other. Reece and Rowan had thought their brother was a killer, and had covered for him anyway. They'd done him a disservice, and they both needed to apologize to him. And Raine had absolutely no idea.

So yes, it was time. Everything had to come out. The brothers had to be honest with each other at last. After that, working together, they would find out the truth about the past.

"So," he said, leaning back in his chair and lacing his fingers together over his chest. "Let's talk about the night Harry Baker died."

ABOUT THE AUTHOR

Leslie Kelly is a *New York Times* and *USA Today* bestselling author of more than seventy-five novels and novellas. Known for their sexy humor, Leslie's books have been honored with numerous awards, including the National Readers' Choice Award, the Aspen Gold, the Golden Quill, the Write Touch, and the Romantic Times Award. She is also a four-time Romance Writers of America RITA finalist, and is a Career Achievement Award winner from *Romantic Times* magazine.

Although she has spent most of her life in Maryland and Florida, Leslie currently resides in Colorado with her husband and two fluffy, yappy little dogs.

DON'T MISS THE NEXT SEXY, SUSPENSEFUL WINCHESTER BROTHERS BOOK, *NOWHERE TO HIDE*.

Detective Rowan Winchester has his hands full protecting brilliant true-crime writer Evie Fleming. She's in town researching old Hollywood mysteries... some of which hit a little too close to home for the family.

Rowan desperately wants to keep the sexy writer safe. But he also wants to keep her in the dark.

Because Evie Fleming might be the one who exposes the truth about everything the Winchester brothers are trying to hide.

Looking for more romantic suspense?

LETHAL REDEMPTION
by April Hunt

Top FBI profiler Grace Steele was just a girl when she escaped the Order of the New Dawn, and she swore never to return. But when Steele Ops needs her help extracting a young woman from the secretive cult's clutches, she's all in...even though the mission requires posing as an engaged couple with the man who broke her heart nine years ago. Includes a bonus novel by Piper J. Drake!

FOREVER STRONG
by Piper J. Drake

Ying Yue Jiang believed her kidnapping was a case of wrong place, wrong time, but she soon realizes that she has become a pawn in a dangerous game. When the handsome and mysterious Azubuike Anyanwu is hired to protect her, he discovers a traitor in her father's organization. As both tensions and attractions grow more intense, Ying Yue and Azubuike will have to test their allegiances and trust in each other in order to stay alive.

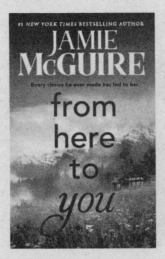

FROM HERE TO YOU
by Jamie McGuire

When Darby Dixon learns that she is pregnant on the morning of her wedding, she realizes that marrying her abusive fiancé would be the worst decision of her life, so she flees to the small town of Colorado Springs...and into the arms of Marine Scott "Trex" Trexler. Trex knows Darby is the woman he's been waiting for his whole life, so when her ex starts making threats, he'll do anything it takes to protect her and her unborn child.

TWISTED TRUTHS
by Rebecca Zanetti

Noni Yuka is desperate. Her infant niece has been kidnapped, and the only person who can save her is the private detective who once broke her heart. "A pure adrenaline rush."–*RT Book Reviews*

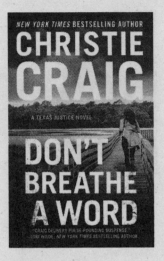

DON'T BREATHE A WORD
by Christie Craig

When special agent Juan Acosta meets his gorgeous neighbor, he knows she's hiding something. As he gets closer to the mysterious woman and her daughter, his investigation uncovers dark secrets that will put them all in danger. Includes a bonus story by April Hunt!